MIRANDA JAY—Her beauty was an obsession with every man she met—and her passport to the dark side of desire.

VICTOR LENRAHAN—Arms manufacturer and confidant of the President, he treated Miranda like a pampered slave—and taught her how the powerful prefer their pleasure.

HAP MITCHEL—A former astronaut, he was a hero who felt like a has-been, until he fell under the spell of Miranda Jay and the sinister truth behind her death.

CLAIRE AVERY—A popular television anchorwoman, she was determined to uncover and publicize everything, even if it meant losing her lover—or her life.

ZOE BALDWIN—A bright, beautiful, and blunt celebrity lawyer, she hid her longing for romance as well as a curious link with Miranda.

◆ ◆ ◆

SILK LADY

◆ ◆ ◆

"Her best, most intriguing, most feeling fiction to date."
　　　　　　　　　　　　　　　　　　**—Liz Smith,
　　　　　　　　　　　　　　　　　　syndicated columnist**

"A page-turner! . . . the luxurious doings of the super-rich as d̲e̲s̲c̲r̲i̲b̲e̲d̲ ̲b̲y̲ ̲a̲ ̲p̲r̲a̲c̲t̲i̲c̲e̲d̲,̲ talented, and playful w̲r̲i̲t̲e̲r̲.̲"

　　　　　　　　　　　　　　　　　　　　　　　Witness

"Unabashedly . . . . **Weekly**

"The most in . . . . all her books."
　　　　　　　　　　　　　　　　　　—Washington Times

SILK LADY

GWEN DAVIS

WARNER BOOKS

A Warner Communications Company

WARNER BOOKS EDITION

Cover design by Jackie Merri Meyer
Cover photograph by Pat Hill

Warner Books, Inc.
666 Fifth Avenue
New York, N.Y. 10103

W A Warner Communications Company

Printed in the United States of America

This book was originally published in hardcover by Warner Books.
First Printed in Paperback: July, 1987

10 9 8 7 6 5 4 3 2 1

For MAUREEN DALY McGIVERN,
who taught me strength under fire.

And for MEGAN,
who taught us all grace.

CONTENTS

1. Le Cirque *1*

2. Miranda *30*

3. The Waldorf Towers *59*

4. Paris *88*

5. La Côte Basque *123*

6. The South of France *153*

7. Trump Tower *186*

8. Watergate South *220*

9. The Equestrian Center *249*

10. Beverly Hills *279*

11. Santa Barbara *308*

12. Century City *338*

13. East Hampton *368*

FRIAR: Thou hast committed—

BARABAS: Fornication? but that was in another country:
And, besides, the Wench is dead.

Marlowe, *The Jew of Malta*

LE CIRQUE

◇

People who didn't know her thought Miranda was aloof. She had the air of a tawny lioness, prowling at her leisure through the social jungle. Ready to unseat monarchs and defrock priests.

Nobody was sure where, exactly, she came from. Along with the ability to find clothes that clung like petals to the slender stalk of her body, she'd picked up a knack for covering her tracks. When the rumblings first began about her and Victor Lenrahan, even the FBI had trouble finding out about her.

Not that she lied, exactly. But she had a smile that made people forget the question they asked. Her mouth was wide and full, with a childish pouting lower lip, as if she hadn't been given the flavor of ice cream she'd ordered. When she smiled, though, all trace of disappointment disappeared, and she was a light in anybody's room. Her mouth tilted up on one side over slightly irregular teeth, left front tooth overlapping right. It was a small flaw, adding to her charm, suggesting guilelessness. A childhood in an artless land where daisies grew, and no orthodontists. Victor Lenrahan had offered to treat her to braces as part of her ''scholarship'' when they first met. She was seventeen to his fifty-five. But after their first two times together, he came to adore her overbite, and never again mentioned that part of the offer.

Lily Masters, as her closest friend, didn't know much

more about her than anybody else. But she loved Miranda, saw through her seeming detachment, felt what a tender heart the young woman really had. When Victor Lenrahan died and Miranda attempted suicide, Lily had flown with her husband on their private jet to rescue her. She had seemed to Lily wounded and harmless, less a sophisticated mistress than a bereaved little girl. The Masters had taken Miranda back to New York, worked together to make her feel better, talking her into wanting to live again. "Your life is just beginning," Lily had counseled her kindly, reeling under the insult that was middle age.

In spite of knowing almost no facts, Lily understood Miranda, as she would have known the reason her child was crying, if she'd had a child. In a way, that was what Miranda had become. Lily had spent days with her arms around Miranda, giving her all the stored-up tenderness she had. Never questioning the past, never passing judgment on the fact that Miranda had been a "kept woman." Something in the girl moved her deeply. It was not in Lily's nature to wonder who else Miranda might move, and in what way.

According to the gossips, Miranda had sprung full grown and sleek from the arm of Victor Lenrahan, like Diana from the brow of Mars. Appropriate, really, since Victor was such an important figure in the world of armaments. Right that she should come like The Huntress from the God of War. But nobody knew where Victor had found her. When rumors of that liaison had shaken political circles uncomfortably close to the president, there were efforts to uncover more about her origins, whispers of covert investigations, rumors of psychiatrists' offices being broken into, all to find out some truth about her. But the only truth that seemed to matter was that infatuation had snuffed out Lenrahan's discretion. There were communiqués from friends in high places, asking him not to appear with her in public. To make her less visible. And Victor had tried to comply.

But it hadn't been easy keeping Miranda inconspicuous. Her eyes were a very pale green, so pale as to look transparent in a certain light. The black iris at the center seemed deeper by contrast, a dart aimed at the observer. The intensity of that look, like her seeming aloofness, came from an astigmatism, a slight cast in her left eye. But Miranda refused to wear glasses, or even contact lenses, afraid they might scratch her pupils. So to bring things and people into perspective, she had to squint and focus hard.

Her honey blonde hair was cut silkily blunt, just above the amber skin of her collarbone. To examine the world, she pulled away slightly and eased her head back so her hair swung, of a piece, to the right. It was that particular posture, along with her long-legged stride, that gave her a slightly imperious air. In a country where no one was sure who the real aristocrats were, politicians, movie stars, the oldest families, or the very rich, an air of being above it all made people sure you were.

But Lily Masters knew that Miranda was really shy, vulnerable. It touched Lily that anyone that beautiful had feelings of self-consciousness. How leveling that the seemingly perfect had the same insecurities the slightly chunky did. Lily had never imagined herself pretty, but she'd always assumed that, had she been long and lean, with a flat belly, gently rounded hips, legs that didn't stop, and a nose that tilted up like that, nothing would be in her path but roses. So the modesty of Miranda, the humility implicit in her air of cheerful apology, made Lily love her deeply. Made her reinforce with cannons of affection the fortresses Fred tried to put up around Miranda.

Lily's love for Fred extended to joy in his friendship, relief when people he admired returned his esteem. He was basically a good-natured blunderer whose only true skill was in business. He was not adept at social amenities, no matter how many parties he threw or how many public relations people he hired. In his background and connections, he was worlds away from Victor Lenrahan, and had enshrined him as some kind of idol. Pictures of Victor hung everywhere in the Masters' apartment, many of them with Fred standing admiringly by: the two of them on private golf links, in booths of exclusive restaurants, in front of the Hay-Adams Hotel, on Victor's yacht. It had thrilled Fred that a man of Lenrahan's stature seemed genuinely to like him. And Lily was thrilled in turn. Sometimes she would come home from uppercrusty parties, where people had fallen all over themselves to make them welcome, and had to lie down, sighing with relief that no one had discovered how simple they were. So Fred's friendship with Victor Lenrahan, one of the great movers and shakers in the country, had been like admission to a royal entourage. Fred was excited as a schoolboy on receiving an invitation to Victor's yacht. Even those in Lenrahan's inner circle were seldom invited on board the *Banana*, since it was there, mostly, that Victor would rendezvous with Miranda. So to allow Fred Masters, whose fortune was cornerstoned on scandal, to become a party to that relationship showed amazing faith.

And the faith was kept. Not even a blind item about Miranda and Lenrahan was permitted in any of Fred's newspapers. The publisher personally cut their names, or even the slyest allusion to them as a couple, from his many gossip columns. He sent down edicts to his staff never to mention them. When Lenrahan had his fatal embolism and the scandal broke about the burial, the will, the threatened lawsuit, and Miranda, Masters' papers played it down, while even the staid *New York Times* was forced to take notice. It was a stripe of friendship as wide as it was out of character. Lily was moved that her husband could feel such fellowship. It never occurred to her his motives might be more complex.

There was not much about Lily Masters that was worldly, in spite of the world she'd been pulled into. She was sophisticated only in that she wore Adolfo suits, lunched with other women who wore them, and went shopping afterward for more of them. But that was only out of a quiet wish to be inconspicuous: she would have stuck out like a sore thumb if she dressed plainly. So it was good nature rather than greed that sent her on buying sprees. She didn't want to embarrass her husband or seem to have nothing in common with her lunch companions. So she tried to make clothes as important as they appeared to other rich men's wives. As Fred was in publishing, her foyer was filled with papers and glossy magazines, among them *W*, a newspaper that suffered over fashion as thinking men did over nuclear war. But she rarely read it, just breezed through the shiny, four-color edition to check if she was in it, to show Fred so he would be pleased. But she didn't have a single seed of artifice. Happiness for her was the essentials: comfort and absence of fear. She was no more impressed with herself in the duplex in Trump Tower than she'd been in the one bedroom in Southfield, Michigan, at the beginning of their marriage, when they hadn't even been sure they'd make it into the country club. People did the grocery shopping for her now, and the cooking. But she felt no sense of having arrived. If anything, she missed picking out the apples herself, checking them out for hardness, as she used to do with Fred on lazy Sunday mornings.

So it had come to her with joy rather than apprehension, the chance of helping Miranda. Because the girl was grieving, because she had belonged to Lenrahan, because he had had the grace to accept and even like Fred. Lily kept telling Miranda over and over again what great things lay ahead of her, never dreaming that one of them would be her own husband.

Now, caught in the middle of what was fast becoming a public scandal, Lily headed for what she was afraid might be another humiliating evening. One where Fred might or might not show up because of Miranda. Along with Lily's confusion at Fred's recent behavior, she was beside herself that Miranda had allowed anything to happen when she seemed to have as much affection for Lily as Lily had for her. Several times she had been tempted to confront Miranda. But confrontation was not in her makeup. And, in a way, Lily preferred to let it remain a puzzle; why love wasn't true, why friends weren't loyal. To have the answers to those questions flat out might make life less than worth living. Puzzles at least sustained your interest, kept the mind clicking so it didn't explode.

She got out of her limousine as it stopped in front of the restaurant, the doorman bowing as he opened the passenger door. Light washed the streets of the city. It was one of those rare New York nights, lit as fully by the moon as by streetlamps. The moon hung low and yellow over the rooftops, as though they were the harvest.

Lily did not take in the crispness of the evening, or the radiant moon. Head bent forward, she made her way directly from the limousine into the restaurant and asked the maitre d' if her husband had arrived. She made a conscious effort to ask the question very softly, but several heads turned just the same and heard the answer with her: Monsieur Masters wasn't there yet. Her disappointment was coupled with embarrassment. No matter how bustling the restaurant was, how busy and intense the conversation, there was a muted quality about the place, maybe because of the rugs, maybe because of the soft fabric on the banquettes. So, no matter how confidential you tried to be, somebody always heard the very thing you were trying to be confidential about.

Not that there was any point in trying to keep it a secret. Gossip was a favorite dish at Le Cirque, preferred to the pasta primavera. And there was no tastier tidbit in New York than Fred Masters and Miranda. Nervously, Lily followed the captain to her table. In the beginning of her husband's social rise, when she first became aware that she was supposed to care about such things, Lily might have noted she was being showed to a choice table, the corner banquette. But this night she was concerned with more than status. Her married life seemed to hang in the balance, as, it felt, did her balance itself. She could feel a queasiness in her knees, as though she were going to faint. That would be all she needed. To pass out cold in the middle of Le Cirque. So everybody could call each other when they got home and chew over Lily Masters' fainting.

The spasm of dizziness passed. She kept her eyes on the leather of her high-heeled, Maud Frizon pumps so she wouldn't have to see the inquiring looks of those who were eating there. Didn't have to answer their unspoken questions, smile and acknowledge their vulture sympathy. Perched all around her, ready to swoop down on the carcass of her marriage, pick clean its glistening bones. Poor Lily, she could imagine their noting, alone again. Having to make her entrance without Fred. Yum yum.

She knew he was with Miranda. Everyone knew he was with Miranda. Fred Masters, whose only obsession had been his newspapers, and the outrageous headlines he set up to sell them, was creating an as yet unprinted scandal of his own.

Dimly, Lily could hear the hum of conversation, the quiet babble of the sleekest buzzards. Vaguely, she saw the Fantasie lights, sprays of wrought-iron deco sconces dancing from between the paneled paintings on the walls. Louis XIII court scenes they were, the satin clothes and white wigs of that era, featuring monkeys dressed as French courtiers. Lady monkeys on swings in palace gardens being wooed by male monkeys in white wigs. Lily found no irony in the decor. What she would have preferred in the way of taste were less bright lights, more space between the tables. Maybe a dim corner where a woman could be invisible when abandoned.

Why was Fred doing this to her? No matter how deeply infatuated he was with Miranda, he loved Lily, she knew he did. They had been together, really together, in the world that preceded New York, the struggle of young married people in Detroit, fearful about their future, caught in the agonies of childlessness, the anxieties of household accounts, car payments. A man who lived a solid life, as Fred had lived with Lily, didn't get caught in the illusion, no matter how seductive it was. An auto mechanic always remembered how the engine worked, even if he got to race at Le Mans. So Fred had to know deep down this was all silly, even as he danced heavy-footed through the dream.

Besides, he had never been the kind of man to risk anything for a woman. Business was his "fix," the thing that gave him juice, renewed him, made him get out of bed in the morning. Women were something he'd never even seemed to think seriously about, considering them one of the "perks" of the power game, an extra, like limos and first-class transportation. Nothing essential to a man's daily menu. But Miranda was not just a woman. She was like a force of nature.

All around Lily were those who struggled for a better table, a better husband, an entrée into better circles. Not a single passion she'd ever shared. It made her sick to her heart that she was capable of jealousy. Worse, because of her love for Miranda. Even now, as she moved to her table, she tried to tell herself she wasn't angry. That it was concern she was feeling, concern because her husband wasn't there yet, and this was such a crucial appointment to him. There their guest sat waiting, with his very handsome, important face.

"Admiral Mitchel," she said as he rose to greet her. "I'm so sorry Fred isn't here yet. I can't imagine what's keeping him." That wasn't true of course. She knew exactly what was keeping him, and who he was keeping. What had happened to Lily that she was twisting phrases, making flip judgments in her head? Had she taken on the colors of her environment? Been changed by all the dinners she had eaten, couturier clothes she had worn, the nails porcelained to the tips of her square, small hands? Had she been transformed from genuine to cunning, so she made cruel puns, like the worldly wise Bunyan Reis? She could see him a few tables away, at a banquette against the wall, being clever, while all around him strained to partake of his wit like sacramental wine.

"You don't have to use the title," Mitchel said, smiling, taking her hand, helping her into her place. "It's a formality that never took. Call me Hap."

She felt intimidated by his trying to put her at ease. Even without the title, symbol of the uniform he no longer wore, he had a military bearing, square-shouldered, broad chested. His looks were clean-cut, particularly American, youthful in spite of his age: Lily knew he had been an astronaut in the sixties. His features were balanced, no confusion or anguish in his wide-set, clear blue eyes. His skin was unlined, with the fresh clear glisten of a baby's.

Remarkable, as if the steel gray hair, close-cropped, was the only indication of the years. You didn't get to be an admiral, even with a title you asked people not to use, if you were a kid.

"I'm sure Fred will be here any minute," Lily said, wondering, wondering. The worst part of being a loyal wife was that Lily hated it when anybody thought ill of Fred, including herself. She still considered him a naughty boy who at any moment would come home repentant, ready for the spanking he deserved.

"I'm in no hurry," Hap said. "It's always a pleasure to be with a pretty woman."

So he was gallant, too. Now she began feeling sorry for Fred, that he wasn't here to enjoy being with them and to direct the conversation. She had no idea what interested military men besides war, no real feelings about astronauts or any way of connecting with them. She remembered once they had been the "A" celebrity, elevating a party as much as a movie star or a Kennedy would have. But that time was over, and even in the midst of it, she hadn't been that caught by the mystique of space. Orbiting. Reentry. Words she vaguely recollected, couched in her brain in the voice of Walter Cronkite.

Nor did she want to step on Fred's business toes and say anything that might be inappropriate about the aerospace industry that Hap Mitchel was now a part of. She imagined Fred's urgency about this evening was somehow connected with that. Fred had lately begun to show a great deal of interest in the business of aerospace, was on the phone a lot of the time about some microchip thing. Lily never consciously took in that kind of information. Fred's business was his own, no matter how willing he was to share it with her, no matter how noisily he yelled into the mouthpiece at his lawyers, accountants, whoever, in some less-than-subtle exhibitionism, power brokering. But she always averted her mind, as a modest woman would avert her eyes when facing a flasher, trying to shut out any real awareness of what was going on. Still, she wasn't stupid. Things seeped in, no matter how she thought she was leaving facts unrecorded, unsorted. So she knew Hap's being there was probably allied with whatever it was Fred was trying to get in on, some takeover that would put him on the front page of the *Wall Street Journal*. But she didn't want to broach anything on that subject, in case Hap was one of those men who didn't think business was any of a wife's business.

Besides fearing for Fred's toes, she was also nervous about stepping on Hap's. She had seen him on a television interview a few mornings before and had noted how angry he became when asked a question he didn't like, when the woman interviewer went in a direction he obviously hadn't anticipated. So Lily edited herself before she said anything that might cause him to take umbrage. She was not one of those women whose brain was connected directly to her tongue. So she chose what for her was always a safe topic: marriage. At least, it had always been safe, comforting, till the business started with Miranda.

"Did you bring your wife with you?" she asked Hap.

"Kate doesn't like New York."

"We'd probably get along. I'm still not exactly comfortable here myself."

A few tables away, at one of the banquettes, Stan Dobson, the literary agent, leaned over in hushed conversation with Marty Fontaine, the singer's son. Lily recognized who all the celebrities were now, even the subtly celebrated like literary agents. She knew Stan Dobson because they were always at the same parties, or he was inviting the Masters to one of his self-styled "fabled evenings." Marty Fontaine she knew because she had been such a rabid fan of his father's, and had always wondered if the children of the famous could grow up without some tragedy stalking their lives. So she had followed Marty's divorces and sort of success in the movie industry, rejoicing that he wasn't an alcoholic or on drugs. As far as she could tell.

Because she still had the soul and the feelings of an outsider, no matter how many gossip columns included her in the center, no matter how many guest lists had her at the top, Lily could observe with a kind of wonder. Marty Fontaine did not look much like his father, but then that might have been due less to nature than the surgeon who had regulated his features, scraping them all into a uniformity that gave truth to the category plastic. Lily did not really approve of men who had their noses fixed, especially those who were behind the cameras, like Marty was. But there was a little line of grief around his mouth that humanized him, made her feel for all his friendless afternoons when a nanny had probably tried to make up to him his father's latest stint in Las Vegas.

Directing her attention back to the man who sat beside her, she asked him about the moon, as one might inquire what Hong Kong was like. Hap seemed to savor her questions, fixing her with his bright blue eyes as if she was the most interesting person he'd ever met, as if being asked what it was like on the moon was fresh to him, an original and brilliant question.

"Illuminated," he said.

"I can imagine," said Lily, not being able to imagine at all. Her mind was not exactly with the conversation, as she wondered why Fred would risk offending a man he was so eager to see. She had overheard him pushing for the meeting, urging Hap on the telephone to stay in town an extra day so they could have dinner. Why insult one of the country's heroes by being late for an appointment he'd all but begged for?

"I'm going to go call Fred," she said. "See what's holding him up."

She made her way past interested eyes, between the cold buffet laid out on a table to her right and the forked tongues on her left. The quiet splendor of the place never failed to impress her. The subtle little luxuries of the rich: high above the buffet table, a giant basket of tiger lilies, spiked blossoms on long, thin stalks, pink, white, yellow, and orange. She remembered the first time she'd ordered them from a florist and found out they were ten dollars a stem. She'd nearly fainted. How provincial she was. How provincial she wished she could have stayed, in fact, back among the roses of northern Michigan.

Several people she didn't know smiled at her in greeting, as she had once sort of smiled at people who seemed to really belong, hopeful they might acknowledge her, pretend they knew who she was. Now everyone seemed to know who she was. Scandal had elevated her to social identity. The soon-to-be-cast-off wife of Fred Masters. The real Other Woman. Bunyan Reis waved pale slender fingers at her, in the camaraderie of the notable, on his albinoish face a smile of interest and compassion, neither of which she supposed he could really feel. Bunyan Reis to Lily was a true celebrity, an artist, even to those who knew little of art, the resident mascot of what some still referred to as Café Society. It was a foreign land to Lily, even though she was now a part of it. She felt always like a ship sailing into some familiar, but not truly welcoming harbor, where a bejeweled statue raised her torch, beckoning, Give me your tired, your rich, your huddled masses, yearning to eat expensive.

At the banquette next to Bunyan, Tia Papadapolis, the second richest woman in the world, traded barbs with her entourage. Lily heard a shriek of laughter from the tall, flamingo-necked, suntanned Greek. Blushed with the certainty that the joke was about her. Strained to hear the words that Bunyan Reis whispered from the next banquette, felt relief mixed with anguish as the syllables eluded her.

She went down the steps, past the corn tree, its dark green leaves lending an air of the tropics to the carpeted stairs, and wondered how it could live, even dwarfed, in only artificial light. Holding hard to the banister, for fear she might fall, she felt a sudden return of the dizziness breaking over her with Bunyan's cackling laughter.

She put coins in the pay phone, dialed Fred's assistant in the office, asked him if he knew where Mr. Masters was. As long as she'd been married, as long as she'd known the people who worked for Fred, she still referred to him with third parties as Mr. Masters, investing him with the respect she hoped they would show him. The assistant told her Mr. Masters had left the office at five-thirty for a cocktail appointment. Compulsive man that he was, taking his workaholic patterns with him even into an extramarital affair, Fred had started carrying it over to Miranda, making a twilight habit of her. Coding it in his diaries as cocktails.

She dialed Miranda's apartment, the one she knew Fred was paying for. A recording sounded: Miranda's smoky voice asking the caller please not to hang up. Her voice seemed obscene now to Lily, heavy with invitation. She hung up the phone and dialed her own number, asked the service if they'd heard from Fred. They hadn't.

Visibly distressed now, perspiration starting to bead her neck where the rubies were, Lily returned to the table. "No one knows where he is," she said to Hap.

At the table in front of theirs the wife of the former governor talked hats with the former wife of a Canadian premier and Sylvia Kranet, the senator's wife. With them was a gossip columnist, also in a hat, who took notes on their discussion. From the banquette next to Bunyan's came a squeal of high-pitched laughter as he leaned across to say something to the Greek. Tia threw back her head and made a noise that to Lily sounded like a whinny, maybe a sign of too much time spent around the horses she collected, along with pornography. Fred was always telling Lily how harmless pornography was, what a decent woman Papadapolis was really, how many and frequent were her charitable acts. But Lily could not help feeling affronted. All that money poured into filth. In her young adulthood, before she married Fred, Lily had been a grade school teacher. She knew for historical fact that pornography had led to the decline of the Roman Empire. Along with decreased salaries to teachers, a sure sign of a civilization's imminent fall.

Why were people so sexual minded? Why such interest in degradation? Lily had never been as sought after before there was all this trouble. Apparently even people who found you boring to talk to found you fascinating to talk about. Never had the buzz in the beauty parlor droned on so endlessly about her. Never were there so many volunteers to help her arrange her charity dinners. Toiling with her over seating arrangements, consoling her across centerpieces they helped her make. Not wanting to say anything, they said, but saying all the same. Why did they offer such sympathy, who were never real friends? Like a funeral, adultery seemed to bring out all the people who couldn't care less on regular occasions.

"I think we should order," Lily said to Hap.

"I don't mind waiting."

"I'm hungry. You must be hungry, too." She signaled for a waiter.

At Marty Fontaine's table, there was a sudden, sharp exchange. "I never said that," Stan Dobson said, a little loudly.

"You promised me the rights!" Marty exclaimed.

"We had no firm deal."

"Don't you welsh on me, you cocksucker."

"How dare you use that language in front of my wife!"

"Since when did you start treating women so holy?"

"At least," said Stan, "I never married a whore."

Marty rose halfway out of his chair, as if it were a saddle on the polo ponies he was used to riding, and splashed his Kir Royale into Dobson's eyes. It was, from Lily's point of view, doubtless meant to be a theatrical gesture. But Marty was not well coordinated, so it was the glass and not just its contents that struck Stan's face, shattering. A gash opened above his eye and there was blood, and a scream from Stan's wife.

"You prick!" Stan screamed. "I'm blind!"

"Perfect!" Marty was on his feet now. "A blind literary agent! What a statement!" He flung his napkin across at Stan, whether to act as a sop for the blood or a further show of rage, Lily wasn't sure.

"I'll have your ass!" Dobson pressed his napkin to the wound. "I'll sue you out of this business. You're finished!"

But Marty was already out of the entrance of the restaurant, onto the street, slamming the door on the excited pitch of conversation that had resumed. "Is there a doctor in the house?" Dobson was shouting.

"I'm a doctor," George Piner said, making his way toward Stan's table. "We better get you to emergency."

Lily felt a sudden, terrible surge of relief. The people in the restaurant were visibly alert, their attention off her, focused on the scene they had just witnessed. As much as she hated violence, it was infinitely more riveting than even the best of gossip, and so served to take the focus off her, to ride like a knight to her rescue. She was sure Dobson would be all right. She would send flowers to his hospital room, if he had to be hospitalized. She would have her secretary check with his wife in the morning. She was confident he would be all right. She knew George Piner and liked him. Understood how long he waited, and in all the right places, for someone to say, "Is there a doctor in the house?"

Still, after war there was peace, and eventually, no matter how good the scene was in a restaurant, people lost their sense of urgency and ordered dessert. When Fred had not appeared by the time the sweets trolley did, Lily's sense of personal panic returned. Her light brown hair, subtly highlighted to disguise the gray by the hairdresser she shared with Miranda, was beginning to curl slightly around her cheeks. There was deep uneasiness in Lily's soul, as on the night her father died and nobody had to tell her. "Something terrible's happened to Fred," she said to Hap.

He put his hand on hers. "I'm sure there's a simple explanation."

"I hope," she said, and shuddered.

"Come." Hap signaled for the check, lifted her fur from the banquette behind her. "I'll take you home."

There was still the gauntlet they had to run on the way out of the restaurant, stares and greetings and intimate looks from those who would never be intimates. At the first banquette, Luke Benjamin, everybody's favorite director again, back from breeding horses to the cover of *Time*, rose to greet Lily, leaning over to kiss her. "You had the best seat in the house," he said. "Front row center.

Did you hear what they were talking about before the fracas?''

"No," Lily said, not remembering really whether or not she had.

Next to Luke, behind the floral arrangement in the center of the white linen tablecloth, Bertram Lester, once the movies' most influential producer, looked up from his soft diet to see what could get Luke to his feet. "That was right what Marty said. A blind literary agent. It does seem correct, the world the way it is."

"Excuse us," said Lily, and hurried out of there.

She was sure she knew where Fred and Miranda were. As many hideaways as he had, including an apartment in the Waldorf Towers, another he'd rented for Miranda, as many hotels as there were in New York to be indiscreet and invisible in, they were probably using Gordon Grayson's apartment. Gordon had been Fred's roommate in college for the one semester Fred had attended, and Fred posted the friendship like the diploma he hadn't gotten. To him Gordon represented literacy, family, all the credentials Fred didn't have. And in the same way, Gordon's apartment probably represented college boy sexuality, irresponsibility, the last bachelor pad among a set all of whose members were long ago married, several times divorced, or out of the closet.

Lily was intimidated by Gordon. As openhearted as she was, he seemed closed to her. He was forever greeting her warmly, telling her how refreshingly honest she was, saying they must get together, and "often." "Often," he was always saying, and then made no attempt to call her, ever. It was not as if she particularly wanted to be friends with him, but with all the people she knew, she still felt very much alone. Fred was so busy in the middle of things, and she was on the fringes, so it would have pleased her to have an intellectual friend who sought her out "often." Or even sometimes. She resented Gordon for what was, essentially, his teasing her. He was like a boy in high school who flirted and then, when it came time to take you to the movies, said he had other plans. Not that she was the person she'd been in high school. But she found as a rule that that was where most men were with respect to women. Few of them were really at ease in the presence of females; not many were grown up. So it was doubly annoying when they dangled arch words at you, like "often."

She distrusted him, then, because she felt hurt. Fred was always telling her not to take things personally, but she wondered how else you could take them. In the part of her that was petty and dark, she harbored little anxieties and irritations, more annoying because she wanted to be a better person, struggled daily not to be petty and dark. Still, in her shadows, where she took things personally and felt rejection like the scratch of a fingernail on a blackboard, she was really mad at Gordon for being a hypocrite: noting how nice she was, but not really seeing how nice she was. So she tried to get Fred to reject Gordon, as Gordon had rejected her. She told Fred all the time that Gordon was not trustworthy, which was certainly the truth. Uncolored, she was sure, by what she felt about him. But as with all men whose backgrounds were better than his, Fred assumed that meant they were also better people. So he refused to recognize Gordon as an opportunist, which was what Lily was certain he was, writer though he categorized himself, serious biographer.

Lily had read that morning in a gossip column of a dinner to be held at Elaine's, honoring a woman *New York* magazine had labeled "Girl of the Year." The label had set off an instant round of parties in her honor, ensuring her becoming what the magazine said she already was. It seemed to Lily a singular phenomenon of New York that people could become famous for being famous. "A well-known escort of . . . ," "a celebrated friend of . . . ," "on the arm of . . . ," columnists wrote all the time, as if the owner of the arm was Venus de Milo, and the arm one that had been missing all those years. So Gordon, famous as he was for hanging around the famous, was sure to be at the party that evening. She could picture him telling anecdotes of the old Round Table at the Algonquin, where his novelist father had sat trading quips with Alexander Woollcott and Dorothy Parker.

"Do you want me to stay till you hear from Fred?" Hap Mitchel asked Lily at her door.

"That's not necessary," she said politely, wishing she could throw away all the amenities and cry out: yes, please, help me, stay with me. "But thank you."

"I'll call you in the morning." He touched his fingers to his temple, the cap he no longer wore, a friendly salute, a habit of respect that had apparently stayed with him.

The minute she closed the door, Lily hurried to the phone, called the restaurant, and asked for Gordon.

"Yes?" he said, picking up the receiver.

Sharp in the background, Lily could hear the cut of celebrity voices, the thrust and parry of smart repartee. "I apologize for bothering you, Gordon, but I'm worried. Is Fred at your apartment?"

"Who's this?"

"Gordon, please. It's Lily Masters. Don't play games. I'm afraid something's happened to him."

"Why are you calling me?"

"Is he at your apartment?"

"I can't hear you."

She could visualize him jammed against the pay phone on the wall by the dark wood, mirrored bar, a crush of the famous at his back, Michael Caine and Liza Minnelli pressed against the leather patches on his jacket.

"Is he at your apartment?" She heard that she was shouting.

"Lily! I can't believe my ears. You, doing something so tacky! Checking up on your husband!"

"Oh, Gordon, for God's sake! This doesn't call for banter. It isn't Noel Coward." She started to cry. "Something's happened to him. I know it. Please. Go see. Something's happened!"

Like most New Yorkers who had lived in New York all their lives and could afford choice, Gordon Grayson had elected to live in a security building. Because he was an artist, or hoping to be considered one, he headquartered himself on the West Side, in a neighborhood still considered desirable, within sound of the gunshot that had felled John Lennon. Since the Dakota, right across the street, with armed guards and a gated courtyard, had been the setting for that bizarre murder, there could obviously be no such thing as too much security. So, besides upper and lower Segal locks, Gordon had outfitted his door with a heavy metal bolt and chain. The service door also had double locks, and was, when Gordon arrived back home that evening, bolted from inside.

Gordon knew from their previous rendezvous that Fred and Miranda had a tendency to languor. He'd been letting them use the apartment since June, and many were the nights he'd hoped to return home early when he'd had to revise his plans. So at first, when they didn't answer his ring, he assumed they were still in the throes of it. But after some minutes had passed, and repeated pressure on the bell caused no audible stirrings inside the apartment, he began to pound loudly on the door. When no one answered, he went to get the superintendent, who broke in the door with a fire ax.

They found Fred and Miranda lying together on a bed in the alcove, a hand-painted silk coverlet pulled up to Miranda's shapely knees. They were both fully clothed, except for their shoes and Fred's jacket and tie. In his left hand, Fred was gripping a .22 caliber automatic, holding it, Gordon was later to write, "as if for dear Death." There was a bullet hole behind Fred's left ear, and one in Miranda's right eye. Their right hands were clasped, like little children in a fairy tale with a terrible, modern ending, two waifs who had fallen asleep in the urban forest.

Gordon phoned the police. He was surprised to hear that his voice was shaking as he told what had happened and gave his address. So little in his life besides his parents' deaths had actually touched him, so many of his relationships were filled with hugs that carried no real affection, conversations that held no real meaning. He had learned to ice skate through his days, skimming across the surface of his life, not even wondering where the depths were, if there were any. Mostly he had pursued events, occasions, dinner party invitations, content to be high on everybody's preferred list, not really caring what he was preferred for. Just happy to be in the hub of things. Death still seemed elusive, distant, something that happened to parents and the old.

Real feelings, like genuine friendships, were something he guarded against, setting a row of social responses in front of his emotions, like capped teeth. When there were accidents on the street, Gordon would simply not look, as if not seeing would deny the tragedies in the world, would put them out of existence. So he was stunned at how genuinely wrenched he was by the spectacle in his apartment, how devastated at the sight of Miranda.

She was graceful even in death, her slender throat a darker, deeper gold than her hair. He put his hand on her neck, where the carotid artery was, and the pulse of life should have been. There was still a touch of body warmth: he could feel the heat that had gone out of her. An unfamiliar sadness touched him, the wish that he had not been too late, that he could stuff the life back in. He who wept at funerals only when asked to give the elegy was unaccustomedly moved to tears at the sight of Miranda's eyes. Open, staring, bloody gore in the right one. Eyes the color of the peridot clip in her honey blonde hair, striped now with russet from the ooze of the wound.

Fred Masters had bought the clip for Miranda the day before, at Tiffany's. "A perfect match for those lamps that light my way to Paradise," he'd written on the note detectives were later to turn up in her apartment. In Masters' jacket they found three tickets for the following night's Metropolitan Opera Gala—the best seats in the house. There was no sign of a suicide note.

The autopsy report that would be filed called Miranda Jay "a well-developed, well-nourished white female, 29, measuring sixty-eight inches in length, weighing 126 pounds. The hair is blonde. The eyes are green." It hardly did her justice. Seeing her lying so, the life draining out of that hideous hole in her eye, Gordon was filled with unfamiliar rage. He felt not a whit of pity for Fred, but a rising tide of distaste that he had done that to Miranda, even if she'd wanted him to. That he'd also killed himself was beside the point. It had never occurred to Gordon that Fred, whose entire empire was built on seeking out the weakness in other men, could himself be so cowardly.

Nor did it occur to anyone else who knew Fred, especially in the absence of a suicide note. Fred had a fetish for notes, the largest collection of stored memoranda since David O. Selznick. The desk in his office, and several filing cabinets, contained a mountain of seemingly unimportant communiqués, over two thousand memos, telegrams and typed responses from business associates, friends, tailors, caterers, passing acquaintances. All of them apparently understood that Masters liked his confirmations in writing. In the center drawer of his desk at the office was a note on beige vellum stationery, in Miranda's florid handwriting, dated the day of shooting, marked, "Deliver by Messenger." It said how much she was looking forward to seeing him that evening at Gordon's apartment and how much she loved her peridot clip.

So it was very strange, considering Masters' passion for notes, that there was no sign of one, especially as suicide should have given him his best opportunity. Nor had there been any hints of despair. Fred Masters had never seemed a complex man. When he won, he celebrated; when he lost, he walked away. No brooding over the past. No meditating on the future. What he did he did like his youthful idol Harry Bell, direct, to the point, no fuss. It went with his blunt, somewhat bullish demeanor, no big to-do, no regrets. At the time of his death, he had never seemed in better spirits, his associates remarked. Excited about his tickets to the opera, New York's biggest night, with him in better seats—he had checked it—than the owner of the *New York Times*.

In Miranda's apartment a new gown hung on the bathroom door, still in its garment bag from Bergdorf Goodman. On the dresser, next to a silver-framed photo of what looked like a high school graduation picture—Miranda at the start of her bloom—was a new, beaded evening purse, and rhinestoned, satin shoes from Yves St. Laurent. All three salesgirls remembered their customer well and said she had been cheerful, excited about attending the gala.

So why had it happened? What made them do it? Why had they, of all people, charted a double suicide? Those who knew Miranda's recent history could accept her as a candidate for self-destruction. But not Fred. Never Fred, whose only connection with melancholy had been as an investor in a musical version of *Hamlet*, which mercifully closed in Philadelphia.

Was it possible she had talked him into it? Anyone who knew him at all well doubted it: she had not been that strong; he had not been that weak. A few ventured that perhaps she had talked of leaving him, and this was his answer. But no one could imagine Fred ending his life over love.

The first headlines hit the street at four o'clock the morning after the deaths, including an ''Extra'' edition of Masters' own tabloid. In the confusion surrounding Fred's demise, a young editor was appointed who was not as squeamish about exploiting Miranda as Fred would have been. He managed to sneak someone into the morgue to photograph her lying on a slab, eyes closed, bullet hole filled with a plastic cap, the powder burns around the eye cleansed, her hair rearranged over where they'd taken the top of her head off. In deference to Lily Masters, who was reportedly suffering a nervous breakdown, the editor waited till Miranda's body was speeded on its pine-boxed way to Los Angeles before the paper ran the picture on its front page. That way it seemed to him history rather than ghoulish. At least he had had the taste to wait till the body was cold, if not the story.

Even without the ensuing sensationalism, the event would have captured popular attention. Why would a man who had it all throw it away? The average New Yorker, indeed, the average American, convinced the handles to life were money and being Somebody, was thrown into a dazed kind of mourning, not for Fred, whom they had not known, but for a shattered conviction. There it was again: money didn't bring happiness, even when accompanied by Power, and—look at the woman—Sex.

Those who knew him were even more puzzled. There had been in Fred no fascination with the shadowy realm of death. Intellectuals who, when he was alive, had considered Fred not even worth dismissing, discussed him now as a burning question. He had not made a habit of reading Baudelaire. Didn't even know who Baudelaire was. Death had no attraction for him. He had not been emulating the poet Hart Crane as much as the publisher Rupert Murdoch. Why would such a man enter into a suicide pact?

Or maybe it was, after all, murder-suicide. Maybe Miranda was really going to leave him. Even a man as thick as Fred had a deep chord of passion in him and couldn't stand to be parted from her. Or maybe, speculated those in the choicest sections of the fashionable restaurants, it went even darker, deeper. Maybe it was some kind of covert, semi-official foul play. Some friends of Victor Lenrahan's. After all, hadn't there been embarrassment in the government about Miranda? Maybe there was a newer, better scandal about to surface that made it necessary to get rid of her.

Almost as steadily as the stream of conjectures came the publishing announcements. Several major hardcover houses heralded books about Fred and Miranda, some making it a three-way package with Victor Lenrahan.

Gordon Grayson threw a cocktail party-press conference in the Grill Room of the Four Seasons Restaurant with his publisher paying, Gordon's favorite kind of party. He stood in his tweed professorial jacket with a smoky taupe ascot the color of his hair, fielding questions from reporters about his coming book, the only authorized version of the Masters-Miranda story. There was no question in anyone's mind that Gordon was the man for the job, being uncontestedly Fred's best friend; not only his college roommate, but owner of the apartment where Fred elected to die.

The head of P.R. for the publishing house, a willowy brunette, at least the top two-thirds, with unfortunately stumpy legs, stood in a subgrouping with some journalists and the producer of "CBS Morning News." "It's almost as if Masters was setting it up for Gordon because he wanted his story in the hands of a pro," she told them.

"That was his favorite expression," the producer said. "We had him on the show last spring. He kept saying how he only wanted to deal with 'pros.' "

"He was like that in business," said a man from the *Wall Street Journal*. "Whenever he was making an investment, he would call around and ask if the others involved were 'pros.' "

"At the paper, too," said a reporter from Masters' own chain. "If we had a tricky story that might mean libel, he was always checking if the guys writing it were 'pros.' "

"I hear that's what he said the first time he saw Miranda," said a cub reporter from the *Post*. "He saw her sitting at a table at 21 and asked the maitre d', 'Is she a pro?' "

And many of them laughed, because they hadn't known Miranda.

By the captain's station, leaning against the reservations book, Gordon's literary agent, Stan Dobson, still with a bandage over one bushy black eyebrow, talked to a stringer from *Time*. "I told Truman, don't write about murders unless you can make it your masterpiece. And he did. I told Norman, don't write about Gary Gilmore unless you can make it Pulitzer Prize time. And he did. And I told Gordon, don't you go near this story unless you can make it Nobel caliber. And he will."

Two paperback houses, gearing up to a speed they hadn't displayed since the transcripts of the Nixon White House tapes, belched out some "quickie" publications about Miranda. They were thin little books, even with the pictures, composed mainly of interviews with people who had known her or claimed they did. Included were a diatribe on her housecleaning habits by her landlord in

Beverly Hills, a former character actor who played mostly Nazis, the kind of food she ate by the manager of the supermarket where she did her shopping. A seamstress who altered her clothes talked about how astonishing her body was: besides those magnificent breasts, there was the surprising delicacy of her rib cage and her tiny waist. There was an interview with a woman who had handled Miranda during her brief career in commercials. But in all the content was unsatisfactory for those who were really interested in who the woman might have been.

The gossip papers at supermarket checkouts did pieces on her doomed affairs with Masters and Victor Lenrahan, and Lenrahan's connections with Washington, both as Chairman of the Board of MercerCorp Aerospace and as a friend of the president's. The Hearst papers ran a series of articles on Miranda, including one composed entirely of ruminations on the clothes left hanging in her closet, which showed how ragged was the quest for real information.

There were plans announced for a television Movie of the Week called *Rich Man's Plaything*. But those were abruptly canceled when the head of the agency packaging the deal got a call telling him to kill it. Nobody would say who the phone call came from, but word was, it was Very High Up. *Very* High Up.

Lou Salerno went to her funeral. A detective from the LAPD certainly had enough death in his life without going to a stranger's burial. But he had seen all those pictures of Miranda, first when Lenrahan died, and now with this so-called double-suicide in New York. They touched his heart, because she was so beautiful. Lou had been investigating a supposed suicide on his own turf—another woman without a suicide note, with a bullet hole in her eye. Lou never believed it when a woman disfigured herself, even in death. They were too vain. So he wasn't quick to close the case, to call it a suicide and shut the file. Instead, he'd talked to the woman's friends, and none of them could say she'd been unhappy. And then he'd gotten hold of all her long distance calls, the records from AT&T, and one of the numbers she had called a lot turned out to be Fred Masters.

He went to Miranda's funeral not knowing exactly what he was looking for, but figuring it never hurt to keep your eyes open. Besides, he didn't mind paying his respects to beauty. He'd had a daughter that looked a little like that, maybe she would have looked more like that if she'd been given a chance to blossom, if some drunk hadn't plowed into her one Saturday night.

The service was held at the Westwood Mortuary, directly behind the AVCO movie theater on Wilshire Boulevard. There was not a particularly big turnout. Maybe twenty people. It made Lou sad that someone who looked like that and generated so much heat on front pages should turn out to have so few real friends. There were a couple of reporters with cameras, sniffing around like Lou was, to see if anybody important showed up. There was an old man who looked like a basset hound, sorrowful and overfed, and they took his picture.

"I'm not here for publicity," the old man said.

There was one big wreath of ribboned gladiolus, the funeral flower, on top of the closed coffin, and recorded organ music coming out of the amplifier. A nondescript minister with yellow hair and a Colorado twang got up and read from the Bible about a time to be born and a time to die. It made Lou mad, her dead and him talking about a time to die. How could anybody think it was a time to die, young like that?

He asked the mortician after the service to let him look at the signers' book, showed him his police ID, copied down the names of those who had attended. Considering what high rollers the girl had lived among, there did not seem to be any glossy names, any movie stars, society monikers. Lou's wife was always reading to him aloud from Suzy Jenks, the local society editor, as if pronouncing the names of the elite often enough would make her one of them. It was a small aberration on her part, one that made Lou laugh to himself, her sitting there in her flannel robe, hair in curlers, drinking coffee, following the adventures of the Armand Hammers.

After everyone had left, Lou went to the graveside with the high mound of dirt beside it covered with a plastic tarp. The old man who'd had his picture taken stood beside the freshly tapped earth that covered the grave, his expression even more hangdog than before.

"You a relative?" Lou asked him.

"A friend," he said. "I knew her when she was seventeen."

"She must have been something."

"A light. A candle flame." A single tear made its way down his cheek.

"Where did she come from?" Lou asked.

"Nobody ever knew, really. I met her in Paris."

"So she must have been around."

"She was fresh. Brand new. Why didn't I grab her then and spare all of us this terrible occasion?"

"Lou Salerno," Lou said, and held out his hand.

"Bertram Lester," the old man said, and shook it.

"The movie producer?"

"Once," he said. "Once when there were movies."

"Whose grave is that?" Lou noted the grave beside Miranda's, the fresh grass growing up bright green from the plot all that marked it as newer than the rest around it.

"I heard it was Lenrahan's. Nobody will say for sure. None of his friends know where he's buried. Not enough a man has to die in this world. People spit on his grave, at least the ones who know where to find it."

"Were you a friend of his?"

"In a sailboat kind of way. We both had yachts. Ships that passed in the marina, I guess you could say."

"You knew her when she was with him?"

"Nobody saw her much after she connected with Victor. He went out of his way to anchor his yacht in places where nobody would ever find them. Shitholes, if you'll excuse the expression." He seemed to be talking to the grave, asking apology for his language from Miranda. "I mean, who could blame him for hiding out when he had *that*?"

He looked skyward, at the sun that seemed to mar the day with its inappropriate brightness. "Christ, this is really disgusting, that she should be here. A precious young girl like that, here of all places."

"It's a nice cemetery," Lou said, looking around the small, square lot edged by a driveway that meandered past the chapel, around some scattered trees, alongside the white marble crypts, cutting back to the parking lot behind the movie houses. "What made them decide to send her body back to California?"

"I heard it was the wife. Lily Masters. She agreed to pay for everything as long as they got the girl out of New York quietly and faster than a speeding bullet. It seems Fred changed his whole will, giving Miranda a lifetime annuity, same as what she would have gotten from Lenrahan if he'd kept his word to her and not been such a prick. Not like Fred to be so generous. More proof how special she was, for all the good it did her. Still, the point isn't even moot, is it, with both of them deceased. Seems like a decent thing for Lily to do, to pay for the hole."

"Very decent."

"I wonder why the earth is all piled up like that?"

"That's what came out of the ground where the coffin went in. They have to give the grave time to settle."

"You know a lot about cemeteries?"

"More than I want to."

"I make it a point to stay out of them. Although the time is not far off when I won't have a choice. Still, if you have to hang out someplace, this is quite a choice location. Marilyn Monroe's here, you know."

"I heard that."

"All these beautiful women. Over there, Dorothy Stratten, the murdered Playmate of the Year. And just below the wax flowers, my old adversary, Darryl F. Zanuck, who would probably get a hard-on if he knew who he was hanging around."

"When did Zanuck die?"

"Just in time," Lester said sadly. "When it was still okay to be a retired giant, when movies were still movies, instead of all this computerized demographic shit, with teenage audiences all that matter. Little boys and girls in workout clothes running studios, not even knowing my name. And if they know it, surprised I'm not dead.''

"I'm sorry," Lou said.

"No sorrier than me," said Bertram. "What would she be, now, Marilyn? Fifty-eight? Fifty-nine?"

"Something like that."

"She was wise to die young," Bertram said, looking over at the white marble wall crypt.

A short, fat, freckled woman holding a book to her breast started running toward them, her left hand clutching the hand of a pale little boy, who struggled to keep up with her. "Where's Natalie Wood?" she called out.

"I don't know," Bertram called back, and shook his head again. "Natalie," he murmured. "What is it about this country that ripens women up so luscious and then cuts them down?"

The woman lumbered closer to them. "Well, I found Marilyn," she said breathing heavily. "She's over there in that white wall thing. There's a vase attached, only there's only daisies in it, with a note from a fan. But no more red roses, so DiMaggio must have stopped sending them. I heard he sent them every week for twenty years. But I can't find Natalie." Her round face was shiny with the exertion. "She's supposed to be here."

"Then I'm sure she didn't go anywhere," Bertram said.

"What's the book?" asked Lou Salerno.

The woman held it out. "*Permanent Addresses*," she read. "'The Final Resting Place of Famous Americans.'"

"Charming," Bertram noted.

"Where'd you get that book?" asked Lou.

"Chicago." She smiled at them. "You live out here?"

"You could call it that," Bertram sighed.

"You're so lucky, so close to all of them." Her eyes swept the crowded graveyard.

"Closer every day," said Bertram.

"Your first trip to Hollywood?" Salerno asked.

She nodded. "We're on our way to Disneyland, but we

came here first. I wouldn't have missed it." She noticed the new grave they stood by. "Who's here? Anybody important?"

"Miranda Jay," Salerno said.

"Oh, I read about her. The call girl."

"What's a call girl?" the little boy asked.

"A woman who takes money for her favors," she told him. "A scarlet woman."

"You got it wrong," said Bertram. "That wasn't Miranda."

He started to walk away. Salerno hurried after him, fell into slow step beside him.

"I hate these fucking tourists," Lester said. "What is it about this country that makes fanatics so fanatic they come to a graveyard and don't even know a whore from a patsy."

"Is that what Miranda was?"

"She was a sweetheart," he said. "A Post Toastie. I should have swallowed her whole in Paris. She would have made me young, and then she'd be alive, and I'd still be making movies." He passed the grave where Darryl Zanuck lay, beside, said the bronze plaque in the earth, his beloved wife, Virginia. "Hey, Zanuck!" he called. "If you could only still wheedle, you old cocker, what a proposition you'd make to who's lying next to you!"

"So what's her story?" Salerno asked. "If she wasn't a call girl, what was she?"

"A symbol for our times," said Bertram Lester.

MIRANDA

◇

At her birth, there were dark and light fairies in the room. Her mother looked up at the ceiling and saw them. Sun and shadow. Good and evil. Raining down blessings, spitting out curses. She knew right away that her child was going to be celebrated.

Lettie was not a superstitious woman, but it had been a very long labor. So by the time the baby's head appeared, her mother was hallucinating. All the same, she saw them very clearly, protecting and damning. Hissing and blowing kisses. "She's not going to be an ordinary person," she told her husband. "She's special."

He was a thick man, with feelings to match his physical shape. Nothing about him was sensitive, except to his own comfort. But it was not a part of the country or a time when women had options, so Lettie never wondered why she married him, or what else she might have done.

Tom Morton had no dreams for himself, so he certainly had none for his daughter. Food on the table and clothes and enough heat to guard against harsh Ohio winters were as close as he came to aspiration. There were layoffs in his town even when times were good; all he wanted was to keep his job, to stay alive. So he paid no attention to his wife's prophecy. All he wished for his child was that she wouldn't cause trouble.

She was christened Honey Miranda Morton. Lettie had been in a high school production of *The Tempest* and loved the name Miranda. Honey was the mother-in-law's choice of a name; Lettie didn't want to tangle with her mother-in-law. Besides, she knew it would be easier for the girl to live with a name that wasn't too fancy for the locals. At least until her true destiny revealed itself.

The name Honey actually suited her. There was a golden tint to her skin even in winter. When it was summer and she ran on the lawn through the sprinklers in her ribbed white cotton underwear, her round little shoulders and face and arms would darken to a color you could almost taste: sweet and juicy and hot. It was all her father could do not to take a bite out of her, a feeling that was to be shared by most men.

They were too quick to notice her, almost as if she gave off a scent. Tom Morton saw that, even through his thickness. When she was nine, he stopped inviting friends home from the factory. He saw how they looked at her, even before she had breasts. Sometimes studying her himself, he would have to run into the bathroom and lock the door, sit on the toilet and jerk himself off. The shame at what he was doing almost outweighed the relief.

One hot summer day, with the weeds taking over their little square of lawn, and Lettie squeezing lemonade, she asked him: "How come you don't have your friends over anymore?"

"They drink my beer," he said. "I don't like freeloaders." He was standing in the doorway watching Honey run through the sprinklers. She shrieked with pleasure when the water hit her, soaking her to the golden skin, her round little buttocks gleaming through the cotton. "She's getting too old to run around in her underwear."

"She's nine."

"I don't want her running around in skivvies," Tom said.

He was enraged at the feelings his daughter generated in him. At night he would go at his wife like a piston, making her cry out sometimes in the quilted squeak of their bed, slapping her when he came, because she was so plain, his cum would trickle out of him, not with the rush he got when he dreamed of the other one.

"Don't I make you feel good?" Lettie would whimper, sopping at the wet between her legs with a Kleenex from the box she kept by the bed.

"Are you still talking?" he said.

The walls were not as thick as he was, so Honey would lie there in her bed, listening to the thumps and thwacks, and the squeaks of the bedsprings, wondering what they were doing in there that made her mother cry. She was confused about life already, because the start of it had been filled with hugs, and now her father never touched her and her mother seemed nervous all the time. The hurt little sounds that came through the wall were like a warning signal to Honey, alerting her to be afraid. The day after, her mother would always be short-tempered and sullen. If

Honey got in her way, there would be slaps, stinging blows across her cheeks and shoulders.

Her father hardly talked to her anymore. When he did speak, he would read the Bible to her, growling warnings. She liked fairy tales better, knowing what she did of the story about her own birth, the magic her mother had told her about, the spell she was surely under. In fairy tales there weren't so many sins to be warned against, to pay for later. All you had to do was to be poisoned by a needle or a witch's apple and someone would come and save you with a kiss. But all Tom Morton read her were black cautions, and all he ever said was "Be careful of strangers. Stay away from strangers. Don't take anything from strangers." But he never warned her about the people who were close.

When she was ten, she went to visit two cousins in Covington, Kentucky. Lying in the bed in the darkness, with her two girl cousins asleep beside her, she suddenly heard heavy breathing close by. Smelled whiskey breath. Felt a hand go across her mouth. It was her uncle. She was too frightened to scream. He fell on Honey, sticking something hard up inside her. She could hear the bedsprings squeaking in that terrible way she heard through the wall at home. And she wondered in her pain if this was what her father did to her mother to make her so crazy. Why would he want to hurt her like that? Why would Uncle Charley want to hurt Honey like that? "You tell anybody," Charley whispered when he was through, "I'll kill you."

She believed him. She didn't know about sex. Lettie had thought it was too soon to tell the little girl about sex, so Honey didn't know it was sex that happened with her uncle. She only thought he was mad at her, that he wanted to hurt her. She wondered what she had done to make him so angry.

"Uncle Charley hurt me," she told her aunt the next morning. She had seen the blood, and the thought of his doing it again scared her more than that he might kill her. "He came into bed and hurt me."

"You terrible child," her aunt said. "How could you make up such a thing?"

"I'm not making it up. He said he'd kill me if I told you."

"You're just trying to get attention," her aunt said, whipping up some pancakes, the whirring of the fork covering her obvious irritation. "I always said that about you. Ever since you were a little thing. Sashaying around. Acting so uppity. Like you was some kind of movie star. Batting those eyes."

Her aunt's anger was as surprising to her as her uncle's had been. "What does that mean, sashaying?"

"Wagging your little butt," Florence said, biting her lips, folding in eggs, dropping a piece of shell into the batter without meaning to, her hand was shaking so badly. Her own daughters were regulation girls. She wondered why her sister Lettie, who had no greater virtue or beauty than she did, should have been given such a gorgeous child. Now that she knew Honey was a liar she felt that much better.

"You mean it was my fault, what happened?"

"Nothing happened, you little liar."

"I'm not a liar."

"Don't tell me. My poor sister. Thinking you were so special. Always treating you like some kind of princess. What could you turn out to be but a liar?"

Now shame was added to Honey's confusion. When she got home, she never told her mother what had happened. She didn't need anybody else being mad at her, doubting her, calling her names. Saying she sashayed.

She refused to go visit her cousins again, ever. But she never told her mother why. When Uncle Charley died in a factory accident, she wouldn't go to the funeral. And while everyone else was in Covington, she went down to the lake and threw rocks in it, whispering to the ripples, "Thank you, God."

When she was eleven, the president of the local bank saw her standing in line to cash her father's paycheck as she usually did on a Friday, and got an erection without any touch stimulation for the first time since he was sixteen. He began stationing himself by the window where she would come so he could almost smell her.

He pressed his daughter into giving a tea for some less fortunate girls in town and made sure the Morton girl was among them. For three weeks Lettie devoted herself to making Honey a dress, pale green taffeta, the color of Honey's eyes, weeping with excitement while she sewed.

"This is it," Lettie murmured to herself, the needle carefully whipping through the fabric, the rustling sound of future fantasies in her ears. "Now begins the magic." She'd been sure it was coming from the moment Honey was born, a life different from everyone else's around them. Here it was then, the first wave of light from the good fairy's wand. It never occurred to her it might be a drubbing from the dark side.

On the day of the tea she dressed her daughter, lifting her arms, smoothing her hair as if she were still a little baby, a beautiful dolly to play with. "You just be polite and speak when you're spoken to," she told Honey when she was almost ready to leave for the tea party. She wound the thick, honey yellow hair with ribbons the same pale green as the dress, turned the girl around, looked deep into the heart-shaped face. She kissed her smooth amber cheek and whispered, "This is where your story starts."

The house where the banker's daughter lived was not like any other house Honey had ever seen, except in the movies. There were silks on the sofas and chairs that matched the fabrics on the walls, pillows of the same thread as footstools, so elegant she couldn't imagine anyone putting their feet on them. The banker's daughter, Amy, seemed just as expensive and untouchable, her mouth pulled into a tight little moue, as though she disapproved of the whole afternoon. Amy did not say a word to her guests, her puckered lips working disaffectedly around the tarts and scones, as though in spite of the sweetness, the raisins within, it was all a bitter pill to swallow.

Her father came into the room. Honey remembered seeing him at the bank, a shortish man, his hair light brown and thinning at the top, nothing very impressive about him, except who he was and the way he looked at people. "Amy, dear, why don't you introduce me to your friends?"

"They're not my friends," Amy said. "They're under-privileged children."

"That's not very nice."

"It's the truth. It was your idea to invite them."

"Now watch what you say. You don't want them to think you're an unpleasant person."

"I don't care what they think," Amy said, and reached for another tart.

"Hello," he said, to each of the girls present, taking their hands. His fingers lingered on Honey's. "What lovely young ladies," he said.

"I hate them," muttered Amy.

"That's a terrible thing to say. Hate is unchristian. Besides, you don't know them well enough to hate them."

Every Monday after that, when Honey went to the bank, Julian would greet her, coming out from his office as though he had just happened to see her and not as if the day had been spent waiting. Some days he would take her for ice cream, ordering her pistachio, the color of her eyes. It became a pleasant ritual between them, even though Honey would rather have had chocolate. But he obviously knew more about what was good than she did.

They celebrated her turning twelve with a bottle of carbonated apple cider, which he said was just a stepping-stone away from champagne. On the Monday after that, he offered to drive her home. But first, since it was such a beautiful day, he said, he suggested they take a drive in the country.

All along the edge of the road he maneuvered in his big black Cadillac were daffodils, sentries guarding the route of spring. He turned off Highway 71, onto a side road, a dirt road, telling her there was something he wanted to show her.

"What?" she asked him, wondering if it was greedy, the hope that he'd bought her a present.

He stopped the car by an apple orchard, its branches fragrant with blossoms. "This," he said, and took her in his arms and kissed her.

She tried to push away. She wasn't sure what it was all about, any more than she had understood what happened with her uncle, made no connection between the two episodes, still didn't know about sex. But in her confusion and panic she intuited how wrong it was. He was the father of another girl.

"Leave me alone!" she cried, as her own father yelled all the time now when she tried to kiss him, to climb into his lap, telling her, "You're too big for this sort of thing." She was terrified of making Julian angry. Enough people were mad at her already. The boys at school who didn't know why she wouldn't let them walk her home, with Tom Morton waiting by the window; the girls who didn't like her because they thought she was stuck-up, just because of that nose. The only ones who treated her with some sort of regard were her teachers. And now, here was this very rich, important man, and if he got mad, her mother would be so disappointed. All her hard work on that dress. For nothing.

"Please," Honey said. "Don't."

He started to cry. "Oh, God, don't you think I'd stop myself if I could? Don't you know I love you? How I dream about you? From the minute you first came into that bank. You think I'm not ashamed? I'd strip off my skin if I thought it would do any good. I'd cut this off. But it wouldn't help me stop thinking about you."

Then he touched her again, but in a different way. Glided his fingers in between her thighs, touched her so softly she caught her breath. He reached inside the elastic of her pants, fingertips brushing her slit. And while his lips pressed her mouth, he found her center. A kind of heat she didn't know was inside her bubbled up and was released.

She wasn't afraid anymore. She couldn't get enough of it.

Every Monday afternoon after that, they drove into the country, Honey relaxed and waiting for it in the front seat of his Cadillac, the safety belt tight around her as they drove, guarding her treasure, he said. She felt like a woman now. With the jump on everybody else because she knew what the secret was, what all the whispers and blushes were about, the sin that was decried at church on Sunday, making her more excited because the next day was Monday.

It pleased her as much as the lovemaking aroused her, the thought that she was putting one over on her father. All the affection she had been denied, Tom's withdrawal from her, and his cold brutality toward her mother was avenged in the backseat and by the fact that he didn't know, couldn't imagine. So busy not letting her be around boys, forbidding her to go to dances or roller skating because the skirts were too short. Not seeing the forest for the trees, the man for the boys he was so afraid of. Sly vengeance seemed the least she could have on him for what he'd done to Lettie. Treating her with no respect or regard. Turning her into a zombie. As though her spirit had packed up and left, with only her body still in the house, doing chores. Laundry. Ironing. Ironing even the towels. Pressing her life into neat little squares. Folding up her days.

That wasn't going to happen to Honey.

Ambition was something Julian taught her, hunger for the faraway luxuries of life. Paris. He would tell her about it over and over while he drove her to the apple orchard.

"You belong in Paris," he told her. "One day I'll take you there. Paris is the place for artists. And that's what you are. A born artist. With your own special gift."

"What is it?" Honey asked him.

"I'll show you," he said, and took her into the backseat.

Now that it was winter, he brought along hot cider and antifreeze and extra gasoline so they could stay warm, keep the engine running the whole time they made love. "What if someone catches us?" she asked him.

"Not to worry," he said. "It's my orchard. In a fiduciary way."

"What's fiduciary?"

"It involves a trust. Our bank foreclosed on the farmer whose orchard this is. He moved away. So there's no one to come and hear us," he said, and made her moan. "Or see me doing this." She sighed beneath his tongue. "It's kind of like having a deaf, blind friend with a motel. Nothing to worry about."

So when he looked up from between her legs and saw the man peering in through the frosted window, his cheeks started twitching. Honey caught the astonished look on his face, the spasm of surprise, and turned to see what he was gaping at. It was her father. He was carrying a shotgun.

"Get up from there, you filthy son of a bitch," Tom Morton said from between motionless lips. "Get up from there so I can kill you, without you messing on my baby."

"You don't want to do that." Julian wrapped his arms around her naked waist, pulled her tight to his chest, holding her between himself and Morton.

"Oh, yes, I want to do that," Tom said. "I really want to do that." He smashed the front window with the butt of his gun and unlocked the door. All at once his face flashed pale. The right side drooped. The gun fell out of his hand and he seemed to watch it slip away from him, as if in slow motion. Then he fell, face forward, in the snow.

Honey started screaming. "Shut up!" Julian snarled. "Shut up and put your clothes on."

"What are we going to do?"

"Leave him here."

"You can't. Oh please. He's my daddy. Don't leave him here to die."

"He's already dead."

"Maybe not. Please. We have to help him."

"Help him what? Kill me?"

"Please. You can't leave him here to die." She tugged

on his arm like the little girl she knew all of a sudden she still was. Finally he agreed to take Tom back to town.

They drove through the freezing afternoon with the window broken open, her father in the back seat with her, dead weight in her arms. She wept, terrified.

"Shut up! Shut up!" Julian kept saying.

He left them at the emergency entrance of the hospital. He dumped Tom Morton like a sack of rotting potatoes at her feet and took off before anyone could see him. She ran inside for help. Attendants put Tom on a stretcher, carrying him into emergency. Doctors did a workup on him, then moved him to Intensive Care.

"Will he be all right?" Honey asked when she came back from calling her mother.

"He's going to live," said the young resident. "He's had a right-sided stroke."

Her father's left eye was a little open. In it she could see how much he hated her.

"What does that mean? Will he be able to talk?"

"We don't know. There are always chances."

She telephoned Julian at the bank, where he was waiting for her call. "Will he be able to talk?" he asked her.

"They don't know," Honey said. "There are always chances."

The day after that, Julian disappeared. It was the biggest scandal ever to hit a local bank. Apparently, went the gossip and some articles in the local paper and the judicial inquiry, he'd taken off with a million and a half in cash and negotiable bonds.

"Imagine a banker doing that," Lettie said, in a momentary respite from personal grief, gossip sometimes serving to heal by distracting. "You remember Julian Randall? You went to tea at his house."

"I remember," Honey said as she watched the blips on the screen of the Intensive Care Unit, giving her father's vital signs. "You made me a green dress."

"The color of your eyes," said Lettie.

Honey knew she would never see Julian Randall again. For reasons she couldn't explain even to herself, she started making sure she was the first one to get to the mail. And sure enough, one day there was an envelope for her, in an unfamiliar but somehow recognizable hand. Inside was an airline ticket to Paris and a stock certificate worth three thousand dollars. And a note, unsigned, that said, "If you ever get the nerve."

As penance, she nursed her father. During school hours he was her mother's job. But the rest of the time Honey did the slavish, stomach-churning things.

When he wasn't in bed on plastic sheets, he sat in a wheelchair. Honey tried looking him in the eyes the doctor said could still see. But Tom would stare past her or look away like he was blind and not just paralyzed. He also pretended to be deaf. So there was no way she could get through to him, to make him know how sorry she was. His shutting her out made her feel like tipping the wheelchair over. Stubborn turned out to be his strongest suit.

The therapist came twice a week to reteach Tom how to talk. But he wouldn't do that either. Honey was glad about that. At least he wouldn't tell her mother about her.

Saturday nights she sent Lettie to the movies. While all the other teenagers were going to dances and movies and parties, Honey atoned, reading to him from the Bible, the way he'd done to her, only the peacemaking parts, the turning the other cheek.

"You hear me, Pop?" In that section of Ohio, as in Western Pennsylvania, they called their fathers "Pop" the same as they did soda. "Can you hear me?"

But he stared and made no sign. "I know you can hear me. Can't you see how sorry I am?" She knelt down in front of his wheelchair, locked up into his expressionless face. "Don't you know how much I love you?" He seemed not to hear.

She got up and went behind him, took a pot from the stove and threw it on the linoleum floor. He jumped with his left side.

"You can hear! I knew you could!" She came around in front of him and fell to her knees, crying, taking his hand, holding it to her lips. "Oh, Daddy, please. I know how bad I was. But give me a chance! Let me at least say I'm sorry."

He pulled his hand away and lifted his left knee, sharply, catching her in the jaw, knocking her to the floor. It was a relief for her, strangely, pain she could actually feel in her body. Liberating. She got to her feet, rubbing her elbow.

"You're a mean old man. I know it's my fault you got old. But you make it worse. You make it harder." She slammed out the door, stood in the patch of burned grass her mother called a yard. Summer was the worst time. The Chamber of Commerce had a brochure about Butler County that said the climate was humid continental. That didn't make it sound as bad as it was. They should have written, summers cook you. Insects come and eat you when you're in your own gravy. She made up her mind in that moment to get out of there.

She would use her ticket to Paris. She had a destiny. Let the dead bury the dead. She understood what that really meant now.

Right after school on Monday, she went to the Butler County Courthouse.

"Hi," she said to the woman sitting behind the concession stand in the lobby. In Hamilton, everybody knew everybody else, so she had to cover her tracks before she made them. "I'm doing a project for civics class. What do you have to do when you want to leave the country?"

"Third floor," the woman said, taking a bite from one of her own mayonnaisey sandwiches. "County Clerk's office."

There was a rack of pamphlets on the counter of the clerk's office with information on how to get a passport. Nobody Honey knew had ever left Ohio, except to go to Niagara Falls for a honeymoon, or Conneaut Lake for a vacation. Certainly nobody had ever gone to Europe, with a passport, except Julian before she knew him. No catching up with him now to ask questions.

"What else do you need besides a passport?" she asked a typist in the corner.

"A ticket."

"Besides a ticket."

"An immunization certificate."

"You have one I can show my civics class?"

The woman got up and took a yellow cardboardish certificate from the drawer. "The doctor fills it in. You need different shots, depending on where you're going."

"I'm not going anywhere. I'm doing a project for civics class."

Sitting in the park, with its green slatted benches bolted to the sidewalk, Honey studied the pamphlet. She would need a certified copy of her birth certificate, two professional passport pictures, and twelve dollars. The only photographer in town took official pictures for the high school, and might tell somebody she wanted passport pictures. So Honey decided to get them taken in Cincinnati.

There was one boy who'd been wanting to walk her home from school from the time she was eight. Now he had a car. She let him drive her to Cincinnati.

"What do I get in return," he said on the way there, and put his hand between her legs.

"Well not *that*," she said, and bent his fingers backward. She thought he would howl in pain, but instead he kind of grinned, embarrassed or pleased, she couldn't really tell.

She had a sad feeling while she was posing for the photographer. It was a sorrow that touched to the core of what limited history she had, because she knew she would be missing her first important landmark, her high school graduation. She would never be in her high school yearbook. The signposts of childhood had been torn up for her, her girlhood over before she'd even understood it could end, and why. Whatever milestones were in a small town existence, the little pit stops of reality, she would never have. They disappeared from her life before her life officially began.

"What's this picture for?" the photographer asked her

as she arranged her legs primly beneath her on the high wooden stool, pulling her anklets up neatly.

"My high school graduation picture," she lied.

"Then try not to look so beautiful," the photographer said. "High school pictures are supposed to look plain."

She smiled at the lens. "That tears it," he said. "You blew out my camera."

"Really?"

"Only kidding, kid. Let's do one more. Throw your shoulders back and sit up straight. Nothing to hide with that body."

"They only want a picture of my face," she said.

"Well that's for them. This is for me."

"Why should I?"

"Make it my treat. Stick 'em up. Do that and you don't have to pay for the pictures."

So the levels you could get favors on were endless. She understood that already, and she was only fifteen. On the way home she let Brian stop the car and kiss her. His kiss was the kiss of an amateur, closed-toothed and awkward. She kissed him back in his own fashion. Enough, she figured, for twenty miles.

Once home, the pictures secreted in the back of her closet, she told her mother she needed a copy of her birth certificate for school. It struck Honey as amazing that you didn't need your parents' permission to get a passport when you needed it for almost everything else. The one vaccination she had to have to go to Europe was smallpox, and she'd already had that. That and her plane reservation. So all that was left was her stock certificate.

She knew better than to cash it at the Hamilton Bank. She made a couple more trips to Cincinnati with Brian, and spotted an old man at the bank. She smiled at him a time or two, so the next time she came he remembered her. It wasn't hard to get him to cash it for her. She understood, in a way, that she was becoming wily.

"Please," Brian said, on the way back from Cincinnati. "Just touch it."

He was really sort of pitiful, with the big bulge behind

his zipper. It gave her a feeling of power over him, a power he didn't have over her.

"Please."

"Oh, all right. No, I better not. You might get excited."

"Please. I'm already excited."

"Oh."

"Please. Please. Just hold it."

"Like that?"

"Oh, yes. Like that."

"Okay."

"Now move your hand up and down."

"What if something happens?"

"Oh, please."

"Like this?"

"Yes. Yes. Like that."

"I think I better stop now."

"Please. Please don't stop."

"I have to. It isn't nice." And tucking him back inside, feeling his anger and his sullen disappointment, she knew he would be good for another ride to Cincinnati.

Her reservation to Paris was for the day of her sixteenth birthday. She'd packed her suitcase the night before, setting it outside the back door, ready for her escape.

The morning of her birthday, she hugged her mother extra hard. Lettie was pretty much sleepwalking through her days, but she wasn't dead. "What's wrong?" she asked Honey. "What's wrong with my baby?"

"I'm not a baby anymore." Panic gripped her. Wasn't she? She was ready to forget about all her plans. But she saw her father looking at her, his eyes filled with loathing. His spite gave her all the courage she needed.

When they were alone in the living room, with Lettie in the kitchen warming up his strained prunes, Honey leaned over and looked into her father's face, straight into the eyes he only pretended were blind. "Good-bye, you mean old man," she whispered. "You paid me back. We're even."

Brian met her down the street to take her to the airport. She could see he already had a hard-on.

"I don't feel like it. I'll miss my plane."

"It doesn't leave till eleven."

"I have a lot of things to think about. I want to get to the airport early."

"You're going to be a big movie star. I just know it. It's right you're going to Hollywood. You're so beautiful."

"Thank you."

"Couldn't you just touch it while I drive?"

"Is that why you said something nice? So I'd do it?"

"I mean it. You're beautiful. So couldn't you just touch it?"

"You'll get all excited and go off the road."

"Then just press against it."

"Okay." She sat with the heel of her hand pressed against him, till her hand fell asleep. How dumb he was, she couldn't help thinking, to believe she was going to Hollywood when the plane she was taking wasn't even heading west. How could he think she was like every other good-looking girl who ever ran away? Why did people suppose everyone's dream was the same?

At the last, just before they got to the airport, she let him pull off the road and touch her breasts, and moan, and beg her. She felt a sort of charity toward him because he was helping her escape. So at the gate, she returned his kiss, opened her mouth and slipped him a taste of her tongue, so maybe he'd get it, do it better with the next girl. That in exchange for the rides.

But no more than that. For the rest of it, she understood now, a girl could get a trip to Paris.

Paris was as cold as it was beautiful, the people and the weather. She felt so bone weary from her trip, she almost wasn't afraid. Almost wasn't panicky about where she would sleep, where she would eat, if they had bathrooms. Wondering if the language was the same as the one she'd studied in school.

Around her, everything echoed as in a dream, sounds bouncing up to the high ceilings, falling down again in a babble of soft-sounding tongues. She let herself be carried

with the crowd to customs and immigration. The man in
the glass booth who stamped her passport asked her how
long she was planning to stay in France. She answered
with the sentence she had been practicing in her head,
telling him she loved France, wanted to learn about the
country and its people. The expression on his face was
frost tinged. "I speak English," he said.

She moved with the flood of travelers putting their
luggage onto the bus. The driver seemed annoyed that she
hadn't changed her dollars for francs, took the bills like he
hated them.

"Where do I get change?" she asked the little gray-
haired woman beside her.

"American Express."

She felt relieved at the sound of the word American.
She experienced a surge of longing for what she left
behind, as little love as there was in it. Familiar pain was
somehow more comforting than pleasure you weren't sure
was coming.

She looked out the window. The sky looked higher. The
sky above Paris seemed a long way away. Higher than the
sky had ever been in Ohio.

The bus moved off the highway, into the city, cutting
through cobblestoned streets lined with tiny shops, unreal,
enchanted, miniature, as though all of it were the paintings
it resembled, windows filled with fresh baked bread, lined
up and leaning, shiny pottery, colorful clothes. She could
hardly believe she was seeing what she was seeing. Paris.

She took a taxi to American Express, gave the driver a
ten dollar bill. He sneered at her like it was not enough.
But when she stepped inside the agency, she saw from the
posted rate of exchange it was four times as much as the
meter had registered.

Around her was all the bustle of a basketball game,
people milling around, crowds in line. "What are you
looking for?" she heard a rich voice say.

She turned and saw him. He was tall, with eyes as clear
as hers, but blue. Yellow hair curled like a cherub's
ringlets around the tanned skin of his big-boned face. With

everything she had experienced of sex, Honey had never felt infatuation. This was a level up. Air in her blood, going to her brain.

From the time she was very young, she had been very old. No time to join in with the inane giggles of her classmates. No opportunity for twelve-year-old love and its accompanying foolishness. She felt all of it now, silliness, empty-headedness, a dizziness that was like an actual presence inside her, an impish child with most of its weight below the waist.

She swayed. He caught her arm. "You must be careful."

"I haven't been to sleep," she said, her voice, like the rest of her, higher.

"How unfortunate for the bed," he murmured.

His name was Alex. He took her for chocolate chaud in a sidewalk café. All around them were lovers embracing. He soothed her fingers, rubbed the weariness from her wrists, rolled his thumbs up her arm, massaged the knots of tension from her neck, curled her hair, stroked her scalp, never stopped touching her. He was a drummer, studying music in Paris. He had wonderful hands.

He took her home. They went up in the slow, ancient elevator to his apartment, and he kissed her through the ride, a lifetime of missed kisses in his mouth, a world of romance in his tongue, tenderness she had never felt in the warm manipulations of his hands. His fingers beat a constant tattoo on her back, moving up and down the flesh inside her sweater.

The elevator stopped. Reluctantly, he moved his lips away from her mouth, butted his head gently toward her face, brushed her cheek with the soft fall of ringlets above his temple. It was hard for her to breathe. She felt like her whole being was between her legs, her nether mouth full, alive, dripping, as though it had overeaten.

He opened the grilled gate with one hand, the other still on her neck, urging her out into the darkness of the landing. Then he let go of her and carried her luggage into his apartment. Started kissing her again in the still of the entry hall, one of his hands moving under her skirt, into her pants, down between her buttocks, coming to rest momentarily on the hole she'd always thought was there just for waste, fluttering it into fire. While his other hand moved and took her hand and pressed it against the hard length of him, he murmured against her mouth, "See what you do to me."

She trembled. He took her to the chaise, propped the pillows behind her. "You must be tired from your trip," he said. "I'll let you sleep."

She almost cried aloud for him not to go, to finish what he'd started. But he was gone into the bedroom and the door was closed.

Eventually she fell asleep. When she woke up it was the middle of the night and she couldn't remember where she was, but she remembered his hands, how they had moved, and how they had moved her. And she wondered what he'd think of her if she simply undressed and went into his bed. Reluctantly, she forced herself back to sleep and woke up to Paris morning.

He was standing over her, his yellow hair tousled from sleep. "How are you?"

"Okay." She had no words in her mouth. Only a sickish, puppy longing.

"I'll fix you breakfast," he said, then showed her where the bathroom was so she could clean up.

They had creamy coffee and warm croissants. His eyes never left her face. She could barely swallow, ravenous as she was.

"What would you like to do now?" he asked her. "Would you like to take a walk and see some of Paris?"

"I don't know."

"But Americans are so good about expressing themselves," he said, in his crisp-edged German diction. "Why don't you express yourself? What do you want to do?"

"Whatever you want," she said, not able to look at him.

"Did you sleep well?"

"I woke up in the middle of the night."

"Why didn't you wake me?"

She swallowed. "I didn't know if it was right."

"But you are American. Americans know what is right. So what would you like to do?"

"I don't know."

"Would you like to go to bed?"

"Yes," she said, wishing she had lies in her.

"Then come," he said, and led her into the bedroom, undressing as he went, waiting at the edge of the bed while she did the same, his erection enormous and purple-tipped. She lay back on the bed and waited for the tender onslaught of his mouth and his hands. But his fingers gripped her wrists, pressed them backward against the bed as he entered her, jutted into her insides.

"Oh. If you only knew how that felt."

"Tell me," she said, and waited for the words that would be as warming as his hands had been.

"It feels right," he said, and, lifting her legs, put her ankles on his shoulders and fucked.

When it was over, he lay beside her, his arm casually over her shoulder, and she waited. "How come," she ventured. "How come last night you never stopped touching me, and now you never touched me at all?"

"Last night was the first half," Alex said, and got up to take a shower.

But when they were in public, he touched her, as all lovers in Paris touched, kissing on the Metro, embracing beside the Seine. As if love exhibited were a part of the art of Paris.

They walked through public gardens, breathing in the aroma of dying leaves, wandered the marbled corridors of the Louvre. "When you can be as mysterious as this," he said, as they stood in front of the Mona Lisa, his body pressed behind hers, his mouth against the side of her neck. "You won't have to worry."

"Do I have to worry now?" she asked, worrying. "Would you love me better if I was mysterious?"

"I couldn't love you better," he said.

They feasted on fish soup lightly laced with wine, crusty bread, and soft, ripe cheese. They would meet his friends, other musicians studying in Paris, for a glass of wine at the Café Deux Magots.

"You rich Americans," said his friend Celeste, a clarinetist who chain-smoked Gauloise, a foul-smelling cigarette that browned her teeth so her mouth looked already old. "How lucky you are. Never to have to ask anyone for anything."

"I'm not rich," Honey said.

"All Americans are rich," said Alex.

"Rich and innocent," said Celeste. "They will never match the sophistication of Europeans."

"Maybe they wouldn't want to," Honey said.

"Freedom of choice doesn't mean you shouldn't see with your eyes open," said Heinrich, a pianist who drank Pernod, his skin the sickish color of the pale, licorice drink.

Then one day Alex told her he was expecting his uncle. "You'll have to stay someplace else. I spoke to Celeste. You can move in with her while he's here."

"Why can't he stay someplace else?"

"This is his apartment."

She moved in with Celeste, who spoke to her only on the day the rent was due. The rest of the time she was silent, her presence indicated only by the piping of the clarinet through the closed door and the heavy odor of Gauloise wafting through the walls like clouds of disdain.

Honey spent her days walking around Paris, sitting in open gardens, waiting in the shadow of Metro tunnels till the best of the melodies the street musicians played had faded. Afternoons she would go to the movies on the Champs Elysées, loneliness improving her French as she listened to the soft Gallic sounds in the darkness, studying the subtitles on American movies so her eye and her ear became schooled. Alex saw her when he could, sometimes for breakfast, rarely for dinner, once to the Comédie Française. Solitude had sharpened her understanding of French, if not the ways of men.

"Why haven't you introduced me to your uncle?" she asked him as they came out of the theater.

"He doesn't like Americans," he said.

Then her period was late. She telephoned him. Another man answered. She hung up the phone, giddy with relief, because all along she had the fear that maybe he was lying to her. That it wasn't his uncle living with him at all, but another woman.

She went to the building where he lived, waited in the courtyard for him to come home. It grew dark. A light went on in his apartment.

She was ashamed of how eager she felt, how filled with apology and longing. She had no patience for the elevator, ran up the stone, circular stairway, pressing the button at every landing to light her way. The door to his apartment was unlocked. She pushed it open.

He sat on the chaise, naked, his arms outstretched against the satin fabric. Kneeling at his feet, between his legs, sucking, was his "uncle."

Shock and grief caught in her throat, hardening into a bitter taste, burning acid on her tongue. "It's true what Celeste said," Honey managed. "Americans aren't sophisticated. In our country, uncles only do that in the dark. And then to nieces."

Sometimes she would go to the Luxembourg Gardens and sit there, hours at a time. Study the cracked brown earth, somehow richer, even in its barren time, than the dirt of Ohio. Trees that were bare seemed more artful than the trees of home, stretching toward the sky, which was higher in Paris. She wondered why it seemed so much clearer there, no matter how miserable you were, how beautiful the world was.

Part of it, she supposed, was where she was sitting. On a wrought-iron chair, graceful enough for the porch of a palace, only it was in the midst of a park. There were twenty of them, set in no particular pattern, on a patch of white pebbles, thin curved legs making them light enough to move so you could face in any direction, sit anywhere you wanted. And nobody stole them. A miracle of Paris. In the parks of Ohio there were green slatted benches bolted to cement so nobody would run off with them. In the Luxembourg Gardens were chairs that were works of art, and they stayed where they were.

Probably, Honey thought, it was a sign of the respect Parisians had for their city. The endless availability of beauty. Every bridge had statues; generals on horseback, cast in bronze; poets with great iron cloaks, commemorating mind. Even the pigeons seemed not to soil them, as though they shared the same respect. Clochards, the drunkards who fell asleep on the platforms of the Metro stations, regained consciousness under glassed-in copies of the art available at the Louvre. So even derelicts had their chance at culture.

Probably, she concluded, a people as proud as Parisians, taking their greatest pride from Paris itself, had no choice but to leave the chairs in the park, not wanting to mess up their living rooms, with company coming. Not that they liked company. It made her sad beyond words. Even the desk clerk at her hotel wouldn't speak to her, didn't look at her when he gave her her key.

"Bonjour," she said to him a few times.

"I speak English," he said, as though her tongue were profaning his language, her presence in the hotel an obscenity. As if she were a terrorist or a whore, entertaining men in her room. Truth was, she couldn't even get up nerve to say hello to a man, because the only ones who talked to her made obscene suggestions.

One French woman greeted her warmly, once, as she climbed the hilly streets of Pigalle to Sacré Coeur. A black girl, dressed in leopardish stripes that clung to her oversized breasts. Honey figured she was probably a whore, but a greeting was a greeting, and it had been a long time since anyone seemed glad to see her. So she returned the salute, smiling. The black girl lifted her skirt and waggled gigantic balls.

Sometimes, Honey would go to the Cathedral of Notre Dame. In Ohio, she had rarely gone to church or felt any true sense of religion. But to go into Notre Dame, to step into that ocean of darkness, felt like being with God. Murmurs, candles, prayers in the shadowy recesses echoed up to the vaulted ceilings, little shafts of blue and red making stained glass wedges in the darkness. Peace making subtle little inroads into her soul.

She lit a candle, always, placed it on the endless rows of white burning wax in the rear of the cathedral, while women with black lace scarves over their heads kissed rosaries to their lips and wept. She asked God to forgive her. Not to punish her baby for all her sins.

Early on, she had tried to get an abortion. Climbing rickety steps to all the slimy offices in Paris, seeing doctors with webs on their eyes and terrible body odor. But no matter how sleazy they seemed, they acted as if they had no idea what she was talking about.

She thought about killing herself. Nights when it wasn't too cold, she walked along the Boulevard Saint Michel with a scarf wound round her face to keep out the bitter winds and the wonderful smells: coffee and Grand Marnier from the crepes they were making in sidewalk cafés. The pleasures of life were nothing she felt entitled to. So instead, she smelled the pissoirs and tried to hate Paris.

Then she came to the river. A million lights reflected on the water. It was still, a ribbon of silvery black, shining back at the night. She wondered how cold it was. All around her were lights, coach lamps illuminating the Pont Neuf, lights strung along the awnings of cafés, in every corner of every column, illuminating carvings.

She started down the steps to the water, walked along the cobblestoned quai, leaned out over the edge, wondering why not. A small boat passed close to her, rippled the water. A young man tipped his hat, bowed to her from the deck.

''Bonne nuit,'' he said. ''Penses de suicide?''

So she wasn't even to be given that, the dignity of killing herself without someone sticking a pin in the moment, shattering it. She backed away, angry and ashamed, and ran up the steps.

In the daylight she returned to the river. The clouds were the color of the cobblestones, lining heaven with the same shade of grizzle as the quai beneath her feet. Below her, off the quai, a police launch brought something into shore. A drowned girl was passed like a limp piece of fish to the waiting policemen. She looked about the same age as Honey, very young, very pretty, even with the blue pallor of her skin, the blue-gray lips, the staring blue eyes with no white in the whites around them.

Honey would know a lot of important and sometimes even great men later in her life, and when the important and great men would be interviewed by reporters and media people who were trying to unkernel the nut of what constituted success, they would usually ask the question, in some form or other, "When did you know you were going to be somebody?" And Honey, in her grown-up Miranda mind, would trace her own moment back to the sight of the girl they fished out of the water. It became suddenly very clear to her, an angry epiphany: either you got them, or you let them get you.

She went back to the doctor who seemed more decent than the others. He told her not to worry, if she couldn't keep the baby herself, they'd find a good family to adopt it.

"Have you talked to the father?" he asked her.

"No."

"Talk to him."

So she walked up the Rue de Rennes, past sidewalk vendors hawking clothes, sweaters, miniskirts, hot pants and jeans, under open awnings, rainproofed against the downpours that were always coming even though Parisians never admitted that the weather was terrible. If it rained or snowed, they would always cluck their tongues and say how unusual it was, that Paris had wonderful weather. But even in photography museums, where sad-faced Frenchmen stood on sidewalks watching the Germans march in for the occupation, the people were all holding umbrellas.

She bought an almond croissant, still warm from that morning's baking, at the boulangerie on the corner of Alex's street. She smelled it, let the buttery pieces sit on her tongue, tasting, as she stood in the shadow of the plane tree in his courtyard. She leaned her head against the yellow blotched bark of the thick, stocky trunk and looked up at the fourth floor window. Stupid to hope that a man would do the right thing when he didn't have decency in him. She left without trying to speak to him.

Some days, she walked from Notre Dame to Shakespeare and Co., a bookshop cater-cornered to the cathedral. She stood in the store for hours at a time, in between stacks of books, reading Hemingway, F. Scott Fitzgerald, all the famous people who'd lived in Paris and been a part of the crowd of Shakespeare and Co. back in the twenties. Nobody seemed to mind her being there, as long as she loved books. It was the nationality of the place, literature, everyone in there from the same country.

She would rent books and take them home, up to the top floor of her small hotel on the Rue de la Huchette, to a room that was more like a cupboard. Parts of the ceiling, at the corners, were as low as her chest. As her belly got bigger, she kept everything she needed in the center so she wouldn't have to bend or crawl. Her bed had a brass headboard, the windows beside it opening in, with gray-painted wood shutters behind them. She would kneel on her bed and lean toward the sky, which was higher in Paris.

It was spring by the calendar, but she couldn't tell it from the air. The doctor who monitored the growth of her belly gave her the name of a place where she could get glasses, because she was reading so much it was affecting her eyes. Reading was all she did now. There was a telephone by her bed, gold painted and peeling, the receiver hanging on a gilded gibbet. It never rang. She would put it on the floor so she wouldn't have to look at it and be reminded there was no one in the world who would call her. Once a day the maid came in to make the bed, and each time she did, she put the phone back up on the table. Honey asked her to leave it on the floor, but it was a battle of wills between them, and the maid was winning.

Honey's feet were too swollen for her shoes now, so she bought a pair of sneakers and lived in those, going for food to the row of markets around the corner. It was spring, finally. She could smell the freshness of blossoms, see the bright fruits and vegetables laid out in boxes, fill her eyes with the colors of tasty little salads, rich mayonnaise spread like icing, dotted with capers, striped with pimentos, rice and vegetables and saucy fish, chez le traiteur.

She spent most of the summer lying on her bed, in the swelter of the attic. Spring had passed in what seemed like an hour. It was hotter than Hamilton, Ohio. She lay there on her back in her underwear, elastics broken and stretched across her belly, wondering who was in there, what was making him jump around like that.

When her water burst, the maid was in the room. She looked at Honey with distaste and went to get a mop. Honey picked up the phone to call her doctor, but nobody answered on the switchboard. She realized that even if there were people all over the world who knew where she was and wanted to call her, they wouldn't be able to get through, and she could die there with nobody knowing.

She reached into the pocket of her winter coat where she hid her money and took out enough for a taxi. The doctor had told her the adopting couple would pay the medical costs. But now that she thought about it, she wasn't so sure she wanted to give the baby up. After all, he was *her* baby. She stuck the rest of the money deep into her boots.

She took a taxi to the hospital. Nuns attended her. The doctor came just in time, to tell her she wouldn't die from the pain. She was on the table in the delivery room, but she had to go to the toilet. She begged them to take her to the W.C. so she wouldn't shame herself, with everybody watching.

"It's a girl," the doctor said.

When she was clean, back in bed, they brought Honey her baby. Love of a kind she had never experienced before flooded through her—not wanting, not needing, not demanding, a love that cared only to give.

"The couple is here," the doctor said.

"I can't. I'm going to keep her."

"You'll be able to take care of her?"

"I have to."

"How?"

"I'll do something. I'll get a job."

"And who will take care of the baby? You have friends who can help?"

"No."

"These people are sympathetic, and quite comfortable. They can give her everything she needs."

"She needs me."

"But you can't take care of her. You can't work and also take care of her."

"But I love her."

"If you love her, do what's best for her. Let them take her."

When the couple came in, Honey turned her head away so they couldn't see her crying. But even out of the corner of her eye she caught the impression of stiffness, formality.

"Oh, but how delicate she is," the woman said, picking up the baby. "But why are her eyes crossed?"

"That happens with new babies," the doctor said. "They won't stay like that."

"Is the mother intelligent?" the man asked, as though it were a dog show.

"Highly intelligent," the doctor said, putting a hand on Honey's shoulder. "And not deaf."

Honey turned and stared at them defiantly.

"Well, anyway, she has pretty eyes," the woman said, appraising. "Maybe the baby will have her eyes."

"Put her down," Honey said. "Give her back to me."

"Perhaps you better wait outside," the doctor said, taking the infant from the woman.

When they were gone, Honey started to sob, pressing her cheek against the small, warm bundle. "I can't. I can't give her away. Not to them. Not to those cold people."

"They'll give her a better chance than you had. A better life than yours."

"How do you know what my life will be?" she asked him, anger now edging out despair. "How do you know what I'll make of myself and what I can do for my baby?"

"The longer you wait, the harder it'll be." He held out

the papers. "Sign these. You can't do anything if you don't have the money."

"Then I'll get it," Honey said, hardly able to see the words on the paper for the tears in her eyes. "I'll be back," she whispered to her baby, and kissed her, and signed.

THE WALDORF TOWERS

◇

Going through Fred Masters' little hideaway at the Waldorf Towers, Lou Salerno tried not to let his observations be touched with envy. When you were a cop on a case from out of town, your per diem didn't exactly pay for the Plaza. Lou had elected to stay at the Chelsea Hotel, which had a certain *éclat* because Clifford Irving had lived there at the time of the Howard Hughes autobiography hoax. Lou knew a lot about the hoax, just as he knew the word éclat, and that it sort of meant style. He had a friend on the *Los Angeles Times Book Review* and they exchanged information: he taught Lou the finer points of literature, while Lou taught him about murder.

There were not too many clothes in the drawers of Fred Masters' apartment, but those that were there were all clean and neatly arranged. Lou himself was not exactly a fashion plate, but he liked to look good. Long ago he had decided to be in the police force rather than in the sheriff's department because he did not really like himself in green.

Lou was following the trail of the so-called suicide in L.A., the woman with the bullet hole in her eye, like Miranda. Women were vain even to the last, so Lou had figured all along that it was homicide. Besides the telephone calls to Masters in the victim's long-distance records, and the similar M.O., all involved were killed by a .22, which really didn't mean that much. They were Saturday Night Specials; everybody had one.

But there was enough of a sense of connection for Lou to get permission from his commander to go to New York and try to find out more about the Masters-Miranda killings. He had a feeling in his gut that it was the work of hired guns.

The New York police didn't exactly welcome him. They were into their own investigation, so they wouldn't tell him a lot, although they feigned cooperation. But they were pushing the fact that theirs was a murder-suicide. Plus they probably sensed Lou's disdain for their methods. The two departments were as far apart as the cities were, New York and L.A. He had been east for one other murder investigation, and where in L.A. there were uniformed officers around the scene and everything sealed off, all very thorough, in New York everybody walked in where the crime was, the cop on the beat, detectives, commanders, everybody stepping all over the evidence. So although the West Coast attitude was more obviously kicked back, Lou considered New York very slipshod. Because in his arena you could take more time, it seemed more professional. In Manhattan if something was forgotten, the mind-set was forget about it. Even their booking process was more store-it-in-a-locker than book-it-into-property. New York detectives seemed so boisterous and demanding, jaded in a way that seemed sorrowful to Lou. Like they didn't even wince at having to pay the policeman who walked the beat to park on the street.

He didn't have to be a detective to know they didn't like his sticking his nose in. The guy who was supposed to meet him at the precinct hadn't been there. But Lou had been extra polite, saying "If you don't mind," so they had to go through the pretense of cooperation. They let him go over the reports, gave him copies of everything they had. Sent one of their detectives, Tuner, with him to Masters' apartment.

"This wasn't the only 'love nest' Masters had," said Tuner as Lou looked in the closets. "There was the place he stashed Miranda, and a house in the Hamptons his wife didn't know about, and then there was Gordon Grayson's apartment, the place where they bought it." Tuner was sitting on the sofa, his hat pushed back on his head. He still wore a hat, as if he had never read Raymond Chandler, Lou could not help noting.

" 'The rich are different from you and me,' " Salerno said.

"Huh?"

"F. Scott Fitzgerald said that to Hemingway. Yes, they have more apartments."

"He said that?"

"The first part, anyway."

"You like living in L.A.?"

"Not bad. Not bad."

"I got a sister in Santa Monica. She says that's where I ought to go when I retire."

"There are worse places," said Lou, checking the pockets of Masters' suits, which he assumed somebody had already been through, but you could never be too sure.

"What's it like to work in Hollywood? You get a lot of glamorous murders?"

"There's no such thing as glamorous murder," Lou said, knowing even as he said it that it wasn't exactly the truth. He had worked on the Sharon Tate case, and even as he waded through the stomach-churning horror, the grisly mayhem, he couldn't help noticing what a great house it was. How well they lived before being slaughtered.

He had the same feeling now as he went through Masters' things, feeling the fiber of the cloth of his suits, noting the labels from Turnbull & Asser.

"How did the crime scene look to you?"

"A little too perfect," Tuner said. "The medical examiner is putting together a psychogram. According to Masters' friends, he was never happier. The physical facts say it was suicide. Murder-suicide, anyway. Closed windows, closed doors. Locked from the inside. Double-locked and bolted. Heavy with prints, all belonging to Gordon Grayson, Masters or Miranda. So nothing wiped clean. No sign of a struggle. No blood anywhere but the bed in the alcove where the bodies were, so they weren't moved.''

"Bally shoes," Lou said, checking the insoles of the black leather loafer in his hand. "They're up to about two hundred a pair. Why would a man with his feet in these blow his brains out?"

"That's the least of it. You should have seen whose bed they were under.''

On the dresser mirror was a Polaroid snapshot of Miranda, her head thrown back and to one side. "Christ, she was a knock-out," Lou said.

"You should have seen the actual package. Dead, she was better looking than most women are alive.''

"Are there any sushi bars around here?" Sorrow made Lou hungry.

"You eat that crap?''

"It's mostly all I eat.''

"Aren't you afraid of the little worms that might be living inside?''

"What do you eat?''

"Meat and potatoes.''

"Aren't you afraid of the antibiotics in the beef?''

"California," Tuner said, smiling. "You sound like my sister.''

On the way downstairs, the elevator stopped and a man got in. He was not unusually tall, but the way he carried himself made Lou stand up to his full six foot three. For a moment Lou was sure he knew him. It was a feeling he had all the time in L.A., because there were so many actors on the loose and he'd seen them on screen or television. So the first flash of recognition always came as an easy familiarity, as though they were a friend or, at least, an acquaintance. Nobody in the elevator looked at each other, although Lou was tempted to make eye contact and smile, something he never dared to do in West

Hollywood, where not only would it turn out he really didn't know the guy, but that he was, more than likely, a fag.

"He looked really familiar," Lou said as he watched the man disappear into the florist shop in the lobby.

"That was Hap Mitchel," Tuner told him. "The astronaut."

"No kidding," Lou said, and stared off after him. "Remember when the world had heroes?"

"Yeah, well I'm not so sure he's that big a hero. I saw him on one of those news shows the other morning, the one with Claire Avery. She asked him a bunch of questions and he wriggled, really sweated, like he had something to hide."

"Every man has something to hide."

"Yeah, well, then you don't go on television with a woman like Claire Avery."

"I wonder why he did it?"

"You ever seen Claire Avery?"

"I've seen her. She doesn't do that much for me. I don't like women who flash their brains."

"It wasn't brains she was flashing the other day. I never saw a guy look more uncomfortable. With her tits sort of hanging out, only very crisp above the collar, she really nailed him. Something about his first orbiting mission. When he landed in the ocean. She asked him whether he didn't get panicked that he was going to drown. Seems he blew out the hatch, so the capsule sank. The Navy gave it out that it was technical mal—something."

"Technical malfunction," Lou said.

"Yeah. But she made it real clear that what it was was Mitchel got scared and fucked up. You should have seen him squirm."

"I'm glad I missed it," Lou said. "I like my heroes to stay heroes. I don't want to know that Kennedy fucked hookers, or how bad his back was, if you get me."

"So why would a guy like Mitchel expose himself like that? Just for a hot-looking woman?"

"All men have dicks of clay," Lou said, and went into the revolving door.

Hap was sorry now he had made the whole trip. He had let Claire humiliate him, gone on the show because he trusted her. He'd believed she wanted him on the air as a lark, the two of them being lovers so long, pretending they were just meeting for the first time. He hadn't known she was capable of such treachery. Which meant he hadn't really known her.

In the flower shop he ordered a big basket of flowers for Lily Masters, to be sent to her apartment, and another, smaller arrangement to be delivered to the funeral at Frank E. Campbell's. He puzzled for a moment whether or not to charge it to his corporate credit card. No question Fred Masters had been doing business with MercerCorp, or at least trying to, buying huge shares of stock of its microchip company, the crown jewel of the corporation. But trying didn't count in business, and the takeover hadn't gone through. So, straight as always, Hap charged the flowers to his personal account.

There was no reason to stay in town for the funeral. There wasn't enough connection to grieve. Still, to have been Masters' last appointment, the one he didn't keep, made Hap feel a grim tie, involved him in an eerie way. Made him curious as to what would have been the subject of the conversation Fred seemed to think was so urgent.

But a floral tribute was enough for such a wasteful, empty exit. Too many men had died for a cause, including Hap's own father, who'd been on the USS *Arizona* at Pearl Harbor. But he did feel pity for Lily Masters, who seemed to him good-hearted, straightforward. And he felt a strange sadness about Miranda.

He hadn't ever met her exactly, but he'd seen her once, thought or imagined he'd seen her more times than that, dreamed about her a lot, like some hot-breathed adolescent. Dreams were something he wished he could excise from his existence. But he wouldn't have minded keeping the ones about Miranda.

As the president of MercerCorp, Hap had had continuous dealings with Victor Lenrahan, Chairman of the Board. Had heard the rumors about Miranda. Had seen her once with Victor. Every time he met with Lenrahan after that, he'd looked for her, trying not to seem like he was looking. The last meeting he'd had with Lenrahan on his yacht, Hap felt her presence. Saw a curtain move. But he knew that might just have been his imagination. Just as there seemed to be spies everywhere when you were in a war, when you were dealing with Victor Lenrahan every shadow contained the beautiful woman.

Miranda had come out of the darkness once for Hap to see clearly, and remember, locking her inside his dreams. Now that she was dead, her picture all over the newspapers, smiling out from countless front pages, so animated, so filled with vitality, it sickened Hap's soul. Bouncing off the slick covers of the scandal papers—out on the streets hours after she was dead—she looked so ready to take life on, Hap couldn't believe she'd left it.

Lively as the black-and-white photos were, it was only color that did her justice. Showed the magic of her eyes, the pale, dazzling green of them. "Set like jewels on the high curve of her cheeks," was how Claire Avery had phrased it that morning, shining up her spot on the show, tacking glamour and intrigue onto what was supposed to be the news. The fact that he still watched her made him angrier than Claire's need to aggrandize herself.

Hap was a strict man, strict with himself as he'd been with his children, all of them grown now. He expected only honorable behavior from those he cared about, was alert for betrayal by designated enemies. But those were political enemies, he thought, in foreign countries, pledged to the overthrow of capitalism just as he was pledged to keeping America ahead, his job in aerospace a continuation of the vow he'd made, when still a boy, to protect his country as his father had. So the last thing he expected was the woman he loved acting like a traitor to that love.

Crucifying him in the same marmalade tones she used to ask viewers to stay tuned.

Crossing the lobby of the hotel, on the way to the limousine waiting to take him to the airport, Hap could feel women looking at him, no longer hiding behind the high creamy marble pillars of the Waldorf to do their cruising. Out in the open now, eyeing him in the same bold way men had, ever since the propaganda told them they were as good as men, which Hap supposed made them believe they had to act in the same low fashion. He knew how he looked to them. He was still spare, with a lean, flat belly, something he worked to sustain. He had a prominent jaw, and too blue eyes, characteristics associated with beauty in men, which very much embarrassed him. Both his daughters complained there was no justice, that their father had eyes like that and they didn't. Looks in a man were an advantage if you enjoyed screwing around, and Hap liked to be faithful. Not to one woman anymore, but at least to one woman at a time.

"Hap?"

He didn't have to turn to know who the voice belonged to. He kept on walking.

"You can't still be angry." Claire's voice was clear, soft but sharp like she was.

From the corner of his eye he could see how good she looked. Light brown hair softly falling around the ingenue face, seemingly incapable of harm. No hint in the wide-set hazel eyes of the snapping turtle that was her ambition. Maybe just a touch of it in the set of her jaw. But otherwise, everything was rounded, light, adding to the impression of innocent curiosity that gave her such credibility with her audience. America, a country no quicker to catch on than he was.

"I apologized," Claire said, her words slightly clipped around the edges, the extra fillip of breeding that spoke of a Seven Sisters education, in her case Mount Holyoke. "I told you on the air I'd misunderstood. That I made a mistake, even though I hadn't." She followed him into the revolving door, crowding him into the same slot of space he was trying to ignore her in. "I said I hadn't quoted you correctly, even though I had."

They reached the open air and the sidewalk. Next to the great gray canopy a bag lady tried to set up camp while the doorway urged her to move on. New York was awash with its own special noises, the whir of traffic, the whines of sirens, ambulances, police cars, the chatter of birds apparently too cosmopolitan to go south for the winter, the splatter of autumn rain on the canvas canopy. Hap tried to take in all of it, shutting his ears to Claire.

The driver of the limousine tipped his hat to Hap. Then, seeing who was with him, he left his cap off, gawking openly. Claire didn't react. She was obviously used to being stared at, fawned over, told secrets on the air most people wouldn't share with their psychiatrist.

Nor was she easily put off. She got into the limousine after Hap, settling herself comfortably beside him on the pearl gray upholstery like the welcome guest she considered herself, impervious to his angry silence. "You can't still be mad."

"I'm lucky you didn't tell them what kind of fuck I was," he said.

"The best. The very best."

"Get out of my car."

"Everybody makes mistakes. People don't think less of you because you made a mistake."

"You heard me talking in my sleep," Hap said. "There can't be anything lower than that, to use what you heard a man saying in his sleep while you slept beside him. Get out of my car."

"Don't be such a sorehead. Not you. Mr. Fairness. Mr. Give Everybody Another Chance. It's a good story. Even after all these years. That you once had a human failing. That you were afraid. That you thought you would drown. That the Navy covered up for you. It doesn't just make you more human. It makes the Navy more human. Don't you think that's good for the country to know?"

"Get out of my car." Hap leaned forward and called the

driver's name. From the angle he sat at, he could see Claire's breasts, the cleavage at the gap of the pin-striped suit she wore, the mannish style she'd adopted, playing against the exposed femininity.

"Yes, admiral?" The driver stuck his head in.

"Help this . . . lady . . . out of my car."

"Okay, I'll go." She turned to the driver, giving him the full intensity of the look she had focused on world leaders, mass murderers. "Just give me a minute, won't you?"

The chauffeur backed away.

"I have just one question, admiral." She used the title like a barb, apparently to sting him.

Even that. The self-consciousness he'd admitted to her about being addressed by a title he'd never really carried in the Navy. Even that piece of intelligence she'd saved to use against him. Was using it now.

Still, as the fair-minded man he was and always tried to be, he considered maybe he wasn't giving her a chance. Maybe because of that last, terrible experience on her television show, the one he'd only agreed to do because of how they felt about each other, because of how long they'd been lovers and what fun it would be to pretend to be strangers, he was failing to keep an open mind. She said she had a question. Maybe she was going to ask him if he still loved her. If he still felt something. Maybe she was going to plead with him not to throw it away. Wasn't forgiveness a part of love? Wasn't what they had together, the added-up total of passion and affection and history, wasn't that more important than either of their mistakes? "Okay."

"You were supposed to have dinner with Fred Masters Wednesday night. What did he want to talk to you about?"

He threw back his head and laughed.

"What's so funny?" She seemed to flinch a little at the sound of his laughter, as though she wasn't used to people not taking her seriously.

"Me. For a minute there, I thought you were going to say something sentimental."

"Masters was a friend of Victor Lenrahan's. So were you. Did you ever see them together, Masters, Lenrahan, and Miranda?"

"You said one question," Hap said. "That's two." He leaned forward. "George . . ."

"I'm sorry, Miss Avery," the chauffeur said. He reached for her arm, his hand trembling.

"I'm going," she said, shaking off his touch. "Just give me one hint, Hap, what Masters wanted to talk about. You owe me that much."

"I owe you a fat lip. Get out of my car." Hap turned away, looking out at the traffic that lumbered along the black, rainslicked lanes of Park Avenue. Some of the stubbornly resident birds took flight from the center lane of trees.

"What did he want?" she almost wailed as the driver pulled her from the car. "Tell me what he wanted!"

"He's at Frank E. Campbell's. Get him to tell you. Jump him in the coffin. That shouldn't be too much for you to get a story, a little necrophilia." He locked his door and did not turn to look at her until the limo pulled away.

She was standing on the sidewalk, jaw set stubbornly, tears filling her eyes. Or maybe he was doing it again, seeing what he hoped would be there, just as he'd waited for loving, contrite words. Maybe all that was in her eyes was rain, or temper at not getting the information she wanted. Probably that wasn't disappointed love out there, but a tantrum.

Like most Americans, Hap had always considered the magic was probably just up ahead. That any minute, everything would change, and all of life would crystallize, and everyone would understand you, and what you felt, and what you were saying. Most of his life he'd been the youngest: the youngest in his class, the youngest at the academy, the youngest on the moon, the youngest to become an admiral. So it came as a terrible surprise to him, turning fifty. Getting older Realizing all at once that

there wasn't a stream of epiphanies up ahead. That this
was it, life, for as long as it lasted. All along he had
thought that his story would sing like an anthem. Now he
wondered if there was even a tune.

He did little things to juice himself up, like reconnecting
with the sky, seeing how vast it was, reminding himself
how small a part of infinity his moment seemed. Because
of the long-ago debacle with his spacecraft, his one brush
with cowardice, he insisted on piloting the plane himself
whenever he flew anywhere. It made them crazy at
MercerCorp. He was much too valuable, they were always
telling him, to take unnecessary risks. He increased the
unnecessary risks by testing out experimental aircraft.
There were constant memos telling him not to do that, from
the members of the board of MercerCorp, from Lenrahan
while he was still alive, from the new Secretary of Science
and Technology in Washington. Everyone telling him to
stop. For a while he cut down on the test-piloting activity,
mostly because the company's test pilots were getting sore
at him, grousing that he was robbing them of their func-
tion. But whenever he traveled for business, he flew one of
the company jets. He'd flown it to New York and had
intended to fly it back to California, until they called from
maintenance to say there was something wrong with the
hydraulics system.

Reluctantly, he made a reservation to fly home
commercially, the first time in years he'd been a passenger. He looked out the window now like a beginner,
watching the movement and heave of the plane. Someone who didn't know him might have thought he was
anxious, instead of just trying to gauge how good the
pilot was.

The young woman seated next to him studied him
studying the skies. "Well, what do you think?" she asked
him. "Will we make it?"

He turned and looked at her. She was young, probably
in her late twenties, although it was hard to nail her age
exactly, carrying as she did a kind of camouflage. Drab
suit, a neutral blouse that blended in with her unmade-up

face, a worried twist to her wide, full-lipped, unlipsticked mouth. Hap enjoyed dazzle in women. Even his wife had a little redheaded brilliance before she burned out. He had two daughters, one of them scared of competition, the other with courage for the contest. So he understood females who were afraid to compete, and spotted the girl sitting next to him as one of those. In spite of her attempt to fade herself out, to try and become part of the gray-beige of the airline upholstery, she was still pretty, clean smelling, freshly shampooed.

"It'll get us there," he said, about the plane.

"This must be very soggy Saltines for you," she said.

"I beg your pardon?"

"Boring. Slower than the speed of sound and all." She held out her long-fingered hand, its clean nails unpolished, buffed into pinkness. "I'm Zoe Baldwin."

"Hap Mitchel. With one *l*."

"I know. I saw you on TV the other morning. With Claire Avery."

"I'm really sorry to hear that."

"Don't be. I thought you acquitted yourself very well." There was a briefcase under the seat in front of her. She leaned over, reached for it.

"Let me get that for you," Hap volunteered.

"Thank you." She tightened her skirt around her very good legs as he leaned down, as if she were afraid he would look between her thighs.

"You're welcome. This is a very important-looking briefcase."

"I thought you were charming, composed, and restrained. I would have knocked her off her stool."

He smiled.

"Why did she go after you like that? Doesn't she like you?"

"I guess not."

"I thought it was very moving, all that stuff about the moon. Did you really feel like that when you stood there, like you could see infinity?"

"I did see infinity," he said.

"That must have been a mind-blow."

"Are you a reporter?"

"Far from it."

"Then I can tell you the truth. What I saw was the design of the universe. And I knew there was no way it could be accidental. Everything planned. Everyone connected."

"I read that cosmonauts who went into space and had spiritual experiences were classified as psychotic," Zoe said. "Because there's no spirit in Russia, they had to be crazy. What did our people think?"

"They made me an admiral," Hap said. "And asked me to resign from the Navy."

"Are you serious?"

Hap grinned. "Well, it was time to move into the private sector anyway."

"Do you have a card?"

"Well, yes, I do," Hap said, a little taken aback.

"I'd like to call you in L.A. You interest me."

"No kidding." He handed his card to her.

"Hillard," she said, reading the name from it. "I'd never have guessed. Where'd they get Hap?"

"I was sort of morose as a kid. My father called me Happy as a joke. I took everything too seriously."

"But you've gotten over that?"

"Still working on it. Some things take time."

"I hope you don't have hang-ups about being the first one to make a move."

"As a matter of fact, I do."

"You'll get over it," Zoe said, opening her briefcase, putting his card in the side pocket. "Now if you'll forgive me, I have a lot of work to do."

"I take it you're not a secretary?"

"I'm a lawyer."

"Corporate? Criminal?"

"A little of everything, including entertainment. Lately, I'm doing a lot of work in sexual harassment."

"By women?"

"Very funny. Don't be afraid." She patted his hand. "I promise I'll be gentle."

Her eyes were a pale, crystal green. He felt like he'd looked into them before. He realized as she turned to her work that she reminded him of Miranda. But pale where she'd been tan, beige where she'd been honeyed, only the eyes the same, broadcasting the beauty.

It surprised Hap that he remembered still, and with such clarity, Miranda's eyes, having looked into them directly only once. She'd been coming out of a restaurant in the Watergate complex in D.C. with Victor Lenrahan. Hap knew he was not supposed to be seeing them. Most of the time Victor was discreet about Miranda, at least as far as his associates at MercerCorp were concerned. So Hap stayed a little distance away, dropping back like a mugger behind a lamppost till they got into their waiting limousine.

Miranda hesitated for a moment, as though she could feel his stare, even through the darkness. She looked directly at him, caught him, caught his eyes with her eyes, hooked him and reeled him in, smiling her slightly crooked-toothed smile. Her look burned the inside of his lids, so intense was the color. Like the Sea of Cortes. The clear pale green of oceans newly divided from earth, nature distilled and set into the eyes of a woman. Then she got into the car.

That was the one time he had seen her. At least the one time he was sure he had seen her. After that, he looked for her whenever he was with Victor, sure that she was someplace nearby, and that if he was cagey, patient, sending out signals, maybe she would reappear.

The last time he'd been on the yacht with Lenrahan, he was sure she was there. The boat was tied at anchor in the marina at Mission Bay, San Diego, bobbing gently in the quiet afternoon, one of a seemingly endless congregation of yachts and well-kept sailing boats, white masted, immaculate, sporting playful names. Victor's vessel was painted with the legend *Banana*, which, according to the scuttlebutt, was an affectionate name for his wife, in the days when there was still a lot of affection between them. Why Victor would keep his mistress on a ship named for his wife was a little beyond Hap's understanding. But the rich were a puzzle anyway. All around him were names like *Vamonos*, *Lazy Day*, as if being able to afford yachts meant you didn't have to have the imagination to name them.

"The business of this country is business," Victor Lenrahan was saying to him as they sat on the deck.

It was a private luncheon for the two of them, with more servants than there were guests, hovering stewards in crisp white uniforms serving cold jellied madrilene and shrimp in aspic. Another curiosity of the loaded, Hap could not help thinking. Salty Jell-O.

The table was set on the shiny, polyurethaned wood planks of the deck. All the way aft, facing out, were two oversized white Naugahyde fishing chairs, bolted to the deck, the large fishing poles of the deep sea fancier racked, waiting to the right of each chair. As far as Hap knew, Victor did not particularly go in for fishing, except perhaps, as Victor's own bible might put it, as a fisher of men, but in high places.

Victor was, Hap guessed, in his late sixties, still a powerfully handsome man. He stood well over six feet tall, with a full head of thick white hair that the sea air curled in slightly Einsteinian fashion. The hair was controlled, or rather suppressed by the yachting cap on top of it. He wore a white sportshirt, open at the neck, showing a vee of his tanned, heavily freckled skin, and the navy blazer of a marina commodore. There were stripes at the sleeve, a touch of gold braid, and, on the pocket, a crest that was either family or an award from some campaign too long before for Hap to recognize.

Lenrahan's teeth were overlarge and dazzlingly white, wolfish, nearly always set on edge or in a grin. The grin, to Hap, seemed to hold the seed of a threat in it, like an aging pirate's, practiced at leaping onto the railings of ships he captured, promising that no one would be hurt if they surrendered their booty and the beautiful women. Hap kept looking around for the beautiful woman, but he couldn't spot her right away. Victor was facing him, the mirrored lenses of his sunglasses impenetrable, flashing back at Hap the bright San Diego sunlight. At his back was the saloon, curtained. She was probably in there. Hap smelled something sweetly, heavily musky that all the sea breezes of San Diego couldn't whisk away.

"Business," Victor was saying, wresting the oversized shrimp free from the patina of gel around it. "That's what we should be interested in. That's what I'm interested in. The economy and our defense ability. Not all these crappy little issues like human rights and abortion." He popped the shellfish into his mouth and chewed.

Hap hardly heard him. They met frequently, and Victor had said pretty much what he had to say: Hap knew where he stood on most issues. Slightly to the right of the prayers-in-school gang, which was okay with Hap. Philosophic questions were not something he concentrated on anymore than he thought, when he didn't have to, about politics. He had a job to do, and if you asked yourself too many questions, it broke your concentration, and that cut back on results. Just as now he wanted to find Miranda, and that required all his concentration. So he didn't give close attention to Victor's ramblings. Sort of paid him ear service, not really taking in the words any more than those who gave lip service to God thought about their prayers.

"Give no quarter to the bleeding hearts," Victor was still going on. "Pepe!" he called to his chief steward. "What the hell crap did they put in this shrimp?"

"Ese aspic," Pepe said, coming to attention like a marine.

"Well, shit, I know it's aspic, but what kind of spice did the new chef put in? My goddamn lips are sticking together."

"I ask him," Pepe said, and went into the saloon. Hap leaned a little to the right so he could see past Victor into the open door.

"That's the thing about these beaner chefs," Victor

said, lowering his voice to less than a boom. "You ask them to do something fancier than burritos and they piss all over themselves. How's yours?"

"Excuse me?" He was sure he caught a glimpse of her, leaning back against the sofa inside.

"Your shrimp?"

"Oh, it's great. Excellent."

"You're full of shit, Mitchel. You haven't touched it."

"To tell you the truth, sir, I'm not much for aspic."

"Me neither," Victor said, and put his fork down. "Beats me why when they get these giant shrimp, they don't just serve them plain."

"Coriander," Pepe said, running back onto the deck.

"What coriander?"

"The spice," Pepe said. "He put it in the aspic."

"Why the hell did he put the shrimp in aspic anyway? These shrimp got flown all the way from Guaymas. Why would he put them in aspic?"

"You asked for aspic, Mr. Lenrahan."

"Well I must have been out of my mind," Victor said. "Tell him not to make it anymore."

"Yes, sir."

"We got any plain shrimp left?"

"I'll ask him, sir," said Pepe and fled. Hap could see her now, yes, he was sure of it, the bottom of a sandaled foot, rocking back and forth. He could almost make out the color of the polish on her pedicured toenails.

"Hangover from my youth," Victor said. "My mother wanted to aspic goddamned everything. Egg in aspic. You never really knew what nausea was, Mitchel, till you tasted that chilled soft yellow center coming out of the ooze. Still has her grip on me, that old lady. Christ, she was elegant. Or tried to be. Shouldn't talk about her, I guess. Corinne always said, 'We who have been well brought up do not talk about family at table.' "

"Corinne?"

"My mother. Tied me to the chair with her apron if she didn't like the way I talked. Children should be seen and not heard and tied to the chair." Victor laughed, a booming laugh.

Pepe ran out on the deck, carrying a plate full of shrimp. "That's more like it," Victor said, and scraped half onto his plate. "Mitchel?"

"Thank you."

"Pass it to my guest."

Pepe came around to his side of the table. To Hap's relief, Pepe had left the door open. Hap leaned to the right, peering into the saloon as he helped himself to the shrimp. If Miranda had been sitting there, where he could see her, she'd moved.

"What were we talking about?" Victor said.

"Your mother."

"I mean before that."

"The bleeding hearts."

"Right," Victor said. "Fuck 'em. You listen to them, this country would be in the toilet. Money and armaments, that's what we're about. And Freedom of course."

"Of course." It stuck in his craw to sound like a yes man, but he knew the drill. Victor was ventilating, not asking for opinions. If he just let Lenrahan run on, like an old engine letting off steam, he'd get comfortable, maybe even relax, think of Hap not just as an employee but a friend, maybe decide it was all right to introduce him to Miranda.

He supposed, in his own way, he was being manipulative, politicking, because really, what was politics but acting in a manner that would get you what you wanted? Hap wasn't that cold-blooded, not even disinterested, really, in Lenrahan himself. He was, after all, his boss, Chairman of the Board of MercerCorp, founder of the organization as it existed now, having merged his armaments business with a small aeronautical concern, expanding it into one of the nation's top aerospace companies. Still, impressive as the man was, in his way, Hap's true fascination was with Miranda. So his attention wandered, went belowdecks, searching her out, opening doors, moving down hallways, in a kind of dreamy slow motion. In his mind, he opened the door to one of the cabins and found her lying on the bed. She got up and came toward him, wafting in green silk chiffon, her arms reaching out, golden arms, tawny skinned, soft, like the silk she was wearing, floating toward him, lips wet, slightly parted, ready for him.

"But Freedom means armaments, make no mistake about that," Victor was saying. "Even if we stopped, the Russkies would keep on building, no matter what they agreed to. All this bullshit about their introducing a freeze. They have no intention of freezing. No way we could check them out, and everybody knows it. They'd keep building. You can't take their word. That's what you have to tell those candy asses on the committee."

"That's just what I intend to tell them, sir." There was a vague air of brownnosing in the way he talked to Lenrahan that annoyed Hap when he caught himself doing it. But it was a reflex reaction, an extension of the respect drilled into him, held for so long in the Navy.

And in truth, he did respect the man, rising as he had to world-class gun dealer, finding wars as other men looked for vacation spots, supplying them, finally cashing in his chips and raising the stakes to aerospace. It was a real American success story, and if not as striped with heroism as Hap's own, at least worthy of regard, some form of deference. Especially when you considered he had Miranda.

That he kept her on his yacht in Mission Bay was an idiosyncrasy that Hap could not quite figure out. He wasn't too up-to-date on the watering spots of the rich, but of course, he'd heard about the Riviera, Cabo San Lucas, some of the glitzier places, and he was sure Mission Bay wasn't one of them. But it was probably one of the few spots Victor wouldn't run into someone he knew, or someone who knew who he was. Standing as tall as he did, as impressive looking as he was, and powerful, there weren't that many locales where a man like that could be inconspicuous.

"When you're talking Freedom," Victor was still going on, capitalizing the word as he chewed his shrimp, "you're saying Money. Money is what keeps this country moving. You let those Russkies have their way, they'll overrun the world, they're sworn to that. There'll be no more capitalism. Don't you forget it. That's their dedication."

"True," Hap agreed, moving his attention to the curtains of the saloon. Someone was holding one of them back a little, watching them. He got an impression of those eyes.

"Free Enterprise is the balls of Liberty. Life, Liberty and Money!" Lenrahan said, his mirrored lenses flashing. "That's what Jefferson really meant when he wrote 'the Pursuit of Happiness.' Money! That was one of his priorities. Money was what he meant. Money and being able to fuck a nigger mistress, even if you're the country's most exemplary man." Victor laughed and threw his napkin down on the table, got up and strode to the rail, looking out at the greenly glittering water. "That's the truth, you know. Jefferson had a nigger mistress."

"I didn't know that." Hap got to his feet, as though imitating Victor, moving closer to the glassed-in saloon.

"Just because a man loves his country doesn't mean he can't have a dick," Lenrahan chuckled.

Hap leaned into the entranceway. But if she'd been there, she was gone. Still, he could smell a heavy perfume, smoky, thick with a memory of lotus flowers.

"Looking for something?" Victor asked him.

"The head."

"Through there and down the stairs."

He'd restrained himself from actually going through the boat, looking for her. It didn't take that much self-control. Lenrahan was outside when he came out of the toilet. The older man walked him back out to the deck, showed him to the gangway.

"Glad you could come," he said, shaking hands as though Hap had had a choice. "So you're clear on what to tell them?"

"I think so, sir."

"The way to keep strong is to keep our allies strong. They go out of business, we go out of business. God had a big hand in starting this country. He means us to stay on top. We are only his instruments. And MercerCorp is his company."

At the bottom of the gangway, Hap turned and waved. And that was when he saw her coming out on deck, her skin so warm a color that Hap could taste her in his mouth. Her legs were so long they looked to him like the glamour photos of World War II, the ones he remembered from the wall lockers of his father's Navy friends, the bighearted sailors who'd taken him in as sort of a mascot after his father died. Young men who only talked about victory, and tail, never mind that there was a kid present. Legs that seemed to go up to her neck: he could feel them wrapped around his hips, had an image of fucking her right there on the deck, her personal heat traveling to his pants.

Her breasts were high and firm, arched over a slim rib cage, moving down to a slender waist and gently rounded hips held tight in brief, white shorts that looked small enough to clothe a little girl's dress-up doll. Hap was too far away to see her eyes, but he didn't have to see them anymore to remember them. He knew what they looked like, knew what they would look like in the middle of a night where she lay looking up at him. He supposed he might have been gape jawed, it was that young, and that steamy, the feeling he was going through. As though Victor sensed it, he pushed her back inside the saloon.

That was the last time Hap had seen her. Lenrahan died a few weeks later. Hap tried to find out where the funeral was so he could attend. But, strangely, there had been no funeral service. Hap would have anticipated a little pomp, some grandeur for the burial, maybe even a military ceremony considering Victor's ties with the Pentagon. But there was nothing. Not even a memorial gathering. That he

wasn't even laid out for last respects seemed very odd to
Hap. He felt cheated. Angry at not being allowed to say
good-bye to a close associate, someone who, in a way, he
considered a friend. He went through all the scattered
irritation of a genuine loss, the lack of concentration that
came with death, the inability to marshal thoughts, the
grievous ache in the pit of his belly that spoke of genuine
mourning. And then he realized what he was grieving for
was not mortality, his own, or Lenrahan's, but the fact that
he hadn't been able to get another look at Miranda. Might
never see her again.

And now she was gone, too. With nothing left but the
picture on the front pages, the remembered heat she had
generated in him. And the indelible impression of those
eyes. Remarkably like the eyes of the young woman who
sat next to him on the plane. Was she going to haunt him
now, Miranda? This woman he had never spoken to,
whose flesh he had only imagined, but never really touched.
He had never even really seen her up close, exchanged
breaths. Now was her specter not just in his brain, but in
the seat beside him?

He considered it very strange, not to fly commercially
for years, and with his first ticketed outing to be seated
next to this bold young woman. Maybe a sign. Not that he
believed in signs, for all his exposure to the mystery of
creation. But maybe it was a sign.

"I thought it was you," a tall stocky man with a bandage
over his bushy eyebrows said, leaning over Zoe. "You
heard what your son of a bitch client Marty Fontaine did to
me." He pointed to his bandage "I'm going to have him
picked up for felonious assault."

"I'm sure it was an accident," Zoe said. "I'm glad
you're all right."

"I'm not all right, and it wasn't an accident. I'll have
his fucking ass. I'll sue him for everything he's got, and
his father's besides."

"You're much too smart to waste your energy on a
lawsuit," Zoe said. "You know how time-consuming and
expensive they are. There must be better ways you can use

your energy. I'm sure Marty would want to make it up to you. Assuming, of course, that he actually did anything."

"Don't try to lawyer-talk me, with your assuming. A hundred people saw him assault me, so assuming your ass."

"I think you ought to watch how you talk to the lady," Hap said.

"No shit. Who are you?"

"Hap Mitchel with one *l*," Zoe said. "Stan Dobson."

"Mitchel the astronaut?" Dobson said. "The head of MercerCorp now, right? I've been meaning to get in touch with you. Ever since the Iacocca biography, business is hot. You had plenty of ups and downs, right? The reading public loves ups and downs." Dobson was suddenly into pitching, the anger out of him now, replaced by eagerness. "You ever thought about writing a book?"

"You'll have to discuss it with my lawyer." Hap nodded toward Zoe.

"Oh." Rage fizzled out of Dobson as business oozed in. "Okay. I'll call you at your office, Ms. Baldwin."

"That would be appropriate," she said, dismissing him with a smile, her attention back on the papers in her lap.

"Great meeting you," Dobson said and shook Hap's hand, retreating to his seat as the seat belt sign went on.

"That was adorable," Zoe said, smiling. "You think very quickly for a sailor. Thanks for the rescue."

"I have a feeling you could have rescued yourself."

"Maybe. But it was nice to have it done for me."

"What was he so steamed about?"

"A little argument in a restaurant."

"Oh, yeah, I was there," said Hap.

"Actually, except for the fact that someone got hurt, it's kind of funny. First outbreak of moral indignation in show business since a producer punched an agent at Ma Maison for suggesting his thirty-three-year-old daughter wasn't a virgin." The plane touched down. Zoe squeezed his hand. Loosening her safety belt, she sprang to her feet, picking out her garment bag from the closet in front of them, and a carry-on bag from the overhead compartment. Grabbing her briefcase, she bounded down the aisle, an athlete on her way to the next event. "I'm late for a meeting, I'll give you a call."

Hap would have tried to keep up with her, but his way was blocked by Gloria Stanley, the legendary film star, and her hairdresser. Hap could tell it was her hairdresser because even though he carried three pieces of hand luggage and a yipping Yorkshire terrier, he juggled his burden so a hand would be free to make neat a runaway lock of the famous hair. Gloria Stanley, a star of such magnitude, Hap could not help but notice, that people no longer looked at her directly, as though ashamed of themselves for invading her privacy. All around her passengers averted their eyes in a deliberate attempt to pretend she wasn't there, thin again, young again, all pulled together. But still sorrowing, maybe, that she hadn't married the sheikh, who, though oily, would have afforded her her own plane and spared her this indignity.

To the west of the Los Angeles Country Club was a rolling section of real estate that had once enjoyed a celebrity as glossy as Beverly Hills. Stretching from Wilshire to Sunset Boulevard, about a half-mile wide, set with stone mansions on grassy lawns, it was called Holmby Hills. It had served for a brief and shining moment in filmic history as headquarters for "The Rat Pack." The group that had clustered around the last days of the great Humphrey Bogart: Frank Sinatra, Dean Martin, Sammy Davis, Tony Curtis, and Janet Leigh were some of its exclusive membership, as well as Judy Garland when she could stay off the sauce. An unofficial club of the best people in town, it unofficially considered itself. The Grand Finale of the Dream. A Hollywood ruled by stars, in residence. And where they resided for the last days was Holmby Hills.

All that had been social archaeology dug up by Hap's younger daughter before she had moved on to become a nutritionist. By the time the Mitchel family moved to Los Angeles, the aura of celebrity glamour had faded. It would have meant nothing to Hap even if he had known about it at the time. He had picked the locale for its proximity to UCLA, walking distance, in case his children, still young, wanted to go there. He was still a citizen of a country where people walked. The curious ways of southern California, with its car-bound civilization, driving even to the corner mailbox, were alien to him.

Even now, ten years after he'd moved his family there, he was no more tuned in to the customs of the community than when he'd first arrived. He considered it a foreign port where he'd been stationed, as he'd been stationed at Canaveral for part of the early time as an astronaut. The habits of the locals were nothing he thought of adopting for himself. But he did like his house, hard as it sometimes was to come home to.

He made his way up the flagstone steps from the driveway where the limo dropped him, looked up to study the facade as one would look up to greet a friendly face. Like most of his neighbors' houses, it was country English, brown wood beams over white stucco, to frame Shakespearean entryways. His older daughter had christened the neighborhood "Stratford on Zsa Zsa." At least she'd picked a more solid path than her sister, getting married, moving to Pasadena, having babies. His older son was out of the drug rehabilitation program, with a job in Washington and a support group. His younger son was in his junior year at Stanford, on the football team. So all in all, his family seemed to have balanced out. Hap considered himself a comparatively carefree parent, and a lucky man, considering the trouble most of his friends had been through with their "young adults," who no longer liked being called kids no matter how much they behaved like them.

The only member of his family that Hap felt really hopeless about was his wife Kate. She was waiting in the playroom for him, as if she had remembered that he was supposed to be home around four and not because that was where the bar was.

"Hi," she said, and kissed him, turning her face away

even as her lips touched his cheek so he couldn't smell the liquor. "How was New York?"

"Peculiar," he said. "My last dinner appointment committed suicide."

"Something you said?" She went to the bar, the lion-footed, carved oak monstrosity that she'd picked out herself, almost as if she needed a barricade to hide behind, something thick enough to insulate her against her dead sensibilities.

"He killed himself *before* we had dinner. Himself and Miranda Jay . . ."

"Oh, yes, I heard about that. That beautiful girl. Sad. Victor Lenrahan's mistress. I remember the gossip when Victor died, and you were so upset that there wasn't a funeral."

"You remember that?" Sometimes she surprised him. So much of her life now was a blunted state of awareness, he assumed she was also insensitive to what he was going through. Certainly not able to remember things. What an amazing woman she still was, what was left, anyway, unmummified.

"I don't understand why you're always so eager to go to funerals. Would you like a drink?"

He shook his head.

"Goody Two Wings. Well, I'm sure you won't mind if I have one?"

He didn't answer.

"Why is that? Why do you like funerals?"

"It's not that I like them. I just need a chance to say good-bye."

"Well, we all ought to say good-bye every time we say good-bye and really mean it. Who knows when it's the last time?" She took a decanter of Scotch and poured it ceremoniously into a wineglass, filling it half full. "Speaking of which, you got a call from the secretary.

"Dwight Efram Jonah." She minced the words, clipping them with importance. "He seemed very annoyed that you weren't at his beck, much less his call. Said you should call him back as soon as possible at the White

House. 465-1414, he told me several times. And then he said the White House again, in case I didn't know to swoon at the number."

"Why didn't you tell him where I was?"

"I thought you were probably busy. I saw you on TV." She took a long sip of her drink. "Are you fucking that Avery woman?"

"Not anymore."

"She's very attractive. I can understand why the nation has taken her to its heart. Or, in certain cases, its crotch."

"I'm sorry," he said very softly.

"You don't have to apologize to me. You're free to do what you want. I've always told you that."

"I mean I'm sorry you're upset."

"I'm not upset." She leaned on the wood of the bar, smiled at him, and sipped. "As a matter of fact, I'm happier than I've been in years. I'm having an affair."

"You think you're having an affair." He started for the doorway, Valpack over his shoulder.

She stumbled after him. "I'm having an affair with Barney."

Hap noted a sad attempt at neatness visible on the front of her gray silk housecoat: the scorched imprint of an iron. She had long ago fired their maid. She'd told Hap that since the children were all grown and gone, they didn't need a live-in anymore, when they both liked their privacy. He heard beyond her words, saw to the truth that she didn't want to have to hide her drinking from a stranger.

"Barney's drunker than you are. There's no way he could do anything." Hap walked into his bedroom and turned on the light. There was still a lot of daylight outside, but this was the dark part of the house, the exterior overgrown with giant hibiscus plants, the limp-petaled, bright red flower with its fuzzy yellow pistil, the only flower Hap had seen in his life that looked truly ugly. He had asked Kate many times to have the gardener cut the bushes back. But she appeared not to remember. He understood that she preferred darkness for her own rooms and the kitchen, so she could sit in them, quietly drinking, with no one seeing her and no intruding sunlight to clash with her mood. But he didn't know why she wanted the gloom carried over to where he slept. Especially as she no longer slept beside him. Still, gloomy and cheerless as it might have appeared, he welcomed the sight of his room, and a bed where he could rest, where no one would coax out his secrets.

Kate stumbled into the bedroom behind him. "Don't be so sure about Barney," she hissed. "He touches me as you've never touched me. Inside and out."

"I'm glad for you." He hung up his Valpack in the closet, unzipped it, and started taking out his suits.

"I think you mean that. You really are." She came closer, eyeing his profile. "What kind of man are you?"

He turned to look at her. A half-inch of gray bordered her face, bright red dye like an abrupt marker ending at the telltale roots. She hadn't even bothered to go to the beauty parlor. Couldn't even get her chops up to get drunk with someone else, boozing her appointment away with the other women whose husbands didn't like them drinking either. That saddened Hap more than the scorch on her dressing gown. He remembered when her clothes had been spotless and starched, as she was, when her hair was its own cherry red, her face cheerful, her spirit quietly resolute.

"Why do you keep coming back?" she asked him.

"This is my home. You're my wife."

"The mother of your children? Well, they're grown now. Gone. I am not the Navy. I don't demand a lifetime of service. I don't ask for loyalty even when the tour of duty is over."

"I do."

"You patsy." She wobbled slightly, tilted to the left, spilled some Scotch on her hostess gown. "Oh, shit. Look what I did. And I went to such lengths to make myself lovely for you." She giggled.

He reached over and steadied her. She stared up into his face.

"Why don't you get old?" she asked, and started to cry. "Oh, Hap, I'm such a mess. Everything's such a mess.

Why doesn't it ever work out the way you think it's going to?"

"That would make it too easy," he said, and held her.

PARIS

◇

So far in her life, brief as it was, it seemed to Honey she had let down just about everybody. After the French couple took her baby, she started to cry and couldn't stop. All around her was the weepy, inexplicable panic of other new mothers, floundering in the sudden disappearance of bellies and euphoric juices. But Honey's turmoil didn't even have a baby to focus on. The nuns at the hospital, used to such outbursts, gave her tranquilizers to lift her mood, shots to stop her bleeding and to dry up the ducts of milk in her breasts. After a while she was pulled together, at least enough to leave the hospital.

Just before she checked out, the administrator asked her if she would be kind enough to help an American who was in emergency, having some problem with the language. Honey could hear him from all the way down the corridor. "Don't any of these clowns speak English?"

There was a terrible stench in the emergency room, the way a war must have smelled, she imagined: the blood of the injured, people vomiting, the suffocating heat. She herself was still in somewhat of a daze. But she wanted to help him, this poor little man, lying there yipping, like one of the wounded. "What kind of hospital is this, anyway? A person could croak here, for Christ's sake!"

He was on a cot in the receiving room, skin gray, his dull little eyes fixed on his short-fingered, manicured hands, crossed on his chest. He seemed to have a stiff neck, till Honey realized it was fear that rooted him, putting blinders on him so he couldn't move his head. Not even an inch, in case he saw something terrible.

His hair was thin and colorless, dressed with pomade that Honey guessed he thought would make it look darker and thicker. It served instead to bunch the meager strands together, so she could see white scalp in between, the dark freckles on the shiny surface. His eyes were small, set close together, webbed at the corners, with thick folds of wrinkles above his lids. She had the impression that if he hadn't been so scared to look around, his eyes would have darted. That was the kind of eyes they were. Nervous, feverish eyes. Like something had escaped him and he was terrified everything else was about to. That whatever it was he had missed—love, peace, contentment—any minute now it was going to stay missed, permanently.

"Can I help you?" Honey asked him.

He looked at her like he couldn't believe she was really there, talking to him. He sat up a little, leaning on one elbow, his neck still rigid, body half twisted to face her. "You a nurse?"

"I'm a patient. I'm checking out."

"That makes you a genius. I figured the only way out of this place was as a stiff. Any sawbones here know what they're doing?"

"Sawbones?"

He sighed. "Doctors. Ham-hands."

"Mine does," she said and smiled. "But he's a gynecologist. I don't guess that would be much help to you."

His little eyes narrowed, but seemed to get some life back in them now that he looked her over carefully. "Who the hell are you?"

"Who the hell are you?"

"I'm Harry Bell." He waited for some sign of recognition, as if it were a famous name and she should know it. "Naw. I guess you're too young."

"What happened to you?"

"Times changed. The public doesn't want the same things anymore. You can bring them spectacle, you can bring them invention, imagination, you can bring them flash and tunes they can hum with words they can remember, that mean something. You can donate art and building wings on museums and own the biggest share of the most powerful communications company in the world, and have some of the most outstandingly beautiful women in the twentieth century crazy about you, I mean crazy about you, even to this day. And they still call you old-fashioned and out of it and tell you you're finished."

"No, I mean, what happened that they brought you here?"

"Oh," he said. "I fainted." He seemed to recover himself. "I was in a restaurant a few blocks from here. I thought first it was indigestion. You know these frogs can sell you just about anything and say it's gourmet." He pronounced it with the final *t*, giving it the fillip a soubrette would have. "Then I realized maybe I was having a heart attack. My limousine driver brought me here. A person could cool just waiting for these jokers to listen if you're still alive or not."

The doctors finally came and checked him out. "They'd like you to rest here for a few days," Honey translated.

"Rest I can do when I'm dead," said Harry, and got up from the cot.

The intern tried to restrain him. Harry brushed his hand away. "Nothing personal, Louis Pasteur. But I didn't come all the way to Paris to end up on a bedpan."

"If you don't feel okay . . ." Honey started to tell him.

"Okay? When was the last time it was okay to feel okay? The world's turning to shit before our very eyes, even without glasses." He took his out of his pocket and studied her. "How old are you?"

"Seventeen."

"Seventeen," he whispered, a reverential echo, and closed his eyes. She could see his lids, magnified through the lenses of the glasses. They were thin, blue veined, almost transparent, so she could watch his eyeballs moving behind them, jumping around as if searching for something in his brain. "Where did it go?"

"Where did what go?"

"Time, you old Gypsy Man," he said, and sang a couple of bars in a reedy tenor. "Friend of mine wrote that song. What did you say your name was?"

"Miranda," she told him, because she knew her Honey days were over.

He had his limousine take her back to her hotel, while he sat beside her in the backseat, studying her with an intensity she could feel like fingers on her face. "Noses like that you're born with."

"Excuse me?"

"You didn't get that fixed, did you, that upturned little map of Ireland?"

"I don't understand."

"Fabulous! Fabulous!" he said, and patted her hand. "That nose and innocence, together again at last for the first time. Why couldn't I have met you a long time ago, when it would have done both of us some good?"

"I wasn't born a long time ago."

"Neither was I," Harry said. "It just seems like it."

The car stopped. Harry leaned over and looked up at the entrance. "What kind of a joint is this?"

"A hotel."

"It looks like a fleabag."

"Well, it's that, too."

"Oh, good, you got a mouth also. That nose and innocence, but also what we used to call in the days when there were still words, a saucy tongue. You staying with somebody here?"

"No."

"You got family in this burg? Friends?"

"No."

"So that makes you independent, just like me. We're a

lot alike, except, of course, I'm prettier. So why go back here? I'm at the Georges Cinq. Best hotel in town. Stay with me. You don't have to do anything, understand. Just be there. In case I pass out again. Or anything.''

He looked so pitiful, her heart went out to him. ''You won't get sick,'' she said.

''When you say that, take my pulse.'' He sort of smiled. ''There was this picture once, called *The Virginian*, and Gary Cooper said, 'When you say that, smile.' So I'm doing sort of a parody. Parody is the sincerest form of no talent. Go ahead, take my pulse. Give me the feeling I'm cared for. See if my heart's still beating.''

One of the things she had learned to do with her father was take his pulse and blood pressure. She had come to do it with distaste because of how he hated being touched by her. But something about this little man moved her, and she reached for his wrist hesitantly.

''Go ahead,'' he said. ''It's only my wrist.''

She took it between her fingers. It made her sad how tiny it was, how threaded with deep blue veins, veins that carried a pulse she could barely feel. ''You'll be fine.''

''I'll be fine if you stay with me,'' he said, and gripped her hand. ''Pretty please with whipped cream on it and maybe a diamond, even if we don't do a thing. My future depends on you. How does it feel to have somebody's whole life stacked on your deal of the cards?''

She thought about her baby and started to cry.

''Oh, Christ,'' he said, and handed her a handkerchief, linen, lightly scented with a male perfume. ''I didn't mean to make you nervous, kid. I wouldn't die on you, I swear. Even if you choose to dump me this minute, which I know you're too smart and bighearted to do. Come on. Give a middle-aged man a break.'' He smiled, his teeth flashing dully. Tiny teeth they were, with a pearly gray cast. ''What you got better on your Hit Parade?''

''Not much,'' she said. ''You sure it's all right to blow my nose in this?'' She had never had a linen handkerchief before, never even seen one except in the banker's pocket, and he'd always been careful not to let her use it, quick to give her Kleenex for her lipstick and for between her legs afterward.

"That's what it's for," he said.

Still, she wasn't sure. She blew her nose tentatively, as if there were a delicate way to do it, not wanting to soil the fabric with something unclean.

"Come on," he said. "Let's hear a real blow. Like a trumpet. Like Sousa would do it."

"Who?"

"Christ," he said. "Blow it any way you want to."

There was a luxury to it, a feeling of waste, of privileged disdain, to blow your nose in something softer than it was, edged with fine patterns of lines. She felt a sudden surge of superiority, the way the rich probably felt all the time, maybe even shitting on silk.

"Get your things and come on," Harry said. "Or leave them. I'll buy you all new ones."

"I couldn't do that."

"Sure you could. Never knew a dame in my life who wasn't right in there waiting to take at the first opportunity, except for my mother."

"Well, now you know two," she said, and slammed out of the car.

"Come on." He leaned out the window. "I didn't mean anything. I was only cracking wise. Can't you forgive a man for cracking wise?"

She went straight into the hotel and didn't turn to look at him. He was pathetic, and old, and that was all she needed at this point in her life, a character who didn't trust women.

When she got to her room, she reached in the boot where she'd hidden the rest of her money. It was gone. She knew the maid had taken it and went downstairs to tell the manager. The manager said the maid was more trustworthy than any American. Then asked her for the rent.

"Get it from the maid," Honey said.

"You'll have to leave."

She started for the elevator. He barred her way. "Without your clothes."

She had no strength for a fight. She took the Metro to the Champs Elysées, and walked to the Georges Cinq. Harry had pronounced it Gorgeous Sink, almost deliberately, like he really knew better but didn't have to since he had the money to stay there.

She called him from the lobby. "Hey, come on up, kid," he said, sounding so glad to hear her she thought he would jump through the phone. He was waiting at the end of the corridor when she stepped out of the elevator, waiting like a little boy. His eyes looked so eager they were almost bright.

"You know what you are?" He pushed the door to his suite open wide. "You're a sight for sore eyes. All my life I heard the expression, but my eyes were never this sore before. I understand better now."

The suite was decorated with gilt and velvet, like one of the roped-off rooms of furniture at the Louvre. Needlepointed Louis XV love seat and chairs were arranged like a courtier's audience, near lightly figured, pale blue walls. A giant mirror, gilt framed (was it real gold?), hung above the marble fireplace. He went to the antique ivory phone and called housekeeping, telling them to send up an extra bed. His eyes were on her face the whole time he talked, like he was making sure she understood he was as good as his word, that he didn't mean for her to sleep in his bed.

The hand on the telephone, like his face, was an otherworldly shade of gray. She felt terrible pity for him, to be that obviously rich and not have been anywhere sunny, not have any color on his face, on his hands, in his life, for all she could tell. Like all there was left for him was hospital pallor, even if your hospital was the Gorgeous Sink.

"I don't know what I would have done without you, kiddo. I coulda died there if you hadn't come along." There were tears in his eyes. "All the outstanding women

I've known in my lifetime, outstanding, and not one of them here by my side because they didn't know how to be faithful. But I'm not sore. Not even at Sylvia. Sylvia married me twice. She was crazy about me.''

"I can understand that," Miranda said, the lying starting to come as easily as blowing your nose in linen.

"Now that she's getting divorced from Lester, I'm thinking of marrying her again.''

"So how come she isn't with you?"

He shrugged a little boy's shrug, withered, an old habit that clung to him. "I wouldn't want her to see me less than perfect. You got no idea how perfect I was before, so what I am now doesn't seem a comedown to you. Does it seem a comedown to you?''

"Not at all.''

"What a doll. What a sweetheart." He chucked her under the chin. "How'd you like a little dinner?''

"That would be nice." She sat back and listened to him ordering room service, everything in English except for the haricots verts.

"And make sure they're plenty verts," he said. "I don't want them overcooked.''

Then he called down to the lingerie shop and told them to send up a peignoir. Something with ostrich feathers. A woman arrived with two negligees on hangers, and he picked the pale shrimp-colored one and told Honey to put it on. "I want you to be comfortable," he said.

"I don't think I could be comfortable in that.''

"Go ahead. Try it out. Pretend you're with Robert Goulet." He pronounced the final t.

There were feathers under her chin, and feathers around her wrists, and feathers wisping up to her nose as she sat down to dinner. Two waiters came and set a table with gold plates and crystal and heavy silver with markings on it, and metal hats on the food dishes to keep them warm. She had never seen—or tasted—anything like it. Harry hardly touched the food on his plate, his attention, his whole concentration focused on her.

"Gusto," he remarked. "That's what I like. Eat, you'll feel better. That's what my Aunt Sarah used to say."

"Then why aren't you eating?"

"You should know what happened to my Aunt Sarah." He smiled kind of feebly. "I'd rather watch you. That makes me feel better.

"Seventeen. You got no idea how fast it goes. Fifty years. It goes like *that*!" He snapped his fingers. "Fifty years. Like the wink of an eye. You don't watch it, you miss it."

"Are you sixty-seven?"

"Why? Do I look it?"

"I don't know what sixty-seven looks like."

"Well, I'm around that. What a lousy surprise. Who knew you got here so fast. This age is the age Barnaby Geer was when I went to work for him, when I was heavyweight steno champion of the world, and I thought he was ancient. Do I strike you as ancient?"

"Of course not," she lied.

"Barnaby Geer was the greatest figure in the world of finance. A legend in the days when legends were really legends, so fine a man you should still hear about him, know about him, young as you are. The greatest money mind in the history of Wall Street. A giant! That's what he was, so it's what I decided to be. A giant! Do I strike you as a giant?"

"Not exactly." He was, she gauged, just over five feet one.

"Good. I like you being honest. Honesty is the best policy except when you can make money by being less honest. The truth is, I'm not a big man. Except a girl I used to see, a real smart ass, said I was tall when I stood on my money."

"That's not kind."

"Kind don't get you bubble gum in this world, kid." He poured himself a glass of water from the green bottle cooling in the crystal ice bucket. "But money does make you tall. When they did the cover story on me in *Life*, they asked me how come I was so successful and I told them I had to be. 'I'm a short, ugly man and I like tall, beautiful women.' That's what I said. I had no choice but to be successful. How tall are you?''

"Five eight," she said.

"That's tall." He got up from the table and went to the window. "So you're how come I had to get rich. You understand?''

"I think so," she said, and wondered if she could tell him about the baby, and ask him for money, and maybe just open the shrimp-colored robe a little and have it all.

"But what I like about you best, you see, what really puts me away, is that you're pure. I can tell. Unsullied. All of the women I knew in my life, they were sullied, up the kazoo. I mean a lot of them pretended they weren't, and sucker that I was sometimes, I believed them. You know, I liked to put women up on a pedestal. And usually the bigger whores they were, the more innocent they paraded. So I got to the point finally when I wanted my whores whores, if you know what I mean.''

"No, I don't.''

"Well, for instance, when one of my 'virgins' dumped on me, what I did was go to the Copa, that was the hottest club in New York at the time, and I'd pick out the hottest-looking girl in the line, and I'd take her to a hotel and send all her clothes to the cleaners, so she'd just be there for me. I'd keep her there for three, four days, until I got it out of my system. Fortunately, you don't have a lot of clothes so my cleaning bill can't be too high. Only joking, you know that, don't you?'' A pallid little smile moved across his lips, flashed like a painful memory. "I mean it's my intention to cover you tip to toe, this is the exact reverse of these stories I'm telling you, you get that, I'm sure, because you're something else. I can tell. There's a lot going on behind those eyes. Of course, there's also probably a lot going on behind that mouth, but I wouldn't dare. I wouldn't even ask for it, though I'd probably give half my kingdom to feel it on me. But you're not that kind of girl, I can tell. Are you?''

"No," she said, because she knew it was what he

wanted to hear, and the truth was she didn't know what kind of girl she was. Not yet, anyway.

"But I could probably do it again just from the touch of that mouth, that sweet little pink tongue, maybe for the last time. I hope I'm not offending you, these are what my psychiatrist would have called erotic ramblings, the putz. He knew as much about me as you probably know about sex. I haven't offended you, have I?"

"How could you?" she said. "I don't know what you're talking about."

"Good," he said. "Wonderful. Anyway, I wouldn't make a move, you have nothing to fear but fear itself. Because even if I did, irresistible as you are, such are the ham-hands of fate that nothing would happen. Some God it must be who keeps all these feelings so young in us while the equipment is breaking down."

"Why don't you sit down and eat something? You'll feel better."

"You can't say words like my Aunt Sarah, not with that nose on your face. You are some beauty. You think you could ever fall for a guy like me?"

She had the feeling when he said "fall" that she would really have to fall, that it wasn't just an expression. That the pedestal he talked about putting women on was higher than the ones that held the statues in the Louvre, maybe higher even than the sky was in Paris. It was Honey's first experience of a broken heart that wasn't her own, and to her surprise, she felt tears coming to her eyes that weren't for herself or her baby.

"Did I hurt your feelings?" he said. "Is it that insulting, my asking you such a question? Because I'm just running off at the mouth, that's all it is. Forget I even said anything." He came over to the chair and patted her shoulder awkwardly, his short-fingered, pale hands clumsy against the soft folds of fabric. "I have the guts of a burglar to even bring up such a possibility to an angel like yourself."

The telephone rang. Harry went to it with the air of a prisoner waiting for news of a reprieve. "Naw," he said after listening for a moment. "Not tonight, Chet," he said. "Tonight I'm having a religious experience . . . Why would I kid you? I almost died today, Chet. I thought it was curtains . . . Okay. Maybe tomorrow."

He hung up the phone. "Not one of them would mourn me. All it might do is interrupt their travel plans, but not for very long."

"All what might do?"

"My death." He shook his head over it, like it was one of the plays he'd produced that hadn't gotten good reviews. "That was Chet Oppenheim on the phone. He's a public relations man. You know what that is?"

"Not really."

"Someone who gets you publicity. Chet handles people so big they hire him to keep their names out of the papers."

"Are you one of those?"

"Well, I'd like to be, angel, but I still got an ego. The bigger it is, the shorter you get." He laughed, a hard little laugh. Then he stopped himself. "Not one of those clowns would mourn me."

"You shouldn't think so much about death."

"Easy to say when you're seventeen."

"Oh, I used to think about death. A lot."

"No shit, if you'll forgive me. Why would a looker like you with those breasts and your whole life in front of you think about death?"

"I was afraid my life would never go anywhere."

"To the moon," Harry said. "To the moon if you want it. That's what I'm going to do for you." He brightened, the light back in his eyes, a glint now, almost possessed. "That's all I really need is a project. I'm going to set you in motion. I did it for the tap dancer. I did it for every one of them I married. Made them larger than life. That's what you got to be in this world, kiddo. Larger than life. It's the only way to beat the fuckers, if you'll excuse me. And you got the potential. I'm going to do it for you!" He raised an index finger in the air. A light spasm shook him and he paled. He sat down and took a deep breath. "If I have the time."

"You have the time," she said softly, and got up and sat on the love seat beside him. "You look a thousand percent better than you did this afternoon."

"Well, that's because of you, kid. You're full of life. I feel better just being around you. What were you doing in that hospital anyway?"

"Female trouble," she said. Alex had told her she'd be better off mysterious. Knowing what she already knew about Harry, how great was his need to have her be pure, she thought this was probably a good place to start.

"Female trouble." He looked at her carefully. "Is it fixed now?"

"Just about."

"Not that it would make any difference, my health the way it is. Not that I would try anything. But is it catching?"

"Not for men."

He exhaled deeply. "I have a confession to make. You know why I came to Paris? To get laid."

"Didn't you know anybody closer to where you lived?"

"Everybody leaves New York in the summer. And there's nobody there even when they're there who could do it for me anymore. If you get my meaning."

"I don't."

"Well, it isn't for men like it is for dames. You can't fake it." He looked away. "And it isn't always like it was when a guy was sixteen and all he had to do was get a sniff of it, and follow it up the stairs and there it would be, ready to go. You don't mind my talking about sex?"

"Talking never hurt anybody." Now that she thought about it, she realized talking about sex was completely new to her. It had been a forbidden subject in her household. Everything she knew she had learned from experience; there were no discussions to draw on. So in Harry's tentative meanderings was something kindly and almost professorial, the air of a teacher who loved his subject, sorrowing over being of retirement age.

"I take it you've had *some* experience," Harry said. "It

isn't important to me anymore girls be total virgins, just that they don't try to play me for a patsy.''

"I've had *some* experience," she said, drawing on his emphasis.

"Well, that makes you more honest than any of the honest women I've known. Not that I even think about them anymore, the whores.''

She could feel all his little-boy anger and disappointment. How sad, she thought, to grow old but not up.

"Whores used to be able to excite me better than whores who admitted being whores. But even that changes. Men can't always do it even with the most exciting woman in the world, which is what I think you are, to be frank, if you don't mind me saying so, since you're in no danger.''

"I don't mind."

"And the older a guy gets, the more he worries about being able to get it up, if you'll pardon the expression.''

"You worried about that?"

"Well, I was. That was the biggest worry in my life. But you'd be surprised how fast it stops being a problem when you think you're going to die. You know how your whole life is supposed to pass in front of your eyes when you're drowning? Well, they were all there. Every woman I ever stuck it to, excuse me, including the countess. A true aristocrat. You know? I thought she was the highlight of my life, like leaking into her would lift me, you understand? Like class was something you could get by swimming in the juices. All of them went dancing through my brainpan like the flickers; a passing parade. And I thought, Holy shit—forgive me—this is what I made all the fuss about?

"So I promised God—not that I'm that big a believer. But I've always been lucky, even for someone as sharp as me, so I got to figure maybe there's something really Big out there, bigger even than Barnaby Geer, that gave me a hand. I mean, why has the sun always shone on your faithful servant Harry Bell? Except where the whores were concerned, and it was my own fault I tried to make them into more than they were and couldn't see they were whores, that was what the shrink said, the putz. And meantime I got to have them, didn't I? So even that was a gift from God, in a way. I mean, after all, He does give us a wang.

"So I promised God if I lived, if I got through the seizure in that restaurant, just before I keeled, I sent up the message, straight from the heart, believe me, that if I made it, if I didn't croak, I was going to stop thinking about my cock—forgive me—I told God I would stop thinking about my cock and start thinking about my soul. How does that sound to you?"

"Like a really good idea."

"Maybe I could build a cathedral. A Jewish cathedral. Why not? Show God I'm putting my money where my mouth is. How does that sound?"

"Great." It was easy to say what he wanted to hear. It was like touching a man where it felt good, to send the right things into his ears, and that was all the comfort he wanted right then, she could tell that. And the truth was, it was easy to be good to this man, who was already more father to her than her own father had been her whole lifetime.

"After all, why should all the big salutes be from the Goyim?"

"What does that mean?"

"No slur intended. It's just an expression."

"But what does it mean?"

"The blue-eyed blondes, like you."

"My eyes aren't blue."

"So I noticed," Harry said. "Where did you get those eyes, kiddo? Are there any more at home like you?"

"No."

"That's probably just as well. I don't know what to do with one of you, so I certainly couldn't handle any more." He looked at her carefully. "Maybe you're it, you know? My answer. I know this one woman, an ex-nun, she tried to hit me up for a donation for some religious group, and she told me no prayer ever comes back void. That a lot of prayers come back and the answer is 'No,' but no prayer goes unanswered. So maybe that's what you are, a sign from God, that he really heard me, wants to know if I mean business. Maybe I shouldn't just build a cathedral of stone. Maybe I should take your amazing beautiful flesh and make it some kind of living monument, to show I'm serious, not just fucking around, if you'll pardon me.

"I like that." Harry seconded his own motion. "I made stars in my time. But while I made them, I made them. This would be different. I really believe it. Maybe you're some kind of heavenly assignment for me. When I saw you in that hospital I thought to myself, here is an angel come to rescue me, and I was right to make a promise to God. Look how fast He acts! The nun was right: no prayer comes back void! He sends an angel to rescue me and test me at the same time. Because if I could only get it up, I'd sure like to stick it to you, if you'll excuse my frankness.

"But there's nothing to worry about, because I couldn't even if I could. You understand? If I could, I wouldn't, because that's my biggest fear now, is going, which you could in the saddle. You understand? I'm too scared."

"I understand," she said, and patted his hand. It felt cold underneath her palm, the flesh clammy.

"So will you sleep with me?" There were little tears of pleading starting to form on the inside corners of his eyes.

"After the whole big speech you just made?"

"That's all I want to do is sleep. Honest to God. May He strike me dead if I have anything else in mind, except maybe weakly. I'm just afraid to sleep by myself. In case tonight is the last night. I mean, if Death comes, I don't want to be alone."

"Okay," she said.

"God Bless you." He hugged her. "And then, in the morning, if I'm still alive, I'm going to set you in motion."

She showered in the marble bathroom, fluffed herself dry in the oversized terry robe, thick and white with the hotel initials blazed on its big pocket in heavy gold thread. Even the embroidery was thicker when it was for rich people. She thought of the meager, careful needlepoint her mother turned into pillows which, artful as it was, seemed anemic in comparison to the luster of the *G* and the *V*. So it wasn't just steaks that were thicker for these people, it was their robes and the threads that decorated them.

The thought of being rich had never before crossed her consciousness, caught as she'd always been in simple survival, trying to keep people from being angry, from hurting or abandoning her, trying to get them to love, or just not punish, not turn away. But held in the luxuriant folds of that robe as the fragrance of the rack of colognes and perfumed soap offered by the hotel (a part of the bathroom, for God's sake!) wafted through her awareness— the fragrance of money—she suddenly understood with blazing clarity that wealth was a buffer. That everybody had pain, but somehow the edge was blunted when you wore thick enough robes.

She put on the cotton twill pajamas Harry had loaned her because she told him she couldn't sleep in feathers. The pants legs came to the middle of her calf. She went into the bedroom. Harry lay on the far side of the king-sized bed, seeming to stretch away from where she would lie down. He made not a very big mound under the covers.

"God must know I'm a man of my word if He's looking at you, kid. To be able to resist the irresistible."

During the night, he cried out. It was a cry of such intense pain, such grief, such loss, that Honey was certain he had died beside her, once she remembered where she was. She struggled through the darkness, found the lamp, turned on the switch. He was sitting up against the pillows, tears running down his cheeks. She could tell it took him a minute to remember who she was.

"Are you okay?" she asked him.

"I was dreaming."

"What about?"

"I dreamed my mother told me to go fuck myself and I couldn't."

She didn't know whether she was supposed to laugh or not. Humor hadn't played too big a part in her life, and from the woeful expression on his face, there hadn't been much of it in his life either. So rather than do what might have offended him, just in case he wasn't making a joke, she was quiet.

"She's a real pistol," he said, wiping his eyes.

"She's still alive?"

"Younger than I am. And still beautiful. You want to snuggle? Just let me hold you. I swear I wouldn't do anything."

"Let's just go back to sleep," she said, and turned off the light.

"I understand," he murmured in the darkness. "I've got a face only a mother could love. Unless she was my mother. She couldn't stand to look at me, she told me all the time."

She turned the light back on. "You're making a joke, aren't you?"

"Anybody can love their children. My mother's an original. Whenever I got too puffed up about myself, she would stick a mirror in front of my face so I wouldn't get too excited about who I thought I was."

"That's the meanest thing I ever heard."

"Then put your arms around me."

"You're making it up so I'll feel sorry for you."

"I wish. Maybe just a hug, huh?"

"Go back to sleep."

"I can't." He turned on the lamp by his side of the bed. "Who would believe this even if I swore on my grave, which I hope I won't have to. With all the women I've had, here I am, in the choicest hotel in Paris, with the most gorgeous girl I ever saw, with her at my mercy, if people would believe I had any, and I'm not even trying to have my way with her. If I could. Ain't life a kick in the head."

"People change."

"I don't think so. I think they just become more what they always were. So maybe my mother was right about me. And what I always was, even though I didn't know it, was a sap. You shoot craps?"

"What?"

"Dice. You ever play?"

"No."

"I got a pair. Sterling silver. The tap dancer gave them to me. That and a hand job at El Morocco." He opened a drawer in the bedside table and took out a tiny red velvet drawstring bag, very worn. "Carry them with me wherever I go."

He taught her how to play sitting on the floor, rolling back the carpet. By two thirty in the morning she had beaten him for two thousand dollars. "I'm starting to feel better," Harry said, and calling for the bellman, had him bring up a magnum of champagne.

They played till dawn, by which time she was very drunk, and had beaten him for five thousand dollars. He seemed revitalized by each defeat, as if by placing the victories in her hands, they would be less shaky. "You sure you haven't played before?"

She shook her head.

"Too big to be beginner's luck. You're just a natural gambler. I wonder how come I feel so good when it actually makes me mad to lose? Every time I signed an alimony check to my wives, I felt like I was dipping the pen in my veins."

She laughed.

"Sure, now you're getting a sense of humor. Now that you've got me nailed. Women always get more relaxed when they see men suffer." He looked at her with hooded eyes and smiled. "Tomorrow we buy you the clothes you should be in. Clothes that offer you up like the bouquet you are, kid. St. Laurent and Coco Chanel. You can afford them now."

They spent the morning in designer showrooms. "Who woulda thunk it," he said, beaming, while women draped her with Diors. "Me dressing a dame after I spent most of my life trying to take their clothes off."

Down at the corners as Harry's mouth was now, Miranda tried to picture it young and pink. Even so, it would have been an unlovely mouth, thin-lipped, ungenerous, caught up in its own appraisal of the world as ungiving, and so ungiving itself. Hard to conceive of anyone's wanting to kiss it. Least of all herself. She wished she could be more unselfish, or harder-hearted, and do it just for the money he obviously had. But she sensed all the conflicts he was going through, all that he had talked about, and some that he hadn't. And she knew that the less willing she was, the more he would want her. And that was what it was all about, really, wasn't it? It was only when they got you, and knew they had you, that they threw you away. When you stayed slightly out of reach they draped you with Diors.

"You're the fairest of them all," he said to her when she came out in a white cocktail dress with beading along the vee of the neckline. "Of all the chicks I ever knew. More fairer by far than Rembrandts I have owned, or similar doodads.

"How great, to cloud men's minds, like Lamont Cranston, just by having a body like that. What a pleasure to be able to buy you such things, only what am I doing being so generous? Maybe you should pay part of it yourself, seeing as how you beat me for five thousand."

"How much is this dress?" Honey asked the salesgirl.

"Forget it," said Harry. "The sky's the limit. Can't you take a joke?" He turned to the salesgirl. "How much is it?"

The woman computed it in francs, and then into dollars. Harry paled when he heard the sum.

"The sky is higher in Paris," Honey told him.

"So where do you want to go for lunch kid? How about the Ritz? They got the crispest haricots verts."

"Whatever you want," she said.

He looked up at the mirrored ceiling of the showroom. "Oh God, what a test. What a test. To have her say 'Whatever you want' and not be able to want whatever I want."

"Maybe we could go to church after lunch."

"You putting me on?"

"Well, if you're thinking about your cathedral, you should see the best. Have you been to Notre Dame?"

"Been to it? I was going to make it into a musical. *Hunchback!* That was the title. Woulda been a great show, but people are afraid to be sentimental nowadays. Woulda tore their hearts out. That poor crippled bastard, in love with Esmeralda. A song, 'I got a hunch I love you.' They got no vision, the people running the theaters now. Realtors. That's all that's left on Broadway. No showmen. No artists. Can't even hear what's creative. All they got is a barn they want to fill. Creeps."

"So you want to go to church?"

"Let's just have lunch. Then we'll see."

They went to the Ritz. There were high marble columns in the dining room. She maneuvered the thick carpets in her new high heels, her feet more arched than she was used to their being, the shoes, like the rest of her attire, whipped magically into the showrooms to complement whatever she was wearing. Even underwear had appeared as if by a magic wand that could manifest anything. Fairy godmothers on staff, when you could afford them.

But the spell allowed filters of true concern to get through her feeling of enchantment. She was worried about Harry, because as soon as they were seated in the crystal-chandeliered dining room, his face took on the same gray tones as the day before.

"Haricots verts," he said to the waiter. "Pour moi, haricots verts. And pour Cinderella here, beefsteak rare, and pommes frites." He smiled at her. "To put a little meat on these gorgeous bones. To build you up for the beautiful life that is now beginning."

"You sound like my mother. When I was born she saw fairies in the delivery room. Like Sleeping Beauty. She thought they were there casting spells so I'd have a magical life."

"She was right. Only Beauty isn't sleeping. She's awake. Although," he leaned over confidentially, "asleep she is something fair to behold, believe me. A man has to sit on his hands, and anything else he's got, whether or not it's working."

The waiter brought green beans, cold, in a salad. Harry

sat up, rigid, combative. "If I wanted haricots verts salad, I would have said haricots verts salad."

"The trouble with Paris," said a well-dressed older woman at the next table, "is that they let anybody in."

Harry leaned forward and murmured, almost inaudibly, "That's what we'll do, is go to church, like you said. I got to speak to God. Make it right. Set you in motion. Do a good deed."

"You probably did a lot of good deeds already."

"Not so they counted. Not in the Big Scheme. I always did them strictly for myself and the glory, like the News of the Rialto. You know what I mean."

"No."

"Like the first dame I ever got stuck on, Rona Jean. I sent her flowers every week. Even after I found out she was a hooker. I don't mean she had the mentality of a hooker, which all women do, present company exceptional. I mean I waited for it and begged for it and courted her for it and when I got it she said all I ever had to do was give her twenty-five dollars. You know, I put myself through the fifteenth century for nothing. There I was being a Knight, when all I had to do was run her gauntlet. But I still kept sending her flowers. Till she died. After, even. I didn't even know she kicked the bucket till the florist sent me a letter. Once in a while you meet an honest florist, which is easier than finding an honest woman."

"That was kind of you, sending her flowers." She wondered how many weeks of her baby's support he'd be willing to pay for if she put it all on the table right then, in front of him.

"Naw. I did it for myself," Harry said, speaking louder now, like a football coach chastising the show-off on the team. "So I'd feel like a sport. A hero."

The woman at the next table snorted. It was an incongruous sound coming from her, sleek as she looked, consummately elegant, the kind of woman who seemed to be wearing gloves even with naked hands. Harry looked at her out of the corner of his eye and then back at his small, freckled hands, slight tints of pink at the fingertips from the pressure of his clenching them.

"Then there were the things I tried to do for my family. My mother especially. Because I loved her so much. Because she was so special. But she was independent. Didn't want me doing for her. Wanted to do for herself. So she got rich on her own, following my advice. And needed me less than ever."

"But that still counts. If she got rich from what you told her."

"Not really. Not so a person could say to himself, I made my mother happy."

A tall, balding man crossed the dining room, his arm already extended, as if velocity plus space covered would give the handshake more meaning. "Here's Oppenheim," Harry said. "The P.R. guy I told you about. Hey, Chet!" They shook hands. "Say hello to Miranda."

"Well, hel-l-o."

"That's what I think, too. Take a load off your feet. How'd you like to make an international event out of this one?"

"It would be a privilege." Chet sat down, the angle of his head and exaggerated interest seeming to reflect light from the inside of his glasses, so it was not possible to see his eyes. Silver discs appraised her.

"Some looker, yes?"

"Are you a model, an actress? What do you do?"

"She's fresh, that's what she does."

"You have any specialty?"

"Life! That's what she has. Vitality!"

"You do any singing? Dancing?"

"That shit can be learned. We're talking about the goods here, Chet old buddy. True beauty. What we called, in the days that counted, Verve. I'm going to make her a monument. I promised . . . " He hesitated, looked carefully over at Chet as if measuring whether he dared to mention God. "I promised myself I'd build a monument. Anyone can make one from stone."

"Got you," said Chet.

"So what do you say? You got an angle how we can launch her?"

"We'll start tonight. Bertram Lester's party."

"Will Sylvia be there?"

"I don't think so. The papers just got filed."

"Good. Because she's thinking about marrying me again, and I wouldn't want to get her steamed, showing up with this stunner."

"You want to marry her?" Miranda asked.

"Well, I always cared for her deeply," Harry mused. "And I'd save a fortune in alimony."

The waiter came with the food. Haricots verts, chaud.

"Serve the lady first, Bozo," Harry said.

"It's all right," said Miranda.

"No, it's not all right. You're a lady. I want you to expect to be treated like one. Demand it!"

The well-dressed woman had gotten up to leave, and passing their table said, "Well, what have we here? School for sluts?"

Harry didn't look at her, his grip on his own fingers tightening. "You want some wine?" he asked Miranda.

"Isn't it amazing. You'd think the world would run out of young, stupid women, but they keep getting younger and stupider." She poised herself for a moment by their table.

"Red or white?" Harry said, his eyes beady, staring at Miranda.

"Something stronger," the woman said. "She'll need to be *very* drunk." She walked away.

Miranda studied the slender figure, noted the well-combed, dark champagne hair cut close to the finely shaped head. "What a beautiful old woman. A shame her face is on so tight."

"Well, Harry." Chet smiled. "I think you've met your match."

"At least Miriam has."

"You know that lady?" Miranda asked.

"That was no lady. That was my mother."

"You're kidding. No wonder you have bad dreams."

"Aha!" Chet said, leeringly.

"Not the way it sounds," Harry insisted. "She stayed with me out of goodness. Purity. No hanky-panky. No touching. This, Chet . . . " He put his hand on her shoulder. "This is the last pure thing in Paris."

"Well, we'll have to do something about that," Chet said.

When Harry told Chet on the phone that he had almost died, that he thought it was curtains, Chet assumed of course it was hyperbole. Hyperbole was Harry's best suit. Something he'd perfected as a showman. Never a mouse onstage when he could have an elephant. But now that he looked at him across the table, in the cruel, direct lighting and high-windowed daylight of the Ritz dining room, Chet realized that curtains was what it probably was. Already he was mourning Harry in his own way, thinking who he would line up for the funeral, who to speak, what kind of coverage he could expect, maybe a segment on the "Today" show, certainly a "Milestone" in *Time* magazine. All this planning took less than a few seconds, and having sort of disposed of Harry, coming to bury Caesar as it were, not to waste too much time on him, his mind skipped to the important issue: what to do with Miranda.

She was as lovely a work as he had encountered in the subtler underside of his profession, angular cheekbones beneath soft flesh that would hold up well, improving her as she ripened, rising out of the babyishness of her face into the woman sleeping there. Rolf Orlovsky would doubtless be crazy for her, but Chet owed no loyalty to the financier. He had kept his name out of the press, gotten him girls, everything he paid for. But Chet felt sorry for Harry, even a little sad. A Lilliputian Hannibal crossing the Alps, but never the right pair of tits. And there she was, his honey-haired, green-eyed Grand Finale. It would be passing cruel to hand her on to someone who didn't deserve such beauty. The least he owed Harry was to put her in the hands of someone even Harry would be impressed by.

He could hear Harry bragging now that she wasn't just gorgeous, she was also clever, speaking French, beating him at craps. But Chet knew that Harry, if he lived, which was unlikely, would grow to resent and even hate her winning. The first thing Chet would do as her counselor, which he now unofficially considered himself, was explain how it was with men. No matter how they seemed to encourage women to be on the top, they liked them better when they were down. In a manner of speaking.

After lunch Chet said his temporary good-bye to Harry and Miranda, telling him he would see them that evening at Lester's party. "Bring her a little early. I want to see she gets absolutely the perfect start."

"The perfect start is good," said Harry. "But more important is the perfect finish."

"I'll do everything I can," said Chet, and meant it. After lunch he went back to his hotel, and put in a call to Victor Lenrahan.

On the Rue de Rivoli Harry found her her own perfume. "None of this Joy shit," he said, smelling. "One of a kind, like you are." He picked out a perfume called Silk Lady, from ancient Oriental oils.

"It smells a little strong," Miranda said.

"It smells like you. Like the you you're going to be. Rich. Elegant. Important. Sexy. A *silk* lady." He bought her three bottles in assorted sizes, one of them a huge, cut crystal decanter. "This one should last you as long as you want to remember me."

As limited as her experience was, she perceived something noble, in a funny little way, about Harry Bell. How courageous he was, how dogged in his pursuit of what he considered excellence. She knew enough to be flattered by his thinking her so special, was raised in her own esteem by his esteeming her. Overwhelmed by the wealth she had seen paraded in the past two days, seduced into being what he wanted her to be, she stroked his ego. "I want to remember you as long as I live," she said.

"Then use it sparingly. I already spent enough money."

* * *

While she dressed and made up for the party, Harry stood outside the bathroom, the door slightly ajar, while he gave her the rundown on who would be attending. "Rick Flinders will be there."

"The movie star?"

"Movie star hyphen playboy prick. You stay away from him. He'll chew you up and spit you out. He messed with Robin McKay and she's never been the same, and she was one of the toughest cookies I ever wanted to nibble on. You're seventeen. You deserve romance. You got to be stuck on somebody in this life or it doesn't mean nothing. Love is what fills us up, and we got to be full, or we're empty. You got me?"

"I got you," Miranda said, putting on mascara. It was very luxuriant mascara, bought at a cosmetics store as lavish for powder as the Ritz had been for food. She'd never used makeup of that quality, makeup being one of the secret forbidden things in her adolescence, lipstick slipped her by Julian tried on underneath her covers, by flashlight and mirror, wiped off before her parents could see. When she'd come to Paris, Alex introduced her to shadows and liners, showing her how to deepen the effect of her eyes with a skill she thought with a trace of bitterness was probably one he wished he could practice on himself. Now she approached makeup with a new, deep dedication, according it the reverence the salesgirl had seemed to give it, worshiping the little subtleties of color and shadow, forming herself out of her own basic clay.

"Then there's Orlovsky," Harry went on. "A true pervert. Stay away from him. I'm talking orgies."

"What's an orgy?"

"I really adore you," he said, and came into the bathroom and kissed her forehead. "God bless you and keep you," he said, and went back outside the bathroom. "I'm talking drugs. I'm talking dogs. I'm talking things I can't talk about to someone as sweet as yourself."

"Then why are we going?"

"Because it's a party," Harry said. "We have to go. Elsa Maxwell will be there. She'll talk about you to the right people, maybe write something about you that'll help you get launched."

"Why do you keep saying launched?"

"Because life is a stormy sea. And we all have to learn to stay afloat. And a beautiful vessel like you should sail the surface with nary a ripple and a star to steer her by. Not bad, huh?"

"Not bad."

"Oh Christ, I wish I could stick it into you."

"I liked the vessel stuff better."

"I coulda been a songwriter, but the returns are too erratic. Still, I did write some songs in my day. Would you like to hear one?"

"Sure."

"My ship came in," Harry sang.
"Unfortunately it's a canoe
And I have to paddle it myself
But at least my ship came in."

"I like that song," Miranda said.

"Maybe just for a minute you could put your mouth on it. Who knows what could happen?"

"Sing the song," Miranda said.

"No, it's okay. You got the idea. Don't forget to put on your perfume," he said, and left the room.

When he came back from the lobby he was carrying a small box. "They call that a jewel neckline, kid." He pointed to the beading around her neck. "So it's only right you should have a jewel."

She opened the box. Inside was a round, yellow diamond on a platinum chain.

"I wanted to get you green to go with your eyes, but emeralds are too dark, and peridot—that's the color that matches them—peridot's semiprecious. Not good enough for you, kid." He looked at her looking at the diamond. There were tears in her eyes. It touched him so deeply there were tears in his. Many women had moved him, but the truth was, now that he was getting close to Truth, he wasn't sure anymore he had really moved any of them. It put him away that she seemed to genuinely care about him.

"Nothing to cry about." He wiped his own eyes. "Except that I'm such a sucker in my old age, I actually bought it downstairs, at the hotel jeweler. You know what the markup is in a joint like this?"

In the limousine, he took her hand, gently, as if even that was an invasion. "So how do I introduce you, Miss Silk Lady. I don't even know your last name."

"It's Smith," she said.

"Too common. We got to give you something more distinguished. What's a good American name?"

"Washington?"

"Too many schwartzes with presidential monikers. How about Jay? John Jay. The first Chief Justice of the Supreme Court. I got a feeling you could make legal history. How does that sound to you?"

"I like it."

"Ladies and Gentlemen of the captivated universe," he said, and squeezed, "may I present Miranda Jay."

At the time he received Chet Oppenheim's phone call, Victor Lenrahan was lunching on his yacht, which was anchored for the afternoon at Monte Carlo. Victor had never much cared for Oppenheim, was unsettled by that publicist's pursuit of him. Lenrahan was a private man, with the kind of power that automatically kept his name out of the papers if he wanted it out, and got him as much space as he desired when trying to help his wife's favorite charities or lobbying for more munitions money from Congress. So he had no real need or wish for a Chet in his life, and, in fact, resented his obvious seeking, not to mention his tenacity. Perseverance and unwavering resolution were the center of Lenrahan's own success. But he hated to see it in someone else, particularly a Jew. Not that he had anything, really, against Jews, they just made him nervous, since he couldn't tell what they were thinking, and he knew they were thinking all the time.

But he knew from a Dunn and Bradstreet he had run on Chet's company that Chet didn't need his business, so he wondered why the relentless pursuit. He was sure Chet made a chart of his whereabouts, always turning up, as if by accident. Now he worried over how Chet had even found him, sequestered as he was in the Rainier lagoon.

Princess Grace herself was taking lunch on the deck, with Maria Callas and Onassis. Lenrahan was not a social climber, but there were some groups that dazzled even him. Some men, handsome as he was, that made him stretch to his full height, be glad he still had that full crop of thick white hair. Some women who cried out for heel-clicking and carpaccio, and two of them were eating at his table. Some businessmen who made his own wealth and enterprise seem like chicken feed, and Ari led the list of those. So Chet's call was more than an intrusion, it was a spell breaker. Lenrahan wished he knew him better, and that the phone was not on deck, so he could tell the pushy bastard off.

But as She was sitting there, Her Serene, glistening like the day itself, like the sun on the pale green water that was her attitude, her patrician brow still unlined, Victor had no choice but to listen and to swallow his rage, like the gentleman he was, in the presence of gentlewomen. So as Chet continued his description, Lenrahan found himself paying more attention than he normally would have, hearing of the beauty and uniqueness of the girl.

"Well, what do you think I ought to do about it?"

"There's a party tonight at Bertram Lester's. 16 Avenue Victor Hugo. You could catch a flight up from Nice. Or, if you had the company plane, you could use the company plane."

Victor gritted his big white teeth, the smile that had launched a thousand gunships, so his guests could not perceive how annoyed he was. Of course he had the company plane. The bastard doubtless knew he'd come to Europe on his company plane. Just as he always knew his whereabouts. Mixed with Victor's annoyance at Oppenheim was a grudging admiration, along with the awareness that

Chet always came up with extraordinary women. Nothing could be lost by taking a look.

Harry and Miranda were the first to arrive at the party as Chet had suggested. The food was laid out, a giant buffet, with chafing dishes of silver, bright flames dancing beneath them as Miranda's heart was dancing. There was a fluttering in her belly like Alex's fingers had fluttered other parts of her, a blossoming hunger that was as strong as what she had felt of lust. Her first diamond at her throat. All around her the flags of money, signaling nothing to worry about.

"So what do you think, kid?" Harry waved his arms, indicating the luxe details of the apartment.

"It's terrific," she said, picking up what she already knew was his favorite word.

"Nothing less than you deserve," he said, and squeezed her hand. He showed her to the buffet table, and taught her how to eat snails. At first she refused to taste them. "Snails are a lot like sex. You have to get over how disgusting the idea is before you can appreciate it's delicious."

"Is that the secret?" Miranda said, nervously slipping the shiny, garlicky meat from the delicate shell with a tiny fork and special twisted cutlery. She closed her eyes and let it touch against her mouth, the look of fear on her face turning to one of gradual delight.

"Who knows what's the secret," Harry said. "If they knew the answer, it wouldn't still be a secret. Don't get butter on your dress, kid." He watched while she licked her fingers. "Would I were the butter, to rest against that tongue."

"Excuse me?"

"Shakespeare. With a few liberties."

"Is this really somebody's apartment? It looks like Versailles."

"I think this is the furniture from Lester's last picture."

"Is he a movie star?"

"A producer. Once a Biggie, on his way to being a Smallie. But who knows? He could fool them again. It's never curtains for smart people until . . ." He sighed. "It's curtains."

"If you don't feel good, we can go."

"After they set up this whole party just so we could launch you? I wouldn't think of it."

"Come on." She saw the discomfort on his face and wiped her hands on the white linen napkin. "Let's go back to the hotel."

"Not on your tintype. This is going to be your night. And a big one for me. This is my last weekend."

"You leaving Paris, Harry?" Bertram Lester came into the room, dressed in a tuxedo that minimized his paunch and emphasized his height.

"I'm leaving everywhere," said Harry. "I feel it in my bones."

"How about her bones?" Lester said, his basset eyes fixed on Miranda.

"Watch your mouth, Bertram. I told her you were a producer, not a scum bag. Everything doesn't have to be innuendo, out the other."

"Don't get so excited," Lester said.

"Then watch how you talk in front of a lady."

"Excuse me, Lady." He clicked his heels.

"Her name is Miss Miranda Jay. Honor it."

"I'm honoring. I'm honoring."

"Don't honor so close. That's a hand, not a sparerib."

"A privilege." Lester bowed over her fingers, and released them.

"That's more like it," said Harry. "That's how I want to spend my last weekend. With people who should know better acting like they know better."

"Stop saying that about your last weekend," said Miranda.

"What do you want to drink?" asked Lester.

"Champagne," Harry ordered. "That's all she drinks from now on. Dom Perignon. Only the best." A pained expression crossed his face.

"You having trouble?" Bertram asked. "I could call a doctor."

"I saw a doctor. A Frog."

"George Piner is in town. I could call him. Isn't he your doctor?"

"I don't need to see him. He could tell me I'm fine. It wouldn't make a difference. Fred Allen had a complete physical, left the doctor's office, and had a heart attack on the sidewalk outside."

"Who's Fred Allen?" Miranda asked.

"I don't know what's more depressing," Bertram said. "How young she is, or how old we are."

"I can tell you what's more depressing," Harry said. He leaned over and kissed her cheek. "Angel. I'm going to see that you're taken care of before I go back to New York."

"Why are you going?"

"That's where I was born. That's where I belong. That was me once, Mr. Broadway. While there was still a Broadway that meant Broadway."

"Take me with you," said Miranda.

"You don't belong with a sick old man."

"That's right," said Bertram. "She belongs with a well old man."

"Keep your mitts off her."

"Well somebody's got to take care of this beauty. A treasure like this shouldn't have to scramble."

"She's not scrambling," Harry said. "She's got nothing to offer but sweetness and beauty and light. No terrible story. No heavy luggage. Who wouldn't be lucky to have her?"

"I don't like being talked about like I'm not here," said Miranda.

"A man would have to be blind and without a nose to think you weren't here," said Lester. He turned to Harry. "Oppenheim called. He said Victor Lenrahan might be flying up from Nice."

"No kidding. Victor Lenrahan." Harry made an impressed moue with his mouth and turned to Miranda. "He might even be good enough for you. A man with true class."

"I don't know. I've heard some funny stories," Bertram said.

"Everybody in the public eye has some funny stories," Harry said. "Live long enough, they'll probably turn up some sleaze about Miss America. Lenrahan is Best of Breed. That's what you should have kid. An aristocrat."

"You know that story, don't you?" Lester said. "About the vaudeville agent booking this family, and the guy asks, 'What do they do?' And the agent says, 'Well the father comes out and fucks the mother and then the sister comes out and fucks the brother, and then the whole family ends up in a moist heap.' And the guy says, 'What do they call themselves?' And the agent says, 'The Aristocrats.'"

"I told you not to talk like that in front of her," Harry said, and leaping to his feet, standing on tiptoes, aimed a gray little fist at Lester's jaw, which connected surprisingly hard.

"For Chrissake," said Lester, holding his chin. "It was only a joke."

"Well, life isn't a joke!" Harry said. "Yeats said we only begin to live when we conceive life as a tragedy!"

"Peter Yates? The director?"

"William Butler Yeats, the poet, you putz."

"Your face is all red," said Miranda, taking Harry's arm. "You better sit down."

The other guests started to arrive then, and among them was Victor Lenrahan. His connection with Miranda was immediate and powerful. The white teeth glistened brighter than his hair, his tanned skin glowed, and the pleasure in his eyes was matched only by his obvious gratitude to Chet Oppenheim for inviting him, and the solicitous way he treated Harry for having found her. Harry, seeing how the great man looked at Miranda, was shaken to his toes. Whatever sadness there was in him he managed to swallow, knowing he was leaving her in admirable hands.

"I'll have your stuff in a suitcase, and leave it with the concierge," he whispered to her at the end of the party.

"But . . ."

"No buts," he said. "Trust me. I'm an entrepreneur. This is as good a one as I ever put together."

He flew back to New York Sunday night, by which time

Miranda was ensconced on Lenrahan's yacht. They found Harry's body on Wednesday. He'd been dead in his town house for two days. The servants were off, his secretary was away, so nobody even knew.

Miranda was devastated when she heard, wailed into the wind off the yacht like a banshee, wept sorrow across the water, wracked with remorse that she hadn't gone with him. But Victor Lenrahan, his big, tanned hands around her shaking shoulders, pointed out that, really, there was nothing she could have done. Besides, by that time they were in love.

So there was that, anyway, just as Harry would have wanted. Happy as she was, radiant, she could be his monument.

September 15, 1985

PERSONAL AND CONFIDENTIAL

Mr. Phillip Slagle, Esq.
Durant, Abbate, and Roberts
1 Dag Hammarskjöld Plaza
New York, N.Y. 10017

Dear Phil,

If anything happens to me, there's a box at Chase Manhattan, under the name of Honey Morton. The key is in a black suede boot in the back of my closet.

Please make sure that the letters in the green silk sack go to my daughter Colette, in Paris. You know how to find her. The rest, do what you see fit. Or unfit. You can turn it over to the authorities, or sell it to Tia Papadapolis, who as you know is hot on collecting porno. You can give the money to Colette. I think I vote for that option. Tia is more honest in her search for trash than most people who are supposedly looking for justice.

Thank you for all your help since Victor's death. I hope you won't have to put this into effect.

Love and truth,
Miranda

LA CÔTE BASQUE

◇

Phil Slagle was still more or less a tyro in the legal business, without glossy clients if you didn't count Miranda. And now she was dead. He had received her letter a week before her death, so it struck him as even more strange, the "double suicide." People who were about to take their own lives, or agree to having them taken, didn't usually write their lawyers a note with the perfume of fear on it.

When he heard of the death, he'd gone straight to her apartment to get the key to her safe deposit box. His signature was already on the signature card, where she'd long ago asked him to sign it, thinking ahead as she always thought ahead. It surprised him how much logic there was in her, how much caution. Looking as she did, it would have been easy to label her ditsy. Women like that, with pale, wide-set, faraway eyes, smacking of seas they'd dreamed of, or dreamed on, didn't usually have so much behind those eyes. But she had been full of surprises, graceful, ease in her long-legged stride, wit in her smile, her reactions, her thinking processes. Not exactly his idea of a kept woman.

Looking in her closet for the key in the black suede boots, he'd felt a wave of sorrow wash over him with the perfume that clung to her clothes. Hard to believe that her essence was gone while her fragrance remained. Once armed with the key, he felt unaccustomedly furtive going to the bank, signing, gaining access to the box without the tax man who was supposed to be present at the opening of a safe deposit box with the owner deceased. But there had been no time for orthodox procedures. He had to get into the box before they knew the owner was dead, before anyone connected Honey Morton with the late Miranda Jay. Her instructions to him in the letter did not survive her death, according to the law. Whatever was in the box might have played a part in what happened to her. Otherwise why would she have had that premonition? Notified him of it?

Going around the law was not Phil's usual behavior, any more than were glittering lunches in places he couldn't afford. But personal loyalty was at issue, not jewels, checks, bonds, whatever the tax man would have been after. Personal loyalty to Miranda. Honey Morton. Whatever her name was. To preserve what dignity was left her in the aftermath of the Lenrahan scandal, and then her too-tidy death and the new and juicier scandal it was giving rise to. No one at the bank had seemed to note anything unusual in his behavior when he signed, got the box, and went into the little room to open it.

When Lou Salerno questioned the clerks, the woman who checked the signature, she hardly remembered that Phil had been there at all, except for the date and evidence of his signing. Nothing nervous about him to make him memorable. Nor could she recollect whether he'd come out of there with anything. It was the job of the people at the bank not to note such things. That was the reason for the privacy of the rooms. Even if she had noticed anything, which she didn't, the woman told Lou, she shouldn't have.

Lou was feeling a little frustrated because it was past lunchtime, and so far he hadn't been able to turn up anything the NYPD didn't already know. It seemed to him they knew very little. Among the reports of Masters' and Miranda's belongings was a memo on the contents of Miranda's purse, its zippered lining containing a receipt for the safety deposit box with a note on the back: "See Stephanie re death." By the time detectives filed another memo to get a search warrant to investigate further, and went before the judge, the banks were closed. So it was the Tuesday following the deaths before they made it to the bank with the warrant. And when an officer of the bank forced the box, with two witnesses present as required by law, the box was empty.

As was Lou's belly. He tried to make it a point never to allow himself to feel frustration when he hadn't eaten, because he knew he would eat too much when he finally got to his meal. It was like a piece he'd read once, in the waiting room of a dentist who'd killed a couple of patients, that claimed women shouldn't go shopping when they were hungry because they'd buy more. A cop shouldn't come to conclusions when he was angry, which to Lou was the same as hungry. So he tried not to let his irritation show as he questioned Phil Slagle, taking in the young lawyer's office, wondering why Miranda, with all her connections, would have hired a kid.

The lawyer couldn't have been older than thirty, chestnut hair cropped like a Republican. "Sorry I kept you waiting," Phil Slagle said. "But I wasn't expecting you."

"Yeah, well, I wasn't expecting you either." Lou sat down in the oxblood leather wing chair opposite the desk. "I figured Miranda would have an older lawyer."

"More of a heavyweight?"

"Now that you mention it."

"I was only her lawyer at the end. I didn't handle any of the California litigation, the fight over the Lenrahan estate."

"That's a shame. I hear that was pretty juicy, as are

most California lawsuits. California's a great place if you're a lawsuit. They grow like oranges.'' Lou leaned forward and checked the wood of the desk. "What's this, oak?''

"Walnut.''

"Oh. From little walnuts great desks grow. Very nice. Very nice. What was in the box?''

"What box?''

"Miranda's box at the bank.''

"It was empty.''

"Your signature was on the card, dated Monday after she died.''

"There was nothing in it.''

"You know the penalty for concealing evidence?'' Lou got up and peered at the framed diplomas on the wall. "Well, of course you do. Dartmouth. Columbia. Very nice. Very nice.''

A cleaning woman stuck her head in the door. "Later, Nellie,'' Phillip said.

"A cleaning lady. I figured your mother would still be picking up after you.''

"She'd be glad to if I let her.''

"You ever hear of a woman named Connie Garrett?''

"No. Who is she?''

"Was. She made some calls from L.A. to Fred Masters. Did Miranda ever mention her?''

"Not that I remember. But we didn't spend much time together. I don't really know who her friends were.''

"How about Stephanie?''

"I don't recall her ever mentioning a Stephanie.''

"Did she leave you any instructions in the event of her death?''

"If she did, I wouldn't have to tell you.''

"This isn't a courtroom, buddy boy. I'm trying to help your mother not have a son who's a lawyer in trouble. You took things out of that box . . .''

"I did not. It was empty when I got there.''

"And she never mentioned a Stephanie?''

"Not that I recall.''

"You didn't socialize?"

"No."

"You were never together socially?"

"Only once. She took me to lunch."

"Where?"

"La Côte Basque."

"Did she send the Rolls for you?"

"No."

"She had a Rolls, though."

"Masters let her use his."

"It wasn't in the box?"

"It wasn't in the box."

"How about jewelry? A hot number like she was, she must have had what they like to call 'important pieces.' Were they in the box?"

"I told you. It was empty."

"Hell, she's dead. Another blonde bimbo with nobody left behind. No family. No heirs, as far as anybody knows. What would be the harm in selling a few pieces of her jewelry?"

Phil got up. "She wasn't a bimbo. And there wasn't any jewelry."

"Was there anything else?"

"It was empty."

"Okay." Salerno scratched the number of the Chelsea on one of his L.A. Homicide Department cards. "Call me if you remember something. And try to remember fast. I'm on a per diem, and the department don't like to let too many diems go by."

For Bunyan Reis, death was the great erotic experience. Artist that he was, raconteur, painter, sculptor, pet of the last remaining doyennes of Café Society, he considered there was no aphrodisiac like murder. Murder made fascinating the lowest of men, recast him, in that glittering second of his passing, as a star. Touched everyone around him, transforming friends and acquaintances into people with a story. Murder was man's darkest Art, and Bunyan loved to dwell on it.

He was sure Miranda Jay had been murdered. No matter how many headlines called it murder-suicide, no matter how many of Fred Masters' own newspapers called it a double suicide, a "pact," a "morbid tryst," Bunyan was positive it was murder.

His spy in the medical examiner's office had xeroxed the forensic report and sent it to Bunyan. From the analysis of the contents of Fred Masters' stomach, he had lived about an hour longer than Miranda. So it might have been murder-suicide. The fatal bullet that had stilled her thinking came from the gun in his hand. Perhaps underneath all Fred's hard-edged bluster there had been some sensibility. Even the shallowest of men at the moment of his death might go deeper, wondering if there was something beyond, trying to let go of the fear. Perhaps Fred, in the crisis of surrendering his life, in his passage through the moment that all men had to face, had experienced some ennobling curiosity. Some instinct to study the death on Miranda's face, to stare on her beautiful shell, empty now, its energy returned to the universe. Perhaps he had tried to stand on spiritual tiptoe, and peer over the transom into eternity, and see what, if anything, lay beyond. Perhaps his death had given him what his life never had, true dimension.

But Bunyan doubted it.

There was nothing complex about Fred Masters, Bunyan had known that from the moment he met the man, nothing webbed or involved except the way he did business, his hearty propensity for takeovers. Such a man studied profit, not death. So Bunyan couldn't buy the scenario.

There was urine on Fred's pants, bloody stool in his shorts, according to the report Bunyan's friend had stolen for him. Battleground reflexes. It seemed to Bunyan very likely that there had been a gun at Fred's head, scaring the shit out of him, literally. As if the soft body of Miranda lying next to him hadn't been enough. A double murder, surely.

But what could the murderers have wanted? Bunyan assumed there was more than one of them. Masters had not been a coward. He would have put up some kind of resistance if there was only one. And there hadn't been the least sign of a struggle, not a bruise, not so much as a ruffled sheet, an out-of-place blood drop on the hand-painted silk coverlet.

Thorough police investigation had yielded no extraneous fingerprints, nothing to dispel the hard evidence of suicide. No flaw in the setup. Locked doors, locked windows. But Bunyan had read and studied enough murder mysteries and actual cases to know there was always a way for the assassin to get out. Had they checked Gordon Grayson's building for dumbwaiters? Ventilator shafts? More than by the unavailability of clues, Bunyan was distressed that it had happened in the apartment of Gordon Grayson. All the clever writers in the world, and Fate had given that story to a suckfish.

Bunyan Reis' life was the kind of life that out-of-towners visualized when they thought about New York. Parties in private rooms at the 21 Club, with votive candles flickering in multi-colored glasses, fresh flowers on confettied tablecloths, expensive favors for all those who attended. Like other accomplished and admired men, he suffered his own agonies. But he didn't sport them. Didn't scream about the loneliness. He tried to dwell, as his devotees would have him, in his public persona, believing his fable as chronicled in newspapers and magazines. His comings and goings were noted by the press, not only in its tongue-wagging components, but in the staid, composed social annals of the *New York Times*. He had made the leap into myth, a man whose life was as fascinating as his work, giving lectures at the Thalia on the movie he'd made with Luis Bunuel, offering Christmas luncheons for orphaned children, one of whom he'd once been. Vain though he was, he was that rare egoist who thought there were more important things to talk about than himself. But one of them was certainly not Gordon Grayson.

Gordon Grayson, who *said* his father had been Robert Benchley's closest friend. Bunyan supposed that a part of his enmity was in not knowing who his own father had been, deepening not only his jealousy of others' forebears but of others' forebears' friends. Still, they were excessive, all those claims of Gordon's sire sitting side by side with the luminaries of the famed Algonquin Round Table, trading quips with Alexander Woollcott and Dorothy Parker. Few were the great things in life Bunyan had missed, but the Round Table was one of them, the scene in time before his time that he most longed to have been a part of. It was a first-rate part of American witty literary history, and it greened Bunyan's gills to have it fall on such a second-rater as Gordon. Because Bunyan had come from nowhere, his boundaries limited only by his own talent and productivity, he deeply distrusted one who traded on the past. And someone else's past at that. With no one alive who could dispute him. No child of Dorothy Parker to whisper that Gordon had never been her playmate. No ghost of Benchley rattling through Elaine's howling, "His father was ne-ver there." It seemed a fiendish way of aggrandizing oneself, friendships with the great dead.

Bunyan had been to the library to check out old reviews, hating himself even as he went to look them up, wishing that love could produce the same enterprise as envy. In fact, he was sorry to discover, Gordon's father had written two novels that garnered praise, some lines of it from Benchley. And, further, Bunyan's own circle of intimates was ringed with some of the best names in international society, most of whose fortunes were inherited. But that was suckfishing of the genealogical sort, to which Bunyan had no objection. What did the rich have to parade, after all, but riches and family names? Touching the born rich were, in their own way, wishing that they'd been born clever. What made Bunyan furious was a man who could consider himself gifted by succession. Talent by association. As if a father's contacts with genius could accrue creative powers to the son.

Now, like salt in the wound, the best death in a decade had taken place at Grayson's apartment. Like Kennedy's murder on L.B.J.'s turf, the death of the most graceful, benefiting the most graceless. Not that Bunyan compared either of the victims to the artful charmer who perished in Dallas. Not that Bunyan thought for a minute in terms of that murder when he thought about Fred and Miranda. Except in the possible combinations that might have been behind it.

Oh, life had been so much more interesting when the Beautiful People were really the beautiful people, young and with a lot of hair done by Mr. Kenneth. Even the vapid ones had been stylish. What were there now but debutante daughters who didn't even have the panache of clumsy mothers. Where had she gone, Baby Jane Holzer? Was she Middle-Aged Holzer now?

Time, that great leveler of men's fortunes. Bunyan made a brief tour of his den, looking at photos of faces that had graced his parties, Louise Felder when she was just starting out on her way to super-agent, Gloria Stanley, three husbands ago, Marilyn Monroe at the height of her beauty and sadness. There was a framed note from Carl Sandburg next to the picture, that Marilyn had left him. Next to that a memo from Albert Einstein on the importance of day-dreams, bought from the Scriptorium in Beverly Hills. Several baby pictures of Bunyan, his face unchanged, the same as it was now, except for the lines of course. Letters from presidents thanking Bunyan for his contributions to the arts. Invitations from Brooke Astor. A printed invitation to Princess Caroline's first wedding. A telegram, because of haste, asking him to the second. All in all, the wall of a man who knew everyone, had been everywhere he wanted. With the possible exception of this year's Rossini festival in Pesaro.

A pile of invitations he hadn't even bothered to answer lay by the stereo. On the rolltop desk were his unopened, unpaid bills. Because he had been so poor for the early part of his life, Bunyan had a phobia about bills. He experienced actual dread at the coming of the mail lest it have envelopes with windows in them, a pull to his stomach when he saw one that did. So the first luxury he'd gotten himself with success was a business manager. From the time he was in his late twenties, he'd never opened a single bill, forwarding them in a fat envelope to Jeffrey, listing all his monthly charges care of Jeffrey's office so he wouldn't have to look at them, think about them.

Jeffrey, who charged five percent for his services, had prospered, escalating from accountant to, as he called himself, "financial entrepreneur." His latest entrepreneurial move had been putting Bunyan and some other clients into a takeover attempt at MicroTel Computer, headed by Fred Masters. Since Masters' death, no one was quite sure what was happening, what would be the outcome. Jeffrey was not available to answer questions, having entered Mount Sinai for a triple bypass. Bunyan wondered whether he was faking.

After all, the puzzle of Masters was more than simply the puzzle of Masters' death. Everyone had wondered in the beginning what he was even doing with Miranda, unlikely Lothario that he was. The wonder was what she saw in Fred. Maybe she'd really loved Lenrahan deeply. Maybe it hadn't been your typical old rich man, young hungry girl. And perhaps, since Masters loved him too, they had shared that bond, he and Miranda. So she'd turned to him like Elizabeth Taylor to Eddie Fisher, after the death of Mike Todd. Maybe Masters could even sing. Who knew what turned people on?

But these were sociological and psychosexual questions, and, as everyone knew, the critical issue was money. Bunyan didn't understand what Masters had been doing with computer chips anyway. They were no more likely a target for him than Miranda had been. And why Jeffrey would have gone along with the move was beyond Bunyan, partnering up with his biggest accounts. (How much had he put in? Bunyan didn't even look at his monthly computer printouts of what he had spent, what invested, what he had left, what it cost him to live. It had to be astronomical, for God's sake, an East River view, all the best restaurants, a business manager living off the fat of the land enough to clog up his arteries.) Computer chips. The only thing that terrified Bunyan more than bills and statements were computers, the dehumanizing of a civilization where human issues were hardly a concern to begin with. Nobody cared about anybody else. Misanthrope though he liked to consider himself, Bunyan thought the hate floating around was excessive. Pascal had said that all men naturally hated each other, but he had been in Port Royal, France. Even he might have been brought up short in New York.

Hatred and fear were allied, Bunyan knew. So the poor hated the rich and the rich hated the poor, which was easier than giving them money, and the rich hated each other because who knew who might be richer, especially with Jeffrey in the hospital.

Anxious as he felt, there was no answer for it but to dress for lunch. Dressing always soothed him. Looking in his closets he could believe what people believed about him. The closet that annexed his pale yellow bedroom was filled, end to end, with pearl gray clothes, pearl gray pinstripe suits, pearl gray ties, pearl gray tuxedos, one morning suit and a set of tails in a slightly lighter shade of gray, satin lapels flashing an echo of life in the elegant fast lane. Grays had seemed to make his wanness less jarring, de-emphasized his almost albino cast. For the rest of it, his brain, his wit, there was more than enough color. He knew he cut a fine enough figure, especially for an artist. For just as once, during the era of Radical Chic, Black was Beautiful, now Fame was Beautiful. People marked his entrance into a party, restaurant, or opening night with the respect the newly arrived Saudi sheikh was trying to buy for his round little would-be movie star. No matter how much money you had for construction, Fame was still the platform. Making short men tall, pale men colorful, but not chubettes into national heroines. And for that, Bunyan gave thanks that it was still America.

The telephone rang. There was a rule among his friends that no one was to call before eleven-thirty, presuming that Bunyan had been partying or gossiping until all hours the night before. An interloper, obviously, someone who had paid to get his unlisted phone, or the nurse at the hospital that Bunyan had bribed to tell him Jeffrey's real condition.

He picked up the phone. It seemed to Bunyan sometimes he had the actual stuff of conjurers: none other than the Saudi sheikh was on the line, as if Bunyan's thinking of him had made him call. Bunyan tried to listen to the voice with the simple excitement a shop girl might, hearing the timbre resonating through it: money money money.

"My dear Bunyan," Sheikh Takesh Al-Miassi said, Oxford diction clipping his words like coupons. "Chanson and I were hoping you could have lunch with us today at Caravelle."

"I'm sorry," Bunyan said. "But I already have an appointment for lunch."

"Well, then, can you have dinner on Friday?"

"Sorry. I'm going to the Hamptons for the weekend."

"So late in the season?"

"Better late than during."

Bunyan could hear the sheikh breathing on the other end of the phone, feel the coils of his sludge-deposited mind interconnecting, hearing the jest, trying to absorb it to see if he should laugh, all the while cowering under the blow that was Bunyan's rejection. Something like pity touched Bunyan. As in the morality tales, money wasn't everything. Here was a man richer than the rich, and just as it couldn't buy them happiness, it couldn't buy him lunch with Bunyan. Or stardom for his dumpling. What it could buy them was an apartment in Trump Tower, with Greco-Roman statues in every room, genitals painted with the brightest pink, pubic hair curling in brown brush-strokes. Remembering that, mercy ebbed, and Bunyan returned to feeling scornful.

"Forgive me for running. But I must dress for lunch."

"Of course."

"But do call again."

"When?"

"Never before eleven-thirty," Bunyan said, and hung up the phone.

It made him sad that he was less than kind. "In the end," Aldous Huxley had said, "what matters is just to be kind." But that was after the bite had gone out of the man's writing, when mysticism had gentled the sneering of the youthful cynic, who had been so clearly a genius. The loving writer had fared not nearly so well. In the same way, Bunyan knew it was his bitchy wit, his disdain, that drew people to him. Had from the beginning, when it sprung from anxiety that he wouldn't be accepted. He'd hungered for acknowledgement as one yearned for an approving parent. When, while still in his twenties, the critic he'd admired most proclaimed him "the finest artist of his day," it was too rich a meal for a starving man. Tolstoy's widow had eaten two pounds of black bread on an achingly empty stomach and died in an agony of indigestion. The most Bunyan hoped for from the critic Jackson Schliessel was recognition as a talent to be reckoned with in future. To be trumpeted as the best was overwhelming and, in Bunyan's opinion, premature. When, a short time afterward, he discovered Schliessel had secretly purchased a number of his works at a very low figure and, by his approval, had driven up the price, it gave Bunyan gastroenteritis of the soul.

Never again did he face life as an innocent. Innocence was what gave art its true impetus, gave the artist courage to get up in the morning, to start the whole unsure process over again. As the Bible proclaimed a little child would lead them, so it was the little child in every artist that gave him the freshness of spirit to go on. The simplicity to hope. Since that time, Bunyan had faced his art with less than faith, preferring gossiping on the phone. Gossip was a way of establishing intimacy without risk, the only social disease that didn't give you sores.

Over the years, Bunyan had come to prefer gossip to sex, and both of them to working. It made him uneasy to think that art was a sex substitute, but he knew it was the truth. All those libidinous energies unfulfilled gave a man more chops for his canvas, Renoir's prodigious output and gallery of mistresses notwithstanding. It was kind of a distortion of the Protestant ethic: a day's work well done. At artist felt guilty if he hadn't painted, just as a full-bodied housewife felt guilty if she hadn't fucked, not necessarily her husband. Combining all those insights,

Bunyan had come to realize that he felt the day had not been wasted if he had either painted, consorted, or, since the coming of AIDS, jerked himself off.

He just hated that, especially since he wasn't attracted to himself. But taking his member into his hands was better than taking his life into his hands. It seemed so grossly unfair, cruel and unusual punishment for such an unhurtful deviation. Bunyan had never been particularly promiscuous, and now he didn't dare be. So rather than take a chance (he put on his ball gag sometimes so he wouldn't cry out, in private agony) he took a vow of chastity. Except for the hours and hours of foreplay and occasional consummation (Eeeeeeeeeeee-yeagh!) of Murder. But why did it have to happen in the apartment of Gordon Grayson?

Now Gordon Grayson was daring to eat at La Côte Basque on a regular basis. La Côte Basque was Bunyan's turf, just as gray paintings were his domain, texture for the sake of texture and design, understood as no one but himself understood it. Wasn't it enough that Elaine's was Gordon's in the evening? Did he have to sully the daytime elegance of La Côte Basque, eating sole meunière with his veal chop mentality?

Bunyan tied his tie and set a gray pearl stickpin in the center of it. Oh, what a well-dressed misanthrope he was. But not really. When he'd loved John Lennon, that gifted boy had sent him on a spiritual retreat where he'd almost learned to let go. To let go of attachment, anger, fear, greed, all the things you needed to get ahead in the world. The retreat was the most difficult experience of his life, especially since he thought he'd hate absolutely every moment and be able to make fun of everybody there. But as it turned out, he had hated absolutely every moment but one, and that was the moment he'd felt, for the first time in his life, absolute peace. A sense of total harmony with the universe. The truth of it had boomed through his entire being. And then he'd come back to New York and that lunatic had murdered John, so Bunyan considered it was, all of it, a cheat. Understanding, knowing, even writing the music, you still were flies to the gods.

The phone had set up a regular jingling beside him, which Bunyan left to the service. Locking the door to his apartment, Bunyan stepped into the hallway. The walls were mirrored deco glass, smoky and etched with angles. The elevator was softened with silver moiré walls, as though waiting a push of the button from Jean Harlow. Mozart was playing in his elevator, soothing, a welcome replacement for Muzak, something the tenants had gotten together on when it was rumored Beverly Sills might be buying there. All in all, the building was the ideal setting for Bunyan, down to its marbled lobby and uniformed doorman, who tipped his hat and went to art exhibitions in his off hours. The singular struggle that existed in New York: everyone on their way to something better, with the possible exception of Stephen Sondheim.

"A man left you this, Mr. Reis," the doorman said, handing him a manila envelope.

"Thank you, Jack."

"And there were two men here asking for you. They wouldn't give me their names. Said they didn't want to bother you. Just interested if you were in town."

"Two men?"

"They didn't look like punks. Overcoats and hats. But they didn't seem like the kind of people you'd be friends with, either. So I told them I didn't know if you were here, that they could contact you through your business manager."

"Very good, Jack. Did you tell them who he was?"

"I have his name on the notification list, you know, in case there's ever any important mail and you're away. So I gave it to them."

"Thank you, Jack." Two men. It made Bunyan uneasy when strangers asked about him, as it had once made him uneasy that they never would. He wasn't a gambler, if you didn't count his "risk-free" investment with Fred Masters. So it couldn't be hit men there to settle the score because he hadn't paid up. Then who were they? Maybe reporters from the *National Enquirer* trying to put the doorman off guard by looking merely sinister. Well, if they meant trouble, Jeffrey would field it. If he lived.

Bunyan felt his pocket, made sure the passport he always carried with him everywhere, even to lunch, was safe against his breast. Flight, he knew, was the salve of the unloved. So always in his breast was the chance of instant departure, in case it got just too depressing, somewhere he could flee to, send witty postcards from. Feeling lean and golden, he could write in a florid hand, from an island in the Aegean, thanking God they were far enough away not to see his paunch or a skin that pinked, never tanned.

"Could you get me a taxi please, Jack?"

"There's a car waiting, Mr. Reis."

"A car?" It was a little jest of Bunyan's, whenever he walked outside La Côte or Perigord and a limousine waited at the curbside, to say to whoever was with him, "Oh, you sent for the car." It was a sally that had started in his youth, when no one he knew could afford a car, and certainly not a limo. Now that everyone in his circle could, and many did, the joke had a certain poignant resonance, as with the Christmases when one present was all there was. Still, he couldn't imagine why anyone would send a car for him, unless it was Tia Papadapolis and the anxiety that even billionaire Greeks had that their lunch dates might not show up.

A driver in a dark uniform, cap set neatly on his deeply grooved forehead, stood leaning against the sleek, frosted brown of the right front bumper, arms folded, thick upper arms bulging, jaw set like the bodyguard he doubtless also was. "Mr. Reis?" He came to attention.

"Yes?"

"The Honorable Sheikh Takesh Al-Miassi thought you might need transportation to your lunch."

"Why, how thoughtful. Or do I mean cunning?"

Expressionless behind opaque black sunglasses, the chauffeur opened the rear door for Bunyan. A blast of perfume struck him in the nose. Already bent to enter, it was too late to back away. There she sat, right in front of his suddenly alerted nostrils, that little round objet de Non-Art, Chanson D'Amour.

Chanson D'Amour. Bunyan believed that was her real
name no more than he believed those were her real tits,
eyelashes, or teeth. He had heard a story once of an
Iranian general who had dared to make a whispered proposition to a mistress of the shah and had never been seen
again. In the same way he imagined the graves of the
Sahara were fretted with the bones of dentists who had
capped Chanson's teeth, plastic surgeons who'd implanted
her breasts, set her eyes wider, broken her cheekbones and
reset her jaw, given her Michael Jackson's nose (or was it
Diana Ross'?) and had not been left alive to tell the Tail.
That, he imagined, was the only real part of her, besides
her round, rather pygmyish legs: her most overstated
rump. *Steatopygia*. A word Bunyan had learned playing
Dictionary, one of his favorite games of the parlor game
era. "Steatopygia," Mel Brooks had written as his definition, "archaic, a threat. 'Stay out of Pygia!'" The true
definition, which nobody had voted for, was "abnormal
growth of fat on the buttocks of African women, especially
Hottentots." Everybody assumed Mel had made that up.
But it was the real one. More real by half on Chanson
D'Amour.

"Bonjour," she said, extending it all to him, the hand,
the bonded smile, the couturier clothes that little elves
must have worked night and day to assemble in munchkin
sizes.

Bunyan had heard all the rumors. Few were the scandal
soups with any stock to them he hadn't tasted, and many
that he helped make up. One that he favored in particular
was that the sheikh had found her dancing in a whorehouse
in Morocco when she was ten. The other preferred by his
group was that she'd been half of the Playhouse Pet of the
Month.

"Bonjour," he said, and bent to not quite kiss her white
gloved hand. "Grace Kelly in *To Catch a Thief*, right?"

"Pardon?" she asked, à la Française.

"Your model for elegance." Why hadn't he run? How
could he not have known instantly that she was in the back
seat of the car when her perfume—the new, overpriced,

overheavy scent Giorgio—should have announced her as a tuba would a parade.

"Is she the one who died?"

"One of the ones," Bunyan sighed, and tried not to grieve that the cliffs of the world seemed always to be waiting for the luminous ones, while those left alive were the Raisinets. Even as she sat there beside him, she did the passive exercises she had demonstrated on "Lifestyles of the Rich and Famous," pumping her plump little thighs together, squeezing fingertips against upper arms, priming her implants for their foray into lunchtime in New York.

"Was she a friend of yours?"

"A true friend," he said, and mourned for some seconds.

"But of course. All the famed are your intimates. Tak Tak was sad you could not lunch with us. You are naughty to be so busy all the time." Her little black eyes were darting fiercely, obviously studying him for secrets, trying to absorb what it was that made him so sought after, even by herself.

Bunyan felt a spurt of compassion for her in between the contempt. He looked at the dark, shiny skin, and wondered if it was thicker for being new rich. Did they not know when they were being avoided? If you pricked them, did they bleed oil?

"So he wanted me to make it convenient for you to go to lunch, even if it couldn't be with us. That is why he sent the car."

"How considerate," Bunyan said as the limousine pulled away from curbside. How could they be so dense, these Saudis, not even knowing how to get close to the people they courted? Imagine the sheikh sending her when he probably had any number of darling little boys he'd bought at auction.

He pressed a button to open the electric window, breathed the thick, wetly cold air. A light veil of fog from the river cleansed the interior of the car of the heavy fragrance. Bunyan could see his obituary flash before his eyes: Dead, rather past his prime, asphyxiated by Giorgio. Hardly fair, after he'd given up amyl nitrate because of what happened to Tennessee.

There had been a spate of publicity relating to Sheikh Takesh Al-Miassi, called Tak Tak by his wife, and Tackey by Louise Felder, the Hollywood agent. He had thus far bought a television station, a recording company, a glossy magazine, and a large share of stock in Marathon Studios, all as part of his campaign to make Chanson a star. She was, from all indications, sublimely untalented. But the couple did have an undeniable brilliance in compiling dossiers. The sheikh's staff had ferreted out information about all important names, people who mattered, how they stood in the community, where they could be found. Bunyan knew he was prominent on the list, and so very hotly pursued. As though social acceptance could make this Ummpa-Lummpa gifted.

"Where do we take you?" she asked him.

"La Côte Basque."

"What a coincidence! Tak Tak and I lunch there, too."

"I thought you were going to Caravelle."

"We go there for dessert."

All bases covered. Bunyan could imagine a little army of burnoosed secretaries making reservations at all the key restaurants while the Moslem CIA uncovered who was going where.

"This most great artist will be going to La Côte Basque, Antonio," she said.

"You flatter me," said Bunyan.

"Yes, I do."

Was she honest, or just stupid? "How direct," he said. "How refreshing." Was she like that about herself, or just other people? he wondered. "Listen, let me ask you something. Is it true the sheikh found you dancing in a brothel?"

"Certainly not," she said. "I was singing. Dancing didn't come till later."

In the manila envelope on Bunyan's lap was a scribbled note from his friend in the medical examiner's office with the caveat that everything enclosed was extremely confidential. Bunyan excused himself to Chanson while he went over the police reports. He read a description of the clothes Fred and Miranda had been wearing when they died, including the shoes that had not been on their feet—one pair of red leather ladies' high heels, size seven, insole marked Charles Jourdan, one pair of men's brown leather loafers, size eleven, marked Bally, black socks rolled up inside—plus the cash in Fred's pockets, $623.77, and a description of some artifacts. In the language of the death reports, these became, "Yellow metal chain, containing nine parts, one yellow metal initial *F*, one white metal chain with clear yellow stone measuring approximately a half inch in diameter." How sad. Not only could you not take it with you, but all a diamond was was a clear stone.

Most resonant of all was a "yellow metal hair clip with six light green stones, with dried brownish red substance." That was what Death made of the sap of life. A dried brownish red substance. How much colder than cold blood was the language of homicide.

Another report included the contents of Miranda's purse. Bunyan made note of the receipt for payment on the safety deposit box, the scribbled reminder "Call Stephanie re death." There was a detective's memo attached to seek out a search warrant for the box, for purpose of further investigation. How very Freudian and appropriate, Bunyan thought, Miranda's box. What secrets wouldn't fly out of there.

"What do you study so hard?" Chanson asked him.

"Mystery," he said, and smiled at her.

"I understand you are trying to find out what happened with Fred Masters and Miranda."

Did they have spies even at the police station? "What makes you think that?"

"I can't tell you everything," she said. "But Tak Tak does have hold of some very interesting information. Perhaps he might be willing to share it with you. Over lunch."

They were shrewd, these little towelheads. "Well. Maybe next week."

"Good," she said as the car came to a halt. "We are arrived."

"One of us, anyway," said Bunyan. Thanking her, he dashed into the restaurant.

Like a Norman cottage, its dark wood beams angling out to a trident above the coiffed heads of its patrons, La Côte Basque radiated a sense of peace. To the rear were the La Motte murals of the harbor of Saint Jean de Luz, fishing boats in the water, creating an illusion of stillness. Gordon Grayson sat taking copious notes on the unexpected beauty of the place, fleshing out Miranda's assumed fondness for it.

But, now that he had his assignment, and it was deductible, he allowed himself to taste the food as Miranda would have done. He had queried the maitre d' about what had been her favorite dishes. He sat at her preferred table while the chef carved some cold salmon for him from a serving cart.

"I know she was a great admirer of your art," Gordon said. "Is it true she once took a quart of your hollandaise home?"

"I gave her some of our sauces," the chef said. "I couldn't give her the recipes, of course."

"Of course." So the hollandaise she spooned onto Fred had come from here, a fact that would make the erotic detail more journalistic, and so acceptable. It was Gordon's intention to make the book as hot as Miranda, but with the unexpected elegance typical of her, and, now that he knew it firsthand, her favorite restaurant.

Erotic detail reminded Gordon of his own humanity, made him feel alive. His father's celebrity, or semicelebrity, his connections to the Algonquin Round Table, had deepened Gordon's early sense of isolation. When Gordon was nine, his parents had reinforced his feeling he was in the way by getting him out of it, sending him to boarding school, where he spent most of his free time at the stables.

The one blessing the school afforded him was the reassuring warmth of the animals. He volunteered for chores in exchange for riding lessons, and at night, when he couldn't sleep, snuck down to the stables. So he began observing not only the horses' grace, but also their intercourse, finding it excruciatingly exciting.

He was a private person, had grown into an attractive man, almost six feet tall, slender and well built, his own credentials starting to accrue with a series of articles and two well-received nonfiction books. And if in the quiet of his apartment he watched cassettes of porno movies, or privately acquired material, that was nobody's business.

Now he allowed the feeling of luxury the restaurant afforded to seep into his bones. He studied how gracefully the food was arranged on the oversized plate, Basket pattern from Villeroy and Bosch, deceptively country and simple if you didn't know the price of a plate setting. He closed his eyes and tried to project himself backward into Miranda's honeyed golden skin, experience all those stately lunches. He would convey not only her death, but a sense of her life, how it felt while the blood was coursing through her. Not to mention the special tricks she had with rope and tongue.

High-pitched, raucous laughter shook him from his reverie. At the table where Bunyan Reis sat, Tia Papadapolis waved her long, fuchsia-fingernailed hands, as though conducting a concerto, accompanying herself on Mirth, like Leonard Bernstein on piano. Gordon was impressed with Tia, less by her wealth than her friendship with Bunyan Reis. He knew Bunyan loathed him, but he couldn't get himself angry enough to hate Bunyan back, he admired him so much. What Gordon wanted more than the best table at Elaine's, or being the center of literary parties, or frequent mention by Liz Smith, or even the fat new contract his publisher had awarded him, was to be a true artist, a genuine contributor like Bunyan was. Even in the worst season of his life Bunyan came up with something, or people waited patiently because there was always the chance he was going to.

Well, maybe Gordon was going to, too. Maybe with this book, he could lift himself to true art. Maybe he could help people. Not naively, with one of those arms-around-each-other songs, but by showing how very human it was, and how gripping, to be caught by sexual desires.

Tia Papadapolis waved her hand, deeply tanned as usual, the rich chocolate of perpetual summer. A shade to inspire fortune hunters. Bunyan simply loved to look at her, the great hawkish nose plunging down to a wide, rather thick-lipped mouth, angular topaz eyes, wide cheekbones, high forehead, the pointed tip of chin, all of it adding up to a majestic face, diamond shaped, or, as the police might have had it, clear stoned. Her skin was as tight and smooth as it was dark. Unlike those from *W* and *Town and Country* who were forever writing about her, Tia never worried about the effects of the sun or the onslaught of wrinkles. Every spring she sailed through the Aegean with her entourage, that lately included a Beverly Hills plastic surgeon. A room on the yacht was outfitted for surgery, and as a bread and butter note to Tia, he would nip and tuck whatever sagged, or seemed about to. So she was flawless, probably the only woman of her generation and class with perfect skin and her own nose, her only imperfection her wardrobe. Bunyan could hardly believe she was in fuchsia, a color he thought had been done away with as part of the Potsdam agreement.

"But you have to do the movie," Tia was saying to him now, while Louise Felder nodded agreement from across the table. "Louise flew in especially to close the deal."

"It's true. I did."

"I heard you had a date."

"You think I'd fly somewhere for a date?"

"Only if he was alive," Bunyan said.

"What a cunty thing to say. Especially since it isn't true. I've been known to go many places with an escort who was already dead."

"Harry Bell?"

Louise sighed. "I really should have married him."

"He was too old for you," said Bunyan.

"Not anymore. Dead, he's just about the right age now."

Bunyan laughed. He reached over and touched her cheek, which to his delight was still childishly soft. Her hair looked shiny and blonde, nothing about her hardening as visibly as her attitude. He had known Louise at the start of her climb to Heavyweight Champion Agent. Now that she had everything she wanted, he grieved along with her that she was still dissatisfied.

To Bunyan's right sat Marty Fontaine, the director. Uncomfortable as West Coast people sometimes made him, Bunyan felt at ease in Marty's presence, since he seemed to have manners, and was, like Bunyan, one of Louise's favorite clients. "Will you be involved in this movie?"

"That's why I'm here," Marty said.

"I'm surprised you aren't afraid to come to New York. I heard Stan Dobson had a marshal all set to serve you with a subpoena."

"He's over it," Marty said. "My lawyer talked to him."

"I think the whole thing was in terrible taste," Bunyan said. "You should never have thrown champagne at him. Nothing better than Coca-Cola."

"He screwed me out of a very important project."

"Don't get defensive," Louise said, patting Marty's arm. "It wasn't important. It wasn't even a particularly good screwing. You want a screwing, I'll give you a screwing."

"Everything works out for the best," said Tia. "Now you're free to do our project. As Bunyan is."

"I don't know," Bunyan said.

"But you have to. It's appropriate," Tia insisted. "It will be Art. So we must have an Artist involved, and you are the greatest living Artist. I'm tired of being just a collector. I want to be active, involved. That's why I'm producing. We'll shoot it on the yacht this coming summer. And the islands. Mykonos, mainly."

"You packaging this porno?" Bunyan asked Louise.

"I'm representing Marty as director, Tia as producer, and you as art director and costume designer."

"I don't really know anything about costumes. Hard as that must be to believe sitting so close to Tia."

"I'm not planning on using any," Marty said. "The whole picture will be done in the nude, except for the dinner party scene."

"Then what do you need me for?"

"Taste," said Marty. "An overall Vision."

"Someone has to get the money," said Louise.

"I'm past that, don't you know."

"Really?" Tia's topaz eyes were skeptical. "I heard you were in on the takeover try with Fred Masters, and no one knows what's going to happen, and your business manager's in the hospital."

"Jeffrey?" Louise asked. "What's wrong with him?"

"His heart. Or so he says. Who's going to be in this filmic orgy?"

"I want names," Marty said. "But it might be a problem with the men. I don't know any male stars who are willing to show their dicks beside Richard Gere."

"What about Rick Flinders?" asked Louise.

"He has herpes. There'll be sores on his pee-pee," said Bunyan.

"I'm sorry to hear that," said Tia.

"As are half the women in the world." Bunyan worried his breadstick. "Who for the female lead?"

"It should be the world's most desirable woman," said Marty.

"How about Gloria Stanley?" Bunyan suggested.

"Get the napkin off your lap," said Louise.

"What do you mean?"

"You're playing with yourself. Gloria's too old."

Bunyan reached for his water, feeling suddenly, desperately dry. Life went by too fast. He had loved her from the time she was a baby star, watched her grow, as close as he had come to having a child, if you didn't count the little boy they tried to sell him in Marrakesh. Now even her own agent said she was past it. *Sic transit Gloria Stanley*. Thank God Tennessee hadn't lived to see this day.

"We need someone who's the essence of female sexuality," Marty said.

"Pity you can't get Miranda Jay," mused Bunyan. "It's going to get even hotter, don't you know. I mean BIG scandal. Victor Lenrahan was merely the tip of the phallus. There's a safe deposit box. With more mischief in it than Pandora's, I'd wager."

"Been thinking about that for a title, oddly enough," Marty said. *"Pandora's Box."*

"Too intellectual," Louise said.

"What's wrong with intellectual?" asked Bunyan.

"You'll drive away your audience."

"Everybody understands Pandora's Box."

"Even the people who know what it is don't know what it is," said Louise. "Even I with my Phi Beta Kappa key that Andre Sherman gave me which he bought in a pawnshop don't know."

Bunyan felt a sudden flood of love for her, for all of them, the people people thought they'd like to be. How filled they all were with a sense of loss, especially Louise. What a good target she made, riddled with deceits she so freely admitted. There she sat, Little Lulu all grown up, trusting in nothing, her whole existence an affirmation of her cynicism. She who had never believed life would work out to her satisfaction, right as usual.

"Prometheus stole fire from the gods," Tia started to explain, "and gave it to man. So Zeus swore revenge, and had a woman made from clay, as a plague to men who eat bread . . ."

"Pass the rolls," said Louise.

". . . as opposed to the gods, who eat ambrosia. The Four Winds breathed life into her, Athena clothed her, the Seasons crowned her, Hermes taught her guile . . ."

"Isn't he the one who choreographed all those old musicals at Metro?" asked Louise.

"All the gods contributed something to her, hence the name 'Pan-dora.' It means 'all gifted.'"

"So educated, don't you know. And all people think of in connection with Tia is billions of dollars and statues with erections."

"You can't judge a dirty book by its cover," said Louise.

"Her husband had a box he warned her never to open. But she couldn't overcome her curiosity. So she opened it. And out came Vice, Lust, Madness, Passion..."

"These are a few of my favorite things," sang Louise.

"All the evils of mankind," said Tia.

"Sounds like Miranda all right," noted Bunyan. Tia laughed.

But Louise buttered her roll and said thoughtfully, "Poor Miranda."

"What, my Lady Disdain?" Bunyan said. "Compassion?"

"We went to the same hairdresser in Beverly Hills. She seemed nice. Very self-effacing. A little too good a body— we all hated her for that, naturally. And beautiful skin. And her own color hair. Some things are unforgivable. But she had a quality—very appealing. A special smile. Rueful, I guess you could say it was."

"Maybe she was trying to play up to you because she wanted to be a Star," Bunyan suggested, capitalizing the category.

"I don't think so. She never auditioned, if you know what I mean. She was pleasant, but it wasn't that suffocating pleasantness where somebody's pushing, trying to impress you even under the dryer. And there was a time, back a few years, where she made a serious stab at doing commercials, or being Christie Brinkley, and she gave it up all of a sudden. So I don't think she had any illusions about being an actress. Or even a Star. No, this was genuine humility, I think. She was sort of apologetic, the way people are in L.A. when they aren't anybody."

The captain came to the table. "You have a call, Mr. Reis."

"Who knows I'm here?" asked Bunyan, putting his napkin on the table.

"Only half of New York," said Louise.

"I hope the right half." Bunyan got up, nearly colliding with Sheikh Al-Miassi, who stopped in his tracks and reached out as though to fold Bunyan in his tent. "Forgive me," Bunyan danced around him, "I have an important call."

He picked up the receiver on the stand by the checkroom. "Yes, hello?"

"Bunyan?" It was his attorney, Ron Abbate. "Bunyan, I'm sorry to trouble you with this at lunch, but I thought you'd want to know. Jeffrey died."

"Oh, God," Bunyan said. "Then he wasn't faking. How terrible. Let me call you later." He hung up the phone, trembling, awash with his own mortality, fearful of what this would mean.

Once, when he was young, he'd run into Marlon Brando walking down Sixth Avenue, weeping uncontrollably. He'd asked him what was wrong, and Marlon had sobbed, "My analyst died." At that self-centered point in his life Bunyan could not imagine anything more devastating. But now he could. All those years, not even looking at the bills, or even the computer printouts. Where had the money gone; where was it going? Somewhere on a hilltop in Switzerland with the fugitive financiers?

Fear chilled his heart into winter. If winter came, could the IRS be far behind?

"You look like you've seen a ghost," Tia said as he came back to the table.

"My business manager died."

"Well, I guess now you have to do the movie," Louise said. "Everything happens for a good reason."

"I wonder if Jeffrey sees it that way."

"I hate death," said Marty, grimly. "Can't we change the subject?"

"Why don't we order?" Tia signaled for the waiter.

"Wasn't there something left in the box?" asked Louise.

"Box?" Bunyan's mind was reeling. "Miranda's box?"

"Pandora's. In case I go back to Vassar for my PhD, I should know."

"Hope," said Tia. "Pandora slammed down the lid and all that was left was hope."

"Man's last comfort," said Marty.

"Except for food," said Louise. "I think I'll have the softshell crabs."

"Comfort?" Tia looked at Marty. "The Greeks have a different view of hope. They think it's stupid and silly, the same as delusion. It's because mankind still has hope that he doesn't deal with the evils that are in the world. He depends on hope instead of the things he should depend on."

"Maybe the veal," said Louise. "Veal is low calorie."

"Symbolically, it could be a warning to men who pry into women's mysteries," Marty suggested.

"Could be," said Tia. "But it all boils down to the same old thing: blame the women. Eve ended up with a world that was no longer Paradise and was left with Shame. The same with Pandora. Only she had hope in her box."

"More than I have in mine," said Louise. "Fuck it. I'll have the pasta."

Lou Salerno stood by the cloakroom of the restaurant, wondering whether he should check his coat or just throw it away. Every man's garment that hung neatly arranged on numbered hangers looked spun from the same magic loom that had turned out Fred Masters' wardrobe, probably all with labels that read "Made in England," which meant expensive.

"Does m'sieur have a reservation?" the maitre d' asked politely, his eyes not really seeming to graze over what Lou was wearing, but grazing nevertheless.

Lou took out his ID and flashed it. The maitre d' looked both anxious and relieved at seeing what it was. Probably glad he wasn't from the Board of Health, Lou thought. "I need some information about Miranda Jay," Lou said.

When the captain showed Lou to Gordon Grayson's table, Gordon was chewing on celery rémoulade, his eyes closed. "Mr. Grayson?" Salerno said.

Gordon opened his eyes. Lou held out his ID. "Detective Salerno. Mind if I ask you a few questions?" He pulled out a chair and sat down.

"Why don't you sit down?" Gordon said.

"Did Masters or Miranda have any enemies?"

"How would I know?"

"You were obviously close to them. They died in your apartment."

"Fred was my college roommate for one semester."

"You saying you didn't know them well?"

"Not as well as I will when I finish my book." Gordon signaled for the waiter. "May I offer you a drink?"

"I don't drink when I'm working."

"Then how about some lunch?"

The waiter, hearing Gordon's offer, held out the menu for Lou. "Merci," Lou said, and looked at the prices. "I'll have a bowl of money. Oil and vinegar on the side."

Gordon smiled. "You like fish?"

Lou nodded.

"Bring him the roughy," Gordon said to the waiter. "The orange roughy is exquisite today."

"Exquisite, huh? What kind of book you writing? A romance novel?"

"I'm writing the story of Fred and Miranda."

"No way is that going to be exquisite."

"You never can tell," said Gordon.

"You know anybody might have been after them?"

"Not really. I mean, if somebody was, I wouldn't know them."

"Well how about the obvious choices. What about Masters' wife?"

"Lily was out to dinner when they were killed."

"Were killed? You don't buy the double suicide?"

"That certainly *seems* to be what it was."

"But you don't think so either. Couldn't the wife have hired a hit man?"

"Not Lily," Gordon said, and sort of chuckled. "She has the right name."

"So who do you think might have done it?"

"I defer to the police. Conjecture isn't my bailiwick."

"Bailiwick?" Salerno said. "You going to use words like bailiwick? How you expect it to sell?"

"Oh, it'll sell," Gordon said. "Don't worry about that. It'll sell."

"Well, at least you're honest enough to admit that's why you're writing it."

"That isn't the only reason."

"What's the rest of it?"

"I feel like this story is a gift to me," Gordon said. "My chance of going beyond all this."

Lou looked around at the high ceilings, the pastelled murals, the mirrors reflecting a peaceful pond of self-satisfied, preening swans. He heard the murmur of the select crowd, lifting gossip into meditation, eating fragrant meals from oversized plates, the food in careful patterns, julienne carrots not touching tiny boiled potatoes, greens set like a brush stroke on a canvas. All of it arranged, now that Lou thought of it, exquisitely. "Yeah, well, I can understand your wanting to get away from all this."

"I'm not talking about escaping," Gordon said. "I mean transcending. Art is a lie that makes us see the truth, Picasso said. There's a truth here, a truth in this book that could change my life."

"What truth is that?"

"Ah, you'll have to wait till it's finished and read it," Gordon said, and smiled, a smile more open and friendly than he was, really. Even he knew it as he smiled. "But I promise you it's stranger than fiction."

THE SOUTH
OF FRANCE

◇

So on a flawless summer morning in the early 1970s, this girl who would later be the talk of New York and the focus of some whispered, urgent conversations in Washington, D.C., awoke in a cabin on a yacht anchored near Cannes. She meant to wake up feeling good about herself. Her life had seemed to change direction with a speed that was dizzying to her. All she had ever wanted, before she had given birth to her baby, was an absence of anger, people around her who did not seem annoyed or affronted by her existence. Now, suddenly, she was covered with affection, and, more surprising, luxury. Never having heard the expression "gold digger," never having read about the Arabian Nights, she would have been as surprised to hear herself described as the first as she was to find herself smack in the middle of the second. Still, there was some gnawing of grief at her psychic bones, some inner instinct that ate at her that all this would not last, that it was only a temporary palliative and the real dose was disaster.

The man who slept beside her was powerful, even in his way of sleeping, the firm, square line of his jaw hardened by a slightly pugnacious set. His teeth seemed a little on edge even as he slumbered. His face, in dreaming, looked trouble free and unworn, a deep tan accenting the white mustache above his wide, thin upper lip, and the thick white hair cascading from his high forehead to the black satin of the pillowcase. His hands were also deeply tanned; huge hands, their rosy nails buffed and shining as though a manicurist rode along on the yacht in his retinue. His fingers clutched the satin sheets, the only hint that he was not as peaceful as his face looked, and perhaps had nightmares and fears the same as the vulnerable did. Maybe he was dreaming he was falling. She reached out to touch him, gently, not to wake him, but to soothe, to reassure him, and herself, that he was safe in his own bed. And she was safe with him.

Safety had not played a large part in their courtship. After the initial grace and charm he offered her, he had introduced her to certain games. Taken her into a secret room he had on the yacht. Even now, thinking about it, she started to tremble, experiencing the same combination of fear and excitement he'd introduced her to. It was a

thunderbolt transition, from the waif she had been in the
Paris hospital, to the Silk Lady Harry Bell had made her
into, launching her into this curious, seemingly carefree
society where people tripped over themselves in their
apparent eagerness to make things easier for you. And then
had come this towering giant, a literal giant of a man,
bigger than anyone who had ever held her. And he had so
respected her pain, so tenderly ministered to her perceivable wound, pressing cool compresses over the part where
the doctor had made the incision for the episiotomy, gently
passing an ice cube over her because, he said, maybe that
would make it get better faster. The ice had made her
scream out in pain. He had been overwhelming in his wish
to console her. Easing her into the sitz baths the doctor had
prescribed, sponging her all over her body with an infini-
tude of patience, as if it were not a full-bodied woman
there but a child.

And only when he had dried her off, swaddling her with
terry towels, did he allow himself to touch her body with a
wanting touch, nibbling her nipples with his big, white
teeth, set gently on edge now, so as not to hurt her really,
pressing his swelling self close against her, but not insinu-
ating, because he knew she was still sensitive there.
Asking her, as humbly as though he were petitioning the
gods, to take him into her mouth, which she did with an
eagerness and gusto she had shown not even with Alex.
Because Alex was always hard when they made love, and
there had never been the challenge to it there was with this
man, who cried like a baby when he came, and thanked
her, never stopped marveling over how, with her, it was
hard. All she had to do was touch him, or let him touch
her, or if that didn't do it, take him into her mouth, and
rub it around its root with fingers he showed her just how
to place, and rhythms he taught her. Rhythm was something she had picked up from the drummer: she had no
trouble at all with that. And much as she missed that fine
Alsatian cock, there was something touching about this big
man's flaccid member, and how she could make it swell,
with enough devotion. Devotion was Miranda's long suit

now. She took what had seeded in her in Notre Dame and let it flower in her mouth, wondering if God would forgive her for being a whore. But that was the gift he had given her, so who was He to judge.

The doctor had also prescribed heat lamps. So Victor bought two in port, and set her up on his massage table and told her to spread her legs. Then he brought the lamps close to her, one in front of each of her thighs, goosenecked, bent in toward her vagina.

"How does that feel?" Victor asked her.

"Good," she said.

"I can see the red light reflecting from your beautiful pussy. God I can't wait to get into there."

"Me either."

"How long did he say you had to wait?"

"Six weeks."

"And how long has it been exactly now, you sweet-tongued, honey creature?"

"I had her August fifth." And I must get her back, she didn't say out loud, because as crazy as he seemed about her, she didn't really have him yet, she knew that. He was always talking about women who put the screws in men, and she didn't want to be one of those. Unless of course that was what he wanted. She was smart enough to follow his lead. She felt obscene and excited, her knees bent, her legs spread like that, with him watching, studying every hair that grew down there, reaching over to twirl a strand at a time near the top of her pudenda.

"Look at that beautiful thing, shining there like a little pink marble. Oh, God, I'd like to wrap my tongue around that. You think there could be any harm in just that?"

"I don't know."

"Well, why don't you touch it, see if it hurts."

"I don't like to do that."

"Not even when you're alone?"

"Please."

"But there's nothing wrong with it. What could be the harm in giving yourself pleasure? Especially if it gave pleasure to me. Go ahead."

"I really don't like to."

"But I like you to. Don't you want to do what would make me happy?"

"Yes."

"Then touch yourself. No. The other hand." He moved in closer. "That's right. Gently. Very gently. Just with the fingertip. And arch your wrist so I can see. Does that feel good?"

"Yes."

"Do you feel yourself getting excited?"

"Yes."

"Now let's take this other hand . . ." He took a silk ribbon from his pocket and tied it around her wrist, loosely. Then he raised her hand over her head, securing it to a metal rung that edged the table. "How does that feel?"

"What are you doing?"

"How does that feel? No, don't stop your other hand. Just tell me if you feel a little helpless."

"Sort of."

"Are you afraid of what I might do to you?"

"I don't know."

"Do you think I would hurt you?"

"No."

"Well, you're wrong," he said, and squeezed her nipple very hard. She gave a little cry. "Oh, baby girl," he said, and brushed his hair against her breasts, and tongued her down to her belly button, and licked the finger that he made her keep on moving.

And that was the start of it.

In between, they went to parties, trod the red carpet the world seemed to lay out for Victor Lenrahan. The party they had chosen the evening before, the one Miranda recovered from now as she lay, champagne soaked, on the bed beside him, was at a villa high above Cannes, peopled with beautiful women, dresses waving in the wind like chiffon sails. Miranda felt shy in their midst, taking in their attitudes and conversations, ill at ease in spite of the deference with which everyone treated her because she came with Victor.

She drank a little too much Dom Perignon, examining the women's confidence, their obvious experience, impressive as the stately cypresses circling down to the sea. One was a European star ("Star*let*," Victor corrected her later), a grapefruit-breasted Austrian with ribs as prominent as her cheekbones, a slender delicate waist, auburn hair down to her full hips. She stared sloe-eyed at the evening, while beside her, her escort-manager-husband fielded the glances of other men, his black eyes challenging them to duels if they so much as dared to think about her without offering a picture deal. Anneka was her name. Miranda had never seen her in anything, but she accepted without question her popularity and earning power, even down to what they paid for her layout in *Playboy*, which her husband did not mean to brag about, he said, quoting the price.

"Oh, Christ," said the woman behind Miranda, a lustrous brunette with royal blue eyes. "I'm still hung over from last night. What am I doing drinking again?"

"You're drinking to forget," said her companion, a short, spectacled young man from a great banking family, Victor had told Miranda.

"Forget what?"

"That you were drunk last night." The two of them embraced, giggling, leaning on each other drunkenly in the sultry wind. Then they reached to include Miranda in their hug.

"You're so pretty," the brunette woman said. "Look at this sweet face. Isn't she pretty pretty?"

"Very pretty pretty," the young man agreed.

"You better not let Anneka's husband get too close or he'll want to sell you."

"She's really beautiful," Miranda said.

"Do you know how she got to be a star?" the woman asked her. "When she was fifteen she heard Gerard Phillipe, the great French actor, was staying in a hotel near her village, so she went to his room and knocked on the door, and when he opened it, she said to him 'I am Anneka.' When the affair was over, along with some roles in French films, she went to London and rode up and down the elevator at the Dorchester till Peter Sellers got in.''

"That sounds sort of cold-blooded," Miranda said. "You think actresses are cold-blooded?"

"Ice wouldn't thaw in their cooze," said the young man, and he and the brunette woman laughed.

Her name was Françoise, and Miranda thought she was wonderful. "Isn't she beautiful?" she asked Victor, staring across the terrace at the dark-haired woman with her pale breast partially bared against the oncoming night.

"You should have seen her when she was young," said Victor.

Grief struck Miranda like a warning. How old was Françoise now, twenty-five?

Later, when they were back on the yacht, Victor murmured his displeasure. "I want you to make friends, Miranda. But try to be selective."

"I like Françoise. She's very funny."

"Peter is an asshole," Victor said. "He's pissing away his whole share of the family fortune."

"On Françoise?"

"Don't be silly. A man doesn't have to spend a fortune on her. Even with inflation, in the very best cities it doesn't cost more than three hundred dollars."

"I invited them to come to lunch tomorrow."

"Here?"

"Well, you told me to consider this my home, your boat."

"Ship," Victor corrected her. "You ought to be more discerning about who you invite." He was obviously angered. But it was nothing they couldn't work out, and did, involving a little more than Miranda had been exposed to so far, this time with handcuffs and plastic clothespins, two for her nipples and one for her labia. She had screamed, and he seemed really repentant afterward, sobbing while he came in her mouth, begging her for forgiveness, saying she could do anything she wanted to, he belonged to her.

And she belonged to him. Because the truth was, there was no one else who wanted her, no place else she could go. And, in a terrifying way, she enjoyed the pain he gave her. It was so much more direct than the torture other people had inflicted on her with their lack of love, the disapproval implicit in the kisses she hadn't been given, the hugs she hadn't received; the uncle who had violated her, the father who'd turned away even before she'd given him reason to despise her. Victor was all the hope she had, and once he grew remorseful enough, which he did immediately and absolutely, he gave up hurting her completely, and led her into hurting him, something he begged for, whimpering, teaching her tricks she could never have imagined. Buying her a very special wardrobe that reflected hot in the overhead mirror of the secret room, lit with its gelled red lights. So all skin looked hot and became pink, even the thrust of his erection, which was there for her now, when she used the tricks. And used them well. "Ah," he murmured as he rode her, black leather gripping his haunches. "Flynn would've loved this. *They Fucked With Their Boots On.*"

But she still didn't ask him to get her her baby back, because it wasn't Christmas yet. She was convinced that this man was literally Santa Claus, come to deliver all the presents she'd never received. She'd never known how much she hungered for gifts, not even daring to ask for them. Hoping that soon enough she could twist him around her finger, since twisting seemed to be one of his favorite arts, as practiced by her.

She got out of the bed she shared with Victor and went into the bathroom, brushed her teeth with the gold-handled brush he had given her, brushed her hair with a silver-handled brush. All along the top of the railed metal shelf above the sink were silver-handled brushes in various sizes, with hard and soft textures of bristles. Silver-backed combs without a spot of tarnish. Her mother had had one silver spoon that someone sent when Miranda was born, and she'd mounted it on the wall, taking it down every few weeks to polish it. It had taken Lettie close to a half hour to get it clean, what with lovingly applying the cream, washing, drying, rubbing it with the soft cloth she kept under the sink for that single purpose. Miranda wondered how long how many people had to work to keep all the silver on this yacht spotless.

In the saloon were silver trophies, awards from regattas his daughters had sailed in, silver goblets for the table. There were silver-framed photos of his children. But she had made him put away all pictures of his wife: she didn't want to know what she looked like. Betrayal seemed less spiteful when the betrayed was faceless. In the sideboard was a tray, every utensil in it curled and curved into intricate, raised designs in sterling silver. Jensen, Victor told her it was called. How many servants were there on board?

Only a few of them were visible during the lunch they served to Miranda and Victor and their guests, that day, Françoise and Peter. Swift little skiffs went by in the water, trailing brown-skinned young men and women on water skis. Victor had set a big ice chest in the center of the deck, and he filled their glasses from it. "Learned this from Errol Flynn," he said. "He and his cronies would rent a boat—" he looked over at Miranda, "theirs was smaller than this."

"Everything's smaller than this," said Françoise, "but the QE II."

"They'd invite a bunch of girls and frolic belowdecks," Victor continued. "And in between rounds they'd come up and stick their dongs in the ice chest to toughen it up for the next go round. I always keep an ice chest on deck."

"I thought it was here for drinks," said Peter. He was wearing white slacks and a white cotton, short-sleeved shirt, open at the neck to reveal an oversized Adam's apple, protruding collarbone, and very pink skin.

"You can use it for drinks if you want to," said Victor. "I just thought I'd tell you about Flynn."

"In like Flynn," said Françoise. "I've heard the expression."

"Hetero-sex was a cover," said Peter. "He was a raging queer. He had a mad love affair with Tyrone Power."

"That's slander," Victor said. "I never met a ballsier man in my life."

"Neither did Ty."

"That's a lie people tell because they're dead and can't defend themselves."

"So can I have a drink?" Peter said. "Or will there be sperm in it?"

"How about a soft drink?"

"Why? Did my parents write to you?"

"What do you mean?"

"They wrote letters to every banker and businessman they knew in Europe telling them to extend me hospitality, but not to give me a drink. Surely you were among them."

"They only asked me to keep an eye out," Victor said.

"Well, I'm not a true alcoholic. I never fall down till after the sun is over the yardarm."

"How about Perrier?" Lenrahan said.

"How about I let you have your deviations and you let me have mine?" Peter stared at Miranda.

"I suggest you keep your nastiness to yourself, or you can get off my ship."

"What makes this a ship, and before you talked about a boat?" Miranda said quickly.

"Anything over a hundred and twenty feet is a ship."

"Well, I don't think Errol was *that* well-hung," said Peter.

"I love your hat," said Miranda to Françoise.

It was huge, made of black straw, shiny, capping her hair like a Frisbee, some spacelike saucer that had come out of the dark Riviera night and settled on her. "Malcolm gave it to me."

"Lord Ormsby," said Peter. "Her British trick. He had a letter of introduction to Françoise from Mandy Rice Davies."

"Stop making fun of me, Peter. You know I'm touchy today."

"Poor Françoise had a really tough night last night. She met this old man. Rather, I met this old man, and even though I have this father complex, I could see he was more interested in *her*. So, always ready to make a sacrifice for a friend, I got them together. Settling the terms, you understand, because Françoise is such a lady, she hates to sully her lips with anything like a price. He hobbled upstairs, his old juices aboil, and a few minutes later, Françoise went up and did the dirty deed."

"Oh, God," Françoise said, and apparently remembering, shuddered.

"Was it so bad?" Miranda asked.

"Well, actually, it was hilarious," Françoise said, and started to giggle. "I went to his room, got into bed, performed my service, took the money from his dresser, and left. It wasn't until I was out in the hall that I looked at the number on the door and realized I'd gone to the wrong room."

"Well, I said to her," Peter started to laugh, " 'What difference does it make?' "

"What difference does it make?" Françoise shrieked, and the two of them leaned forward in their chairs, sighing and moaning and gasping with laughter, slapping at each other's hands as though it was merriment that linked them instead of despair.

"From now on, sweetheart," said Victor as he watched the dinghy taking Françoise and Peter back to land later that afternoon, "*I* pick your friends."

He was as good as his word. Guests on the yacht that summer besides European dignitaries, American politicians, and Oriental businessmen, whom Victor called Gooks, but not within their hearing, included Dwight Efram Jonah.

Jonah was a big man, almost as tall as Victor, with a barrel chest, as if he worked out lifting weights in between figuring out how to put satellites in orbit. He was considered among the most brilliant of the new breed of physicists, a disciple of Edward Teller, the physicist who did not like being described as the father of the H-bomb, but who had come up with the engineering step that made it possible. Like Teller, Jonah was an avowed hard-liner, quoting Teller's describing himself as having been part of one "shipwreck"—Nazi Germany taking over Europe—and not wanting to be part of another: Russia taking over the United States. Like his mentor, Jonah was fearless in presenting his convictions, echoing Teller from his much junior vantage point, that America had to stay strong and very much ahead. It was Victor Lenrahan's pleasure to help see that it did so.

Jonah was currently serving with the Atomic Energy Commission, a post requiring an intensity of vacation equal to the pressures of the job. So it was that Victor had invited him to spend two weeks on the yacht that early September. It was a glistening time on the Riviera, the sparkling water quiet, the crowds of August having retreated to their serious stomping grounds.

"I think that God Septembers in the south of France," Jonah said, looking out over the water, bourbon and branch water in his hand. It had been specially stocked on board for his arrival, honoring his Carolina origins. "What better place to watch the ebb of summer?"

It titillated Miranda, the way he talked, full of poetry and words that had no thrust to them, like someone playing with her ears, fingers touching inside her lips. She seemed to be in a state of perpetual heat now, because the air was sultry and the sun was warm on her skin and she knew what she and Victor did downstairs. The hypocrisy excited her, the passing of renowned men and representatives of great and small nations, who celebrated civilization on deck with champagne and caviar, while belowdecks Victor begged to stuff her with crème caramel and eat it out of her, but not until after she spanked him for daring to want her.

She would spread her legs in the sunlight, the line of bikini protecting her from all but the most insolent of glances, and let the sun beat on her, warming up her juices. She was awash in them, ready for it all the time, her erotic imagination burgeoning as her experiences did, her mind replaying his sucking her, pleading for it. The submissive role of her sexual adventure was over now. He had run her through it very quickly, then abandoned it, explaining that he'd only taught her that part so she'd know how he felt, so she would temper her ministrations with compassion, but not too much. If he really thought she felt sorry for him, it would flag, like determination. But there was a large triangle of liquid heat now always in her crotch. She almost thought she could hear it washing when she moved, like waves lapping on the shore, and she wondered if Dwight Efram Jonah could hear it, too.

"This is the perfect setting to collect energy for autumn," Jonah said. "I think this is where He must go."

"God knows He needs a vacation," Victor said, and went downstairs to take a shower.

It did not occur to Miranda that she would ever be unfaithful. Other men were only other men, pawns in the chess game Victor played, some of them with erections that Miranda imagined, because cocks had become a source of fascination to her now, knowing how caught up even giants were in whether they could get hard or not. Dwight Efram Jonah, she conjectured, would probably have a military cock, stiff and very clean, coming from a patch just this side of a crew cut. Jonah's hair was black, with one or two renegade strands of white invading it. He did not tan quite as deeply brown as Victor, his skin having a slightly ruddy cast, so he was more Indian looking than anyone else in their party.

Those included his wife, who had very pale skin and a tendency to burn. So she spent a lot of time belowdecks. At least that was the reason she gave, although Dwight and Victor both knew it was because of Miranda.

Miranda knew it too. Edith Jonah was a friend of Victor's wife, and so was obviously edgy and uncomfortable. They'd introduced Miranda as the girlfriend of one of Victor's aides at MercerCorp, invited along on the trip for just such a cover. What they called in cheating circles a "beard" although, in Allen's case, he was extremely clean shaven. Not enough to fool Edith, however, since she wasn't stupid. She saw how Victor looked at Miranda.

And so did Dwight Efram Jonah, with his very sharp, gray eyes, the color of steel, the color of battleships, the glint of gun barrels on battlefields. His own eyes were full of Miranda. He respected Victor and honored him, but she was a painting, and he understood that Victor had her on display. With her arched, perfect breasts—the nipples protruding underneath the skimpy cups of the bikini—and her legs spread there in the sunlight so you could see the outline of slit. Like most driven men he did not allow himself time to be highly sexed, and put his fucking into ambition. But it was, after all, vacation time, and there she was, spread like a feast, and if he ate her only with his eyes, Victor wouldn't be offended.

"Have you ever been to Saint-Tropez?" Dwight asked Miranda.

"No," she said. "I haven't been many places, really. I did live in Paris, though."

"Is that where you met Victor?"

Victor was belowdecks, so it was just the two of them, if you didn't count the stewards who were refilling their drinks and serving hors d'oeuvres. She had already absorbed Victor's capacity for seeing the working class as invisible, not out of any snobbery, but out of a certain wish for discretion. As languorous as she felt, as turned on by her sexual flowering, she was not an exhibitionist. Victor's passion for her still embarrassed her when he showed it in front of the servants. So she had adopted his attitude of not being conscious of them.

To all intents and purposes, then, she was alone on deck with Dwight Efram Jonah. Although the servants, unseen, were the only ones in front of whom Victor showed his feelings for her, she did not imagine Jonah was fooled. His intelligence was palpable: She could see it sticking out of him as easily as she could have his erection, poking into everything, sifting, weighing. Of Victor's associates, only Allen, that red-haired, freckled, clean-shaven "beard"

purportedly knew what was going on between them. But
Miranda understood Jonah knew. Still, it was something
she was not permitted to acknowledge, Victor had warned
her. They had to be circumspect. You didn't give these
people any extra ammunition, no matter how friendly they
seemed to be, no matter how close they were. "Not that I
don't trust him," Victor had said. "But business is tick-
lish, and you have to be careful who you give a feather
to."

"No, I didn't meet Mr. Lenrahan in Paris, I met him in
Cannes. When Allen brought me to the yacht." Miranda's
mouth was a little dry from the effort of dissembling.
Deception was not one of her attributes. As adept as she
was becoming at games, those were about teasing. Pretending
anger, disapproval, making a man feel naughty and punished
to get him excited, that was different from telling a lie. In
her own way she was a highly moral young woman.
"Wasn't it nice of him to let Allen invite me on this trip?"

"Very nice," said Dwight. "But that's Victor for you.
The soul of generosity."

"Not to mention the heel," said Edith, coming onto the
deck. She was swathed in white gauzy pants and shirt, a
white hat with a large brim shading her face, which was
creamed with sunscreen. She wore oversized Carrera sunglasses, so Miranda could not see the expression in her
eyes. If they had any expression at all.

"Would you like something to drink?" Miranda sprang
to her feet as though in the presence of a schoolteacher.

"Well, how nice," Edith said. "Victor has a hostess."

"Oh, I didn't mean to act as if I was the hostess. I just
thought . . ."

"How unusual," Edith said. "For someone of your
calling."

"Edith . . ."

"I mean, you are a model, or something like that? Don't
you think it's commendable, Dwight dear, a girl who looks
like Miranda, able to *think*?"

"Why don't you tell the steward if you want a drink?"
Dwight said, grim-faced.

"Maybe a Seven-Up. Does this little pleasure cruise have Seven-Up?"

"Have a real drink," Dwight said. "Maybe it'll relax you."

"I'm perfectly relaxed," Edith said. "Women aren't like men. Self-indulgence doesn't make us feel better about ourselves."

"A little self-indulgence on occasion doesn't mean you aren't a virtuous person," said Dwight.

"Oh, I couldn't agree more." Edith sat in the chair under the canopy. "Self-indulgence is fine, as long as you practice it moderately. Perhaps once a week. And only occasionally in the morning." She put her glasses slightly down her nose and peered over them at Miranda. "Myself, I only do it after the children have left for school."

"How many do you have?"

"Two. A boy and a girl."

"How lucky. That must be the nicest thing in the world, raising children."

"Not the nicest. But certainly one of the most challenging. And then you start getting older, and you have to worry about what happens now that the children are grown. Mrs. Lenrahan for example. Such a lovely woman. And what a fabulous job she did with those girls. What are a woman's rewards, I often wonder."

"Edith . . ."

"Well, surely you can't object to a little philosophic musing, Dwight. A little philosophic musing never hurt anyone any more than a little self-indulgence."

"It must be hard getting older," Miranda agreed, sitting up stiffly, her electric blue bikini bright against the day. She was sorry now she wasn't in black, which would cast her more as the villain this woman was making her out to be. It would also make her tan look darker, emphasizing the contrast between her and Edith Jonah, an emphasis she devoutly wished for now. Edith Jonah with her white skin and her unforgiving attitude, tight and judgmental like her mouth. No mercy to it. No understanding what Miranda was doing, saving Victor's life. He told her that all the time. Making his life worth living, and so saving it.

The steward brought Edith her drink. The ship lurched slightly, spilling some of it onto her hand. Miranda was on her feet again, handing her a napkin, the impulse toward caring and politeness stronger than the irritation she felt toward this woman.

"Why thank you," Edith said. "How thoughtful. Not only thinking, but thoughtful. A rare combination, certainly among those in your trade. I expect you do a little acting?"

"Lay off," said Dwight.

"An interesting choice of words."

"You're going to love Saint-Tropez," Dwight said to Miranda. "Though it isn't all that 'in' anymore. Brigitte Bardot made it popular at the height of her fame . . ."

"And her breasts," said Edith.

". . . but I find it curiously beautiful. You have to get in tune with what's going on underneath the feathers and sequins. There's a strange feeling of regeneration . . ."

"I find that, too," said Edith. "But then perhaps I'm regenerated by the knowledge that even sexpots get older."

Victor finally came up on deck. But instead of riding to Miranda's rescue, he moved uncomfortably to another part of the ship with Jonah. The braver a man was with other men, apparently, the more cowardly he was with a cutting woman. That much was fast becoming clear to Miranda. Her eyes were so hot with anger and embarrassment at Edith's attack on her that she practically paid no attention when they went into port, which should have been the highlight of her trip, according to Jonah. People watched their coming from the shore, riveted, suntanned faces staring at the ship moving into dock as though it were the naked line at the Moulin Rouge. All of them envying Miranda. And Miranda had to miss it, so caught was she in her own discomfort.

She went down to her cabin and locked herself in. The steward knocked on her door and told her Mr. Lenrahan wanted her up on deck.

"Tell him I don't feel well," she said. Malingering was no more a part of her personality than deception was, but she was a fast learner, and the brooding and anger of Edith Jonah had not been lost on her, the effectiveness of whining as a weapon of intimidation had not gone unmarked.

"Now come on," Victor said, opening the door to her cabin with a key he kept in the deep pocket of his shorts, so entry to her was always within touch of his member. "Don't you turn into a brooder on me."

"You heard how she talked to me. Why didn't you tell her to stop?"

"She's a guest, just like you are. I can't be rude to my guests."

"You can if they're being awful to your other guests. If you really cared about me, you could."

"Oh, sweetheart. You know how much I care about you. The world could know for all I care. But I can't afford to let that happen. You're a smart girl. You understand what's going on here. Edith's a friend of Vivian's."

"You don't have to tell me that," she said, and reached inside his shorts and scratched his scrotum with her fingernail, not enough to really hurt him. Just a sharp reminder of what she could do to him. Later, if he behaved himself.

"Just be kind to her, like you would a sick cat."

"I tried. She's just awful."

"She's the wife of one of my dearest friends. Don't make it tough on me."

He handed her a packet of crisp green bills. "There's exchange places all along the dock. Banks and agencies and camions where you can get francs. Go and have yourself a great time. Buy something as gorgeous as you are."

"Aren't you going to come with me?"

"I can't."

"Because Edith might be watching?"

"Not only Edith. Dwight is a friend of Vivian's, too."

"He knows. He's a smart man. He knows I'm not really with Allen."

"Well, let's not make it harder on him to pretend he

doesn't know. You go have fun." Victor patted her on the head.

"Don't pet me like I'm a dog," she said, and pushed his hand away.

She tried to keep the pout in her soul when she went up on deck, but the dazzle of the day overwhelmed her. She could hardly see, even with dark sunglasses. She stood for a long moment on the deck, squinting, adjusting her eyes to the panorama they were roped to: Along the dock, deeply tanned, overly made-up, wildly dressed and un-dressed young girls paraded, cowboy boots on their other-wise naked, brown legs, peacock feathers, chandelier crystals hanging from their ears in mad innovation. Young men in cutoff jeans browsed among them, appraising. Artists sketched in charcoal the faces of tourists for fifty francs a sitting. Children tugged on balloons and their parents' arms. Directly in front of the ship, past the swell of people, rose brightly colored awnings, open air cafés, side by side with boutiques, rods of miniskirts hanging out like flags of greeting. All along the dock stood the bald-faced curious, eyeing the latest yacht to drop anchor, trying to see who the passengers were as the rumors made the rounds—Miranda could hear the excited urgent whispers that Ursula Andress was on board. She studied the people lined up, staring up at the gangway connecting the *Banana* to the dock, their imaginations aching like the stomach of the Little Match Girl, nose pressed against the bakery window. Knew for the first time in her life what it was to be the fresh bread. Coveted.

"Are you going to go shopping?" Edith was behind her, suddenly, dressed for port, her sharp features made more angular by the madras plaid scarf around her head, completely obscuring and flattening her lifeless brown hair.

"I don't know what I'm going to do," Miranda said, not daring to think the woman was looking for company.

"Well, I'm sure you have *lots* of money to spend."

"That's right," said Miranda. "I do." She walked down the gangway, the cotton skirt she'd put on over her bathing suit gently brushing her calves.

There was a flow of people in the narrow cobblestoned alleyway off the main quai, a stream that went against Miranda. She looked in windows, leaned against them, letting the tide go by, taking in the noise, the happy chatter, the barking of dogs, the complaints about the heat, too many people, all of it a singular symphony in French, a language that made even discontent sound like praise, an affirmation of life. In a bakery window a plastic white marker penciled with the legend, "Tarte Tropezienne, 2F," pierced the white cake, the custardy confection it advertised. In the boutique next to it, a young, chubby blonde hung white lacey blouses in a fresh display. Everywhere were notices that promised sales, sacrifices. From the open arcade came the scent of the spices of Provence, drying flowers in colorful clumps in round straw baskets. Cosmetics and perfume dotted glass windows like jewels on display, at discount for export, read the aviso.

"E veramente magnifico, si?" said a young man standing near her, his naked feet brown against the leathery thongs that separated his toes. There was an arc of white skin in the V between his big toe and the one next to it, and his toenails were a little sooty. But it was not so much dirt as the track of the town recorded by his wanderings, she could tell that. He looked very clean, black lashes thickly edging his dark blue eyes. His eyes reminded her of Françoise. She felt a sudden, aching nostalgia for Françoise, the only friend she'd been allowed to make on this seemingly splendid voyage.

"I'm sorry," Miranda said. "I don't understand."

"Mi dispiace," he said. "Non capisco."

"Pardon?"

"What you said. I said it in Italian."

"That's very clever of you."

"Yes. I am very clai-ver."

"And modest," she said.

"I don't know what is this word."

"It's all right," Miranda said. "You'll do fine without it." She started walking up the alley, looking in shop windows. He trailed a few feet behind her, watching her

movements. She could feel his eyes on her back, appraising. The sun was hot on her shoulders. She was used to
men studying her by now, but this was very open, straightforward. Refreshing after the clandestine flavor of what
she'd grown used to in the past few weeks, longing
disguised as polite interest when there were other people
around. She was enraged by Victor's behavior. Gallantry,
charm, and good manners in public were what had drawn
her closer to him, made her feel really secure for the first
time in her life. All through her childhood she'd missed
that carrot of esteem most fathers held out for their
daughters: the affection, the regard. What she had seen in
Tom Morton's eyes was a cold signal that the world
wouldn't like her any better than he did. Well, maybe that
was the truth about life, that the world didn't love you any
better than your parents. That was as good as it ever got.
So if it started out sorry there, it could only get worse. But
with Victor she felt all that changed: at last she was
comforted, protected. So how could he fail to be gallant on
her behalf when it was gallantry that made her love him?
Gallantry that had made him pledge his devotion, promise
her a rest of her life that angels could sing about? How
could he say all that and not intercede with that woman?
Why hadn't he shielded her with his big, white-haired
presence from Edith's darts?

"I invite you for a drink, yes?" the young Italian said.

"You invite me, yes. I accept you, no," Miranda said,
and kept walking. Angry as she was at Victor, she could
not act out of spite. Besides, she was starting to see that
men didn't really provide shelter, one better than the other.
What you had to do was figure out how to shelter yourself.

She moved through the square, the Place Des Lices it
said on the blue enamel sign wedged deep into the stone of
the corner building. In the shade of the thick-trunked,
patchy yellow and gray-barked plane trees, old men played
boule. Sorrow pulled at her throat: she remembered the
plane tree in Alex's courtyard in Paris, wondered how her
baby was, if her eyes were turning yet to the color of
Miranda's own. Blue they had been at birth, but all babies'

eyes were blue, the doctor had told her. "Maybe her eyes will be like the mother's eyes," the bitch woman who'd come to adopt her had said. In pained recollection, that unlovely face appeared a lot like Edith Jonah's. They all had the same face, really, the women with no love in them, the one whose only energy was drawn from hate, and envy of young girls.

She hiked up the winding, cobblestoned streets to the top of the town, paid her few francs, and marched through the naval fortress that capped the village. How small they must have been, the sailors who walked through those short, cut-off doorways, who leaned against those stones. Everything seemed in miniature, the maps, the plans for naval assaults and naval defenses framed on the walls. Out in the air again, she could see, far below, the harbor, from the ancient overlook that guarded the Gulf of Grimaud. The water was wrapped in a sudden, surprising mist, as sailboats skimmed across the smooth surface, stripes in bright colors challenging the gray.

She could feel a sudden heat behind her, like a spot of sun through a magnifying glass, burning her shoulders. She turned and saw the Italian boy.

"Are you following me?"

"Yes," he said.

"I am not interested. Can you understand that?"

"Non capisco," he said, smiling.

She wondered at the thickness of them all, at their conviction they were irresistible. Fury at Victor and his insensitivity melded with a general rage at the rest of them, and she wondered if, when she took the little Plexiglas whip and tied the ropes tighter there wasn't more excitement in it than she even allowed herself to feel, if it wasn't revenge at how cruel they were, how unfeeling. Pain to get back at the pain they caused. Power over the powerful. A kind of spiritual uprising, a gladiator charging from the arena to slay those who dared to sit above them in judgment, putting thumbs down.

She looked at the boy's royal blue eyes and remembered Françoise. And remembered her mother. And remembered her baby. A great female loneliness and longing came over her, and she wished she had a breast to weep against. To cry on because of how alone she was. How alone they all were.

He seemed to sense what she was feeling, as a puppy could pick up on pain. He reached out his hand to touch her hair, tentatively, with fingers that looked to be clumsy but weren't, so all they touched was a single curl that fell beside her cheek, barely grazing her scalp. He had big hands, massive hands, broad at the base, with long, thick fingers, the fullness at the base of his thumb and the mound above the wrist to little finger like a sort of inverted bowl of flesh against her cheek.

"Don't," she whispered.

"It is only . . ." he said, and his fingers cupped the side of her face, but gently. "You look so sad."

"Well, that's because I'm sad," she said, and started to cry.

And his naked arms, brown and tanned, jutting sleek and shiny from the cut-off sleeves of his T-shirt took her in an embrace, more respectful than passionate, more comforting than wanting. The soft thickness of his hand gripped her shoulder, started working the taut, strained muscles at the back of her neck where the tension was from trying to hold her head up, pretending a pride no one had left her. There was a muskiness coming from the hollow above his chest, honey edged with salt, the coarse masculine smell of countries where men did not struggle to seem cleaner than their thoughts. For a moment she was caught in it, caught in the tenderness, caught in the honesty even of his smell. And then she pulled away.

He stared at her with eyes that licked her face, his focus moving along every inch of her eyes, as though he would touch it an eyelash at a time, moving over the lids to the bridge of her nose and across the other eye. Then he studied her mouth, first the top lip, coming to rest at the corners, moving along the bottom lip slowly, resting on the slight cleft in her chin. It was more tactile than touch, his look, his longing.

"I have to go now," she said, curiously breathless.

"Good," he said. "I go with you."

"I don't think you understand."

"I understand," he said, and held out his hand without touching her arm, his thick fingers almost, but not quite resting against her skin as he guided her down the steps, guardianlike, ready to catch her if she stumbled.

He fell in step beside her, the long, streamlined muscles of his thighs shiny beneath the cut-off fringes of his jeans, the tight pull of fabric across his fly boldly outlining his masculinity. No problem getting that up, she bet herself, sick at what a tramp she was, filled with the same kind of heat she had felt since the start of this crazily erotic voyage. Turned on by kindness and interest as she had been by luxury and power. Was that it? Was that all a man had to do was look at her with something that seemed like affection and she was ready to fall into bed with him, the only thing holding her back some perverse sense of loyalty? Loyalty to what? A man who did not prize her enough to slay a dragon he himself had invited on board. Was she so tuned up by all that had transpired on the *Banana*, that all anyone had to do was hum and the music started inside her? Had Victor tied her up just to set her free as the whore she really was? Was Edith right about her?

"You think too much," the Italian boy said, studying her profile. "You need to eat. When the stomach is full, it is easier for the head to be empty."

He bought her a ripe red apple from the open marketplace. Washed it from the faucet alongside the fishmonger's iced display of that day's catch. Wiped the fruit shiny and clean, polished it with the cotton of her skirt, his eyes fixed on her ankles. He held it out and let her bite into it, closing his eyes with the sound of her crunch, took it into his own mouth and bit into the space beside her teeth marks. Then he passed it back to her again. Back and forth it went until there was nothing left but the core and the juice on their fingers. He took her hand and put it to his lips, licked the liquid from her fingertips. Then he put his fingers to her mouth. She ran her tongue along the sweetness that dripped from them.

He moved to take her in his arms, but she pulled away. "What kind of a game do you play?"

"It's not a game," she said, being very adept at games and wishing, in fact, she could play with him. But some awful knot of decency she did not understand and had yet to acknowledge in herself twisted her insides, cut off her wanting, monitoring it, making her afraid. Making her angry at what she really wanted.

"I belong to somebody," she said. "Do you know what that means?"

"I thought it was a free country, America," he said.

"Only sometimes," she whispered, and rising on tiptoe, kissed him quickly in the shadow of the plane tree, and ran up the cobblestoned street before she could taste how sweet his mouth was, how soft his lips were, the impression of them still warm on her lips.

She was in a rage of loneliness, a fury at her own limited sense of liberty. There was a sweater in a shop window to the side of the courtyard, and because of the crystals of tears still left in her eyes, it seemed to have a special radiance. Well, there was that for a solution, anyway: shopping. Victor thought it was an answer. She went inside and tried it on, her malaise easing, disappearing in the colorful folds of the sweater that felt, for a moment, like the young Italian's sweet, warm arms. Was that what clothes were then, hugs? Was that why women cared so much for style, consoling themselves with fabrics when there should have been embraces?

She asked the salesgirl the price and was stunned at the cost of it. "But you look so beautiful in it," the young Frenchwoman said. "You must have it. It is the only one like it. Handmade."

There were threads of angora like puffs of smoke coming out of the main weave of the sweater, in pinks, blues, and grays. Miranda saw herself in the mirror. She looked as though she were cloaked in sky. Just after sunset, in one of the better places.

She bought it. When she got back to the ship, it was twilight. Edith was sitting on deck wearing the same sweater.

Miranda clutched the bag containing hers closer. A sliver of moon crept above the harbor. "Papa, la lune!" cried a little girl on the dock, pointing skyward. A tall sunburned youth in rolled up jeans flashed luminous whips against the evening, whirled metal disks, making stars from friction, hawked them among the crowds, softly calling out "Ma-gic."

Miranda slammed belowdecks, into Victor's cabin. "Are you crazy?" he said. "What if someone saw you come in here?"

"What if they did," she said. "Who do you think we're fooling?"

"My little angel . . ." he said, and reached for her with hands that suddenly seemed old.

"I want my baby," she said, and pulled away. "I want you to get me my baby back. I want you to give me money to buy her, or whatever I have to do. But I want you to get her back for me, or I'm leaving you."

"Precious angel . . ." he said.

"Precious angel my ass," she said. "I'm your whore, and if I'm going to be your whore, and be treated like it and insulted by that bitch up there, I want my reward."

"Anything you say . . ." he said, looking suddenly pale beneath his tan. "Anything you want . . ."

"Well, you better mean it. You better be ready to do whatever you have to do or it's over between us."

Tears started welling in his eyes. "Oh, please. Don't even say that."

"You're a very bad boy," she said as he fell to his knees in front of her.

"I know. I'm such a bad boy. I need to be punished."

"Later," she said, and back in control, returned to the deck.

"Ma-gic," the sunburned young man was still crying, spinning his sparks against the oncoming night. Well, it was magic, wasn't it? That much lovelier, pronounced in

French. That much more enchanted on the Riviera. There she was on the deck of a yacht, while a few yards below her crowded those who would have been in her place, necks craned for a better look at how she lived. And there among them stood the dark blue-eyed young Italian, a sorrowing look on his open, square-jawed face, as though she had betrayed him by being Rich People.

Edith saw him staring up at Miranda, saw the recognition on Miranda's face. "Did you have a spiritual experience in Saint-Tropez?"

"As a matter of fact, I did," said Miranda, clutching the bag with the sweater in it. "Did you?"

"Oh, I always have a spiritual experience in Saint-Tropez." Edith stretched her long, athletic legs, their shape retained and strengthened by regular tennis games in McLean, Virginia. "You see, it's just as Dwight said. You have to look underneath the feathers and sequins . . . to penetrate the gaudy. See through to the simplicity of this place to restore your soul. Connect to what is eternal . . . Shed like a tougher skin your material longings."

"Except for that sweater," Miranda said.

"Except for this sweater," said Edith, and smiled. "You are a bright little thing. I can understand why an old man would make a fool of himself over you." She drank from her gin gimlet. "And a young man," she added, and looked down at the dock.

It discomfited Miranda to be with this woman, this wry, judgmental creature who, simply by pronouncing her bright, made her feel stupid. They were a different breed, the people with education. It was ammunition that could not be acquired, unlike money and clothes, the security of knowing how smart you were. So no matter how Victor might cloak Miranda in luxury, no matter what promises he kept, even if he got her her baby back (Would he? Would he be that kind, that unfailingly generous, letting the small creature into their lives?), he could never really protect her from women like this. "Is anyone else around?"

"Victor is below, which I'm sure you already found out,

and if by anyone else you mean my husband, I trust you have the good sense to stay away from him."

"I meant Allen," said Miranda, reddening.

"You don't have to keep up that little charade for my benefit." She pronounced it sha-rod. "I know what's going on here. And I am much too fond of Vivian to add to what must already be her considerable agony by telling her. But keep your distance from my husband."

Miranda let herself see how very unbecoming the sweater was to the angular, sharp-featured woman, her dull hair shampooed for evening, but still flat, as if her disagreeable nature had spread to her follicles. The little puffs of angora coming out from the main weave of the soft, threaded wool looked on Edith like angry shocks of electricity in a comic strip, where someone had put their finger in a socket.

"How could he possibly be interested in anyone else when he has such a warm and lovely wife?" Miranda asked, and flounced belowdecks.

"Dom Perignon?" Victor Lenrahan said to his assembled dinner guests, as if he were really offering it to all of them, thinking about all of them and not just worrying about pleasing the palate and newly acquired tastes of Miranda.

For God's sake, he was fifty-seven years old and she was only seventeen. But what a seventeen: blossomed, full-blown on that magical, fluorescent shore like one of the twisting sparkling things the tanned young man in rolled-up dungarees was hawking on the dock, something to cut luminous spirals into the darkness, to catch the eye and the heart and lift it. Lift everything. But it was a little late for him to experience the feelings Miranda elicited in him.

He found himself trembling sometimes in her presence, like a leaf in a twilight wind, like a boy whose dream of love had never been set aside. He could hardly keep his hands off her, the touch of her warm, honeyed flesh like a tonic to his fingertips, sending energy through his whole body, even to his dick, which, strangely, amazed him. There was something lyrical about her, musical, so that even he who had never cared for music, who hated opera and slept through it rather noisily when he was forced to go, all at once understood the reason for symphonies, and, in his way, heard arias. Would have sung them to her in his froggy voice if he knew the tunes, if he could make manifest the melodies that suddenly played inside him. It was embarrassing for a barbarian, which he knew damned well he was, to have all these delicate things going on. He hoped to hell it didn't show.

He was still not sure that he could trust her. This new business of the baby discomfited him completely, and he wondered whether that was it, whether she was playing him for all she could get. It would have been okay if it hadn't included a brat. What would he do with a baby on board? Or even in a flat in Paris, were he to stash Miranda there. Or stash her anywhere. She was his treasure now, and a baby would be worse than a mother-in-law. Still, he made a mental note to talk to some lawyer, because a promise was a promise, whether or not you intended to keep it. You had to go through the motions so a person wouldn't know they were being fucked.

But his feeling for her was genuine enough that he thought he wanted to please her, make her happy. She excited him like no one in his life had excited him. So it was doubly hard, doubly devastating to him that there were obstacles to their contentment. That she wanted her wailing bastard. That she was angry and hurt at the way Edith treated her. That they were dining in candlelit splendor on the deck of the *Banana*, still tied to the dock at Saint-Tropez, while below them strolled the ordinary people. And he could see in Miranda's eyes she would rather be among them.

Edith Jonah was several sheets to the wind, though the yacht was motorized and anchored. She sat, or rather leaned to Victor's right, between him and Allen Hewitt, his subordinate from MercerCorp, the purported boyfriend of Miranda. Allen was a genial former newspaperman who'd written a favorable profile of Lenrahan for his paper and promptly been offered a job. He had no Ben Hechtian dream of a newsroom, with its busy hope of a better world beneath the copy. His deepest principle was survival, so without hesitation he accepted.

He had not been earth-shattering as a journalist, and was no more so in aerospace P. R. But as less reached print in this job, he was less likely to be exposed as not very good. He was flattered by his fronting with Miranda, who was more woman than all the women in his life, including a mother, a wife and an ambitious mistress who all thought him more important than he was.

Next to Allen, cornering the table, was Miranda. She had put her new sweater on out of spite. On her right, opposite Victor, was Senator Kranet, who'd motored up from Cannes from a villa where he and his wife Sylvia were houseguesting. Sylvia, opposite Miranda, was dressed in satin, hand-stamped to look like snake curling around her high-breasted, long-waisted body like a second skin. It emphasized all her best points while ensuring that her husband wouldn't be set upon by endangered species groups. The closest Sylvia had come to personal tragedy was not being able to walk the streets of Manhattan in her leopard coat.

Next to Sylvia, his steel gray eyes warily appraising the extent of his wife's drunkenness, was Dwight Efram Jonah, equidistant from Edith, who sat across from him, and Miranda. It was lucky, Dwight thought, that Edith could not see her, looking as she did so much lovelier than Edith ever could in the very same design. He knew his wife had spent more than she spent even on gowns for this sweater. The huge fluffy thing that now, with the image of Miranda in identical garb, looked to be vomiting Edith out of it.

"Caviar!" said Sylvia Kranet. "Isn't this dreamy, Senator? Here we are sitting in Saint-Tropez on a yacht, and we even get to have the authentic Russian."

"We don't know for sure it's Russian," Victor said quickly.

"That doesn't make you unpatriotic," the senator said, his yachting cap, bought especially for the evening, set at a rakish angle above his aging boy's face. "To enjoy the good things of the Soviet Union makes you a citizen of this planet, which might not be a bad thing for people to be."

"He's a sucker for balalaika music," Sylvia said fondly, an affection in her tone that disputed the blind item in a gossip column that had her coupling indiscriminately in the backseats of moving taxicabs. "And Chekhov."

" 'A sky full of diamonds,' " the senator quoted wistfully, looking above them. "The most poignant speech in all of drama, what his niece promised Uncle Vanya. Ah, if we could understand that deep melancholy and combine it with our get up and go, what a nation we would be!"

"What a nation we are already," Victor said.

"No question," said Sylvia Kranet.

"But we're afraid of sadness," said the senator.

"No question," said Sylvia.

"Whereas it is the most ennobling of all human attributes to be able to go into sadness deep enough, to face it, confront it, see that it's our greatest humanity to feel it. To go deep into the throat of sadness and pull from it the tonsils of joy."

"Ouch," said Edith.

The senator looked up astonished from the potato skin on his plate, larded with sour cream, sprinkled with raw onion and egg white and dollops of caviar. He was not used to being reacted to, or, a lot of the time, even listened to, so much of his life had been spent filibustering. He was not sure whether the woman was, in fact, addressing what he had been saying or if she had hurt herself. Victor Lenrahan seemed to have the same concern, leaning solicitously toward Edith.

"Not to worry," she said. "I just spilled my portion of Baltic Sea into my crotch."

"Let me help you," Allen said.

"No, no, it's all right. Stay with the crotch you're pretending to be assigned to."

"Edith . . ." Dwight said.

"Helps to pass the time, don't you think? If you're not sure how to pass your time in port, you can always spill something on yourself and spend the rest of the evening trying to get it off." Edith rubbed at her lap with her napkin, and got to her feet, wiping angrily. "How does that look?"

"I can't even see it," said Dwight.

"Well, thank God I didn't get it on my sweater," she said, and sat again.

The steward brought the second course. Gleaming china soup bowls filled with steaming moules marinières.

"Ah," said the senator, tasting. "If only we could eat life like a mussel. Sucking the tenderness out of the shell. Having the patience to work out the chewiest part."

"Mussels are a specialty of Saint-Tropez," said Victor.

"I noticed that this afternoon," Edith said. "You should have seen the set of pecs that showed up following Miranda. All in a tank top he was, so browned and blue-eyed. What was he, dear?" She leaned forward so she could see past Allen to Miranda. "A Turk? They are reputed to have the bluest eyes, not to mention the biggest . . ."

"Edith!"

"Well, I'm only quoting popular speculation. Perhaps Miranda can tell us if it's true."

Miranda did not speak, but used an empty mussel shell as pincers to extract the meat from another mussel. She closed her eyes and chewed.

"Did you meet someone in port?" Victor asked, an attempt at joviality on his face but not in his voice. Edith leaned forward, a little too far, her face nearly to the table, watching Miranda for the explanation.

"I went sightseeing," Miranda said, "and I bought this sweater."

"Shit!" Edith said, as her bowl of mussels spilled into her lap. She jumped to her feet, the clattering of shells and overturned, breaking china splitting the air like her expletive. "Ruined! I ruined it. Oh shit!"

Miranda giggled.

"Are you laughing at me, you little tart? You little trollop!"

"Edith!" Dwight was on his feet. "For God's sake."

"Oh, ease up. Nothing's at stake here. Your relationship with Victor isn't going to end because I lay a little truth on your venerable host and his admirable company."

"You better go down below and change," Dwight said, and took her by the arm.

"Let go of me," she said.

"Excuse us," said Dwight, and pulled her toward the stairs.

"It's ruined!" Edith said, and started crying. "It's ruined, and she's glad, did you hear her, how she laughed? She actually laughed at me. The most gorgeous thing I ever owned, and it's ruined!"

"We'll find a good cleaner," Dwight said. "They'll fix it."

"I never want to wear it again," she sobbed as they went down the stairs. "She bought hers just to torment me."

There was silence on deck for a little while. Below on the dock was the strolling murmur of the crowd, a light oboe concerto from street musicians playing Beethoven, the tenacious chant of the boy who sold sparklers: "Ma-gic."

"I believe this is the most colorful place on all the Riviera," Victor finally said.

"No question," said Sylvia Kranet.

"Cigarette?" Allen offered one to Miranda.

"I don't smoke," she said, and blushing, added, "But of course you know that."

He held the packet out to Sylvia. "Ooo," she said, making a face. "Gauloise. No thank you. You always think you could fall in love with a Frenchman till you smell their cigarettes."

"How long are you staying here, Victor?" the senator asked.

"We'll probably cast off tomorrow. But I'll miss it."

"Me, too," said Sylvia. "I don't get to spend enough time here. I truly love Saint-Tropez. I think I'd like to grow old here, if I had to grow old . . . But of course I'd keep my top on."

* * *

After that summer, Miranda told Victor she would accompany him nowhere "fashionable," not even on the yacht. He would have to find more obscure places to anchor if he wanted her company. And speaking of company, she'd gone on, she wanted no more of his friends invited on the yacht who didn't like her, in front of whom she couldn't be herself. And where was her baby?

By that time, she had Victor by the proverbial short hairs, which he'd shown her exactly how to pull. He hired an attorney in Paris who wrote him frequent reports about the progress he was making with the infant's adoptive parents, whom Victor was relieved to note were completely unwilling to give up the child. Still, he told Miranda he would not weaken. That the lawyer would keep working and they'd think of something.

And meanwhile, if she didn't want to go to fashionable places, that was fine with him. He was glad to abide by her dictum. If that meant cutting off friends and their wives, that was better than cutting off his own cock. Which was how deep she went in him. So none of it was a sacrifice, really.

And as long as Honey—she'd told him her real name, finally—Christ, as long as Honey had the talent she did, as long as they had their own secret room, what the fuck did he care if he wasn't in the South of France? It sure felt like he was.

TRUMP TOWER

◇

Most mornings, when the wound was still fresh, when the excision of his body from her side was brand new, Lily would wake up and not remember Fred was dead. For the past several years she had gotten used to waking up alone, because he would be up at the crack of dawn, as he himself liked to put it, the day's chiropractor. Leaping out of bed with the boundless energy he had for accomplishment. On the telephone in the den to London, Paris, Istanbul, Japan, all the places he did business. So when she would reach for him, as she had every morning of her married life, he'd usually be gone. It was the snuggling that gave substance to marriage, the cozy proximity of two bodies and spirits familiar with each other, buttock that curved into pelvis, a design as correct and ordained as fetus in womb. There had been that between them for all the good years. So loved by her she hadn't really cared if there was the welcome intrusion of a hard-on against her back anymore.

Even when he'd changed the manner of their early mornings and been out of there too fast for her to feel him when she wakened, there was always his warm imprint on the sheets, the scent of him on the pillow, a mixture he'd had blended specially by Caswell-Massey, apothecary and toilet water maker to George Washington and some other apparently immaculate Founding Fathers. Somehow splashing himself with the same lotion made Fred feel more an American, sprung from Revolutionary soil. It was a light fragrance, subtly nutlike around the edges, with a touch of fruit, but unmistakably male. Lily would wake from her drugged, dark dreaming, pulling herself into consciousness reluctantly, reaching first for the warmth of him. Then, like a hurt animal sniffing out its own, she would struggle to pick up his aroma. Not smelling it, she would think he was out of town, try to remember what trip he was on. Then she would realize it was the longest one.

Fear pulled at the base of her belly, a roller coaster propelling her into wakefulness. Waves of panic would seize her, as if she were at the edge of an abyss, looking down, with nothing to stop her falling. For a moment she'd be held in midair, suspended, while a new thought manifested itself: she'd only dreamed he was dead. That was the why of the unreasoning terror. She'd had a nightmare, the kind people who were sure they had no imagination were always having, more convincing than reality itself. Fred was fine. He wasn't dead at all. She'd only dreamed it.

So reassured, she'd sit up a little against her mound of goose down pillows, while her pores opened, and relief flooded through her, and she broke out in a sweat. Then she'd see the bottles beside her bed, each of them filled with pills, for sleeping, waking, mood elevating, the prescription seesaw modern medicine provided. The truth would hit her, feeling like a literal blow, deep in her throat: It wasn't a dream. Her husband was dead.

She lay there without even the strength to get out of bed. Considered letting go completely, falling over the edge. Madness held out dark arms for her now, attractive as the latest breed of movie Dracula, an enveloping cloak that would hide her before fangs sucked her dry. She tiptoed on the brink of it daily, flirting with insanity, letting it go down on her, masturbating joylessly, searing her thighs with the metal hand vibrator she'd once used to ease the pressure on Fred's skull when he had his headaches. Life was an ache for her now. The only way she could even get her motor going, remind herself that she still existed, was orgasm. But she didn't really want it. She would grit her teeth, try to get it over with, dully raging for release. Finally release would come so faint and fluttering it didn't really bring relief. And so she would get out of bed.

Guilt played as deep a role as despair. Maybe if she had been more, he wouldn't have gotten mixed up with Miranda. Perhaps if she'd put her finger in his sphincter he would have stayed contented in their bed. Who was she to think what was disgusting, she whose heart only started to beat these grim, mournful mornings when she acted like a woman in some European movie.

She did not believe in an afterlife, so when religious well-wishers appeared at her bedside and tried to console her by telling her Fred was now in a better place, she threw them out of the apartment. For some reason she thought Lou Salerno was one of those.

Obviously he had given his ID to the doorman, the elevator man, her own personal maid. Clearly he had some calling to be there that had moved him past all of them. But even as he introduced himself to her as a detective, she failed to hear what he said and saw him as some kind of priest, some minister, some well-intentioned sales rep of a bright Hereafter. He had a nice face, webbed as it looked from the pressure against her eyes, the ice she'd been holding over them to take down the swelling. That was the worst part of waking. For a moment she'd think she was all right, that the grieving, acknowledged now, was under control and she'd be able to go on. And then the heaving would start, great deep sobs that came from a place she didn't even know was in her, a pit of separation and loss, abandonment, all the people who'd never loved her, even a sewing teacher she'd had in the eighth grade who thought she was clumsy with her fingers out of choice.

"Forgive me," she said to Lou, pressing the cold pack against her eyes. Her maid brought it to her first thing in the morning, with grapefruit and a rose in a bud vase on a tray. A little Mardi Gras number the pack looked like, light blue plastic, shaped to fit just over the eyes like a sleep mask, kept in the freezer all night, delivered with breakfast. She lay back against the pillows and felt it defrosting, lifting it to look at this man, an interested expression on his big-featured face as he hovered, uncomfortable, close to the door. "I wasn't expecting anyone."

"I can come back later if you want a chance to get dressed," Lou said.

"What for?"

"Well, I have a few questions."

"I mean why would I want to get dressed? Where do I have to go?"

"I'm sorry to intrude on your grief," Lou said.

"Is that what it is?" Lily sat up on one elbow, caught a glimpse of herself in the mirror on the sliding glass door fronting the closet next to the bed, the one Fred started looking in when they made love. He'd been boyish about it, sneaky really, narrowing his eyes as though in ecstasy, stealing little glances out of the corners until she finally told him not to be afraid to watch straight out. Sexual innovation was something that came late to them, because it never occurred to her that he needed it till the business started with Miranda. She'd rushed to have the mirrors installed, bought black lingerie, studded the room with soft lights, and told him to go ahead and watch. "Can you see?" he'd whispered, naughtily transfixed, "Can you see it going in and out?" "Yes," she'd answered, even though she couldn't, because that was part of it; she understood that, his need to think she was growing kinky along with him instead of just older. In truth what excited her was that he was excited again, that her resourcefulness had reasserted itself and she wasn't just good for centerpieces. But it hadn't been enough to keep him alive. And now what she saw in the mirror, rather than uplifted legs and the half-closed eyes of a man entranced with the thrusting of his own swollen penis, was a woman with a bloated face and a very red nose.

"Would you like me to come back later?" Lou asked.

"What church are you from?"

"LAPD," he said. "Homicide."

"Ah," she said. "A new denomination. Like devil worship, I guess."

Lou looked at her carefully, trying to figure if she was kidding. "Sacrificing starlets by the light of the full moon," he said in an attempt at joviality.

"Well, you're a little late. Our starlet has already been sacrificed." She sat up and drew her blue wrapper around her shoulders, one of the robes that the charity bunch had sent her for the comeback from her reported breakdown.

"Did you know about your husband's affair with Miranda?"

"I'm not blind."

"Did he have a lot of affairs?"

"No. She was the only one."

"You sure about that? I mean, Masters moved around a lot, didn't he?"

"He moved around, yes."

"Spent a lot of time in L.A.?"

"Some time, yes. Not a lot of time."

"You ever hear of a woman named Connie Garrett?"

"No."

"Didn't she call him here?"

"Not that I know of. Who is she?"

"Isn't anymore. But some of her long-distance calls were to your husband. A few to his office, some here to your apartment. He never mentioned her?"

"No."

"So, in fact, he might have been seeing more women than you know?"

"Fred was too busy. The wonder was he even had time for Miranda."

"You sure he was as busy with business as you think? Maybe business was a cover-up, so he could fool around."

"It was very extensive for a cover-up, Mr. . . ."

"Salerno. Lou Salerno."

"Over four thousand employees, seventeen major companies. I mean, Miranda was beautiful, but it seems a little much to go to all that trouble just to cover up."

"You ever confront him about the affair?"

"Confrontation isn't my style."

"What proof did you have that it was going on?"

"I didn't need proof. I knew. Everybody knew."

"That must have made you pretty mad."

"What are you getting at?"

"Didn't you want him to stop?"

"Of course I did."

"So how come you didn't try to get him to stop?"

"I tried in my own way," Lily said, and sighing, looked at the mirror.

"But you never actually hit him with it, told him to stop. Tried to do anything to force him to stop?"

"No." She took the ice pack completely away from her face now, dried around her eyes with a linen napkin, tried to focus more clearly on this man, understand what he was getting at.

Lou, in turn, studied Lily Masters, x-rayed her, looking for deceit, revenge, finding neither. He'd already checked her bank accounts to see if there were any large withdrawals, either at the time of the Connie Garrett death or the death of Miranda and Masters. Some big sum paid to hired assassins to wipe out first the West Coast mistress, then the New York mistress and husband both. But there'd been no evidence of any such withdrawal, no stocks sold as far as he could find out, no jewelry unloaded. And no sign in Lily of the kind of calculating, angry woman who could follow such a path. She seemed more shattered than vengeful.

He was, by his own fair appraisal, just another human being. That was all a detective was. Sometimes a case would be like a novel, which, because of his friend on the *Book Review*, he sometimes tried to raise to Lit-e-ra-ture. You got into a crime scene and had to make a story out of it. Not just pick up innuendos and rumors, but try to nail facts. It took two items to make one fact. So far all he had was a .22 bullet in two women's right eyes and a couple of phone calls maybe linking the deaths. And a knot in his gut that said hit men and murder.

"Who were your husband's business associates?" Salerno asked.

"He had a lot of them."

"All in the newspaper business?"

"Fred was spreading out," Lily said. "Business was a game to him, and he was trying to cover the whole board. His attorney can tell you these things better than I can. Who his friends were. His business friends I mean."

Lou could feel her torpor, the sadness slowing her words, giving them a slightly drugged tempo. Although, looking at the bottles by her bedside, he wondered if sadness was all of it. In spite of the pity he felt for this woman—not just because of her pain, but because there was something so honest about her—he wished he could goose her into talking faster, spitting out the information that would make things clearer for him. He was, after all, just a nine-to-five guy, and there were answers you had to have, if only to give to your superiors when they asked you what the hell was taking so long, what was keeping you in New York, using up all the money?

The maid came to the doorway. "Mr. Holt is here, Mrs. Masters."

"Oh, I'm not up to it," Lily said. "Ask him to forgive me, but . . ."

"Forgive my buns," the young man said, and pressed in from behind her, carrying a plastic footbath. "If you think I'm going to let you lie there and rot, you're crazy." He maneuvered toward the bed, not even seeming to see Lou, caught completely in his act of balancing the sudsy water.

Lately Lou had begun to feel a whole lot more compassion for them. Sometimes, passing the Mother Lode, a bar in West Hollywood where gays stood hungering in their tank tops, he would be moved to terrible pity, feeling how afraid they must all be, how powerless to stop, how terrifyingly lonely. He understood how strong a drive sex was—but wondered what it felt like to take a chance on dying for it. How could there be a need so deep you could risk intimacy with strangers knowing it might be lethal?

"Come, come," the young man said, and set the footbath on the floor by the side of her bed. "It's time these little piggies went to market."

The mask slipped from her eyes. "Detective Salerno, Steve Holt, my hairdresser."

"Remodeler to the stars," Holt said, and reached to shake Lou's hand, wiping some of the suds on his jeans, offering a dry palm.

At least Lou hoped it was dry, with no sweat on it. No one was that sure, really, about the nature of the virus, and though Lou knew it was spread through semen and blood, how could you be sure it wasn't in their sweat or their saliva? What if some faggot waiter didn't like the way you acted to him and spit in your food?

"I love your haircut," Holt said. "Where did you get it cut, Chino?"

"A little barber in Pasadena," Lou said.

"Oh, I know the one. He's married to the little old lady in sneakers who drives all those secondhand cars. Well, give him my compliments. It really shows off your skull." His attention moved back to Lily. "Up, up, my flower. Let us seize sadness by the roots." His fingers separated the strands of her hair near the crown of her head. "A little golden brown, a little brownish gold, and life will be good as new."

Lily gave a faint chuckle.

"Well, it's true, pussycat," Holt said, and lifting her chin, looked into her swollen eyes. "It won't be the same, but it will *be*. That's what life is about. Win some, lose more. But you continue."

Slowly, Lily eased herself into a sitting position, lifted the bottom of her wrapper and set her feet in the warm, sudsy water. "Good girl," Holt said, and turned to Lou. "Toesies are not my usual line. Pedicures." He made a face. "We are not into *feet*. But we can't have her turning into Howard Hughes. Curlicues, for God's sake. Did you see the cartoons of those toenails? Well, it's just not going to happen to my Lily."

"What would I do without you?" she said.

"Were there any other people doing business with Fred his attorney might not know about?" Lou asked, anxious to get out of there. The young hairdresser had launched into a Carol Channing impression, singing "Hello, Lily" in place of "Hello, Dolly," and the truth was, Lou could not help admitting, he did it rather well, strutting his five feet eight as though it were six feet of showgirl, telling Lily how nice it was to have her back where she belonged. He was, Lou noted, sort of funny and talented, probably what rich people meant when they said someone was "amusing." Still, Lou was uncomfortable, and needed to cut the visit short if there wasn't any more information to be gotten out of it.

"Bunyan Reis, the painter," Lily said. "He kept calling

after Fred died. But I couldn't talk to him. I couldn't talk to anybody.'' Tears started down her cheeks again.

"Now stop that!" Holt said, as Carol Channing. "Let's not dwell on the past. Let's get those little toes ready for a party.''

"Oh, I couldn't," Lily said.

"Of course you could, and you can, and you will! Bunyan's giving a party downstairs in the lobby next week just to make it easy for you. The most coveted invitation in town, if you don't count Elizabeth Taylor's next two weddings.''

"I just want to stay in bed," Lily said.

"With these toes? Are you kidding? I know thirty women who would kill for these feet. It's a sin to have them out of commission. These toes should be dancing!''

"I'll be back," Lou said. "Thank you for your time.'' He started out the door, into the hallway, the hairdresser rushing after him.

"Listen," Holt said. "Sweetheart. Fuzz, darling. Can't you stay out of her hair, if you'll forgive the pun? The woman is obviously suffering. The less she has reminding her of the past, the better off she'll be. We've got to think about *her* now. We have to save her, yes? Everyone must do everything they can.''

"You have your job, I have mine," Lou said.

"Mine is not a job, it's a calling," the hairdresser said, as Lou went out the door.

When Holt got back to Lily's room, she was in tears again. "Now you've got to stop." Holt said.

"I can't even look at his closet," Lily said. "I was wandering around last night, and I went in his bathroom. And seeing all his things . . . his toothbrushes, his shaving lotion . . . the suit he was going to wear that last night to dinner, hanging up on the shower rod like he wasn't even really gone . . . I nearly died. I ran out of there and closed the door.''

"You should call Goodwill and have them pick up all his things.''

"I can't have strangers in the apartment. As it is, I can hardly stand friends. You're the only one. The only one who makes it easier."

"I'm going to come and do your hair on Thursday, and take you with us to the party. I'm going with Sylvia Kranet. And you're coming along."

"I can't. I can't go anywhere."

"All right." He sat on the bed beside her and put his arms around her, tentatively, fraily, like a child. "Maybe it is too soon. Though why you should mourn for that unfaithful shit is beyond me."

"Don't call him that. It wasn't his fault. She was so beautiful."

"Really." Tears started forming in his own eyes. Sometimes, late at night, he would find himself weeping for Miranda. And for himself, too, he supposed. Because his only measure of greatness was his art, such as it was, the only reflection of his talent the heads of his customers. And the best of them, hairwise, was gone. So all he could be was mediocre, style-wise. And he wondered what it all meant, life-wise.

Bunyan reckoned the perfect place for the party was the lobby of Trump Tower, with heavy security, so the police would feel sort of at home. The motif was, NEW YORK'S FINEST MEET NEW YORK'S FINEST, black tie optional, uniforms optional, it said in the lower right-hand corner. Raised lettering on the best white stock, at discount since the printer himself was promised an invitation. Bunyan had his friend at the precinct, his spy, figure out what would be the best night of the week, the evening police would be most likely to attend and scheduled it for that evening, after checking with Donald Trump that the place was available, naturally inviting Donald, too.

The party was being catered by Dino De Laurentiis' Food-show, which Bunyan himself had been overheard knocking while buying deli at Zabar's. But it was right downstairs on the garden level, a gorgeous decadence of marble and plants and beveled glass and brass, providing the perfect party atmosphere, along with steps people could throw each other down if the thing became political. And Bunyan was fond of Dino. So why not give him the business? Even though he doubted Dino would appreciate it. The party looked to be that magic combination of good food, drink, and luminaries that even luminaries were hard put to turn down, a taste of celebrity even in the eats. Bunyan lamented he would have to pay standard prices for them, Dino being unwilling to *hondle* unless it was over a movie.

The cost of the party was something Bunyan could not begin to think about. He had bought a rolltop desk at auction the previous Saturday, stuffed its upper portals with all his unpaid bills, computer printouts of his credits and debits and bank balances, the reports that Jeffrey had sent him monthly that he'd always ignored. It made him physically ill now to even try to look at those things. He'd rolled the top shut on his accumulated financial garbage, closed it like he was hiding a body in it. After that, he didn't go into the room where the desk was except to dump new bills in it, like recovered parts of a dismembered corpse.

Bunyan was not poor. He couldn't look for the bottom line of the last computer printout he'd received before Jeffrey's bypass to establish what exactly he did have—but he knew whatever it was, it was more than most people had. Friends collected his work to show they could afford it. His price, when he could finish something, was high. But Christ, the expenses. The investments. The gambles he'd made not even knowing what the risks were, or, really, what the deal was, because he'd had so much trust in Jeffrey. A trust as deep as his fear of bills. He'd invited the Secretary of the Treasury to his party, in case the IRS was going to be after him. How long would they take to be on his trail? The two men who'd been to his apartment building had been back again, according to the doorman, refusing to state their names or their reason for being there. He'd had some calls from a cop named Salerno. He hadn't been able to check him out through his friend at the precinct, though Salerno had obviously checked him out, getting his unlisted number, showing up at his apartment building. Thank God the doorman had told him Bunyan wasn't at home.

After putting him off, why was Bunyan nervous? Had he done anything wrong besides not knowing how much money he had? He'd finally thought to invite him to the party. After all, it was for the police wasn't it? And Salerno was a cop, wasn't he? Or was he undercover, a spy for the IRS? Did they do those sneaky things like the CIA? Have covers? Pretend to be what they weren't while you let down your financial trousers and they checked your pockets, not to mention your pee-pee.

How could Jeffrey have been so disloyal as to die? This clerk who had saved Bunyan from reality, this pastel man with his Dickensian life of ledgers, checks and balances, double entries. Who would have thought him colorful enough to cool? Leaving Bunyan in chaos, not knowing how much he had where, or what was taken care of. Maybe he could ask the Secretary of the Treasury for the name of an accountant. That way, the man would feel some personal involvement, so when they came up with the stiletto at IRS, he would intervene and tell them not to plunge it in too coldly. Or even—dared he hope for it—forget? Pay no attention to the man behind the green curtain, as the Wizard of Oz might have said, when discovered. Pay no attention to this man who can't account for his life, since the one who knew all the details was gone, via the same funeral parlor as Fred Masters.

Bunyan had gone to Jeffrey's funeral service at Frank E. Campbell's. The coffin was closed. Jeffrey's widow said it was closed because of the toll the surgery had taken, but Bunyan was starting to suspect that maybe the reason it was closed was that Jeffrey wasn't in it. Maybe he had fled, with all his clients' money, to Lugano, meeting up with Marc Rich. Maybe he was off in the Bahamas with Robert Vesco, planning the next campaign of Richard Nixon. Maybe he was in Zug, with Alan Saxon, who'd mulcted everybody of cash for gold, and then purportedly committed suicide, cremated by his wife so fast no autopsy could be performed. Maybe they were all atop the Matterhorn, eating fondue. Getting ready to buy their own country—Transylvania, probably, where nobody would notice the supposedly dead still walking around.

It was a paranoia that continued to haunt his dreaming and caused anxiety attacks by day. His doctor had given him a little white pill called Ativan to slip beneath his tongue when it threatened to overwhelm him, but Bunyan knew the only real medicine was giving a party. For, as in the ancient Spanish maxim that living well was the best revenge, giving a party, it seemed to Bunyan, was better.

Especially when Gordon Grayson wasn't invited. Bunyan knew that Gordon had read about it, had petitioned common friends for an invitation. He tried not to be too gleeful when he told them no. At the top of the invitational list were Bunyan's favorite columnists, so they'd write it up, as they wrote about everything Bunyan did, with the special glow those who didn't really need publicity seemed to give off for journalists. A glow translated into newsprint, feeding the fuel of Gordon's envy. Gordon Grayson: first to the divorces of Gloria Stanley, first to the drowning of Robin McKay. Well, at least he wouldn't be first to New York's Finest, after this evening. The police would be in Bunyan's pocket after the party. His tuxedo pocket. That was a nice touch. Coming in his formal pearl gray, even though black tie was optional.

Everyone notable had been invited. In all of New York, only Jackie sent her regrets. Only Tia, that Trojan clotheshorse, was out of the country. The evening of the party twilighted clear, the lights of the city already feverishly bright, no mists or clouds or haze softening them into impressionism, the gentled-down shimmer of the paintbrush. New York was flat-out incandescent, Disneyland for the driven.

He walked into the glistening, glass-enclosed lobby of the Trump Tower, its rose marble rising like Venetian palaces over elegant entryways burnished with brass. To the rear of the lower lobby, already bustling with a built-in air of festivity, Bunyan's specially hired security guards were checking out the credentials of the food crew, to make sure ingenious party crashers weren't getting in carrying trays. Bars were set up on either side of the lobby and at the bottom of the polished staircase. The escalators had been halted with the closing of the shops at the end of the regular business day so the party could take place on the ground floor and the garden level one flight below. On two stories. Symbolically as good as a conversation taking place on many levels. It was all so Samuel Beckett in sequins, didn't you know, symbolism on a splashy scale. As Bunyan had learned when he went on the retreat to mollify John Lennon, the material world was an illusion. But what a convincing illusion it was, in this glittering, glass-enclosed, rose-red marble lobby. Trump Tower. Even the name was perfect. Restoration comedy correct. He pictured a Divine Bridge game. "I lead with a Heart," says God. "I Trump," says Donald.

Guests were starting to arrive, droves of them, obviously eager to enjoy what was already the party of the year. To his own pique, he had been forced to invite the Sheikh Takesh Al-Miassi and his little Chocolate Baby, since a lunch had no longer been sufficient for an exchange of information once they'd heard about the party. The sheikh still hadn't told him what it was that he knew about Fred Masters and Miranda, but he had not been so anxious to find out. Besides, if he was honest with himself, which he had to be inside his own head, they were really an addition, in their eccentric way, the emperor and his little nightingale, whom he hovered over as they entered, beaming with sure pride that she was best, although fashioned from brass.

Next through the big glass doors, to Bunyan's delight, came Dwight Efram Jonah, truly a heartening sign. If the Secretary of the newly minted cabinet post of Science and Technology came, that meant the party had significance in Washington, even though the president and Nancy regretted. So the Secretary of Treasury might indeed be coming, and Bunyan could ask for a good CPA, maybe even a cousin. And his troubles would be over. Nearly every one of Bunyan's close friends had a business manager or accountant they highly recommended. But just getting together with any accountant would not do. To begin with, Bunyan would have to explain things to them, and he couldn't.

Bunyan pushed through the blossoming crowd to personally greet Jonah, smiling at well-wishers, nodding at columnists, throwing kisses as he moved. Government figures were key to an important party, lending an air of serious business to the frivolity, as they did to Washington, in between receptions. Clearly the most attractive of the presidential appointees, Jonah was tall, athletic, slender, barrel chested; his hair the reassuring salt and pepper Americans took as hard evidence of maturity, giving to the nuclear buildup the same air of sex and dignity Kenny Rogers gave to country pop.

"Mr. Secretary," Bunyan greeted him warmly. "How flattering that you would come all the way from Washington."

"Well, I'm flattered that you would invite me," Jonah said, little buds of magnolia still clinging to the branches of his diction. He was dressed in the standard government style of the District: dark suit, white shirt, striped tie. The back of his jacket was deeply wrinkled, like some Dark Badge of Courage—the sign of the traveler, the mover and shaker commuter.

Bunyan was loath to ask him directly whether the Secretary of Treasury was coming. All cabinet members, he supposed, were intimates, hanging out in the same locker room, pals of the same Fellow. But rather than seem eager and transfer his panic to the department where it didn't belong (though of course in the event of a nuclear war the IRS wouldn't come after him), Bunyan led Jonah to the bar.

He seemed pleased to see Claire Avery, the television journalist. She looked bright and alert, intelligence radiating from her eyes where most pretty women showed only irises, her surprising breasts peeking naughtily from the closing of her starkly man-tailored suit. Bunyan could feel a sudden electric attention in the man beside him. He guided their steps to where she stood, light brown hair curling around her face like curiosity.

Oh, it made Bunyan feel so much better about America, didn't you know, that the powerful had adolescent chinks. Even the man with his arm around the shoulders of the man with his hand on the button could act schoolboyish in the presence of a pretty woman. Not that she was just a pretty woman: it was her media celebrity that gave Claire her real potency. Government people, Bunyan had come to observe, were giddy in the presence of stars; witness Washington's falling to its knees when Gloria Stanley moved there. The business of politics had finally come down to the business of Show what with the ascendancy of Reagan, who, truth to tell, hadn't been anywhere near the star Gloria was.

Bunyan felt absolutely world-shaking, introducing this nuclear genius to the woman with the largest rating on the television news. "Secretary Jonah, may I present Claire Avery."

"We've met," she said eagerly, holding out a well-manicured hand, pinky decorated with her college ring, its motto carved out in Latin. "I'm a friend of Hap Mitchel's."

"Oh you don't have to remind me, lovely lady. Well I remember."

It startled Bunyan that Claire would give anyone else for a credential since the world knew who she was. It was the first and only indication he had ever perceived in her of self-consciousness. He was touched because he hadn't suspected there was any insecurity in her, and it pleased him that he was wrong.

"Well, I know I've left the two of you in the best possible hands. Please excuse me," he said, and wandered off toward the bar opposite. Suddenly he was caught in a pocket of spun cotton, the security men of the Sheikh Takesh Al-Miassi having formed a burnoosed wedge around him. " 'Toto,' " he said. " 'I have the feeling we're not in Kansas anymore.' "

"Pornography," the sheikh sort of whispered, his full lips pursed close to Bunyan's face.

"I beg your pardon?"

"The deaths. There was pornography involved. Fred Masters and Miranda."

"How do you know?"

"Someone called me and offered to sell it to me. Some writings, highly erotic, she said. That would have reverberations in high councils and chambers."

"That does sound sexy," Bunyan said. "I've always hoped to have my chambers reverberate."

"You want information," the sheikh said. "I told you I would give it to you. We are most grateful for the invitation to this glorious party. We trust you will let us reciprocate in kind."

"So are you getting hold of it? Will you show it to me?"

"Chanson and I collect only Greco-Roman art," the sheikh said. "We are not excited by modern erotica."

"I could tell that by her outfit," Bunyan said, smiling to take the sting from the words. But if Takesh had felt the prick he did not show it. The security men salaamed and moved away.

"I know," said Louise Felder behind Bunyan. "It's the road company of *The Desert Song*. Or is it the musical version of *Lawrence of Arabia*?"

He turned and hugged her. "I love you for coming."

"I love everyone for coming," she said. "Did you see Chanson's video? She moves like Michael Jackson, cut off at the knees."

"Don't be unkind."

"Why not? It's why you love me."

"I love you because you are steadfast. Because you knew how important it was to me that you be here. So you're here."

"Rick Flinders is pissed. I was just in the middle of closing his deal. He said if I left L.A. he'd fire me. I told him to go fuck himself."

"That would give him herpes," Bunyan said.

Behind her, Lou Salerno, face strained with concentration, studied the conversation around him with the fixity of a graduate student. Bunyan saw him staring, perceived the intensity with which he listened.

"Do I know you?"

"Lou Salerno."

"I thought you were a novelist from how hard you were eavesdropping. This is Louise Felder, the famous agent. Lou Salerno, the famous detective."

"I know who Miss Felder is. I'm from L.A."

"What brings you to New York?" Louise asked.

"Murder."

"Oh, liveliness!" Bunyan said, and clapped his blunt little fingers together. "Then you think so, too."

In a group by the bar clustered the fashion people, the men's designers. Most of them were handsome, their bodies kept in shape to look good in their own blazers, which several were wearing, their signatures on their breasts, double woven in gold and colored threads. They stood like tall, silver-haired birds, plumes on their pockets. All around them people crowded in, their faces lined with what poets might describe as character, but which Bunyan marked as the strains of upward mobility.

Deep in conversation with them was Luke Benjamin, the theatrical director, looking very relaxed, having been personally extolled twice in the past six weeks by the toughest critic in the history of the *New York Times*. He was asking their advice on how to dress his staff at the Santa Barbara ranch where he planned his annual auction of Arabian horses. Luke was wearing black tie, which he rarely sported even for his own openings, so Bunyan felt affectionate toward him, even though he was planning this fuss over horseflesh. It offended Bunyan's artist heart that animals could bring such prices, millions on millions, all the more galling because they were referred to as "art." Genetic Art, according to their multimillionaire owners. Art passed on through the genes. A market sustained at outrageous levels simply because people were willing to pay those prices for *horses*. Bunyan would have been deeply outraged at the whole idea of the auction had he not himself been planning to go. He just adored Santa Barbara. All those descendants of the nation's finest families, making you so glad you came from nothing.

"You think Miranda was murdered?" Louise asked Salerno.

"Detectives are not paid to think. We're paid to put facts together. That's what I'm trying to do."

For a minute Bunyan was tempted to tell him about what Sheikh Tackey had said. But there was no point in helping the police, certainly not this interloper from the West Coast. It was his own delicious undercover project, private and exciting, more arousing than frottage, finding out the truth about Masters and Miranda. Besides, if he was going to share his theories with anyone it would be the host of the "Tonight Show."

What a setting! What a night! he could not help thinking, his wily imagination popping back and forth from group to group, concentration darting from murder to hors d'oeuvres. To the right of the bar the present mayor chatted with a handsome former mayor, while two uniformed policemen stood self-consciously by. What a spectacular place he had chosen, Trump Tower, with its red marble and fountains, water dripping down the walls. Plants to the left of them, Bucellati to the right of them. Into the valley of Wealth rode the Four Hundred.

But studying the expression on the faces of the police, Bunyan wondered if he'd made a mistake with his choice of place. He'd had decorations of his own brought in, besides the great bouquets of flowers carved from cabbages and turnips and lettuce and radishes, an ingenious touch that DDL provided. There were huge blowups of famous movies about cops, from *Rogue Cop*, Bunyan's favorite Robert Taylor movie, to Paul Newman in *Fort Apache, The Bronx*, mounted on poster boards and set around the lobby. The posters were Bunyan's attempt to make his police guests feel as glamorous as his celebrity guests. But all it did, really, he saw now, was point out to the police how very unlike Paul Newman they were.

That didn't seem to bother Lou Salerno. "Mr. Reis," Lou said politely. "I realize this is neither the place nor the time . . ."

"Neither the place nor the time?" Bunyan said. "How lyrical. You sure you're a cop?"

"I have some questions."

"Excuse me," said Louise, and moved away.

"If you can't take the heat, run away from the policeman," Bunyan said. "Coward."

"Lily Masters said you kept calling her husband . . ."

"Oh, *that*," said Bunyan.

"Yes, *that*," said Lou. "What was *that*?"

"My business manager got me into some deal with Fred Masters. Some microchip thing. He was trying to take over a company, and Jeffrey put me in with him."

"Can I talk to Jeffrey?"

"Not unless you know a good medium."

"He's dead?"

"Natural causes," said Bunyan. "At least that's the story they gave out. Anyway, it was all perfectly innocent. Business, don't you know. I wasn't really involved. I mean, I was involved, but I wasn't involved. Jeffrey did all my business thinking for me. I'm an artist. I have no left brain. Or right brain, whichever it is that's logic, that's the hemisphere God left out of me and gave to Jeffrey."

"What was the name of the company?"

"Oh, Christ, I don't know. I have no head for names either. I'm an artist. And a party giver. Please excuse me." He was feeling faint suddenly, panic thudding onto him like a dropped brick. How dare they all die on him, Fred and then Jeffrey. How dare people leave him like that, like his parents had done, with no consideration, no caring about what was to become of him. What was to become of him? Oh, God, what was it doing right in the midst of all this sophistication, that self-pitying, fairy-tale phrase? He was the man of the hour, the decade maybe, giving the party of the year. Where was this little-boy anguish coming from?

Looking back over his shoulder, he could see Lou

Salerno was perfectly at ease, feeling right at home, scooping a giant chanterelle mushroom from a tray a waiter was passing. Five dollars a fungus, Bunyan noted, but what did Salerno care. It was only money, or as Dino would put it, soldi.

"Sweetie," said Hillary Dobson, the slender, blonde wife of Stan Dobson, the literary agent. "You look absolutely pale."

"I'm a pale person," Bunyan said. "Albino is my natural color."

"But you look pale for you," Hillary said. "You look pale even for Andy Warhol."

"You need a drink," said Stan Dobson. "What are you drinking?"

"Hemlock," said Bunyan. "Weren't you in on that Fred Masters takeover try? Jeffrey told me he put you in it, too."

"Yes," Stan said. "I was in. What's the problem?"

"I don't know what's happened to the investment," Bunyan said. "Is it deader than Freddie?"

"The company's sound," said Dobson. "The stock is still high. The takeover didn't happen, but we have our shares, and they're worth plenty. There's no technology without computer chips. It's better than gold."

"That's what John DeLorean said about the cocaine, and look what happened to him."

"Nothing happened to him," said Hillary.

"Why don't you call my broker if you're worried?" Stan said, and suddenly catching sight of the tall man at the other side of the bar, touched Bunyan's arm. "Is that Dwight Efram Jonah?"

"That's who it is."

"An interesting man," said Stan Dobson. "I bet his life would make a fascinating book. The public can't get enough of business since Lee Iacocca," he said. "I hope he's had some ups and downs." He headed toward the secretary.

It was clearly a successful party, but Bunyan felt anxious and depressed. Where was the Secretary of the Treasury? As a woman in love, surrounded by men, still hungered for the beloved, so Bunyan's antenna picked up the fact that Treasury was missing. Everyone else had shown up. In the midst of a group of young police officers, Chanson D'Amour seemed to be casting some kind of spell, aided by what looked like several hundred yards of lavender tulle, a pastel web to weave them into. Sheikh Tackey stood close by, beaming proprietarily, his bodyguards forming a kind of arc around him. Bunyan hoped he would not confuse his invitation to the party with social acceptance. Exchange of information was all it was, an opportunity for campiness in an era when camp was a thing of the past, except for her wardrobe.

Chanson was dressed for belly dancing, as an athlete invited to a picnic would wear Nikes, assuming he might be called upon to run. Spangles shimmered from the band around her forehead. A large amethyst glittered in her navel. Around her puffed lavender tulle, thinly spun with silver. Attached to her hands were a set of bells, the Tangiers version of mariachis, Bunyan supposed. Every time she laughed, her fingers spasmed, and little bells in her palms and on her fingertips tinkled. But where was Treasury? Maybe—oh God, why did he think of it now— who Bunyan should have invited was the Attorney General. Would it go that far?

"I've had enough Rome and Venice," said Luis de Louis, the woman's designer, to the group that argued vacation spots. "Even Greece has lost its simplicity for me. Too much smog. The Acropolis is being eaten away. Where I'd like to go for my next holiday is someplace I don't have to think about splendor vanishing. Where I don't have to think about clothes. Where the women have no self-consciousness about their attire, no concept of fashion, no thoughts about their bodies."

"Queens," said the wife of the former mayor.

Bunyan threaded his way through the crowd, trying to collect himself. Lou Salerno moved in casually behind him.

"Are you shadowing me?" Bunyan said.

"Sort of."

"Well, why don't you poke around where it'll do you some good?" Bunyan said. "Why don't you find out what was in the box?"

"Box?"

"The safe deposit box Miranda Jay kept at the bank."

"How'd you know about that?"

"A friend of hers told me Miranda had a box," Bunyan lied. "And what about Stephanie?"

"Stephanie who?"

"I don't know her last name. But she was a friend of Miranda's." It made him sick that he was spewing out clues, but he had to get Salerno off his back. The big marinelike detective probably knew some of this already. Next to him now he saw Claire Avery, smiling. "Dear heart," he said, and stretched on tiptoe to kiss her, as if she were a relative on visiting day at prison. "Are you having a wonderful time?"

"A wonderful time," she said, her eyes on Lou Salerno. Behind her Stan Dobson talked contract to Jonah, told him how anxious the publishers would be to have his story.

"Who's that guy there?" Salerno asked.

"Stan Dobson."

"The literary agent?"

"You certainly have ecumenical interests for a policeman," Bunyan said.

"Excuse me." Lou eased his way through to Stan Dobson, tapping him on the shoulder, introducing himself. "My friend on the *L.A. Times Book Review* told me you're the biggest force in publishing."

"That was kind of him," Stan said, his attention focusing back on Jonah.

"You handle Joseph Wambaugh?" Salerno persisted.

"No."

"I thought you handle all the best-selling authors."

"Not that one."

"He got very rich from his police experience. A lot of men would probably think it wasn't fair, writers making millions while the police get nothing. But Wambaugh never got to be Homicide, like me. Never got to the V.I.P. murders. That's what he really wanted."

"In your opinion."

"Yeah, sure. In my opinion."

"Are you working on the Masters case?" Claire asked him.

"Sort of."

"Then what was in the box?" Bunyan asked. As long as he couldn't get rid of this man, he might as well garner some information.

"It was empty. Her lawyer got there first."

"What's his name?" Dobson asked.

"Phillip Slagle. He said it was already empty when he opened it."

"You can believe him," said Dobson. "He has integrity."

"In your opinion," said Salerno. "I've been thinking about writing a book."

"Really," Dobson said.

"I was on the Manson case, Sal Mineo, the Hillside Strangler, the Lennon Sisters' father. I got a lot of good stories. My friend at the *Times* said I ought to write a book. You be interested in handling it?"

"I'm sorry," Stan Dobson said. "But I have too many clients. I must husband my time."

Claire Avery dropped back and smiled at no one in particular, flushed with the information she'd picked up. But she still felt a little embarrassed at how the evening had started. Bunyan had not been the only one surprised when she cited her friendship with Hap Mitchel to the secretary. Claire herself had been stunned at the words falling out of her mouth. She and Hap had spent most of their time at the Paris Air Show two years before ducking out of everyone's way, especially Jonah's. Sitting in different parts of the plane going over on the Concorde, taking separate cabs to their unchic hotel. Playing their little game all through Paris, hanging out at opposite ends of rooms during the official cocktail parties of Hughes and Grumman and MercerCorp. Imagining that none of the aerospace and government people present, there to parade their weapons for sale as St. Laurent showed his designs, would know they were lovers, with Paris their greatest rendezvous. Only once had anyone caught them together, in an unlikely neighborhood restaurant. Fortunately, their hands weren't all over each other, the way it usually was between them, so they both held the hope that Jonah might have thought they were just friends.

No one was more aware of her own celebrity than Claire was. Everyone in the country watched her on the news, saw her interview specials. So to remind Jonah that they'd already met, and that she was a friend of Hap's was demonstration of a humility not in her character. She was a tough-minded woman who saw things as they were, and as it was with her was that she was important. As high profile an independent woman as lived, and pretty in the bargain. Thirty-two years old, never married, in spite of princes and tyrants and barons with banking names who'd pursued her. The truth was the truth: She didn't need anybody. No man's arm to give her support, no man's name to lend her identity. So it boomed very deep in her, the little girl rush that had made her underwrite herself to Jonah with Hap's name. Like a letter of introduction from a sophomore. She couldn't imagine what dark cellars were part of her foundation, defining herself as relating to her man. Especially since he wasn't her man anymore. Not taking her phone calls. Not talking to her or letting her apologize. Not that she had anything to be sorry for.

No one in her life, no matter how much she thought she loved them, had ever gotten through to her, before Hap. No one had touched her as deeply as he did—she hadn't even known how deep—until she stood there like a pigeon-toed adolescent with Dwight Efram Jonah, giving him her Hap credentials. How could she not have known how much she loved him, how important a part of her life he was, that he defined her, even a little, to herself?

Still, she would not waste her time sorrowing over him. Grieving was not her style, especially when there was a news story hatching. She could smell how foul it was, the still-hidden scandal, the truth about Miranda. She could hardly wait to help pull it all together.

Across the room, Chanson D'Amour had started dancing. "What's she doing?" someone asked.

"I can't see," Bunyan said, and mounted a flat marble bench so he could look over the heads of the party goers. He held out a hand to Claire and helped her up. They could hear Chanson's bells jingling against the murmur of conversation, cutting through the high-pitched laughter, see the gawking of the young policemen.

"What do you think Stephanie knows about Miranda?" Claire asked.

"I haven't the foggiest," Bunyan said, and craned his neck. "God, I wish Chanson wasn't such a dwarf."

Passing alongside the bench that Bunyan and Claire stood on, Sylvia Kranet, her slender torso sheathed in black jersey, rattled slightly in a tunic of chain metal. "What ho!" Bunyan called. "My lady knight! Whither goest thou?"

"Home," she said, dark red fingernails clutching the arm of her escort.

"But why are you leaving? Is her body that bad?"

"She's afraid you might get raided," said the young man with her.

"By whom, you adorable thing? The police are already here."

"All the reason she should have more sense," Sylvia said, while in the distance someone yelled, "Down in front!"

The hum started building, like a chorus, a tune Bunyan could only identify as "They Don't Wear Pants in the Southern Part of France."

"Oh come on, Sylvia," Bunyan said. "Stay. How badly can she dance?"

"If there's a scandal and I'm here, the senator will be cross."

"He doesn't mind your going out with Harry Handsome here," Bunyan said, and smiled at the young man. "Why would he mind une petite scandale?"

"This is my hairdresser. Steven Holt. Bunyan Reis."

"How are you?"

"Take it off," they were shouting, the men up front, in unison now.

"Come, we must go," Sylvia said, pulling Steven by the hand. "Time is of the essence."

"Really," Holt said, and hurried away with her.

Claire Avery got down from the bench and started after them. "Now don't tell me *you're* offended," Bunyan said.

"I have to be up at dawn. Love you." She blew a kiss to Bunyan. "Thank you for a super party."

Bunyan turned sadly back to face the crowd. He absolutely hated it when people started to go home. He got down from the bench and climbed the escalator so he could better see what Chanson was doing.

She reared back her naked shoulders and shimmied against the ranks of thunderstruck police. "What a surprise," Bunyan muttered to himself. "I could have sworn they weren't real."

"Now," Claire Avery said on her television spot the next morning, "in addition to the rest of the unanswered questions about this so-called double suicide, comes the revelation that Miranda Jay had a safe deposit box. And whatever was in it—what was it? Stock in MercerCorp, Victor Lenrahan's aerospace company? A secret slush fund? Proof of a government bribe?—whatever it is is mysteriously missing. The police seem to be without clues.

"And who is Stephanie? Miranda's closest friend, who must know some, if not all, the answers. Not to mention the Secrets. Who is Stephanie, and why hasn't she come forward?"

She was off the air at eight-fifteen. It was a little early in the day for items of the Rona kind, but it was legitimate in its substance, or lack of it. It was more than anyone else had. There was that for her rationale.

Having discovered the terrible extent of her longing for Hap the night before, she ran back to her dressing room the minute she was off the air and called him at home in California. They'd agreed long before that she was never to phone him there, but all agreements were off now that she really loved him.

It was only five-twenty in California, but she didn't have to be afraid of waking him. Now that she knew how desperately she wanted him, her only real fear was losing him. Not hearing his voice. The only danger was his being alert enough to duck her call.

The last of the Good Old Boys, and she had messed with him. A breed you didn't endanger. Like eagles, so rare they had to be preserved. She was filled with regret that she had ever had him on the air. She loved him. She understood that now. Love had history in it. An evening had been empty because he wasn't there, her protector. Who would have thought she would want that?

"Yes?" His voice was heavy with sleep.

"Did I wake you?" She could picture him, close-cropped gray hair slightly matted, curly, tangled from the pressure on the pillow, the heavy fringe of gray eyelashes half-closed over bright blue eyes.

"No, as a matter of fact, I was just on my way to lunch."

She laughed.

"I asked you never to call me on this number."

"Unless it was life or death."

"You wouldn't recognize anything that basic."

"How about love? You think I would recognize love?"

"Only if it had an overnight rating."

"I'm dying," she said. "I've never been so lonely. I'm dying for you. You've got to believe me." There was a click on her line, signaling a waiting call. "I love you, Hap. Don't hang up. Are you still there?"

"I'm still here. I guess that makes me dumber than I thought."

"I'll get rid of whoever it is." She touched the button, and the line rolled over. "Yes?" she said impatiently.

"Miss Avery? This is Stephanie. Miranda's friend."

"Hold on." She pressed the button. "Hap? I'll have to

call you back." She tried not to hear his bellowing laughter as she hung up the phone.

When he got to the office, Hap told his secretary to expedite two new, unlisted phone numbers. One for his home and one for the office. For the rest of the day Claire kept calling him, and he tried not to notice the light on his phone, waiting for his secretary to get rid of her.

He was mad at himself because her voice had still moved him. He had all the externals of a contemporary corporate tough guy, an office free of frills, a mound of paperwork in front of him, a rubber plant in the corner he wasn't sure was artificial or not. The workspot of a man who was straight to the point, not easily deceived. Not one of those flowery Century City aerospace hotshots. Close to the guts of the industry, within earshot of the rivets. A president's office only because he was president. So how could he have been fooled?

Clarity had always been his best suit. It was his own choice to be near the factory, past the lines of sleek, windowed towers belonging to Hughes and Grumman and MercerCorp, near the LAX airport. He liked to go inside the hangars, watch the static testing, the real action of aerospace. Liked even better testing the planes out himself. Chance was the only thing worth taking. He knew that much. How could he be so clear about that and so confused about her?

"As soon as we get the new number," he said into the intercom, "phone everybody on my personal Rolodex and give it to them. Except Miss Avery."

"She's on the line again," the secretary said. "Says she has something urgent to tell you. Says it's a matter of life and death."

"I'm not here," he said, and disconnected.

His private number rang again. He let the secretary pick it up. How foolish he'd been to give her that number, the one the Pentagon had, the one Dwight Jonah used to call him from Science and Technology. There he sat, hesitating to pick up the receiver, when it could be a national emergency.

The intercom buzzed. "It's a Zoe Baldwin," his secretary said.

"Who?"

"*Ms*. Zoe Baldwin. An attorney. She said she was your seatmate coming back from New York."

"Get a number," Hap said. "No, wait a second. I'll take it." He picked up the receiver. "Hello, *Ms*. Baldwin, Esquire."

"You have a sexy voice. I didn't remember that part."

"I didn't remember your voice either." He tried to think what he did remember about her. Mostly her eyes, and her smell. Very fresh.

"Isn't it nice we both have one. How are you?"

"Okay," said Hap. "How are you, besides aggressive?"

"Does that bother you?"

"I don't know yet. I think I find it entertaining."

"Are you up for dinner? I thought I'd be doing some contracts tonight, but I've gotten a reprieve. I'm unexpectedly sprung. Can I buy you a veal chop?"

"I like to buy."

"Good. I'm tired of it being the woman who pays."

"But I have a dinner meeting tonight." He was surprised that he felt actually disappointed.

"How about afterward?"

"I won't be finished till nine-thirty, ten."

"I enjoy eating late. You can watch me."

"I'll leave room for dessert," Hap said.

As he was on his way out of the office, his secretary told him Claire was on the line again. "She says it's an emergency. She sounds like she's crying."

"Tell her I'm gone," he said. "I'm out of here."

He was unaccustomedly distracted during dinner, impatient for it to be over. Business as a category actually bored him. It was the real business of defense that captured him, not striking compromises or negotiating with men. When he thought about it, he realized he often preferred the company of women, something he admitted not even to them. And not just for sex. Bright women were a source of delight to him. Kate, his wife, had been the brightest girl he knew. He'd taken secret pleasure in his second daughter testing out as cleverer than his sons. Men had the edge, he understood that, so it seemed only fair for women to have hidden ammunition.

He hurried to the restaurant where he was supposed to meet Zoe, a bright little corner café in Beverly Hills, decorated in Art Deco, sharp angles and curves to the low chairs and tables. A space station for the thirties: Joan Crawford playing Sally Ride. He found himself curiously impatient to see Zoe again, wondered if she was as sharp as he remembered.

She showed up exactly at the appointed time. When she smiled he noted how white her smile was, long eyeteeth at the corners. It made her look like an innocent, but with vampire potential.

He ordered a bottle of wine for her. She offered him some. "Are you trying to seduce me?" he said.

"You only have to ask." She smiled again, wider now, banishing the grays of her clothes, shimmering from behind her drab disguise.

She ate with the gusto of his son, the football player at Stanford. It pleased him to see such an appetite in a woman. Brains and gusto. He delighted in it.

"How old are you?" she asked him, seeing him watching her.

"Why?"

"Well, I imagine you're from that era when a woman didn't give herself too quickly or easily to a man, or the man thought she was easy."

"Those standards don't apply anymore."

"Sure they do. Just because a man has been to the moon doesn't make him sophisticated. The truth is, I'm sort of a traditionalist myself, and I wish I had time to court you. But attractive men in this town are at a premium, and I've got a very heavy work load."

"You've really thought this out."

"I really think everything out. That's my curse. But you seem smart enough so I can short-circuit my doubts that you'll appreciate how unusual this is."

"I appreciate everything about you."

"Do you?"

"Especially that you think things out. I don't consider that a curse."

"I do."

"Then maybe I can free you from it."

"Can you do that? Can you break the spell?"

"I can try."

"But first you'll have to free yourself," she said. "That's the way curses work. Are there any women in aerospace?"

"Not too many."

"And probably none in positions of power."

"I don't want to get into this discussion."

"A woman should be in charge of the button. A woman wouldn't push it."

"I don't know about that. Women have less mercy than men."

"That's true."

He was surprised that she agreed with him. Even Kate in her rare moments of arguing the virtues of women was intractable about admitting their shortcomings.

"Men don't talk about other men the way women talk about other women," Zoe said. "And women in business cut each other out more cruelly than men do."

"Then why do you think they wouldn't push the button?"

"Because they give birth. They value life too much. A woman couldn't give the order that would kill millions of people. Men think in terms of territorial rights. Space. Boundaries. Women think in terms of families. Relationships." She looked at him directly. "I'd really like to go to bed with you."

"See, there's the main reason women shouldn't run the world. They can never come straight out and say what they mean."

She laughed, and touched his fingers. Little darts of electricity moved through the hairs on the tops of his hands.

"Dessert is on me," she said. "Would you object if I bought you an ice cream?"

"Not at all."

"Ice cream is for innocence," she said, taking his arm as they walked down the street to Häagen-Dazs. "Just like rosemary is for remembrance. Lean your head down, would you?"

He lowered his head and her palm pressed against the top of his hair. "That's what I wanted first," she said. "To touch that. I knew how silky it would feel, even though it looks so strict, like you do. I want to feel that all over my body. Against my face. Under my arms. Between my thighs."

"You're driving me crazy," he said.

"Good. First we have to have ice cream. That way we can pretend we've known each other a long time. That we've been through our adolescence together. All those nervous little feels in the front seats of cars. Ice cream will give us a feeling of history."

"You're adorable," he said, and stopped there on the street and brushed his hair against her cheek, under her nose, across her lips.

"I can't wait," she said, a little breathless.

There was a television on the rear wall of the ice cream parlor, and from the corner of his eyes, Hap saw Claire's face flash across the screen. He was used to being buffeted with her likeness. The network was unflagging in its promotion of her, making spot announcements, telling the viewers who she would be interviewing the following morning. This time it seemed to Hap a particular intrusion, a pushy move on her part, personally, trying to get into this evening, when he could feel himself moving just from the words and the closeness of this fresh new woman. When the heat was already in his groin and his juices were flowing in a healthier direction. When he couldn't wait to touch this new skin and breathe this new smell all the way in. When he was already getting hard just at the thought of it.

And then the announcer's words got through to his brain: "Her body was recovered from the Hudson River.

The police chief said apparently Miss Avery drove past a sign warning against proceeding further. It was raining, and visibility was poor. The car went off the bridge and landed upside down in the water. Miss Avery was strapped in a seat harness at the wheel."

"Oh, Jesus," Hap said.

Shortly after the late night news recapped the accident in greater detail, the police station in Palisades, New Jersey, received a phone call. "Did you find the papers?" the caller asked the officer on duty.

"What papers?"

"The ones Claire Avery had in her briefcase."

"Who's this calling?"

"A friend of justice. A friend of Miranda's." There was a click on the line.

Later, when the sergeant was asked to try and remember details about the caller, something to give them a clue, any kind of clue, he said he thought he could detect a New York accent. Not very pronounced, as it would have been if the person was from Brooklyn, but definitely New York. For the rest of it, though, he was vague. Because her voice was probably disguised, he said. It sounded muffled to him, as though she were speaking through a handkerchief.

WATERGATE SOUTH

◊

Their first few years together, Victor was content to abide by Miranda's wish to be in "unfashionable" settings. But the truth was, getting there was not half the fun. Victor was pressed for time. So finally Miranda agreed to move to Washington, where it would be more convenient for him.

He set her up in Watergate South. There was no stigma to the address, in spite of the brouhaha about the break-in and the resignation of Richard Nixon, which had recently taken place. The circular gray complex rose, terraced and shining, in the crisp autumnal sun, one of the best apartment buildings in the district. It was a haven for diplomats, if they were rich enough, congressmen if independently wealthy or corrupt enough, international businessmen, and women whose careers were sometimes ill-defined. Many of them said they were in public relations, which was sort of accurate, anyway.

Victor seldom took Miranda out, even though she was willing to be seen in public now. Eager to be seen with him, really, because it had been enough time, and he was dragging his feet about getting her her daughter. She knew it, no matter how many lawyers' letters he showed her, and in French. She figured if she pressed him to take her where people could see them together, he would negotiate for something else she would rather have, and that would be Colette.

So she begged for an outing, the two of them at the Jeffersonian, her favorite place, really. The setting where she felt most comfortable, special. It was luxuriously exotic, trimmed with red velvet hangings, filled with seductive alcoves in which luscious dinners were served on pewter plates, wine in crystal goblets. The waiters wore white gloves, as though the guests were royalty. But Victor didn't trust the owner, Hiro Takeda; for him Orientals were still Gooks. As far as he was concerned, the place, no matter how elegant and peppered with former attorney generals, several of them resigned during Nixon's time, might have been strung with foliage hiding UHI Hueys, which Victor's company had manufactured for that—still, in his opinion—Great Engagement.

Second only to his obsession with Miranda came love of

country, and Lenrahan considered it a great mistake that the U.S. had pulled out of Vietnam. He blamed the failure not so much on the unpopularity of the conflict as on the fact that you could never figure out what the little yellow bastards were going to do next, as Korea had demonstrated before it. Victor still hadn't gotten over Truman's calling MacArthur back, not giving him a chance to stamp them out, once and for all. He still got mad from time to time that MacArthur hadn't won out, as general, or as presidential candidate. That had been Victor's first political involvement, the beginning of his crusade for the perfect candidate, the one who would best express his political philosophy: Fuck 'em where they breathe.

His political credo was not so different from his sexual one, as Miranda had learned very early. But at least he had transformed her as he'd never yet been given the opportunity to groom a candidate, taking her from the willing innocent he'd found in Paris to the gifted mistress of the Great Man she thought he was. The externals were there in her apartment at Watergate: Savonerrie rugs bought at auctions she'd started attending; custom sofas, thick with pillows stuffed with kapok and down, $150.00 each, not counting the fabric.

But Miranda was lonely, filled with outrage that expressed itself in long weeping jags, distressing to him unless they were part of a game. So rather than have her start talking about her daughter again, he would blindfold her and stuff her mouth and her vagina with chocolate-covered marshmallows, and lusty little girl that she still was in that one part of her, and hungry woman in the other, she would get caught up in tasting and chewing while he was tasting and chewing her. And the danger would pass.

Momentarily. She was no longer satisfied with the lawyers' letters, so he hired private detectives to follow the little girl, to check on the parents. Anything to increase the number of reports. Small pieces of news seemed to serve to calm her a little. Detectives reported that Colette was healthy, coming along as nature intended, pretty, from the pictures they'd taken from across the street from her home.

Miranda started to write her letters, explaining why she'd given her up, telling her how much she loved her, how fervent was her hope that one day they would be reunited. She never mailed them. She would read them to Victor aloud when he got back to town, and he would tell her what good letters they were, how much they touched him. In truth, they did touch him. Not because he could understand her affection for this child she had hardly seen, but because they were so laced with longing to express herself. From the beginning of their time together, she'd written poems. As little as he understood softer yearnings, he knew when something was sweet. And that's what her poems were, with unself-conscious rhymes. The letters gave him more pause, because they mentioned names and places. Telling of Victor's activities and associates, besides their candy box content. Even though she said she was not going to send them, it bothered him that there was such a record. "You have to write her about me?" he said.

"How can I leave you out? You're as much my life as I am."

"I liked the poems better."

"Why?"

"Because they're more like this."

"Doesn't feel like poetry to me."

"That's because you're not in my fingers," he said to her.

She would sit on his lap on those tender occasions, climb into a favorite position in the chair he'd had specially designed. She was feather light on him, the warm softness of her nourishing, making him feel like a bigger man than he was, even there. He cradled her like the airy creature she was in spite of herself, her weight miraculously suspended by a variety of devices, so when he was ready, he could go at her with his mouth, without any pressure, real or implicit.

"I could do this all night," he said.

"Then do it," she would answer. And he wondered if there wasn't some anger around the edges of her words, along with the light, delicately fishy taste of her on his tongue.

At such moments he would forget about any fears he had about the public part of their lives together, lose any objections to anything she did, wanting only to satisfy her. She could only enhance his life, he was sure of that. The truth was, there was probably no activity he engaged in that a number of official sources couldn't report on in full detail, with the exception of this one. So the letters were really harmless, especially as she had no intention of mailing them. In the final analysis, it was appropriate to encourage her, asking her the minute he got back in town what letters she had written to Colette and if he could hear them. Promising her that he would see she had enough money to buy a house in the country to raise the girl in, one day. After he was gone.

Their erotic play began to have a certain desperation to it. She was anxious, especially in view of the new promises, to do anything that would please him.

So they began spending more and more time in the secret room. The locked one, where the cleaning lady wasn't allowed to go. Most of the smaller items in there had been brought from the yacht. The larger devices were custom ordered through proprietors of private clubs in London and Paris. The trick was getting them into the Watergate apartment without anyone knowing what they were. Some of it was too large for the elevator and had to be hoisted through the window, like the grand piano he had also bought her, as if that were her true virtuosity, what could be practiced on a Steinway. She spent an uncomfortable couple of hours when the latest equipment they'd ordered shed part of its brown paper wrapping only halfway up to her floor, and hung there partially exposed while she fretted that someone might look out a window. But fortunately, few in Washington paid attention to scenery, no matter how beautiful or bizarre it was, their attention focused solely on politics.

She had lost the sense of duality she'd felt at the beginning of their relationship, the unspoken discomfort

almost equal to her willingness to learn, her eagerness to
please him. With the bait of her daughter being dangled in
front of her, there was nothing she wouldn't do to satisfy
him. He was all she'd known of generosity and paternal
warmth, except for Harry Bell. Besides, it excited her,
seeing what power she had over him. Power, in her
experience and vocabulary, had always been in other people's hands. That she found herself so much in charge,
even while he taught her what the moves were, made her a
little drunk with herself.

Drunk, she threw herself into their scenes with the same
gusto with which she ate, the same hot, excited stretch she
gave to her bubble baths, the same exhilaration she took
from walks in the park. Life was all of a piece to Miranda,
a feast to be indulged in. And if there were certain dishes
that gave her pause because they might burn her tongue,
well, it was just like being blindfolded and fearing the
worst, like Victor was always teasing her, that what was
about to go into her mouth was sheep's eyes, and having it
turn out to be chocolate-covered marshmallows.

And he would come with a frenzy somewhere between
death and deliverance, dying to the world with her hand on
his cock, her mouth on his, her thighs around him, her
words coiling in his ears. And he would moan and scream
and say that was how he wanted to go, like that, with his
energy feeding into her, crucified by the balls with her
nails. And he would make joyful lament that in all the
world there was only one Miranda, while men passed
through their lives and their peckers without ever finding
out what either was for.

"Christ," he'd say, "I feel so sorry for Dwight. You
could blow his head off."

"I'm only interested in your head," she whispered to
him, because it was over and there was no need to
humiliate him anymore, make him feel bad about himself.
All right to let him know he was good enough for her. All
she wanted. Because it had passed out of her ken, romantic longing. The adolescent was dead forever, and all she
wanted was her chops satisfied, and her child.

Melissa Mae August was curious about their relation-ship. "The dude is three times your age," Melissa Mae said over softshell crabs at Sans Souci. All around the room were staff from the Ford White House, who were keeping the restaurant in favor, making the transition from Nixon painless, at least for the maitre d'.

There was an elegance to the decor that matched its patronage: the soft dark green of the walls, the antique bronze fixtures, the portable white telephone with aerial before there were portable telephones in any other part of the country, so if Kissinger came in, which he did, and often, he wouldn't be inconvenienced and have to get up for his calls. In case there was a crisis, which there was, and often. But not so often as in the last part of the Nixon administration. Melissa Mae told Miranda she didn't feel nervous about what would happen to the country, since Kissinger was really president.

Witty words about politics made no real impression on Miranda. Politics seemed a. game to her, as it apparently did to any number of politicians, and the dictionary, which used it as an example of a plural noun construed as a singular e.g.: *politics is a game*. Miranda had begun spending a great deal of time with the dictionary, studying it as other dreamers did the stars, making sure her spelling in the notes to Colette was letter perfect, since it was to be the child's only exposure to English and she didn't want her to think that her mother was uneducated or lame. At moments of excruciating loneliness, when Victor wasn't in town, and Melissa Mae wasn't in her apartment right down the hall, and there was nothing on TV that absorbed her energetic attention, Miranda would consult the book. *The Random House Dictionary of the English Language* sat on the big lectern Victor had bought, to add the hint of the mind, of serious thinking to the lush atmosphere, white and green and red chintz pillows, mirrored sideboard, Steinway. Miranda would close her eyes and lift a great sheaf of the onionskin thin pages and let them fall as they might, placing her finger, eyes still closed, on a word. She would take the word for her counsel, what to do with her day, her life, her imagination, casting the pages as ancient Vikings did their runes. *Self-mastery* came up more than once. *Sense*, defined: feelings or perception produced through organs, *touch*, *taste*, etc., 2/sanity.

Melissa Mae was a genuinely educated woman, a Harvard MBA who'd given up her investment career to "hostess" for Hiro Takeda. The quotation marks were her own. When she drank too much, which she usually did late at night, she would call herself his bimbo, breaking glasses, flinging things into the fireplace, which was seldom lit because she had a fear of setting herself on fire. She was a superstitious woman, for all of her education, and when she was haunted, as she was in her dreaming, she would believe herself condemned to burn in hell. The way she felt, that could just have meant Washington.

But lunchtimes she was chipper, bright, her big breasts flattened to fit into stylish clothes, elegantly cut, high-fashion ensembles she wore only when she wasn't with Hiro. It was her roundness he loved, the feminine lines of her body, not voguish ensembles. Oriental men, she explained to Miranda, were tyrants with their women, expecting to be obeyed. In Korea they made wives eat human excrement for talking back to their husbands.

"But I suppose I shouldn't say that while we're having lunch," she said now to Miranda.

"It doesn't bother me."

"I know." Melissa Mae tilted her big head, black hair cropped close to her impressive skull, huge ebony eyes with their luminous blue-whites shining. "I'm trying to figure out what does bother you. You seem so pulled in, so composed. It can't be from getting fucked regular."

"Why not?"

"He's an old man. That may make him wiser, but it sure don't make him hornier."

"Don't bet on it," said Miranda.

"Well, if you're getting your sauce stirred up by that old chef, then my hat is off to him." Melissa Mae started cutting into her asparagus with a fork, but changing her mind, picked up a stalk and started eating it, slowly, from the top. "I'm always surprised when there's as much action in this town as there is. Everybody is so busy suck-ceeding."

"Don't you make love?"

"Oh, honey, I make as much as I can, but Hiro is in bus-i-ness. I keep telling him everybody else is into power and sex at the same time, but he doesn't seem to be as much of a juggler as the rest. Take those Watergate guys, for example. You think any of them were heavy into pussy?"

"I didn't know them."

"Well you saw their pictures. Haldeman looked to me like the toughest one, the most repressed, so he's probably the coldest fuck. It's those chopped hairs, you know, the marine sergeant Nazi types that truly like to stick it to a girl. But without imagination.

"Erlichman is probably more generous. I had the feeling about him that he might even care if he got a woman to come. Still, I can't picture any of them going down on you. Probably they'd consider it beneath them, so to speak. Drinking pussy juice."

The woman at the next banquette leaned slightly away from Melissa Mae, crowding toward her escort, creating an embarrassed kind of intimacy. None of it seemed to register with Melissa Mae, who just kept talking and chewing, delicately wiping her mouth with the white linen napkin, in between chews and hypotheses.

"Gordon Liddy would be the most demanding and selfish . . ."

"His mother says he was a good boy."

"Yeah, but she never had to fuck him. Far as we know. Mitchell would have been the pits. I don't think it's just this town and the lies that made Martha crazy."

"You really think there's that much sex going on?" Miranda asked.

"Shit, honey, you should talk to my shrink. Behind closed doors you wouldn't believe what's happening. Half the men in this town are into whips and chains."

"Really?"

"Goes with the territory. If you can survive one kind of beating, you can survive another. So it sort of gets them in shape for the next election. Sadomasochism, he says, is mother's milk to politicians."

"Who woulda thunk it," Miranda said.

"Then there are the orgies." Melissa Mae buttered her bread. "Naturally you never think of Republicans practicing group sex. It's so full of sharing. But there's all these groupie types, you know, the ones who couldn't find rock stars, so they come to D.C., catch the evening news and go after the stellar players. Who could resist them? Certainly not these little equerries that carry the coattails of the bosses."

"Equerries?"

"Schleppers, to use a New York word," Melissa Mae explained. "An officer of the household who takes care of the horses, or, in certain cases, press secretaries."

"You'd think they'd be a little worried about their reputation."

"Well, yes, you would think that, Miranda. But sex in Washington is like the draught of forgetfulness. Swallowed to ease your woes. Nobody's really as discreet as you'd expect they would be if they had any sense. An honored tradition that goes back to J.F.K., who, as the joke goes, did for fucking what Eisenhower did for golf."

"I wonder if he was any good."

"The worst, from what I've heard from a good many women who are in a position to know. Wham bam, thank you, ma'am. Or up against the wall, I only have two minutes. Of course, there was his bad back, so the girls had to do everything, but not for very long. Friends of mine in Georgetown had tape recordings they made through the wall when he was punking their roomer. 'Are you ready for this?' he used to say, and she would say 'I'm ready.' Women always lie, you know. Women don't want men to think it takes that long to satisfy them, and men don't really give a shit if they do or not. So with all his charm he was really contemptuous of women. Fucking them, he really fucked them."

"I'm sorry to hear that," said Miranda.

"So am I," said the woman at the next table, and signaled for her cheek.

"No, this is on me," said her escort.

"Lucky you," warbled Melissa Mae. "He must be a Democrat."

"I've never talked about sex with a woman before," Miranda said. "I never imagined women talked about it in detail to each other."

"Shit, honey, you should be in my yoga class. Savitri, who teaches serenity to all of Washington. They hang out and stretch and do their standing BoPoli and try to reach *samadhi*, then go to lunch and talk about sucking ass. I almost dropped my teeth in the car pool the other day. I mean, there was Ginny Mason, you know who she is, the ex-wife of Paulie Mason, Johnny Fontaine's best friend. Anyway, there she is in the backseat of the car, and out of nowhere she says, 'I sucked the most gorgeous ass the other night.' "

"A man's or a woman's?"

"Well, far as I know Ginny isn't a dyke, and she's been running with ski instructors, so I assume for the sake of what little decency there's left in this world that it was a man's ass. But who knows. How degrading. I heard the Nazis really liked that: as a sign of contempt for the women of the countries they conquered, they used to make them lick their assholes."

"Do you mind waiting till we leave?" asked the woman at the next table.

"Oh, honey, I'm so sorry. I didn't mean to make you jealous." She smiled her bright red-lipsticked smile at the man who sat beside her.

Miranda really loved Melissa Mae. Besides her sauciness, there was a great freedom the woman had, a kind of thumbing her black ass at people who didn't amuse her or didn't have a sense of humor, a waving good-bye with her bottom, mooning them with her clothes on. The woman at the next table had a bright red face now, which did not go very well with her tight blonde hair, pulled back into a chignon at the back of her blistering neck. She was dressed in black, which made her face look twice as fiery, as if it and her clothes were opposing players in a game of checkers.

They paid their check and got up to go, the woman knocking over a glass in her hurry to exit. The busboy came and cleared their table, wiped up the spill, and started to set places for the second sitting. There was in that restaurant the atmosphere of a transatlantic liner, with its cosmopolitan passenger list and crew that understood that, in spite of storms and difficult passages, the ship would always, except in the event of war, of course, get to port.

Most regulars came for lunch at twelve or twelve-thirty, depending on the feeling of urgency that swept whatever administration was currently in power. There was a steady menu of local celebrities, television commentators, newspaper columnists, best loved of whom was Art Buchwald, who sat at a banquette a few tables down from Melissa Mae and Miranda. Tourists, P.R. people, movie stars coming to the city for location shooting of their movies, and those who did not have the fixed schedules of the working locals were content to accept the later sitting, arriving for lunch at one-fifteen or one-thirty if the restaurant was busy, which it almost always was.

Melissa Mae posed thoughtfully over her asparagus spear. "Did you happen to read Buchwald's column this morning?" she asked Miranda.

"Not yet." In fact, Miranda never read the Washington papers. She continued to subscribe, stubbornly, to the *International Herald Tribune*, which she had begun the custom of reading in Paris, finding its content clear, condensed, and closest to the second definition of sense, sanity. Sometimes it arrived as many as three days after the date on the masthead, by which time the news in the headlines had already been resolved, so she lived free of an atmosphere of crisis, probably the only one in Washington who did so.

"You know, Buchwald used to live in Paris," Melissa

Mae said. "He and his wife went back for a visit recently, and he told about it in this morning's piece. He said to his wife—they were eating out in an ordinary Parisian restaurant—'Shall we order the white asparagus, or shall we send our son to college?' "

"What a funny man," said Miranda.

"That's the secret of sanity," said Melissa. "Being able to laugh at yourself."

"Can you do that?" asked Miranda. "I can't do that."

"Well, I probably could if I stayed up late. But I have this tendency to pass out." Melissa looked up as the maitre d' greeted some new arrivals. Poised on the threshold of the dining room were two women, one with the face of the perennially young and well-exercised, dimples deepening with pleasure at the warmth of her reception. The other was tall, with constricted elegance, a streak of white darting across her dark hair like a part. "Don't look now, but there's Ginny Mason herself, Paulie Mason's ex-wife, from my yoga class. I don't know the woman with her, the dark one."

"That's Sylvia Kranet. The senator's wife."

"That streak makes her look like the Bride of Frankenstein."

"Not fair to the senator. He's a nice man. No monster. I think she's beautiful in her own way."

"I don't like women who wear suede. There's an arrogance about them, like they're not going to spill on their clothes. Anyway, capes are out. Look how cute Ginny looks, with that tight little body and the curly hair and the dimples. Like Shirley Temple, isn't she?"

"That's before my time."

"Hoh-ney, it's before everybody's time. But there are some things you just know about. Race memory. Paul's bringing them over this way."

"Darling!" Sylvia Kranet said to Miranda. "Quelle coincidence!" Sylvia bent over toward Miranda, offering her cheek, making the kiss easier. It was not so much an exchange of affection as a brush of air, the stirring around of the atmosphere with habits of social friendship, lips never touching skin, makeup unimpaired.

"Ginny, you look fabulous!" Melissa Mae said. "Do you know Miranda Jay? Ginny Mason."

"Hi," said Ginny, her voice abounce with the over-optimistic lilt of a cheerleader's.

"I've heard so much about you. Sylvia, this is my friend Melissa Mae August."

"Enchanté." Sylvia moved to the adjoining banquette as the smiling maitre d' pulled out the table. The two women sat and ordered a drink.

"Ginny, you're glowing! You been doing an extra set of yoga?"

"Something like that," said Ginny, and dimpled.

"How's the senator?" Miranda asked Sylvia.

"Crusading."

"Such a nice man."

"We haven't had relations in several years."

"Maybe we should order first," said Ginny.

"Miranda's one of my dearest friends," said Sylvia.

"How's the crabs?" Ginny asked Melissa Mae.

"Succulent."

"I'm always nervous about ordering crabs for fear God will hear me and strike me with the kind I didn't order. That happened to me once when Paulie was on the road with the band and I went along. I got them from a toilet. It was some hassle to make him believe me."

"Sex wasn't that important to me until recently," Sylvia said. "I was content to be in a marriage of ideas."

"Paulie had a prick of a lawyer at the time. Johnny Fontaine's lawyer. He called me and said Paulie wanted a divorce and I should waive my community property rights or he'd give it out to the scandal papers that I had crabs, which he said you couldn't catch from a toilet seat. I said in that case, maybe I had gotten them from Paulie."

"Venereal disease is so unfortunate," Sylvia said. "They have such a hard row to hoe getting funded. You wouldn't believe the terrible time the little girl has who lobbies for government aid. No one wants to contribute to syphilis or gonorrhea. The names have no magnetism."

"Crabs has a certain simplicity," Ginny said. "Though I must say it's a terrible shock the first time you look down there and see these little critters playing in your pubic hair."

"Are you ladies ready to order?" the waiter said, giving them their drinks.

"I'll have the vichyssoise and an omelet," Sylvia said.

"I'm going to have what Miss August is having," said Ginny. "But without the asparagus. Maybe a salade des tomates, nature, on the side."

"As an appetizer, or with the main course?"

"Have it as an appetizer," Sylvia said. "I hate to eat alone."

"In that case you should have been with me last night," Ginny said, and told the waiter to bring it as an appetizer.

Sylvia sipped her double martini. "The truth is, I never realized how much sex meant to me until I started to be without it."

Ginny raised her margarita. "Salut." She drank. "I was thinking about calling you last night, Melissa Mae. There were so many of them, and only one of me. But I guess you're still keeping up this farce of being faithful to Hiro."

"It isn't a farce. It's somewhere between high drama and romantic comedy."

"Lucky you. Still, I thought you might have liked the boys I was with last night. Visiting firemen from Europe."

"Europeans have such heavy crotch smell," Sylvia said.

"They were more into mine than I was into theirs. It was my first experience with a gang bang, if you don't count the football team. And I never do. We were all so young and silly and in high school, and they were lousy. All around eighteen, with low IQs."

"You think that has anything to do with how good men are?" asked Sylvia.

"The smarter a man is, the better lover he is. Intelligent

men get their satisfaction partially from outwitting a woman. Surprising her.'' Ginny took a long drink from her margarita. ''We know delicacy is the key. Who of us is into beef anymore, once we taste caviar?''

''So how was the gang bang?'' asked Sylvia.

''Good and bad,'' said Ginny. The waiter came with their appetizers, and she was silent till he had left. ''Good was the bulk. The frenzy. You can't beat it for excitement, all those men turning each other on. There was a hush. I expected it to be very noisy, but they had the good taste not to cheer each other on, the way the football team did. There was something almost reverent about the way they waited their turns, although you could see they all had erections. But only one of them took his out before it was time.''

''I never did it with more than one man at once,'' said Melissa. ''I don't think I missed anything.''

''That depends whether you like to get it front and back. The crowding is what makes it so terrific. Like a festival for all your thin membranes. And of course not only are they having you, but they can rub at each other's cocks through your walls and not feel guilty about their homosexual yearnings.''

''I have a friend,'' Sylvia began, ''who made love with a homosexual. She said it was the most extravagant sexual experience of her life. Compared it to being a rice pudding with someone going after your raisins.'' She spooned some vichyssoise toward the back of her cup, touched the underside of the spoon to the rim of the china, gracefully removing any drops before raising it to her lips.

''My special friend is Loren Aggrizi, the well-known novelist and pederast,'' said Ginny. ''He says his favorite is fucking a man who's fucking a woman.''

''I couldn't handle being at the bottom of that club sandwich,'' said Melissa Mae.

''Well, I always wanted to do it with Loren. He's so subtle. So the last time I was at the Villa D'Este, he and a friend, a lovely young count he was crazy for, paid me a visit.''

"And?" Sylvia's spoon was halfway to her lips.

"Highly erotic. In the best literary sense. Quantum leaps, as far as imagination was concerned. When you're creative in one area, it extends to another. My nipples were stiff for days."

"So what about last night?" Miranda asked.

"Well, if you're going to moist heap it, I think the ideal way would be to choose who was going to be in the moist heap with you. For instance, I would like to select the cast for my gang bang, and the order of performance."

"Who would be the curtain raiser?" Miranda asked.

"Warren Beatty," suggested Sylvia.

"Oh, no, you'd save him for further down the road, because he has staying power." Ginny smiled at the waiter as he offered her the pepper mill, nodded. He ground. She waited. Then he moved to Sylvia and grated black flakes onto her soup.

"Ryan O'Neal?"

"Oh, that's because you're so young. I wouldn't lean too heavily on movie stars. They don't really worry about you. Unless it was being filmed. They don't care if you toot your whistle."

"That isn't true about Rick Flinders," Sylvia said.

"Well, he has a reputation to hold up. Women *belong* to him. He literally fucks their brains out. The smartest of them gets tapioca where her gray matter used to be."

"What about Johnny Fontaine?"

"Well, we never did it because of him being best friends with Paulie. But I know a lot of girls who have, and they said it was very long and skinny, and they had to do everything. He just lies there like some kind of Oriental potentate. No harm meant, Melissa Mae."

"Oh, you're not bothering me," she said. "What goes on between me and Hiro is outside categorizing."

"I hear you have him by the balls," said Ginny.

"I wish. To have an Oriental by the balls means you can count on everything you want and need in this life."

"How many of them were there?" asked Sylvia.

"Last night? Six."

"How did you meet them?" Melissa Mae asked. "Did they just come up to your door and ring the bell, and say, 'Hey, lady, you want to fuck?' "

"Not exactly. I met two of them at a reception at the Iranian Embassy."

Sylvia shuddered. "They smell of camels."

"These weren't Iranians. They went there for the same reason I did. Because Iranians have the good caviar. Anyway, they were cute, Yugoslavs I think. And they asked me if I would join them for dinner, and I did, and suddenly there were six of them."

"Where did you do it?"

"Back in my apartment. All very jovial, and, in a way, innocent. They took me to my door and wished me good night. Then the first two started to kiss me, chewing at my face, and the next thing I knew, they were all inside the apartment."

"Did you do it on the floor or the couch or in the bedroom?" Sylvia asked, her color high.

"A little of each."

"And they just waited their turns?" asked Miranda.

"They were very well mannered. Though the sodomist in the group, the one with his big dong exposed from the beginning, he made it into a party. Come to think of it, they couldn't have been Iranians. They weren't circumcised."

"I hate foreskins," Sylvia shuddered. "So unhygienic."

They resumed their attentive silence while the waiter cleared their appetizers and gave them the main course.

"Excuse me," said Miranda. "I have to go to the ladies' room."

"I don't wonder," said Melissa Mae. "After this conversation."

Miranda made her way back toward the rear of the restaurant, a fixed smile on her face in case she passed anyone she knew and didn't recognize. Victor had told her how many people thought she snubbed them simply because she hadn't seen them. Her growing astigmatism had come as kind of a blessing to her, dulling her awareness of being stared at. For too long a time she was made uncomfortable by the way men looked at her, which did not serve to flatter or make her feel good about herself. It was still a puzzle to her, men wanting her as much as they did, and as she was faithful to Victor, she preferred not to know about it. Not being able to see unless she focused hard and gave it her full attention helped her spin through public scenes without that peculiar heat in her belly, feeling herself being undressed, desired. There was no question of her getting glasses. Ignorance in this case was certainly bliss. Still, she smiled, in case she passed someone she knew.

"Miranda?"

She tilted her head back and pulled away slightly, bringing into focus the face of the man who addressed her. It was Allen Hewitt, Victor's employee, the man who'd been the "beard" for them, that long-ago time on the yacht.

"Allen," she said, surprised. "What are you doing in Washington? Is Victor coming?"

"No," he said. "I'm here on personal business."

There was a man sitting at the table next to the stairs, and because Miranda had come back from her unfocused drift, she saw how he was looking at her. He appeared youngish, in his middle thirties, but there was a portliness to him, a premature signal of age in spite of the full head of hair and the liveliness of his eyes, which were all over her. "Miss Jay?" he said, and got to his feet.

"Do I know you?"

"Fred Masters," he said, and took her hand without her offering it. "I'm a great admirer of Victor Lenrahan." His fingers on her were oddly childlike.

She squinted, to try and see what he really wanted. "So."

"So naturally I know who you are."

"Well that puts you one up on me."

"I'm a newspaper publisher."

She pulled her fingers back as though she had been stung. Masters blushed like a boy.

"I'm not looking to make any trouble," he said. "Like

I told you, I admire Mr. Lenrahan. The country needs men like him. I was just curious . . ."

"I'll bet," Miranda said.

". . . about what you ladies talk about at lunch. I mean, I couldn't help noting what an attractive and lively bunch you seemed, and I thought it might make an interesting feature, what Washington women talk about while their men are changing the face of the world."

"The other part of it," she said, and went down the stairs to the ladies' room.

Inside that small domain, Allen Hewitt's personal business sat weeping on a petit-pointed bench. Jacqueline Trimble Forsythe was a redhead, trim from the waist up, her hips having run slightly out of control, like her affair with Allen. She and Miranda had become friends at a distance.

"Jacqueline . . ." Miranda said.

The woman looked up, little crystals of tears hovering in her eyes. "Oh, Miranda. I would have called you. But I didn't know till yesterday I was coming here. I thought we were going to meet in New York, and then his wife got wind of it." As she talked, tears fell from her hazel eyes at a slow, steady rate, like her words, which were marvelously executed. Jacqueline had been a speech major in college, and had carried it out into the corporate world, becoming an elocution teacher for highly paid executives, training them, rehearsing and practicing delivery of important speeches, adjusting their verbal stance before the public. "I've got to end it," she whispered now.

"How long will you be in town?"

"He's flying back to the coast this afternoon. I was going to go straight to the shuttle from here."

"Stay in town. Let me cheer you up. I've got a couch in my living room." She was surprised by her own effusiveness, feeling suddenly how lonely she had to be to so eagerly invite this woman.

"What an angel you are," Jacqueline wept. "Why aren't there any men around as nice as women?"

"Listen," Miranda put her hand on Jacqueline's shaking shoulder. "Get yourself together and join us after he's gone."

"Oh, he's already gone. I was too much of a coward to say good-bye, to watch him walking out the door. He'll have paid the bill and left by now."

"Wash your face and come upstairs and join the ladies. It'll make you giggle. If you don't mind talk about sex."

"Sex?" Jacqueline looked up from her Kleenex.

"There's a woman I never met before today who described in vivid detail her last ten orgasms."

"Orgasms?"

"All of them occurring in the past two days."

"I'll just go and wash my face," Jacqueline said.

Upstairs, the restaurant had settled into the relaxed buzz signaling the end of heavy traffic, a return to the serious business of the day, lobbying, policy-making, the thrust and parry of decisions everyone wanted credit for, provided the outcomes were favorable. On the raised platform to the rear, a round table filled with people from the Kennedy Center argued the next spring's production schedule. There was a light hint of combat to the atmosphere, as sociable as it clearly was, as gourmet festive.

At the two side-by-side banquette tables where the women sat, however, there was an aura of clubbiness, spa. Jacqueline Trimble Forsythe introduced herself to each of them by her full name, giving it the French pronunciation, Jock-a-leen.

"Well, rest it there," said Ginny Mason, who had been moved to introduce herself back as Virginia Ann McGeary Mason. Jacqueline seated herself across from Melissa Mae and Miranda, on a chair angled toward the two other women. "Have you eaten?"

"Yes, thank you."

Ginny ordered everybody an after-lunch drink. "As I was saying before we were so elegantly interrupted." She nodded her head at Jacqueline. "After he had the bypass, Hiram couldn't get it up. He and Tatiana were married for a century, probably the only couple in California together that long. But after the triple bypass, he couldn't get an erection.''

"Fear," said Jacqueline. "Many men imagine they're going to die in the saddle."

"Garfield did, you know," said Sylvia.

"Hiram was really in a panic, Tatiana told me, scared he might die if he fucked her, die if he didn't. Afraid they'd cut out his manliness along with his cholesterol deposits, if you know what I mean."

"We know what you mean," said Sylvia and Melissa Mae together, and laughed at the sound of their chorus.

"He made Tatiana sit and play with his limp prick for hours at a time. She was exhausted. She started getting arthritis in her tongue."

"He should have gone to Palm Springs," said Sylvia. "There's a plastic surgeon shoots silicon into penises so they're hard all the time. It must be awful to run around with one of those in your drawers, but he does at least four hundred a year."

"Is that like the little blower they have to pump it up?" asked Ginny.

"No," Sylvia said. "That's a different operation. They insert a little plastic inflatable bag in the cock, and there's a rubber hand pump with a hose, and when it's time, you connect it and blow up the inflatable plastic bag so the penis seems to be erect."

"How do you know all this?" asked Miranda.

"Well, the senator's always getting appeals for funding. Help to lobby in congress. You'd be surprised at the kinds of things he's approached for."

"So what happened to Tatiana?" Miranda asked Ginny as though she knew who Tatiana was, sex establishing an intimacy even when you were only talking about it.

"Tatiana had this very best friend, Babette James, the famous hooker-starlet who was in Rome for La Dolce Vita time. She'd become an artiste, she said, and Tatiana, that innocent, used to listen to her cry about how Hollywood wouldn't accept her, and people change. So she started inviting Babette over all the time, letting her hang out at the Bel Air mansion. I asked Tatiana how come she spent so much time with Babette, and she said, 'I feel sorry for her. And Hiram finds her very exciting.' So I said to her, 'Get rid of her.' But she didn't listen.''

"So he started fucking Babette," Sylvia said.

"Not exactly," said Ginny. "He left Tatiana for her and then couldn't get it up with Babette either."

"Praise the lord!" cried Melissa Mae.

"It must be very hard on men, if you'll excuse the pun," said Jacqueline. "Worrying about that all the time."

"No harder than it is on women, worrying they won't receive," said Sylvia. "I have one friend, a woman I went to high school with—she's become a famous poet. She spends every penny she makes hiring limousines to drive her to motels in the country. She has transportation, a bodyguard if she needs one, and someone to fuck: Imagine. She fucks the drivers."

"Not a bad idea," said Ginny thoughtfully.

"So did Hiram ever do it with Babette?" Miranda asked.

"She took him to a sex therapist," said Ginny.

"You think they help?" asked Jacqueline.

"Well, most of it is skills and techniques," said Ginny. "Hit the right fantasy and you'll get yourself going."

"I have a little trouble with orgasm myself," said Jacqueline, downing her second stinger. "A friend of mine just had a clitoral circumcision, and now she comes just putting on her pants."

"That must be very romantic," said Melissa Mae.

"I thought about having one of those. Right after Paulie and I split up, when I was going with Tony Candella . . ."

"Is he really that *macho*?" Jacqueline asked.

"Macho?" Ginny touched her pinky to her dimple. "The guy was hung like a butterfly!"

The five women laughed, a hearty chorus of guffaws that echoed through the restaurant, which was nearly empty by now. "I guess we ought to be moving on," Melissa Mae said.

Standing on the street, waiting for a taxi, with Ginny

and Sylvia gone off in Ginny's two-seater silver Mercedes, Miranda shivered. "Excuse me," said Fred Masters, coming up behind her. "Can I give you ladies a lift somewhere? I've got my limousine."

The wind was chill and blustery around them, although the calendar said it was spring. Miranda wrapped her scarf tight around her throat, did little quick dance steps in her high heels on the pavement, hands deep in her pockets. "No, thanks. We'll wait for a cab."

"I don't mean anything by it," Fred said. "I don't even have to ride with you. I can send you wherever you're going, and Granville can come back for me."

"How sweet," Melissa Mae said, and eyed him curiously. "Do we know you?"

"Fred Masters," he said, and held out his hand.

"The scrofulous publisher!" Melissa said. "Hiro would be appalled that I even talked to you. He said you're absolutely scrofulous."

"I'm afraid I don't know what that means," said Masters.

"It means what it sounds like," Melissa said. "Like whatever you got is full of scrofles. I hope it ain't catching."

"I'm cold," said Jacqueline. "Why can't we take this kind man up on his offer?"

"Did you touch your scrofles to the seat cushions?" Melissa Mae asked as the limo pulled up.

"I try to keep them inside my pants," said Fred, and smiled good-naturedly.

In the end, he took them in his limousine to the Jeffersonian Club. It seemed to Melissa Mae the decent thing to do, to invite him inside in return for his kindness, even though he wasn't a member, and Hiro would never let him join, no matter how much money he had. "He mistrusts the sensational press," she explained to Fred, once they were settled in the plush low red velvet sofas, while serving men in eighteenth-century colonial garb with white wigs and dress coats hovered over them, pouring champagne. "He has so much respect for freedom of the press, it makes him sick when you people go too far just to sell papers."

"That's probably just self-defense," said Fred. "I got a lot of scandal I could unload about Hiro."

"But of course you won't."

"I never dish about friends," said Fred, his eyes glued to Miranda.

After a second bottle of champagne, Jacqueline and Melissa Mae helped each other to the ladies' room. "You understand what I'm trying to tell you?" Fred Masters said.

"You speak a funny kind of English," said Miranda.

"I mean with all that I know about you and Mr. Lenrahan, and I got a lot of stuff, you understand, telephoto pictures on the yacht, stuff like that, hotter than Burton and Taylor. With all that, I'd never think of printing a word, much less a picture, because of how important I think Mr. Lenrahan is to the welfare of our country."

"That's very high-minded of you," Miranda said.

"That's why I'm doing it. Exactly. High-minded. Yeah. I like that."

"And I'm sure you don't want anything in return."

He looked at her legs. "Well, I can't say I don't want it. But I have too much regard to even try for it."

"That's a wise decision."

"But since I do admire the man so much, I'd like a chance to talk to him."

"You want *me* to introduce you to Victor?"

"Oh, we already met. He knows me. I'd just like you to tell him how high-minded I am. And how very much I would esteem his deeper acquaintance."

"What an ignorant jerk you are."

Masters blushed and got to his feet. "I guess I really ought to be going."

He left. It was time for the first sitting of dinner. In the Jeffersonian Club that was served with an elegance and style that existed nowhere else, with the possible exception of genuine palaces. White-gloved footmen and white-gloved waiters carried in service trays, rearranged place settings, put fresh flowers into crystal vases, while with white gloves holding scissors they snipped off leaves and petals not fresh enough to meet with Hiro's approval. Dining at the Jeffersonian was one of the district's high echelon treats. Membership was private and expensive, although Hiro Takeda, its owner, was gracious about extending it as a gift to congressmen and politicians whose official salaries could not quite support such lavishness. But only if he liked them. Or, as the less beneficent tongues in town put it, if he wanted something from them.

According to private dossiers on Hiro, which were not quite as detailed as Hiro's own dossiers on most of the important people in the town, besides having heavy industrial connections in the Orient, and unofficially lobbying for increased trade, Hiro was an unquenchable enthusiast. There were some who were sure that his graciousness was not self-serving, that he simply hoped to number among his friends the best-loved people, which, according to his training at American colleges and American dinner parties, meant the successes. This might have been a fact that escaped cynics, that it came naturally to him, from his American education, wanting to be with those who were, as a local rock group put it, Hits. Critics and members of the Justice Department who were later to conduct their investigation of him missed that part of his character completely, the boyishness that was rife in him, in spite of his being an Oriental. Fervor was nothing he easily expressed, any more than the truth that he was a fan of celebrity. And in Washington, the politicians were the movie stars.

One of the few who understood that about him was Miranda, since they were feelings akin to what she sometimes experienced herself, little-girl flutterings of the heart in the presence of greatness, most prominently exampled in Victor. But some others set admiration stirring in her, and giddiness, as openhearted as the opposite toughness with which she could deal with people like Fred Masters, dismissed by her because she was sure Victor would consider him scum. So, understanding Hiro's feelings, even though he never expressed them, she liked him, almost as much as she did Melissa Mae.

Hiro never looked directly at Miranda, not even now as

he kissed her hand and told her how honored he was that she and her friend were gracing his club. To look directly at someone, according to Oriental custom, meant you considered them your equal. Hiro wasn't as arrogant as that. Not with beautiful women. Even after having been with Melissa Mae for years, even while expressing annoyance with the sullenness and temper she showed from time to time, and her jealousy—once she had actually dived across a formal dinner table and placed her hands squarely on the throat of a woman she thought was making a play for him—he would not presume to look directly at her when he addressed her.

"It's lovely to be here," Miranda was saying. "This is my friend . . ."

"Jacqueline Trimble Forsythe," she introduced herself.

"Will you join me for dinner?" Hiro asked them.

"We'd be delighted," Miranda said, and then looked inquiringly at Melissa Mae. "Unless you two want to be alone."

"Hoh-ney, even when we're alone we're not alone," Melissa Mae said. "We got a roomful of his ancestors' spirits, not to mention the living spectres of his not-yet-dead parents, who would turn over in their graves they ain't in yet if they saw what their little boy wasn't bringing home to mother."

"I'm afraid a little too much wine has loosened your tongue," Hiro said, checking the bottle of Dom Perignon that sat cooling in the brass stand beside their low red sofas.

"That's mine," said Miranda. "I'm the one who had the champagne. Melissa Mae's hardly touched any."

"That's right," she said. "Do these look like the lips of a woman who's sipped champagne?"

"I wouldn't mind if you sipped. I'll just go tell Mr. Carmen to set up our table." Pulling at his starched French custom cuffs, Hiro walked away.

"I don't know why we go on pretending these fuckers really care about us," Melissa Mae said sadly. "What are you doing here, Miranda? How come you're not away on the boat?''

"Ship. His wife and the girls are with him for Easter."

"Hypocrites," Melissa Mae said.

"They can't be direct as women are," Jacqueline Trimble Forsythe said.

"Well, well, Dwight," said a sharp woman's voice. "Look who's here! Rebecca of Sunnybrook Whorehouse."

Miranda looked up and saw Edith Jonah. Behind her stood Dwight Efram Jonah.

"What an unpleasant surprise," said Miranda.

"For me too," said Edith. She was dressed in challis, a light costly wool, what Washington matrons called a dinner dress. No hint of festivity to it, tight and severe as she was, its only formality its length.

Jacqueline was on her feet, her smile eager, her hand extended. "You probably don't remember me," she said to Jonah. "Jacqueline Trimble Forsythe."

"Good to see you," he said heartily, no hint of recognition or lack of it on his face, shaking her hand.

"Jacqueline Trimble Forsythe," she said to his wife.

"Edith Jonah."

"Edith Persimmon Lips Jonah," Miranda said. "Since we're using full names."

"You keep your sewer shut, you festering hole," Edith said, cheeks flaming.

"Your mother sucks eggs," said Miranda.

"How dare you."

"Now don't get mad, Edith," Dwight said, trying to lighten the moment, smiling. "The truth is the truth. Your mother does suck eggs."

"Don't you dare! Don't you dare be on her side!"

"But, Edith . . ."

"It's all your fault. Ruining my sweater. Destroying that summer. And now my evening. You . . . Fancy Woman."

"Better fancy than plain," Miranda said.

Edith turned her back and threw her challis shawl across her shoulders, the end of it catching Miranda square in the face. Miranda did not move. Just stared, her pale green eyes reflecting the candle flame, irises yellowing.

"I'm so sorry," Dwight said as Edith moved away.

"Don't apologize," said Miranda. "It's not your fault. You've got enough to feel bad about."

She didn't ever tell Victor exactly what had happened that evening. But she told him Fred Masters was dying to get friendly with him, and personally she considered him a putz. Victor said not to judge him too harshly. Someone like that could come in very handy if you used them right.

And the next time they went into the secret room, she let it fall on him, sort of casually, that if he really meant what he said about Dwight Jonah, if he really felt sorry for him, that he was missing out on something, if Victor was so fond of him that he didn't mind sharing, well, then, it would be all right with her if he joined them at their play. And where the hell was her daughter?

Not long after that, the scandal broke about Hiro and he committed suicide, throwing himself off the balcony of the Savoy in London. When Melissa Mae followed suit a year later, flinging herself from her terrace at Watergate South, Miranda decided she'd had enough of Washington. Really, it had soured for her since that night at the Jeffersonian Club. Now that her best friend was gone, and the town had done it to her, closing her out, driving her off the side of the building, Miranda was filled with acid. Hatred for people who couldn't see what other people really were, who judged them from inside challis dresses.

Besides, the truth was, Miranda looked best with a tan. As bad as people said Los Angeles was, at least the sun shone nearly all the time. So she wouldn't have to wait for Victor's yacht to restore her honeyed glaze. L.A. would put her closer to him. MercerCorp, after all, was headquartered out there. And there were plenty of marinas for the yacht. Mean as that town was supposed to be, it couldn't hold a candle for viciousness to Washington.

So he set her up in an apartment on the border of Beverly Hills. Just a few blocks from where the jogging path was, so her beautiful legs wouldn't atrophy. The legend was Marilyn Monroe had lived in that apartment, which was how the landlord got away with not replacing the worn white carpeting.

THE EQUESTRIAN CENTER

◊

The *Wall Street Journal* was not Lou Salerno's kind of paper any more than polo was his kind of game. Nonetheless, he had spent a lot of hours in the public library while he was still in New York, reading that publication's back issues, trying to adjust his eyes to the very small print, his mind to the way they told stories, jumping around from long articles in the first and second sections to capsulated world events in a single column on the front page, sort of reconstructing in his head what had happened with the Fred Masters takeover attempt of MicroTel Computer. The Almost of it blossomed like a very exotic tropical flower, with twisted stems and intricate, strangely shaped branches that, when pieced together, made a plant, albeit one that had withered and died. But he more or less knew who had been involved with Masters—the reporting in the paper was as investigatively thorough as a detective would be. So whether or not people wanted to be publicly a part of the deal, the *Journal* seemed to have turned them up, just as it had turned up villains on its own staff, and profiteering. So besides Masters himself, Lou knew that heavy participants had been Bunyan Reis' business manager, who had put in several of his clients, some Middle Eastern types, and some West Coast people, including Johnny Fontaine and his son Marty. Which is how it was that Lou found himself on his way to the Equestrian Center to watch a polo game. Not exactly his cup of Oolong.

Marty Fontaine had been avoiding his calls, not answering the door bell when Lou appeared at his apartment, even though Lou knew he was home. You could always tell when a guy was really home. He had a particular stubborn fix on getting through to Marty because, like most Americans of his generation, he was a fan of Marty's father and wanted to see if the kid had turned out okay. The way a man's children turned out was a source of great interest to Lou, since he'd never had a chance to see how his own turned out because of that drunk on the freeway. It eased his ache a little when men he admired had kids who did them credit. Or even when they didn't. Continuity was important to him, since the underbelly of the world had kept him from having continuity. So although he'd sort of given up on being able to talk to Johnny—there was too much protection around him, lawyers, security guards, everything short of spear carriers—he was determined to get through to Marty. When a guy was that elusive, you found out the one thing he couldn't do without, the one place he had to be. And Marty's fix was polo, and the ponies.

Lou had found out that Marty owned a couple of horses, that he kept them at the Equestrian Center, and that he was planning to play in the season opening that evening. There was a fanciness to the whole excursion that lifted Lou's spirits, put a certain starch in his attitude. The New York trip had come up, as far as the department was concerned, as having yielded nothing concrete or even, for that matter, as his friend at the *Book Review* would have put it, ephemeral. But he felt himself getting closer to something. The telephone book of Connie Garrett, the West Coast woman with the bullet hole in her eye, had a number that turned out to be an employee at MicroTel. The man was no longer working there. No one was sure where he'd gone, including his landlady, who said he'd just packed and left one night without any word. So Lou was pretty sure the puzzle had to do with that company. Then he'd turned up a twenty-five-thousand-dollar deposit in the Garrett woman's account, made just before her "suicide." So whether or not someone was paying her off, it sure looked like someone was paying her off. Maybe not the same one who paid her off in the eye.

Driving through the thick interchanges of the Los Angeles freeways, concrete lanes twining like spaghetti strands in a smoking pot, a casual visitor could imagine himself condemned to some infernal punishment. As if, not having taken the right road in life, he was damned to travel the wrong one forever. A kind of motorized No Exit with smog. Lou, of course, was as far away as a man could be from a casual visitor, priding himself on being from L.A. Much as he hated smog, after the Beautiful People settings of New York, it seemed to him preferable to hot air.

Still, it made him sad, air you could see most evenings, even in the twilight, a light brown shroud clinging to the hills. He thought of the wars that men had fought in the name of what was holy, the people who had died. What was holy in Los Angeles was the car, and for it, people killed the atmosphere. Once there had been an easily joyful song about the San Fernando Valley, crooned by Bing Crosby, carrying the same lightheartedness as the area, the stuff retirement dreams were made of. Now it had become a center for the foul air trapped in the mountain-edged basin, a place of relentless heat, endless miles of straight boulevards like bowling alley lanes, with stores on both sides flashing the message of a life consecrated to just getting through. Philosophy wasn't Lou's bag, but he sort of understood how important it was to be living your life, not just passing through it, when he drove in the valley.

The car Lou was in was not exactly a symbol of the town's dedication to the mark, a low-level product on the Chrysler line, good for getting him where he was going and back, which was what he thought a car was for. His wife, suffering as she did over Suzy Jenks' column, knowing that the rich and elegant were in rich and elegant cars, whined around for a couple of years till he got her a Peugeot so she could speak French to herself on her way to Ralph's market. All around him on the freeway threaded shiny BMWs, an occasional stretch limousine, Porsches, Mercedes, in between workmanlike Chevies and Fords, and invader Toyotas. The woman who zipped in and out of the traffic just in front of him drove a silver two-seater Mercedes. Lou thought she had a hell of a nerve, driving so flashily, boldly really. How much faster would she get where she was going, moving in and out of the lanes so impatiently? What did she need to get anywhere that fast for, really, taking a chance, driving like a guy, and in a car like that?

Sitting beside the woman in the Mercedes, Hap Mitchel was of the same opinion. He watched Zoe skeptically from the passenger seat. Trying not to seem too obviously pressing his hand against the dashboard, waiting for the impact. Testing the latest in experimental aircraft was to Hap more risk-free than women drivers. Besides the old-fashioned prejudice against them, Hap carried his own reserve of statistics once compounded as a sort of joke by researchers at MercerCorp. They proved that while women thought more quickly in many instances than men (they'd blacked that line out) their physical reflexes were a fraction slower. In addition to not being at all sure about women behind the wheel, Hap was still unsure about Zoe, period. He had tried hard to be in charge of the evening, to make it into one that allowed for the opportunity for intimacy, quiet talk, dim lights. But instead she had pressed on him the importance of her being at the opening of the polo season that evening as a courtesy to her client, Marty Fontaine. Worse, she had called for Hap, picking him up to take him there, making him feel as though she was in charge of the "courting" and it was he who was the "date." Had she been tougher, with a harder perceivable

edge, he would have considered maybe it was some
womanly way of trying to put him in his place, which
seemed to him unaccustomedly obeisant to hers.

She turned the car off the Buena Vista exit toward
Riverside, the dry arroyo where once, long ago, a river
had run, leaving the inhabitants with only a wistful name
for their boulevard. Night tinted the leaf-heavy branches of
pungent eucalyptus trees into black, lush shadows. The
wind carried the last traces of a Santa Ana, the several-
times-yearly struggle of shifting sands to return from the
desert to the sea, tearing a ribbon of heat through the
basin, temporarily purifying the air. There was a hush to
the evening, an unaccustomed tranquillity, as though what
they drove through was a genuine suburb and not just the
outlying sector of a desiccated dream.

Hap marked the seeming expertise of her driving, tried
to suspend his conviction that none of them was any good
at it. He struggled to relax a little in his seat, leaning his
head back against the raised leather headrest, at the same
time making sure his safety belt was secure, his hand
braced against potential impact. He reminded himself of
the salutary effects of deep breathing, took in the smell of
eucalyptus and Zoe's perfume. It was not like her. Little as
he'd had a chance to observe her, little as he knew her,
really, there were certain things he could already intuit as
characteristic or foreign. He had noted that first time on
the plane how fresh smelling she was, as if her scent were
a Peter Pan collar, carefully washed and ironed. Crisp and
straightforward, as she seemed to be, girlish by virtue of
the innocence of soap, the scrub that went along with it.
Now, suddenly, a heavy fragrance obscured her. As if she
were in disguise, had donned another persona, like a
mask, and with it, this stranger's aroma.

She wasn't dressed like herself, either. Hap was already
steamed at whoever it was they were going out of their
way to see, figuring the client was behind her transforma-
tion, her dressing up like that. Both times Hap had been
with her before, first on the plane, then the night of Claire
Avery's death, Zoe had been muted, in colors that drabbed

her out, no makeup on her, her graceful body obscured by tweedy, bulky fabrics, with no more life to them than she seemed to want to advertise in herself. He knew it was presumption on his part, thinking he could come to conclusions about her, knowing her so little. But she seemed so open, so out in front, and he had missed so much about Claire, he had resolved to notice everything now about whatever women he trafficked with, flirted with, passed by the borders of, or, as soon as he could manage it with Zoe, went to bed with. Much as he wanted her, he had already adopted a mind-set to run her through his consciousness like a computer, coming out with clear, unequivocal answers. If you could ever get anything clear and unequivocal on a woman. Assuring himself this planned process stemmed not from any capacity he had for affection, but from potential adversarial relationships, he tried to grit his mental teeth against Zoe, to arm himself, just as he set his body for the car crash he was sure was coming. As he could tally from the two times he'd been with her, the woman he thought she was, he wondered who this lovely, soft thing beside him could be. Which was the disguise: the plain creature or this subtly radiant one? And was it this Marty Fontaine character that had brought her out of her nubby chrysalis?

Banana-colored silk clung softly to her body, the long line of tunic and loose folds of pants emphasizing her height, the gentle curve of her breasts, the length of her legs. In his mind she was already pigeonholed as conservative, her usual dress reflective of her business habits, professional and efficient and unsentimental. So he was knocked off balance by how she was now, her fluid femininity, the easy rock music floating from the car stereo, a breath of mellow youth that jarred him. She seemed suddenly filled with contradictions, as pointedly expressed as by her hand, with its long fingers and pale pink oval nails manicured and buffed, lightly iridescent in the glow from the stereo, so expert on the stick shift.

Seated, she seemed small, even though standing she was

nearly as tall as he was, something that always surprised
him. Always. Two times before and now made three. He
wondered if women were as quick to make generalizations
as men were.

Her no-nonsense attitude seemed also to have been
amended to some nonsense. Her beige hair fell shoulder-
length and full, brushed in a kind of loose sweep away
from her head so she looked more airy, carefree. As
appealing as she was, so unexpectedly breaking out of a
mold he thought he could set her into, he made a steadfast
resolution to keep it strictly a sexual exchange. Romance,
sentimentalizing, all those things he had never suspected
were in his character, that had almost shot him down,
were over now, banished, gone down the riverbank with
Claire.

Even dead, she was not completely forgiven. Treacher-
ous though she'd been, he had gone into a nosedive of
grieving, because it had never occurred to him that she
could die. Even if he hadn't cared for her as much as he
did, she'd been young, beautiful, smart, filled with potential, all things that made death seem a graver insult. He
felt anguish and guilt because they'd never had a chance to
work it out between them, like a parent who died before
you could tell them how much you loved them, or how
much they'd hurt you, or both. It had been his intention to
scald her out of his body with somebody new. But it never
occurred to him he wouldn't have the chance to do that
while she was alive. No living, pulsing creature to wreak
revenge on. Death had carved a statue to her, raised her
concrete and stately in his head, a solemn, inflexible
monument.

Grief, he understood now, was more powerful than
anger. Making men into junket, taking the steel out of
getting even. So there'd been no seduction of Zoe their last
time together. He could not even think to touch her, the
night he'd heard about Claire. He had started to weep right
in the middle of Häagen-Dazs, with its celebrity auto-
graphs on ice cream cups hanging, ribbon-strung, behind
the counter. Richard Gere's scrawled greeting in massive,

angular handwriting seemed to scowl its disapproval, censuring a grown man for crying in public. In an ice cream parlor, no less. Worst of all, for a woman who had betrayed him.

There was still no clear explanation of the tragedy. No detail that threw light on what, exactly, had happened. According to journalistic reports, it was assumed by local police at the scene of the accident that Claire had gone the wrong way out of a restaurant parking lot in a blinding rainstorm. Visibility had been poor that night. Not the first time cars had gone off the bridge, into the river at that place. Presumably she hadn't seen the warning signs. The car had been found upside down in the water, so the pressure on all sides must have been enormous. Hap was sure the accident wasn't alcohol related. Claire drank little, except when she was celebrating. And clearly there was nothing to celebrate that night. That was the part that ate at him. If he had taken her call, would she still be alive?

Had it been tears, besides the rainstorm, that clouded her vision? His secretary had told him she was crying. A matter of life and death, she'd said. If he'd listened, she might still be living. No way around that, except rage at Claire. If she hadn't been such a liar, he might have believed her.

There had been no sign of anything in the car besides her purse and an empty briefcase. The question had naturally arisen why a crack journalist would be carrying a briefcase with nothing in it. But no follow-ups, no answers. Whatever the truth was, Hap's own deliberations were unremitting. Guilt wasn't anything he was used to feeling. But he scraped at that last moment of her calling like a sore. How unlike him that was, how anomalous to his American character. Guilt was a heavy, Russian thing. It was why we should believe their pledge in the U.N., the pacifists were always whining, that they wouldn't make a first strike, answer it with a similar pledge so they wouldn't be affronted. It had always sounded like propagandist bullshit to Hap, but now that he was having his first experience with guilt, he began to understand how powerful a force it could be.

Humming softly along with the light rock ballad that issued from her stereo, Zoe turned the wheel to the right. The car shimmied up the long, wide gravel driveway leading to the Equestrian Center. Floodlights marked the white-painted, slatted wood entranceway, standing thirty feet in the air above them like a false-fronted barn. At the base of the entranceway red-painted sandwich boards announced the availability of season tickets.

A young man stood waving an oversized flashlight. "Valet or self-parking?" he asked Zoe.

She turned to Hap. "You mind hoofing it a little?"

"Not at all," he said. "I'm not wearing heels."

"Self," Zoe said, smiling.

He directed them toward the right hand lane. About eighty feet up the gravel road were fenced corrals being used for parking lots. Zoe pulled into the first, turning off the lights, opening the electric locks on the doors, shutting off the motor with one deft, continuous motion.

"You're a good driver," he said.

"For a girl?"

"You don't smell like a girl." He leaned closer to her. "You smell like a woman."

"I feel like a woman."

He touched her cheek. "You certainly do." His fingers moved to her lips. She turned her face toward his and opened her mouth to receive his gentle, exploring kisses.

"Oh, good," she said in a heavy whisper. "That's what I thought."

Then, crisp again, she opened her door, slid out and reached into the backseat for her coat. "We don't have to stay the whole evening." She smiled at him. "Just greet the client, eat supper, and watch one chukker."

"Chukker?"

"Like an inning or a quarter. One period of a polo match. Marty's playing in a preliminary tournament before the Lancers game. We don't have to stay for that. We'll just watch him play a little."

Above them, renegade stars sparkled, as they had sparkled on long-ago nights before the gaseous roof closed over the basin. A thick wedge of moon lit the clear sky, sentried their footsteps crunching through the dry dirt. He moved toward her, taking her arm, guiding her by the elbow.

"Gallantry," she said. "How lucky can you get?"

The tips of his fingers touched her breast and she trembled, moved closer to him. Her hair brushed against his cheek. He stopped her in the moonlight. Shadows played across her lashes; light glinted from her pale green eyes. A warm rush of breath issued from her mouth, washed his chin, lips, before he moved in to kiss her, a light play of tongue now on her inner lips, dancing with her tongue. She looked flushed in the iridescent air as she pulled her face a little away to speak. "One chukker isn't very long, thank God," she said, and moved her body close against his so he could feel every inch of her. "And they better make it fast."

Marty Fontaine had inherited his father's spare good looks, but not the same lawyers. To avoid conflict of interest, Johnny had given his sons shares in his various corporations and the names of attorneys who were not as tough as his. Marty adored his father, but when he found Zoe he still went to church and lit a candle. From the minute he recognized how feisty she was, how unimpressed by cloaks of influence, he was armed for the world that up until then he'd thought his father controlled. The first thing he did after becoming her client was to raise the rent on a warehouse Johnny had given him, in which one of his distribution companies stored its liquors.

"How can you do this to your own dad, when he gave you this gift?" Ben Michaels, Johnny's attorney, shouted over the phone. "It isn't right."

"Call my lawyer," Marty said, giving the name, waiting for the explosion when Ben heard his lawyer was a woman.

"You'd do that to your own father?" Ben exploded, as anticipated. "Pit him against some bimbo?"

"She isn't exactly a bimbo," Marty said, wishing he could be a fly on the wall when Ben had his conversation with Zoe. He sent her a hot pink satin bowling jacket and a sparkle-covered bowling ball, with the legend "KILLER" in raised letters on each.

He was excited as a boy that she was coming to the matches this evening. Having people he admired admire him back was the only thing that gave Marty a sense of peace. His expectations of affection were based, like the trade papers he had grown up on, solely on the difference between what he announced and what actually materialized. So far he had made four pictures, which to nearly everyone's surprise had been quite good. He offered them like little Stonehenges of accomplishment to a God who seemed to like him on occasion, sending friends like Zoe. Proportionate to his age, Marty was still several pictures behind his idol, Stanley Kubrick, although he did share with that genius a fear of car crashes. A phobia about going too fast, except careerwise. He tried to deal with that particular neurosis by playing polo, which somehow made automobiles seem impotent, a joke. Polo placed him high above the ground, presenting him as someone to be taken seriously. In control, if not of his destiny, certainly of the reins.

He knew what hubris it was for him to play polo, what a finger to the gods of class and station. He had studied the history of the game, as he had studied cinema, knew the sport was the domain of aristocrats. Coming down through the years from ancient Asian chieftains, setting their underlings to mounted play in pursuit of the little *pulu*, liking the game so much they'd unseated their subordinates, restricting it to rulers. A small exclusive club, Kiplingesque in its elegance. Society bluebloods who played their horseback hockey in the thirties and the forties, men with names like "Boozey" and "Froggie," old boys who slid privileged through Princeton and Yale, excellent at polo, so not required to be good at anything else. The world's most select membership, offering haven and instant welcome in the unlikeliest places. Manila, Rangoon, where all one had to do to enjoy acceptance and any number of invitations was to be a player. Perennial houseguests at the watering holes of the very rich: Southampton in summer, Palm Beach in winter. A Wasp entertainment.

Certainly if there was one thing Marty wasn't, it was a Wasp. Not all the perfumes of Arabia could give him that smell, the vanilla breath of Episcopals. Playing polo, though, he felt he could almost pass. On the back of a local glossy throwaway magazine called *Ranch and Coast*, there was an ad for polo that said, "For Everyone who's Anyone, and those who wish they were..." It had a certain snotty sadness to it, as if the whole civilization, if such it could be called, had learned nothing from Theodore Dreiser, the tragedy inherent in trying to rise above your class. Marty felt beyond the asshole rhetoric. He was Anyone, son of the Big Anyone. There was no way he had to *wish* he were. But there were some things in life that could not be won, earned, or bought, that came in the genes: grace on ice skates, hollow vowels, rushing a river on a raft. Any one of a number of pleasures and refinements seemingly restricted to Wasps.

On the field, though, he could feel himself shining with seeming Protestant polish. In the uniform of a polo Adept, he was secure. He was a trim man, on the small side, who gave the impression of being tall because of how proudly he held himself, and because of his neat good looks. He wore his chestnut hair full and to his neck, the streaks in it lightened by afternoon rides in the bright California sun. He had grown a mustache early in his maturity to distinguish himself from his father: It added to the impression that he was bigger than he stood. His body was lean and well developed, impeccably suited to the soft polo shirts tucked into tight white pants and knee-high leather boots with a zipper up the front, buckled across the top. Suited up like that, catching a glimpse of himself in his dressing room mirror, he would swear he was Gilbert fucking Roland, the fair version.

Three nights a week he worked out at the gym, bench pressing one hundred and eighty pounds so there'd be good definition to his pecs when his shirts got a little too small, which they always did when the maid had a run at them. After his last divorce settlement, he'd moved to an apartment on Doheny Drive, bordering Beverly Hills, not big enough, really, to require the services of a maid. But Lupita had worked for him all through that marriage, and his wife didn't want her. Lupita was a frightened, bleak-eyed woman with a pale Salvadoran face, so Marty understood she knew what real trouble was. He took her on full time, though there were just two and a half rooms, with worn white carpeting. Not that much to clean, so she spent a lot of time laundering in too-hot water. Without making protests, he wore his shirts too small and worked on his chest. As close as he could come to the Mother Teresa concept of Christianity: to care for the uncared for. He carried his sensitive feelings over to his horses, wondering if he was a burden for them, if they resented the imposition, if it was too much for them, playing polo.

He imagined it was hard being raced up and down the field, charging after the hollow rubber ball. In every other equestrian sport, a horse knew what to expect. A racehorse knew when the gates opened, it was time to run, a jumper to jump, a rodeo horse to chase a calf. But in polo it was always changing. A horse ran full speed for thirty feet and was suddenly reined in, stopped, pulled in the other direction. So there was no way to learn a pattern of behavior.

But there were "perks" for the horses, he knew that, too. Little extras they got for their specialness, as if they were heads of studios. They were catered to and coddled and preened for six days of the week, and only had to work on Saturday. The roars of the crowd, the pleasures of the game were palpable. He could feel the animals getting tuned up for it, psyched up like athletes, pawing the ground before a game, their adrenaline shooting like his was. Liking the contact, the crowding as though they were football players. Anticipating some of his moves. Enjoying their workout in the spotlight.

Horses were a breed for which Marty felt enormous affection, since they, like Zoe, were not intimidated by his father. It also made him feel more like a man to do one thing his father, that versatile giant, wouldn't dream of doing. Marty was a better horseman than polo player, but he was learning. And no one could suggest that Marty could ride like he did because Johnny had influence with the horses, that it was his glue that kept Marty in the saddle. But he wasn't content just getting good. He needed to be outstanding. So, accelerating his natural aptitude, he bought superior horses, from eight- and nine-goal players, polo being a handicapped game the same as golf was, a ten handicap equaling perfection. The term made Marty smile; as though anyone could be considered to have a handicap when he was lucky enough, coordinated enough, rich enough to play polo.

He stood now outside the stalls of the stable where he boarded his horses, watching the groom preen Sidewinder, the gelding he intended to ride in the first chukker. For the tournament he'd hired as his teammates an Argentinian and a Texan, coolheaded players who rode like Comanches.

It was important to Marty that he look good to Zoe because she always looked so good to him. Not so much her appearance—he hardly saw what she looked like; all the women who had let him down were regulation Rodeo Drive, dresses by Lina Lee, faces by Georgette Klinger, bills by his business manager—but how she conducted herself. She was like a soft version of the army sergeant he'd never had but always wanted: stringent, exacting, quietly compassionate. But always there. That was the thing about her that kept him going, how consistent she was, how unflaggingly supportive. Always, when she said she'd be there, she was there.

And she had humor. That was what he loved best about her, how irreverent she was. Most people dealt with Johnny like he was the Pope, including, as Marty had once been present to see, the Pope himself. But Zoe treated him like it was all a joke and a game, everybody taking Johnny so seriously.

From time to time, Marty considered falling in love with her. He knew she was smarter than he was, but that didn't bother him. He had never had a sexual relationship with a woman who was smart, and he imagined she'd have warm and witty things to say afterward. But he'd never made a move on her. The last thing he wanted was to make a fool of himself, although he knew she was too gracious to dump him professionally. But he hoped with all his being that the pace of the contest would heat her up as he'd never had the nerve to try and do.

"You better make me look good to Zoe," he said to Sidewinder, rubbing his shoulder, enjoying the hard warm contact, the compact sturdiness of the animal, a horse slightly scaled down from a regular jumper, just a touch smaller, neater, the way Marty was. Stepping to the doorway of the stall, he caught a flash of Zoe underneath a floodlight, moving toward the stables. Her beige hair swirled like a cloud around her head, bouncing along with her quietly energetic step. He waited for the skip of his heart that would signal infatuation. Instead, he felt a pull of anguish at the base of his belly as he saw the man with her. How dumb he'd been not to tell her to come alone.

In his fantasies of the evening, he'd pictured her as a latter-day, fresh-faced Ava Gardner, himself as the Burbank version of a matador, presenting her with whatever would serve as an ear. In his visions she had been alone in the stands while the crowds cheered and he bowed in front of her box, and she rose slowly to her feet while the fans rained flowers on him. He hadn't pictured her with a man who looked that good, even from a distance, as spruce as he himself was, and not even in riding clothes. She was such an independent woman, it never occurred to him she would feel the womanly compulsion to travel in pairs.

He wondered why he hadn't dealt more honestly with her, honest as she was, why he hadn't made his intentions known. Why was he so dazzled by women's accessories? The apartment he'd moved into after the divorce was very much a woman's apartment, with smoked glass mirrors above the fireplace, the soiled white carpeting he promised himself he'd replace as soon as he got organized. There were other sad little feminine touches around the place, crystal sconces on the wall, elaborately carved moldings. Marty didn't want the responsibility of a house; an apartment was all he needed. But its atmosphere depressed him, along with the legend he heard: on those matted down tufts had danced the bare feet of Marilyn Monroe.

Marty couldn't verify for sure whether she'd lived there. Whether or not that had been her actual domicile, Marty was sure if it had, she'd been caught in the crap. The fading glitz of the crystal fixtures, pockmarked with accumulated dust, the little touches that spoke of vanished glamour, and dreams interred, vaulted in white marble the way she was. An apartment of feminine ghosts.

There had even been a giant carved crystal decanter of perfume deep in one of the cabinets far back in the bathroom wall, unopened, as if left there as a spectral gift for The Starlet to Come. The bottle was marked with the legend "SILK LADY" and sealed with golden twine. Curious, Marty had opened it. It was a scent he had never smelled before, heavy, musky, Oriental, aggressively feminine. He'd put some under his nose and masturbated and thought about Zoe. Then he resealed the bottle, had Lupita polish it, and gave it to Zoe, telling her it had been left to him by Marilyn Monroe.

He held out his arms to her now as she approached the stall, noting how good she looked, as he had never noted her appearance before he decided to maybe be in love with her. She hugged him, a friendly hug, straightforward like she was. He smelled her perfume. "You're wearing it."

"Marty Fontaine," Zoe introduced them. "Admiral Mitchel."

"Hap," Hap extended his hand. "It isn't necessary to use the title."

"I like it," Zoe said. "It impresses me."

"Colonel Fontaine," Marty said, shaking Hap's hand.

"I didn't know that," said Zoe.

"Neither did I till I heard titles impressed you."

She laughed. "You look very smart in that outfit."

"I look *good*." He touched the collar of his bright green team shirt. "You look smart. And you smell gorgeous."

"I'm wearing the perfume you gave me."

"Marilyn Monroe left it to me," Marty told Hap. "Said I should save it for someone who was woman enough. Took me all these years to find her."

"Doesn't perfume go bad?" Hap asked.

"Not if it's sealed and kept in a dark place. I kept it in my heart."

"False advertising," said Zoe.

Behind them, a tall, heavyset man lumbered out of the shadows, his head bent forward a little bullishly. "Marty Fontaine?" he said.

"Yes?"

"Detective Lou Salerno," Lou said. "I been trying to get hold of you."

"Detective?" Zoe asked.

"LAPD Homicide. You been ducking me," he said to Marty.

"I missed the homicide part. I thought you were someone my ex-wife sent."

"What do you know about MicroTel?" Lou asked.

"You don't really want to talk business," Zoe said, smiling at Salerno. "Have you been to many polo matches?"

"Not even one. It's a little elegant for my blood."

"You'd be surprised how fast it heats up," Marty said. "Elegant or not elegant."

"So what do you know about MicroTel?"

"I don't even know what it is."

"It's a stock. You were in for several thousand shares. What can you tell me about the company?"

"I don't know anything about it."

"You in the habit of buying thousands of shares in companies you don't know anything about?"

"I didn't exactly buy it."

"You were listed as one of the participants in the *Wall Street Journal*."

"It was a gift," Zoe said.

"Who are you, his mother?"

"His lawyer."

"Anyone can have a mother," Marty said.

"So what can *you* tell me about the takeover?" Lou asked Zoe.

"Not very much. We did what everyone else does. We sold when the price was up. If you have any other questions, lieutenant, why don't you call me at my office?" She handed him a card, and smiling, took Hap's arm, and Marty's arm, and walked them away.

"You didn't tell him my father just bought it in my name and how he almost shit when you sold it," Marty said.

"That isn't any of his business," said Zoe. "Can we get something to eat around here?"

"There's a restaurant over at the club. I have to stay here with my horses."

"If the lieutenant asks you anything else, change the subject. Or tell him to call me," Zoe said. "You don't have to talk to him."

"I don't have anything to hide."

"But we don't know what he wants. It's never smart to say too much to people when you don't know what they want."

"I know what I want," Marty said. "I guess I should have told you." He turned to Hap. "I'm sorry we didn't have more time to get acquainted."

"Me too," Hap said. "I enjoyed the light-type patter."

"Here, we call it light-type bullshit. You don't look like a man who minces words."

"I don't like to use profanity in front of a lady."

"It isn't profanity. It's a very descriptive word that says exactly what something is when it's bullshit."

"I didn't realize you were into semantics. I thought you were a movie director. Who knew you were a man of so many parts?"

"What part are you?" Marty narrowed his eyes.

"The romantic lead," Zoe said.

"I would've cast him younger," said Marty.

"Fortunately it's not your movie," said Hap.

"You stationed out here?"

"I guess you could say that. Been a lot of years since I was in the service. But my company's out here, so so am I, most of the time. Same thing I guess as movies. You have to be where your business is."

"My business is all over. I'm planning a movie this summer to be shot in the Greek islands."

"That wouldn't be hard to take."

"None of it's hard to take once you get over the prejudice against it. Sort of like bright women."

"I never had a prejudice against bright women," said Hap.

"I never knew one before Zoe."

"Well, there's nothing to be afraid of, as long as you stay a little ahead. Like with the Russians."

"Oh, you're that Mitchel," Marty said. "You really believe that crap? That we have to have all those weapons?"

"I really believe it."

"But how about terrorists getting them, or what if the button goes off by accident, or the computer in the Pentagon breaks down, the way it has over a hundred times this year, and they think we're under attack, or what if a flock of geese sets off the alarm?"

"That's not going to happen."

"But it already has. Didn't you hear about the geese?"

"The rest of the system showed error," Hap said.

"That was that time."

"It won't happen again."

"I wish I had your conviction."

"I wish you had it, too. But there's no way that everybody can see things the same, so why don't you leave it to the people in charge?"

"Because I don't think the people in charge know their ass from the button they're ready to push," Marty said. "They actually think a nuclear war can be won. You cowboys and the Big Cowboy are going to turn this whole planet into the O.K. Corral."

"I think you should leave weapons management to us and save your passions for the movies."

"I hope I'll have that chance," said Marty.

Zoe took Hap's arm. "We better go have our dinner if we're going to be finished by the time the match starts."

"Won't you join us?" Hap asked politely.

"I can't. But please sign my name. You're my guests."

"I can't allow you to do that."

"You can't *allow* me to do anything else. It's members only. Your money is no good here."

"I feel uncomfortable about that."

"Well, I feel uncomfortable about the fact that greedy corporations and trigger-happy military men and covert assholes are playing games with my life. But sometimes we don't have a choice."

"Up yours," said Hap.

"It was nice meeting you, too," said Marty.

The Members Only dining room at the Polo Club had the atmosphere of thrown-together chic of one of Los Angeles' most famous restaurants. The similarity was not accidental. Both places were run by a Frenchman who had discovered that the key to success in that curious corner of the continent was a seeming indifference to whether people patronized you or not. The restaurant in Hollywood had soared to popularity despite cheap tenting over garden tables, aluminum silverware, and dishes a notch above Melmac, its greatest distinction a snobbism outstripping its clientele's, including the local celebrity tic of an unlisted phone number.

The Members Only Restaurant at the Equestrian Center offered a bit more hospitality. The menu was serviceable, with the restaurant's better salades on the buffet, next to a cut-glass vase garlanded with spiked gladiolus, drooping slightly, as if left over from a bar mitzvah. A terrace alongside overlooked the covered arena, its tables cheerfully laid with bright yellow linen and small vases with fresher flowers. But Hap and Zoe elected to eat inside, where the captain advised them the service would be quicker. The terrace, he counseled, was better for afternoons.

"Maybe we'll come another time for lunch," Zoe said as Hap pulled out her chair for her.

"To spend more time with Marty?"

"Sorry about that," Zoe said.

"It's not your fault." Hap sat down to her left. "If there's one thing I can't stand it's these knee-jerk show business liberals who think they understand the arms race."

"At least he's not too caught up in himself to feel concerned. It's an issue that has to torment sane people. Aren't you afraid of what could happen? Why are we still building weapons with all there already are?"

"They're ahead. We have to catch up."

"That seems to be the party line, and you deliver it very well. But I happen to think it's baloney that they're ahead. And what about this 'Star Wars' stuff? Laser beams in space, for God's sake."

"That would help us nullify their advantage. Our advantage is accuracy. We could stop their missiles. Get back to balance."

"What's balanced about asking for nuclear war? You make toys, boys use them. You're a smart man. You must have grave doubts."

"I have grave doubts about tonight," Hap said. "I thought it was going to be a pleasant, superficial evening."

"You left out passionate."

"A pleasant, passionate, superficial evening."

"Okay," Zoe said. "I can be superficial if you want."

"How about passionate?"

"What do you think?" Zoe looked at him so hard he forgot what it was he drank when the waiter came to ask for their order.

Behind them chattered a table of Beautiful People, women with jewels that might have more aptly graced royal tables, diamond necklaces that the late Mrs. Gould might have worn touring the Cambodian jungles, just as inappropriately. Their shoulders draped with fingertip-length furs, as though having supper before the opera, the women smiled and exchanged recollections and shopping tips. The men with them wore custom jackets and the tailored trousers of country gentlemen.

Someone called out Hap's name. He turned and caught the smile of Dwight Efram Jonah, the salt of his hair saltier in contrast to a fresh, deep tan. He got up and came over to Hap.

"Thought it was you," he said.

"Mr. Secretary." Hap stood as they shook hands.

"Couldn't imagine what you'd be doing here," Jonah said. "Used to finding you places you're not supposed to be, but usually in the air. I didn't know this was your turf."

"It's not." Hap indicated Zoe. "Mr. Secretary, Zoe Baldwin. Dwight Efram Jonah."

"I'm honored," Zoe said, holding out her hand.

"On the contrary," Jonah drawled. "It is I who am honored. Are you the lovely reason for his being here?"

"You're very flattering."

"Flattery carries with it a hint of deceit. There is no deception here, unless my eyes deceive me."

"Mercy. And me not even from the South."

"That is the South's disadvantage," Jonah said, and let her hand go with a visible show of reluctance.

"What brings you to town, sir?" Hap asked.

"Kind of a sentimental occasion." Jonah's opaque gray eyes misted slightly. "A year ago at this opening, I was here with Victor Lenrahan. Excited as a boy he was. His favorite game, polo, in his own backyard. He couldn't believe it. Shame he couldn't be here to watch the place grow."

"A shame," Hap echoed.

"By the way, I'm sorry you lost the contract."

"I'm not. I'd like to talk to you, sir."

"There's going to be a second go-round on the 'Star Wars' research. Even more money will be involved. I assure you I'll give you the inside track."

"I appreciate that, sir. But I really need to talk to you."

"I'm at the Wilshire. Call me on Monday. Meanwhile, enjoy the game. Maybe you'll have a drink with us after the matches."

"If we're still here, we'd be happy to."

"Still here? Watched much polo?"

"Only once, a long time ago."

"You won't be able to tear yourself away." His eyes moved back to Zoe. "Then again, maybe you will." He went back to his table.

The match was set to start at eight, but the crowd seemed in no hurry to get to their seats. Hap and Zoe were the first ones in their box, two sections of four rows each, metal chairs soldered into concrete steps, each section separated from the one next to it by metal railings. The whole arena, the size of a football field, was canopied by a metal roof, the sides open to the air.

"They're playing three men on a team," Zoe told Hap. "They play four on the open field, but in the arena they play three."

"I suppose you want me to root for Marty's team."

"Do whatever you want."

"He's in love with you."

"He's grateful for my help is all. That was a real sticky one with his father. Johnny bought all those shares in Marty's name so people wouldn't know how deeply involved he was in the takeover try. I had a feeling it was going to get ugly. I just had a hunch. So I cashed him in just before Masters died."

"I was supposed to have dinner with him the night he committed suicide."

"You think it was suicide? We heard all kinds of rumors."

"I never listen to rumors."

"I always do," Zoe said. "I just don't believe them. Anyway, it turned out to be very lucky, my getting him out."

"I don't think I'd want to tangle with you," Hap said.

"Sure you would."

"Sure I would. But I guess I'll have to wait my turn in line."

"How funny. You imagine men are after me."

"If they were smart they would be."

"Forgive me," she said, and patted his hand. "But they aren't that smart. There's no one in my life right now."

"Then get rid of the perfume," Hap said. "It's too heavy for you."

The loudspeaker went on. An announcer welcomed the onlookers to the Equestrian Center, giving the names of the two teams in that evening's preliminary tournament. People started coming down into their seats. Below, in the arena, a man on a tractor flattened and sifted the dry brown earth, making it smooth for the coming event. From the gate next to the scoreboard at the far end of the field, a rider entered on an Arabian horse. The announcer introduced it to the crowd. Like the show creature it was, the white Arabian reared on long, graceful hind legs, flashing its tail, shuddering its mane, flaring wide nostrils and whinnying. The crowd applauded. An aging starlet in very high, spiked heels and long, glittering gown, came out and sang the "Star-Spangled Banner." She exited, her heels awkward on the turf as she held up her skirt and tried not to stumble, followed by the tractor. Then the announcer called out the names of the players on the team as they cantered in on their horses.

Marty's team, the Burbank Bengals, were dressed in kelly green shirts with a wide stripe diagonally across, green saddle pads, and matching leg wraps on the horses. The opposing team was shirted in light blue, their horses similarly saddled and wrapped, colorfully civilized. Stylishly swinging their mallets in practice moves, exaggeratedly in slow motion, the players lined up for the first throw-in. But when the ball was thrown, all trace of civility disappeared and the game exploded into violence.

There was a fierceness about the way they moved down the field, a thundering rowdiness that dispelled the air of refinement, blistering the atmosphere. The one polo match Hap had seen when he was stationed in Florida had been

played on a field three hundred yards long, two hundred
yards wide, twice as wide as this arena was long. There
was only one less player on each side in this game, one
less horse, on a field a seventh of the size. The arena
seemed to Hap too short to handle the speed of the
mounts, the physical presence of six horses, which once in
the arena appeared in no way diminutive in spite of being
called ponies. Hap got the impression the field was not
enough of a stretch for the horses, that they would all
collide into the far wall before their riders could rein them
in. It was one thing having a field that size for football or
hockey, but not this mounted, medieval combat, sportslike
as the players tried to make it seem. Too short by far for
these fleet-footed, powerful animals, setting off as though
riding in a derby.

But to his surprise, the horses made quick stops and
turns, as Marty's team recovered the ball from the other
end of the field. And then they were at the far end, the
crowd roaring, and a point went up on the scoreboard. All
of it happening so fast, Hap wasn't even aware of the
yellow ball hitting the goal.

No less surprising to him was Marty's grace and ease on
the field. Even knowing as little as he did, Hap had
appraised the horse as way above Marty's head, much
more horse than Marty was horseman. But that was doubtless smallness on his part, he had to admit to himself,
trying to see the man as less because of his jealousy over
Zoe.

Now the other team had the ball, the blue-shirted riders
coming down the field like invading marauders. Marty's
eyes momentarily flashed over to the seats where Zoe and
Hap were. He drove his horse in the direction of his
opponent, trying to move off the line, to take possession of
the ball. Half a ton of horse riding toward the man at forty
miles an hour. Marty hit him at a forty-five degree angle,
driving the full weight of his mount into the other man's
knee. Hap could feel the man's teeth rattle. A game of
intimidation, domination. Like warfare. The whole thing
made him uneasy.

But not quite as uneasy as it seemed to make Marty's opponent. Hap could see him struggling to get back his wind, riding toward Marty, attempting to regain possession of the ball. Over his shoulder, Marty saw his opponent bearing down on him and tried to get his horse out of the way. But the horse didn't move fast enough, and caught off balance, went down, with Marty underneath him. Hap could see Marty's foot hit the dirt, toes first, heard the splintering of bone. Heard the screams of the crowd, the loudest beside him, Zoe's.

The horse rolled back, got up on its legs and started to gallop in panic, with Marty's foot still caught in the stirrup, dragging him skidding along on his elbows. People shrieked in horror as Marty flailed to get out of the way of the flashing hind legs. The rest of the players watched him helplessly.

"Stop him!" Zoe was shouting. "Somebody stop him!" Mallet still in his hand, Marty reached out, and with it caught the horse's drooping reins, finally pulling it to a halt.

The ambulance was there within two minutes, driving straight onto the field in the arena. Paramedics put an inflatable cast around Marty's leg and, lifting him onto a stretcher, got him into the ambulance. By then Zoe was on the field, Hap right behind her.

"Let me talk to him," she said to the paramedic closing the ambulance doors.

"Sorry, lady. We've got to get him to the hospital."

"Tell him I'll be there," she said, and called out loudly, so Marty could hear her, "I'll be there. I'll be there."

"I'm so fucking embarrassed," Marty said when the doctors let her into the room. He'd been two hours in emergency at St. John's, while doctors set his foot, a telescoped break from front to back, every bone in it smashed.

"I thought you were incredible," she said, and took his hand. "Why didn't any of the others try to help you?"

"If they chased after the horse, it just would've run faster."

"That was very impressive, reaching up and catching the reins with the mallet."

"Not quite as impressive as the fall."

"Are you in much pain?"

"Only when I dance."

She laughed and kissed his forehead. "What can I do for you?"

"Go home. I can't stand for you to see me so helpless. I wanted you to think I was a hero."

"You are a hero."

"Go home." There was an IV in his arm, bandages around both his elbows. "They gave me something. I can't keep my eyes open."

"I'll call you first thing in the morning." She leaned over again to kiss him.

"I love you in that perfume," he said, and fell asleep.

"How the hell can I compete with that?" Hap said as they got into Zoe's car. "A man stopping a runaway horse with a polo mallet."

"Well, you could stop the arms race."

"Get the needle out, kiddo." He slammed the car door.

"Don't you think you could do it?" She saw the look on his face, the shadow of uneasy despair. "Okay. Then I guess I'll just have to ask that you be good in bed."

"I want to be as straight as you are," Hap said when their clothes were half off and his palms were cupping the outsides of her breasts, fuller than he had imagined, rounder than they looked in her clothes. "I want to be as direct."

"Try me," she said, her fingers undoing the belt on his pants while her mouth never left his face, her lips moving along the strong line of his chin, half tracing, half sucking, till she got to his ear and chewed on the lobe.

"I won't sleep with you," he said. "I want to make love . . ."

"Oh, I know that," she said, and unzipped and freed

him, her hands moving around him, touching. "I can certainly tell that."

". . . but I won't spend the night with you."

"You don't like soft sheets?" she asked, and led him to them, leaned her body down toward her bed and eased him down with her, pulling his pants over his buttocks so he could get out of them, while he moved the elastic band that gathered her banana silk trousers down over her hips. Flashed his hand across her mons.

"I like soft everything," he said, and burrowed his head gently between her breasts, brushing the short crop of his hair across the rise of them, circling, one at a time, with the crown of his head, beneath, and to the center, letting his tongue flicker across her stiff, palely rosy nipples. "But I have certain ground rules. When it's over, I go home."

"You want me to draw up a contract?" she asked, and cupped his ears, drawing his face up to her face, darting at him with her tongue.

"Don't be a smart ass," he said, and fell into her mouth.

"I can't help it," she said when they could breathe again. "That's what I am."

"Doesn't feel so smart to me. Turn over."

She did. He traced his hair slowly down her backbone while his hands moved along the sides of her breasts, her waist, her hips, the outside of her buttocks, gently trailing along the curve of her bottom cheeks, coming to rest in between, spreading her. Then he was at the bottom of the bed, and his hair moved against the high arch of her left instep, and he sucked her toes, and she sighed, and stretched, and called out for him. And he moved his hair up the inside of her leg, circling, lightly, his forehead brushing the silky skin of her inner thigh. And she opened for him, and called out his name again, more urgently now and said, "Yes," and then, "Please." But he grazed past the warm, wet place and started down her other thigh till he lay against the hollow behind her knee, and washed it with his tongue. And he could hear her murmuring, and

feel her hands stretching down to reach for him, but he
eluded her, continued the movement of hair and mouth till
he came to her other foot. And he drank in her toes, one
by one, flicking his tongue over the delicate skin between.
And he could hear her cooing now, somewhere between a
purr and a sigh. He sat up on his haunches and touched
her.

"How come you're so wet?" he said.

"You've got to be kidding," she answered, her words
drawn back tight as an archer's bow.

And he reached around to the front of her hips, raised
her slightly, straddled her, and plunged inside. She cried
out, lifted herself on straight arms, strained backward,
moving herself against him, pumping slowly, as he pumped.

"Easy," he said, and gentled her down, the fleshy part
of his thumbs joining at the hard round tip of her, kneading.
"Don't want it over too fast."

"Don't want it over at all," she breathed, and turned
her head, stretching her long, graceful neck, and reaching
for his mouth with her mouth. And they filled each other's
openings.

She tensed, cried out, spasmed against him. "Oh, my
God," she said, when she lay in his arms. "And I thought
the Navy wasn't supposed to be subtle."

"Well, don't forget I'm Air Force."

"I'll say." She traced the angles of his face with the tips
of her fingers.

"But I can't spend the night."

"So you said."

"Nothing personal."

"Okay."

"It's just how it is."

"Whatever you say," she said.

"I wouldn't be comfortable."

"Relax," she said, and kissed his nose. "A deal is a deal."

"But I guess I could stay for a little while," he said,
and trailed his fingers across her armpit. "Just don't let me
fall asleep."

"Oh you can count on that," Zoe said.

* * *

Sometime during the night, Marty Fontaine thought he saw someone coming into his hospital room. He was in the midst of an erotic dream about Zoe. As he believed in the power of dreams, he thought maybe he'd conjured her, so he welcomed whoever it was. He couldn't speak, drugged as he felt, still heavy with sleep. But not so foggy he couldn't pick up on his own confusion and realize it wasn't Zoe at all. The person in the nurse's uniform was heavy-set, putting something in his IV. He experienced a sensation of burning, and tried to cry out. But he was so tired and depleted, he just blacked out. When the morning nurse came to check him, he was dead.

The autopsy revealed no apparent cause. Marty's heart, the doctors said, had just stopped beating. But Lou Salerno didn't buy it for a minute. He went to Marty's apartment with a sick feeling in his belly, like he could have saved the kid if he'd only been more cooperative, and if Lou had only known. Known what? Wouldn't you think whoever they were, whatever they were trying to hide, they'd be a little wary of too many bodies piling up, have a little shame, a little caution?

In the bathroom of Marty's apartment, there was a wall broken out. Hammers and what was later concluded from the fingerprint reports to be gloved hands had smashed and pulled apart a false fronting of plasterboard to get to the hidden wall safe behind it. The safe had been broken into and was empty.

Lou talked to Marty's neighbors. One of them, a plump, tired woman, told Lou without his even asking that she had failed in television because she couldn't pee standing up, and that was how come she never got out of her robe. She stood in the courtyard, leaning against azaleas that had grown into trees, clipped into hedges now, fuchsia blossoms splattering across the smooth green surface like spilled paint. A thin stream of water wisped up from the lips of a bronzed Cupid in the fountain in the center of the courtyard.

"I lived here for twenty-five years," she told him. "Way before those fuckers pretended they didn't mind women executives and women in power, even though they had no real intention of letting them have any."

"Interesting," Lou said, wondering if she was a dyke.

"This building has real history," the woman said, and drew the belt of her chenille bathrobe tighter. "Who lived here once, in that corner apartment, was Marilyn Monroe. I guess you could say that apartment has Sanpaku eyes."

"What's that?"

"You know, when the whites show underneath your pupils. The Orientals call that Sanpaku. It usually means disaster. That the person is doomed. I guess you could say that about that apartment. It has Sanpaku eyes. First Marilyn. And now Marty . . .

"And who lived there right before him . . ." She stared beyond the fountain at the high double windows, the shades behind them drawn. "If you could call it living, I mean, she was more like a prisoner. Hardly ever coming out of there except to water her flowers. Who lived there before him was the late Miranda Jay."

BEVERLY HILLS

◇

In the mornings, Miranda would wake up very early, as though she had some purpose to her life. There was so much despair and dissolution in the community, there were so many people who had their hopes pinned to balloons, that she resolved not to be like them, to make every day of her life have meaning. Not the easiest thing in the world to do when you believed so little in yourself.

But all the same she would whip out of bed, or try to, and barring the occasional hangover or Valiumed sleep, she would slip into her Nikes with the same automatic motions she brushed her teeth, put on shorts and a T-shirt and canter down to Santa Monica Boulevard. On the north side of the street was a dirt jogging trail, a leftover bridle path from the days when Hollywood was young and full of real dreams and a number of horses. Running from Doheny Drive, the eastern border of Beverly Hills, to the intersection of Wilshire Boulevard, the path was lined on either side with lacey-leafed Brazilian elm trees that feathered over like a spikey arch, pieces of smoggy sky visible between the branches. Miranda would follow it at a brisk walking pace, her ears filled with the puffs of joggers coursing by her, their retreating bottoms trailing, in the mental image she conjured to amuse herself, long rodent tails. So what they were getting in shape for was the rat race.

She did not regret moving to Los Angeles. As deadly dull as the town seemed to be, she had had enough of the deadly lively. Her spirit was still seared by Washington and the suicide of Melissa Mae. There'd been no other friends there to speak of or part from, except Jacqueline Trimble Forsythe, who'd come in strictly for assignations with Allen Hewitt, which she wept over afterward on Miranda's couch. And all that served to do was remind Miranda how foolish women were to listen to men's words instead of seeing what they did.

So she was content, in her way, to be living on Doheny Drive, on the border of Beverly Hills, where the rest of the nation thought it would like to be. The town had formidable specters. From the Standard station on the corner of Sunset to the Hughes market on Beverly, there was the unspoken conviction that everyone filling their tanks or their shopping carts might bump into the ghost of Sidney Skolsky, who'd tap them on the shoulder the way he had

Lana Turner, and say, "Kid, you're a star." No matter how unattractive or untalented they were, there was always that off-the-wall chance. Especially now that the game had changed to include the ugly and the freaky, often making them into box office favorites.

A kind of foolish ambition rose in Miranda to be Somebody. Foolish because even as she wanted it, she knew how dopey it was—like someone with cancer in the family who needed a cigarette. But there was a woman living across the courtyard who kept asking Miranda why she didn't give herself a shot at becoming an actress.

"You're certainly prettier than most of the ones who make it in this town," Roz Goldwyn said, watching Miranda garden.

There was a quadrant of earth around the brass Cupid fountain in the center of the courtyard that was tended once a week by an indifferent gardener. Lately Miranda had started visiting nurseries in the area, as if they were nurseries of another sort. She would come home trailing sacks of mulch and potting soil, putting them around the plants outside her window, getting a spray attachment for the hose that coiled like a snake by the corner of the small apartment complex.

"Pretty doesn't mean much," Miranda said, making a hole for an African violet plant she found outside an office on La Cienega. On her outings she'd been noticing plants instead of people. She'd seen it there in too much sunlight. On her last visit to Trashy Lingerie, next door, she'd checked the soil at its base, and finding it dusty dry, dug it up with her fingernails and brought it home.

"Why are you doing that?" Roz said. "It's not your responsibility to garden." Roz was a former agent, an orphan who'd legally changed her name to Goldwyn because she was convinced that was who she was, the illegitimate spawn of one of the founding families of Hollywood, put into an orphanage because she hadn't been pretty or clever enough. Now she was in television, associate to a former network executive who pretended to like women, no matter how overweight they were, or what good ideas they had.

"I like it," Miranda said.

"You ought to get out of those shorts and put on a dress and go see some casting executives. Or leave the shorts on. If I was still in the agency business I'd handle you myself." She'd been watching Miranda from the upstairs window. She'd noted that the girl seemed always to be home, and that a limousine came at night and parked in the alley. "You should be doing more than taking care of flowers."

"I love flowers," Miranda said, getting to her feet, taking off her gardening gloves.

"Everyone loves flowers who isn't the head of a network," Roz said. "That doesn't mean you have to take care of them."

"What do you do now?" Miranda walked to the hose and connected the spray, turned it on and let it gently arc through the air and wash the earth around the violets.

"I work with Eddie Wax. We have three series in development. Eddie knows where the bodies are buried. Lucky for him, since he's a necrophiliac."

"I don't know what that is."

"Someone who likes to fuck the dead."

"Oh. You're making a joke."

"I don't think so. I found his little black book once, and he's got a listing of all the funeral parlors in town, and the home numbers of the morticians. That way he can find out who's hot off the slab."

Miranda laughed.

Roz checked out the girl's smile, as spectacular as the rest of her. "It sort of distinguishes him from the rest of the people in this town who only fuck the living."

The telephone rang inside Miranda's apartment, and she turned off the hose and ran for her door. "I mean it," Roz called out after her. "I'd like to help you."

"How would you feel about my trying to get work as an actress?" Miranda asked Victor the next time they were together.

"Oh, I don't know," he said. "I wish I could show you off more. But that's different, you know, *my* showing you off. How come you want to do this all of a sudden?"

"Because I have to be *something*," she said, and started to cry. "I'll never be a wife. I'll never be a mother."

"You'll be a mother, you'll be a mother," he just about shouted at her, and pulled from his briefcase the latest correspondence from the lawyers in Paris, including their bills, which were exorbitant and marked paid. "They offered them money, look, see, they offered them a pile of cash, my pile, but they refuse to give the kid up. So now they're checking into the legality of your signing her away."

"I'll never get her back," Miranda sobbed.

"You will. You will."

"Just like I'll never get the goddamned house."

"I have an order in. Realtors all over the country are seeking out a paradise to raise Colette in."

"She's ten years old," Miranda raged. "She's practically raised."

So all in all, it seemed a more constructive fantasy for Miranda to imagine she might connect in show business. Victor gave his blessing. Roz set up a number of appointments. But auditions were agonizing for Miranda. All of life seemed to be a weighing of whether people loved you or not, so to stand there with a piece of paper in shaking hands, trying to make people care for you, approve of you, by acting a part, tore strips in her soul. She went to the interviews in Victor's limousine, had her pictures taken for a portfolio by Harry Langdon, who had photographed in gloss everyone from Ann-Margret to Nancy Reagan. She took the chauffeured limousine not to impress agents and producers, who rarely if ever saw her to her car, but because when she went to these appointments she could hardly drive. She had come quite close on a number of occasions to having accidents, she was so anxious at the thought of not being wanted. So it seemed judicious to allow herself to be taken on her rounds.

She got a few jobs in commercials, where her glow

connected somewhat, especially in an ad for a new and advertised as erotic perfume. But none of it seemed to nourish her. She would come home depleted, not very up for her scenes with Victor, no longer eager to don the costumes, to pretend the anger. Anger was welling up too real in her to play at it.

"You know what you need?" Victor said, his face between her legs, his practiced tongue having little effect on her. She seemed distracted, even as she stood over him, ordering him to do what he was doing, not even pleased that he was doing it, forgetting to make him feel like scum while she hid her own pleasure. Neither the loathing nor her supposedly growing excitement seemed real to him, and real was essential in a fantasy. Especially with his tongue stroking the underside of her tip, and no sighs forthcoming.

"You mean besides this?" Miranda said, seeming to come back to where she was, hearing him at least.

"Besides this, honey pot," he said, and dipped in deeper to illustrate. "Would you undo my hands so I can touch you?"

"You're not good enough to touch me."

But her heart was obviously not in her words, so they didn't excite him. "You need a day at Elizabeth Arden's," he said.

The red door rose on the east side of Rodeo Drive, a spiritual beacon for the weary seeking a different kind of church, where all would be soothing and comfort, with no risk of judgment as long as you tipped. There were silk print dresses on mannequins in the huge glass windows glittering transparently on either side of the door. Miranda hesitated for a moment before entering, pretending to look at the clothes. Then she stepped on the woven rubber mat with the huge initials and crossed the threshold.

There was a silence inside, a curious lack of activity, an absence of people, except for one Oriental salesgirl who sat behind the cosmetic counter. "I'm supposed to have a massage and things," Miranda said.

"Fourth floor," the dark-haired young woman said, pointing to the elevator.

The elevator seemed a continuation of the curious tranquillity. Miranda could hear no buzz as it ascended, feel no motion as it moved, the only sign that she'd been lifted at all was the glow of the number four above the door. The double doors opened with a faint squeaking, the one indication that there was anything mechanical going on, besides the quest for beauty.

But at the desk all was activity, a ringing of telephones, a flipping of pages, as women stood in their Arden robes while the desk girls checked the scheduled appointments.

"And that was for a manicure?" A curly-haired blonde with very round eyes asked the woman in front of her, a slim, elegant redhead in her fifties.

"Herbal wrap and massage," the woman said.

"I'm sorry," said the round-eyed blonde. "I'm new."

"I wish I was," said the customer.

"And the massage was with . . . ?"

"Hilda. And then I have a leg wax with Ann."

"Oh, I'm sorry. Ann just called. She won't be in till this afternoon. Can I schedule you with someone else?"

"I'm used to Ann. I could come back at the end of the day."

"Excuse me," Miranda said to the other girl at the desk. "I'm supposed to have a day here."

"Go change into a robe." The girl indicated the dressing room.

Once inside, Miranda started taking off her jeans, noting the clothes that were already hung there. As many designer suits as had decked the showroom in Paris all those years ago when Harry Bell had waltzed her into this dream. A sudden sadness passed through her as she remembered him and wondered if he'd be as disappointed with her as she was with herself. Her only potential couldn't have been as a whore. Though he'd obviously been a patsy about some women, he couldn't have been so far off about her. New resolution started to flow through her. It wasn't just her outside that she'd retrim this day.

She looked at the beige paper scuffs lined up on the floor. "Am I supposed to take off my shoes, too?" she asked the red-haired woman, who was just coming in.

"It's like Let Go and Let God," the woman said. "You have to surrender everything."

After her herbal wrap, where they sprinkled her with attars and what smelled like spices and felt like medicinal lotions, and wound her round with an infinity of rubber sheets, stiffing her arms at her sides, mummifying her entire length—to cleanse her of her toxins, the attendant explained—after they toweled off her strangely rank sweat, they gave Miranda a sheet and took her to the massage area. There were three stalls, separated by dividers but with no doors. The dividers between did not go all the way to the ceiling. A slender woman lay on the massage table in the center stall, talking rapidly as her masseuse worked on her. In front of the far stall waited the red-haired woman, wound round with a sheet as Miranda was. They nodded at each other as their masseuses came out to greet them.

Miranda let herself be led to the table, helped up, laid out, unwrapped, covered lightly with a towel. Over the transom she could hear the woman in the center stall talking.

"And the story was that she was the mistress of Ho Chi Minh. That he'd seen her when she was twelve years old in a detention camp for Europeans, picked her out and said, 'Send me that one,' and it had been going on for a couple of years till she got the money together to flee and came to Chicago. Don't ask me why, Chicago. So here was this mysterious Swede, or whatever she said she was, and this fabulous legend started filtering down through Chicago society that she had been the mistress of Ho Chi Minh. Next thing you know, she knocks off the heir of one of the meat-packing families.

"I think she started that Ho Chi Minh rumor herself. I mean, who would know? It's not like the *National Enquirer* was working Vietnam for hot gossip. But imagine the patience she had, taking all those years to merchandise herself. It's brilliant, really.

"I think I'm going to start that rumor about myself. A Russian is always good. Whose mistress was I? A friend of mine went to work at the U.N. looking for a foreign involvement, because they work so well when they're behind you, but all she had was an affair with a United States senator, and of course he was married. That doesn't count, especially with someone native. Maybe Khrushchev was who it was. He couldn't keep his hands off me. How does that sound? You think he was too old?"

"I don't remember much about him," the masseuse said.

"He was very fatherly, but that couldn't hurt. A hint of incest is always exciting. Anyway, after she dumped the meat-packing guy she went to New York where she now has this crown of Ho Chi Minh and a regular American multimillionaire. Next thing you know, she knocks off this billionaire, Bummy Vonnocken. Now she has an affair with their chauffeur, and Bummy catches them, and he takes her back anyway. Then she rehires the chauffeur, and Bummy finds some papers that they're planning to bilk him out of his fortune. And he still takes her back. Imagine that. Finding papers."

"Some people like to get caught."

"But imagine him taking her back. They go out to dinner at 21 and she watches him eat and says to his friends, 'You believe what a pig he is?' They go out dancing and she grinds her machinery up against his best friend on the dance floor. His *best friend*. The poor man is so embarrassed he can never ask her to dance again, but she's always asking him. And the dodo still stays married to her."

"Some people like to get punished."

"Maybe it was Gromyko."

"Who?"

"Who I had the affair with."

"Is he still alive?"

"Yes."

"Can you do that?"

"Well, what is he going to do? I mean, it's just a rumor. Nobody's going to print it. He probably won't even hear it, unless he goes to lunch at the Bistro."

Miranda left her stall after the massage and saw the redhead again. They exchanged amused glances, both having heard all the same stories. For the rest of the day Miranda was oiled and preened, fed a light lunch, Scotch-hosed. This last was a procedure with a pressure hose, where she stood at the end of a long, tiled shower room while the woman who shot it at her told her to cover her breasts and turn slowly. It was a not-so-gentle pummeling all up and down her body, and she wondered if it had indeed originated in Scotland, or didn't more appropriately start in Germany, where they could have really gotten into it, turned up the pressure, and maybe spread-eagled people while they were getting it. Then she was taken for a leg waxing, manicure and pedicure, a facial, makeup, and, finally, hair styling.

"You're *not* really here for a makeover," the young hairdresser said.

"A friend of mine gave me a day here," Miranda told him, smiling.

"Because you're already divine. You know that. They should make everybody else over into you. What am I going to do with this hair, besides run my fingers through it? Up, down, cut, what?"

"How good are you?"

"Well, I'm going to be the best," he said. "But I don't like to mess with perfection."

"Do whatever you want."

"Fling myself at your feet? Who are you, besides gorgeous?"

"Miranda Jay," she said, and offered him her mani-cured hand.

"Steven Holt," he said, and kissed it. "Your ser-vant."

* * *

Dressed again, finished now with her day, Miranda stood in front of the desk, handing her tickets to the curly-haired blonde with the round eyes. Next to Miranda, the red-haired woman, sleek in a red suit that looked like Chanel, handed her ticket to the brunette. She and Miranda smiled at each other, old comrades now.

"Cash or charge?" asked the brunette.

"Charge," said Miranda.

"Charge," said the elegant redhead.

"How does the charge read?" asked the brunette.

"Who to?" asked the blonde.

"Victor Lenrahan," said the red-haired woman and Miranda together.

"It was the most humiliating experience of my life!" she screamed at Victor. "You did it on purpose! You wanted to get caught. Some people like to get caught, and you're one of them! You did it on purpose!"

"I didn't know she'd be there today!" he said.

"But you knew that's where she goes! That that's *her* beauty parlor!" She caught a glimpse of herself in the smoked glass over the fireplace, and the hate and rage of her face frightened her. She looked all twisted, distorted, like she was always playing at being in their games, but there was nothing she could do to get that expression off her face now, to tear the awful feeling out of her stomach. "You degraded me!"

"I didn't mean to. Honest to God."

"Then why did you send me where your wife goes?"

"She always looks so good," Victor said.

"You shit!" She slapped him. "You incredibly stupid shit!"

"But I love you," he whimpered, holding his cheek. "I'm so proud of you. I wish I could show you to everyone."

"Is that it?" she screamed. "Your way of showing me off? To parade me to your wife?"

"I didn't mean to. I just wanted you to feel good. To be happy. I like people to see you. You're so beautiful."

"I am not an exhibitionist!" Miranda screamed, and started to cry. "I'm a person! I'm a person!"

Shortly after that, Miranda gave up her show business career. She started doing cocaine in the morning, a line when she got back from her walk to get her through the day. Victor saw what was happening, and encouraged her to join some charity group. SHARE, he thought, might be a good idea.

"Does your wife belong to SHARE?" Miranda asked coldly.

"No," he said, and didn't look at her.

So she joined for a little while, went to some meetings, started rehearsal for the SHARE show, where the wives and associates of show business notables made their annual kick line, showing what good shape they were in for wives. It was at the third such rehearsal that she stood beside Alicia Farrell, wife of the powerful producer, who was discussing the charity she chaired with a friend.

"Every time I think of those poor little things," Alicia was saying. "With their empty bellies, and the flies in their eyes, I have to think twice before buying another jewel."

So Miranda didn't go back there anymore, either.

"I have to be *something*," she said to Victor. "I have to be more than I am."

"But you are wonderful," Victor tried to assure her.

She felt empty all the time. The coke didn't help that. It gave her a lift at the beginning, but by the time her day was half over she knew that she was nothing again. She didn't want to be like the people she'd seen around who were into it all the time now, telling themselves and each other that coke wasn't really addictive, that they could stop anytime they wanted to, while their whole lives became centered on cocaine and how they could get it.

So she started driving to UCLA in the little gray Porsche with the plaid interior that Victor had given her for her twenty-sixth birthday. She would park and read the an-

nouncements on the bulletin board near Slicter Hall, as
though she were a graduate student looking for a roommate. And in between the notices for antirape workshops,
and nutrition classes, and used motorcycles for sale, and
nuclear seminars, she found the flyer for Nick Zetta's
Creative Writing Workshop. She called to ask what she
had to do to take it, and Nick's assistant told her besides
the tuition fee, she would have to submit a sample of her
writing. So she picked out one of the letters she had
written to Colette.

Letter 241

Washington, D.C.
March 12, 1976

My darling baby girl,
    My heart aches sometimes so I can feel where
it is in my chest, like a ball of grief that will
never unwind until I hold you again. What a fool
I was to ever give you up.
    I heard on the radio today on some entertain-
ment program that this is Liza Minnelli's birthday. And I started thinking about the children of
famous parents, and what a tough row they have
to hoe. Her mother was Judy Garland, who was
the greatest performer of her day, and from the
records I heard, and the couple of movies I saw
on TV, maybe anybody else's day besides. And
my heart went out to Liza Minnelli, with her sad
dark eyes and her sad dark inheritance—her mother
died much too young, abusing herself with drugs
and alcohol, abusing her beautiful voice, and her
own sad dark eyes—and I thought, well, at least I
didn't do that to you. Become famous.
    I remember when I was living in Paris waiting
for you to be born, and I would read all the great
American writers who had lived in Paris—mostly

Hemingway and F. Scott Fitzgerald, who also died from too much alcohol, because as good an editor as he had, a man named Maxwell Perkins, nobody ever edited out his self-pity. I think self-pity can kill you faster than alcohol, especially if you're a writer. But when I think about you, I'm covered with sorrow, and I know what I'm feeling is not so much grief for you as pity for myself, because I was so young and stupid and may not ever hold you in my arms again.

Do you think about me? Do they tell you you are not their baby, that you have a mother somewhere? Do you wonder if she loves you? Do you hate her, because she gave you away? It wasn't so much giving, try to understand, as confusion. Because I didn't know, because I couldn't think, because I wanted you to have a better life than I did. A better chance than I could give you.

What a chance I could give you now, in this seat of power. Men here twist each other's arms with things they know about each other, and that's called big business and government and that's how deals are made and wars are on the verge of being started. If only women could do that in the name of country. There's no way they couldn't get their babies back.

Try to forgive me. Every day I try to forgive myself. But maybe you are more generous than me. I hope so.

And maybe there's a chance. And maybe there's God, and He will smile on me and the little girl who was in my belly in the great dark womb of Notre Dame. And maybe soon—oh please, can I pray for it—I'll hold you in my arms again.

I love you,
Mom

She was accepted in the writing workshop. Nick Zetta was predisposed from the letter to like her, but he fell in love with her the moment he saw her. Although he noted the limo that waited for her Wednesday evenings in the shadow of the arch, he was young enough and cocky enough to figure he could take that on. So he kept asking her to stay after class, to talk about her writing.

It didn't take her long to figure out what he really wanted. He began giving assignments of a more and more autobiographical nature so he could find out everything about her.

Also in the class was Tracy Fine, the movie star, who considered all the assignments directed at her, since she imagined that he, like *McCall's* and the *Enquirer*, couldn't get enough of her life story. Tracy had invited Nick to tutor her separately in poetry writing, which offer he declined. When, about three months into the course, Nick suggested the class do an exercise in erotic writing, Tracy supposed he wanted her sexually. It bothered her, since it was her greatest wish to be taken seriously in spite of how ditsy she seemed on the screen. Also, in her relationship with teachers, she was dealing from her Higher Self, something her psychic, who read the Tarot, assured her was shortly to come into full flower. So to deal from her Lower Self, her sexual shakra, seemed literally beneath her. Although the psychic assured her that in all the communications with those who had died, the only thing they grieved for, in their peace, contentment, and radiant joy, was the absence of bodies, hungering for touch.

Tracy raised her hand in the workshop, which was conducted around a long, oval wooden table, with comfortable chairs, like a conference room. "Is this erotic writing supposed to be autobiographical?"

"It can be," said Nick. "But the guise of fiction is always more freeing."

"I hate pornography," Miranda said.

"Erotic is not pornographic," Nick said, his windbreaker beige against the dark wood of the walls and the blackboard behind him. He had a tendency to pace during the workshops, keeping up the stretch of his long, lanky legs. His eyes were dark and very liquid in his angular face, as though taken from another person, one who wasn't as rigid as his cheekbones and jaw would seem to indicate, or so composed. The eyes seemed always on the verge of tearing, as if it was only the sadness of life they saw, not the comedy. He had double rows of black eyelashes that served as a not very effective fan so he wouldn't seem to be looking at Miranda. "Pornography is meant solely to arouse. Erotica is a key to character. If you get deeply into someone's sexuality, it can be the door to their soul."

"Ha!" said Miranda.

"No, I believe that, I believe that," said Tracy, who had just found true love for the fifth time.

"Anyway, this is a course in *creative* writing. You're permitted to make things up." The class laughed. "Or you can use the roman à clef technique."

"What's that?" asked a minister from Westwood Presbyterian.

"Something that started with a writer named Mrs. Mary Delariviere Manley in 1709. *Secret Memoirs and Manners of Several Persons of Quality* was the title of her book. A bold satire on the great personages of her day, with their names concealed under pseudonyms, revealed at the end in a key. So you can write about people you know and disguise them, if you have a point. It's a literary tradition that honored writers have been doing ever since. From Proust to Saul Bellow."

"How down and dirty do we get?" asked Miranda.

"I'd rather say deep and sensual than down and dirty," Nick said. "Sexual isn't dirty."

"Tell me about it. How down and dirty do we get?"

"Whatever feels right to you," Nick said, and held her with his eyes.

After class he tried to stop her under the Moorish arches. He saw how tight-lipped and angry she looked, reached for her arm. She pulled away from him in the darkness. "Why are you so mad?" he asked.

"You were supposed to be better than the rest of them." She walked away.

EASTER BRUNCH

by Miranda Jay

To begin with, I made him take off all his clothes in front of everybody, and stand there naked while I wrapped a long chain around him. Not tight enough to hurt him, not sticking it anywhere it would cut, carefully avoiding his already engorged manhood. I twisted it under his arms and over his shoulders and down to his glistening buttocks, and then I said, "Spread, you scum." I could see his little starry anus contracting from the excitement. What he likes best is being degraded. I twisted the chain under his scrotum, but left it slack. I didn't want to cut him. Then I brought it under his belly and around his hands and clamped it together with a padlock. Then I took a paintbrush and dipped it in Mercurochrome, and painted his now fully erect cock red. Then I wrote "SLUT" with a brush across his naked belly while I told him how stupid he was. Stupid, and a wimp, and a coward.

"Aren't you?" I asked him, crossing the *t* with my brush. "Aren't you a coward?"

"Yes, ma'am," he said, shaking and shivering.

"Not ma'am, you fool. Mistress. I am Mistress Elizabeth to you."

"Yes, Mistress Elizabeth," he said.

"Now, kneel, slave," I said to him, and he knelt in the corner, quivering, his organ bobbing up and down like a buoy in a stormy sea. His eyes were half-closed now, the tempo of his breathing increased.

Over by the terrace, one of Mr. X's friends, who I will call Lloyd Henry, pretended to be only vaguely interested, but I could see the bunching at the front of his pants. He was by the buffet table, filling up his plate as though what he was really there for was Easter Brunch.

Mr. X had it catered. The apartment was borrowed from Remy, a Parisian Master, and personal friend of Ann Pierce, the leading Dominatrix in New York, who makes guest appearances several times yearly in the leading B&D clubs of England and L.A. The food was first rate, as it always is when Mr. X arranges things, with a full buffet, deli, and for the Christians present, hot cross buns. These hot cross buns were from a place called the X-rated Bakery, and they were molded into real buns. I mean buns. So they could celebrate Easter while they were biting into miniature, sweet, plump, round-ass cheeks. Lloyd Henry seemed to find them very tasty. I could see his mouth moving over them with maddening slowness.

There were three other girls besides me: Mistress Victoria, Tess and Misty. They were dressed the same as me, black lacey tight corselettes with garters attached squeezing up their ripe, rounded female flesh, emphasizing the swell and curve of their hips while the garters below framed their mounds of desire. Over the corselettes they wore black leather skirts with chains around the waist for belts. Misty had a red leather bow on the center of her bra, coordinated to red lace stockings, with stiletto heels about four inches high, while the rest of us wore boots. Mine come to the center of my calf, with very high heels and pointy toes. Victoria's are mid-thigh, and Tess' go all the way up, so you can just see the edge of her garter holding up her black net stockings, and when she stands over you, her coralline slit. Nobody wears pants except Misty, who's so cute.

I guess people seeing how we dress might think we were whores. They don't get that what this is about is to attract certain fantasies. To make people feel better about themselves, to get to know themselves. I know if you ask Misty about it, she considers herself performing a necessary service. A very real, honest, and true occupation. Many times she told me how she stopped rapists and terrorists and people who would otherwise bomb the U.N. One of her regulars is a high government official, and instead of beating up his little girl, he comes to see Misty, who dresses up like his daughter; he tells her what she's done wrong, what a bad girl she is, how she hasn't made her bed, etc. Then he turns her over his knee and spanks her hard. That way when he gets home he doesn't abuse his child. People are under a lot of pressure.

I mean the truth is, the whole world is doing what we did in that penthouse, B&D. Bondage and Domination. Everybody is into it, they're just not as open and honest as we are. As Khrishnamurti says, it is the truth that liberates and not our efforts to be free.

Lloyd Henry was over by the terrace, looking down at Central Park. From the apartment where we were, you could see the frosted domes of Tavern on the Green, where the Best People were having Easter Brunch. Except I would bet we had some more Important Names at our brunch than they did across the street. Mr. X arranged this for his friends, like the gracious gentleman he is. I called Misty to tell her we were coming to New York, and Tess set it up at her master's penthouse. This is a true network, the people who are into this, all of us pretty much knowing each other, understanding it is not so much an activity as a way of life.

Tess and Misty are "slaves" to Remy, who keeps bringing over some of the latest refinements from Europe, where they are heavily into B&D. Remy has a true sense of history. From him I learned how Catherine the Great of Russia died, which was from a horse falling on her while she was fucking it. He says that every time there is a queen in England, Dominatrixes are on the rise, which is why I am glad I am living in the time I am.

That's me. I'm a Dominatrix. In the beginning I did some things Submissive, and now I can do Switch, Dominant into Submissive, if that's what they really like. But I'm faithful to Mr. X, and only do this as a favor to him, when he needs to impress his friends or wants a favor from them.

The man in the chains (I'm doing this roman à clay, like you said) I call the Cockmaster General. He was kneeling the way I told him to, sniveling, the rigid pole of his male flesh the only proud part of him. I yanked at his chain, and he yelped, and I said, "What do you say?"

And he whimpered, "Thank you."

And I said, "Thank you, what?"

And he said, "Thank you, Mistress Elizabeth."

I picked the name Mistress Elizabeth because what we are trying to do here is bring back an era. Many of the girls have extensive wardrobes in velvet. Texture is very important. Tess has ten thousand dollars in rubber for those who are into Latex, as well as thirty thousand in leather for those with more traditional fantasies. It's not hard to think of spending that much on clothes when you consider that a good pair of custom boots for this costs $700. Polished British kidskin, handmade, so shiny it looks like someone just licked it. With five-inch stiletto heels. Boots are the priciest item, as they say in jolly old England, where a lot of this stuff originated because they're so proper on the outside, and then the minute the doors are locked, they go bananas, or, not to mix a metaphor, whips and chains. Dresses can run $500 up for leather, velvets start at $400, and so on. At Trashy's in L.A. they have satin robes for those who are Edwardian in their hang-ups, people who long for the sentimental working girls of yesteryear, with Trepunto work—appliquéd flowers stuffed and raised—that run as high as a thousand. Lucky we all have rich fathers. Ha ha.

I took my little Plexiglas buggy whip then, and told

the Cockmaster General to turn around, and he did,
whimpering the whole time, still on his haunches. I
whipped him twice across his milk-white ass. There
were bright pink traces of the blows. From the corner
of my eye I saw Lloyd Henry put his plate down. His
own natural endowment was really straining his pants
now, so I thought it was time I paid him a little
attention. After all, he was the star of this show. All of
this arranged for his benefit. Mr. X wanted me to get
together with him for a long time now, and after a
recent incident in D.C., which is another story, I thought,
"Why not?"

"Would you like to go inside?" I asked him.

"Yes, please," he said, and because he is no dummy,
added, "Mistress Elizabeth." It's good that so many of
those in high places in government are quick learners.

"Now you stay there and wait for me like a good
boy," I told Cockmaster.

"Yes, Mistress," he said. I'm not without feelings,
even when I'm doing my Bitch, so I threw a couple of
magazines at him to look at while I was busy. Some
publications are available that not everybody is familiar with. Swastika Snatch, for instance. His hands were
still in front of him, bound by the chains, but when he
leaned over he could turn the pages with his little
fingers. He opened Swastika Snatch and there were
two leather-skirted, bare-breasted dykes shoving a
long hose up a man's rectum. Cockmaster got a real lift
of the cock from that one. He's always begging me for
an enema, but I don't do water sports.

"Come with me," I said to Lloyd Henry, and led him
toward one of the bedrooms that had been converted
into a dungeon. "Have you been to a dungeon before?"

"No, Mistress," he said, very meekly. A lot of men in
positions of authority have a terrible need for balance
in their lives. Always having to act so dominant out in
the world, they really need a turn at being submissive.
I remember when I first met Mr. X how he really got it
on was when I would ride his back and use a tie like

reins and make him play Horsie. Being submissive like
that helps them get rid of their frustrations and anxieties, and then they're not so filled with resentment. On
a more even keel. Making less trouble than they ordi-
narily would. I like to think I make the world a better
place.

I signaled Misty to follow us. It's important to find out
what the person's fantasy is. That's the key. To find out
Lloyd Henry's big fantasy so he can have the orgasm
of his dreams. My hunch was Misty would be it. I
could already see him giving her looks. Misty, like I
said, is very cute, white skin, lightly freckled, her milk
white globes jiggling above her tight Victorian corselette,
her waist sucked in to twenty inches. Misty is a size
34D. I know because I bring her lots of lingerie from
Trashy's, since she is always so willing to play with us.
Trashy's bras start at twenty-five dollars, the masks at
a hundred and twenty-five, and the corselettes at a
hundred and a half, size 34D for Misty. From the way
Lloyd was eyeing her, certainly worth every penny.

He was also eyeing me, but not directly, which is as
it should be. First of all, the Dominatrix, the Mistress, is
a virgin in this game. Up on a pedestal. The only way
he can have her is through her Sub, who's a surrogate.
Lloyd seemed to understand that right away. Besides,
he knew I belonged to Mr. X, who is his closest friend.

"Now, this is the first dungeon," I said to him. "We
call it Pegasus." The walls were hung with dark red
velvet, even over the windows so there is no natural
light at all. This is traditional in B&D, going back to
medieval times, when they didn't have many windows
to begin with, and probably didn't want the neighbors
looking into those they did. It certainly heightens the
atmosphere, or, in this case, darkens it. Many people
involved in this sort of thing have guilt, in spite of how
healthy it is. In the center of Pegasus was a huge oak
four-poster bed, with leather straps and clamps on
each of its posts to attach ropes and cuffs to. Suspended
above it was a black leather swing for those who are

into leather and flying. Which is why the dungeon is named for the mythical horse.

Off to the side of Pegasus was a cell, converted from a sauna, with a long wooden bench and metal spokes to tie the penitent to, metal cuffs for the feet, chains, all the extras, and a thick wooden door to close him off so you can't hear the screaming. "Have you been a bad boy?" I asked him. "Would you like to go in there and think about your sins?"

"No, Mistress."

"No, thank you, Mistress." As ready as he was to play, I knew he didn't want to play alone. So I took him into Dragon, the second dungeon Remy so kindly set up. There was a bondage bed, with stretch racks at the bottom and top, and a wheel to tighten the racks, and a cross for those with religious fantasies. Tilted to the side so Born Agains wouldn't be offended. In the middle of the floor was a large wooden triangle, three dimensional, constructed especially for these games, room to crawl inside or just be attached to the outside, with about a hundred eyehooks driven into it at every four inches so chains or cuffs or collars can be tied from any part of the body and tightened. Tightening the collar is a big one in B&D, since the most intense orgasms come when the carotid artery is pressed tightly, but hanging is too dangerous (We've lost a few friends that way!). There was also a whipping post, or better, two, His and Hers. And an artist's stool. "Won't you have a seat?" I said, indicating the bondage bed, not a real bed but a camping bed, canvas stretched onto the frame. He sat down, and Misty went into the corner. Then I pulled up the artist's stool close to him and sat on it, the one bright light in the room shining down on me, while he was in darkness, in shadow. Right away me being higher than him and the light I was in made him feel weak. As I said, this is an Art.

Usually, when I'm with Mr. X, I sit beside him on the bondage bed because we're very flirtatious. But with this man, the game was to bring him down from his lofty pinnacle. "Are you comfortable?" I asked him.

"Yes, thank you, Mistress."

"Would you feel more comfortable kneeling?"

"I don't think so, Mistress." They usually don't unless they're real head cases. At first they have to pretend they don't enjoy being submissive. But once they're really into it they can't wait to put on women's clothes and serve you.

"Well, what do you like? Spankings? Whippings?"

"I don't know." He was telling the truth, I think. Most people have no idea what they're going to find out about themselves, how once you get into this, five hundred doors open, doors you didn't even know were there. Fear making you more excited. Being tied up intensifying orgasm because you don't know if you're going to get out of it alive. He looked so anxious I was tempted to go into my Bitch with him. But I don't really like the cruelty part as much as the game, the affectionate part of playing, the loving part, like spanking and whipping. I'm not a Dominant who likes to say, "Your cock isn't big enough," or "You're pussywhipped," or "You're not even good enough to be a shit, yet." If I do cruelty, I prefer mental Domination, telling him he's not good enough to look at me, that his intellect isn't big enough. That he's not intelligent enough to be my slave. That kind of put-down.

I don't get a kick out of making men feel like pigs, even if a lot of them are, in love with feet and ass, heavy into body smells. Those are the kind that like a lot of degradation.

"Come here, Misty," I said, and she did. "Take off your corset." Fear was already livening up her alert little face as she unbuttoned the tiny buttons in front, bottom to top, her gloriously round, big globes bursting free. "You've been a very naughty girl. Take down your pants."

"Oh, please, Mistress, don't hurt me. Don't spank me, please." But even as she spoke she took off her cute little panties, and as she raised her leg to step out of them, there was a flash of her sexual temple, behind the pale auburn mound.

I indicated my lap. Obediently, she lay across it. "Oh, look at that lovely white bum," I said to Lloyd. "Wouldn't you love to take a bite out of it?"

"Yes, Mistress."

"Well, first we'll have to warm it up for you." I started spanking slowly, like the calm tempo of a leisurely fuck. She was protesting and whimpering, little sobs of hurt and fear coming out of her, but I just kept it up. I could see where his pants were almost being pulled apart now from the growing excitement.

"She loves it," I said. "She's like a bitch in heat. If I let her, she'd have everybody in this whole apartment. Listen to her begging me to stop. But if you touched her, you'd find she was all sticky and wet. You absolutely love it, don't you, my little darling? Well, that's enough now. Go over and show him how nice and pink your bottom is."

She did.

"Isn't that lovely and pink?"

"Yes, Mistress," Lloyd said, his breath as tight as his pants.

"Remember how she cried she didn't want a spanking? Look at her nipples. Touch between her legs."

He did.

"Isn't it all sticky and wet?"

"Yes, Mistress. Lovely and sticky and wet."

"You want to play with her, don't you? Shall we let her beg us for the orgasm?"

"Oh, please, Mistress." Misty was almost crying. Not just cute, but really knows how to beg. "Please."

"What do you want? Do you want your orgasm? Well you're a good little slut, so maybe we should give it to you." I forced him down to his knees with the pressure of my hand, while he gave a token show of resistance. His face was in front of her sweet red thatch and he was on eye level with her bud of passion. He reached over and touched it. Misty moaned.

"Oh, yes, please."

Eagerly, he started stroking it. "Use your tongue," I said.

"But I don't like to..."

"Use your tongue," I said, more urgently now. With seeming reluctance, Lloyd leaned over and opened his patrician mouth.

But I could tell from the rigid set of his shoulders that he wasn't into cunnilingus, so I got up from my stool and went to the chest of drawers. It is filled with all kinds of wonderful compartments, like the mind. In one was the Hitachi Magic Camera I asked Remy to make sure was there for me. The Japanese are so clever. Even their vibrators are ahead of ours. And of course the vibrator and dildo lobby in Washington will never be listened to, so there will always be a flood of Japanese equipment on the market. But the truth is, they're not really innovators, so we have to invent first. But then they really make improvements. I find that the Magic Camera can bring a woman around in less than thirty seconds, especially if she's been warmed up like Misty was.

"Well, what do you think?" I asked Lloyd. "You think you'd like to do this for her?"

"Yes, please, Mistress," he said, and grabbed the vibrator out of my hand. Then he moved it over Misty's pale red bush, spreading her with one hand. She was screaming with pleasure in twenty seconds according to my Rolex.

I went over and kissed her pink mouth. "It's okay," I whispered. "It was all just for fun." That's a very important part of B&D, making sure they have their orgasm. The orgasm makes it okay. A very important part of mental well-being. The kiss was a little extra for Lloyd. Men love it when they think women want each other. On my part, it was just affection, because she's such a good little slut.

"Would you like to kiss her nipples?" I asked him.

"Oh, yes, Mistress, please."

"Well, first I think she should kiss yours. Crawl to him, you slut." Misty crawled on her knees, opened his shirt, and started to lick his nipples. He threw his head back like a little boy when his first puppy bit his ear. An ecstasy he didn't quite understand. "Now take off the rest of his clothes."

She did.

"Oh, please, Mistress. Can I suck it?"

"In a while," I said, then addressed myself to Lloyd, who was on his feet now, standing naked before us, his great cock at full attention, as though someone had just played the National Anthem. "If you want to kiss my girl, you have to get down on the floor and kneel with her." This time he did it without even a token show of protest or resistance. Partly what this is about is retraining. You have to get their minds away from horny, because this isn't really about sex. It's about fascination. Seducing the mind.

"You have to keep your hands behind your back," I said. He put them there, and before he knew what was going on, I had cuffs on him.

"Hey, wait a minute," he said. "I don't like this."

"How do you know till you've tried?" I stuck the tip of my stiletto heel between his ass cheeks. Then I snapped the collar around his neck and irons on his ankles. He was protesting the whole time, the way Misty did.

"You played with my girl," I said. "Now you're going to have to please me." I sat down on the stool and nodded at Misty. She helped him up and put him across my knee.

"Hey wait..." he said, but I started swatting away. "That's enough," he said, when twenty swats had gone by.

"Take him over there," I said to Misty. She led him to the whipping post.

"I told you I've had enough of this. Get me out of these things." But his organ was totally erect, inflamed.

"When I'm good and ready," I said, and manacled him by his ankle irons to the whipping post. Then I made Misty put her hands around the one next to him and tied them behind her.

"Please," she said. "Don't hurt me anymore."

"What are you going to do to her?" he asked.

"Sweet that you're worried about her. I think you'd better worry about yourself."

"What are you going to do to me?"

"Don't be afraid," I said, my mouth close to his. "You're mine now, and I won't hurt you any more than you need." And I gave him one good crack of the whip across his flank, and then ten pretty hard ones to her, harder than any he got.

Misty was sobbing then, so I let her loose. "Poor darling," I said. "You've had a lot of pain. There. Rest at his knees." I could see now he had a touch too much, so I let him loose, untied and uncuffed him, took the collar from his neck. "Why don't you comfort each other," I said.

And so I left them. I went out into the living room, where Mr. X was waiting for me. "How did it go?" he asked.

"Okay, I think." I like to try and keep some humility with Mr. X. He's done so much for me.

"Would you like something to eat?" he asked me, and I said, "Yes, please." Mr. X made me a plate, and we went inside to Pegasus. In the closet was a maid's uniform, Mr. X's size. And he got into it, and the wig, and the five-inch stiletto heels. He really has great legs for a man his age, and when he wears black stockings with garters, a lot of women would envy him. I tied a little rope around the head of his cock, with two ends to pull it by. He got a hard-on when I tugged on it. So cute, his little short black taffeta skirt sticking out from the erection he had.

I walked to the bed slowly, leading him after me, and sat down on the edge of the bed. "Kneel, Jessica,"

I said. When we do this, he likes to play my maid whose name is Jessica.

"Yes, Mistress Elizabeth," he said, his voice shaking, the hand holding the plate shaking too. I held the plate for him while he got down on his knees, because even when I'm playing the Bitch I can't help being merciful. I gave the plate back to him when he was down there, and leaned over, my mouth at an easy angle for him to feed me, the tip of my leather boot circling his glans while he brought the fork to my mouth. And every time I touched it with the hard leather tip, it bounced.

"Oh, I love it when it jumps," I said.

The salad wasn't bad, but I was disappointed with the Eggs Benedict, which were cold. I think when you pay that kind of money for catering, the chafing dishes should keep the food hot. Anyway, it was hard for him to get the food to my mouth, his hand was shaking so much, so I told him I wasn't hungry anymore.

And then, because it was time for dessert, I took the rope off his corona corona and replaced it with a lovely soft piece of red satin ribbon and made a darling bow. "How does that feel?"

"Fine, thank you, Mistress," he said, fucking the air in little spasms, trying to catch the feel of taffeta against his cock.

I got down on my knees and kissed the tip of it. It didn't take long. It was time to rejoin the others.

Lloyd Henry was back in the living room, dressed, looking a little sheepish. So I winked and whispered, "That was pretty sexy," and let him off the emotional hook. What these men are really afraid of is that someone will think less of them for enjoying being Submissive. My wink, and what I said, puffed him up again. The point is to bring them down from their pinnacle temporarily, but you have to put them back up there once you're back in the daylight or they resent you. So to cap it off and make it neat, I said, "Do you like my boots?"

He looked down at them and said, "Very much."

This established the flirtation between us. He might have played with Misty, but who he really wanted was me, and all I would have to do in future was to mention boots or wear them, and that would be a signal between us, and he could remember my heel in his sphincter. These guys freak out when they understand who and what really has power over them, because they always thought power was their game. So whenever I wear boots in the future, that will be stronger than my hand on his cock. Except, as I can't emphasize enough, none of this is really about sex.

The sun was filtering through the windows leading out to the terrace, the kind of brilliant day New York has every once in a while that reinforces New Yorkers' opinions they'd be crazy to live anywhere else. Remy put on some music. A Barbra Streisand record. I could hear her voice, very sweet and searching, and you knew from the sound and the energy that it wasn't easy, even for strong women. But, after all, it was Easter. A day of joy and hope. No reason to think that we, too, could not rise again.

SANTA BARBARA

◇

It was a lot like being a college student, Lou Salerno could not help thinking, which was what his daughter had been when the drunk plowed into her. So rather than resist all this learning of new subjects he was having to do, he sort of brightened himself up by thinking maybe he was the continuum of Marcy. That her spirit would be inside him, keeping up with its homework and sense of discovery, and that way there was a challenge and excitement in having to pick up all this new stuff at his age.

He'd been out to MicroTel to talk to the president of the company, as cool a living stiff as Lou had met up with. He'd assured Lou there'd been no panic at the discovery that Fred Masters was trying to take over. "Based on Masters' past behavior," Coolidge Ransom said, looking like a steel gray composite for the next issue of *Fortune* or maybe *Architectural Digest*, his office a chrome, angular extension of the man himself, "we determined that he didn't have hostile designs. But it did put us on notice that we needed to address the broader issue of maximizing shareholder value. And of course we knew not to be quick to surrender our position."

"But of course you didn't have to," said Lou, "on account of he died."

"Yes, that's true," said Ransom. "But even before that unfortunate occurrence Masters decided to pull out. We expressed to him our unwillingness to be acquired. So he halted his accumulation and agreed to sell his stock back to the company at the current price."

"And did he?"

"He was just about to, when . . ." Ransom tilted his head to the side, to indicate how tricky life was. "But even if he'd succeeded in taking over the company, it would have been a victory in name only. MicroTel is simply a subsidiary of MercerCorp. There was no way he could strong-arm his way in there, not even using this as a power base. Masters wasn't as shrewd as people think. The really savvy raider learns to cover his tracks. He was so visible even a novice could spot the buying pattern. And by knowing who was buying our stock, we were able to communicate our intent. Otherwise you have to let the other side play all the cards, while you're sitting in the dark, not even knowing there's a game going on."

"Only this game was called on account of death . . ." Lou said.

"You keep trying to bring it back to that, lieutenant.

Maybe it helps you from the point of view of the Homicide Department to try and weave in these gloomy threads. But as I pointed out, we were already in friendly negotiation to buy the stock back when he killed himself.''

"He didn't kill himself," Lou said, and got up, wandering around the office, checking the matted prints on the wall.

"I heard talk to that effect. What really happened?"

"Who was Chuck Dresner?

"A man in our Quality Control Department. Why?"

"What happened to him?"

"He got fired."

"Why?"

"Why do people get fired? He wasn't doing a good job. What made you ask about Dresner?"

"He had a girlfriend named Connie Garrett who took a bullet in the eye. Ever hear Dresner talk about her?"

"We didn't socialize," Ransom said.

"So then you weren't *stunned* by his disappearance?" Lou tried not to let sarcasm eat into his voice. But now that he was this middle-aged college-boy, these Princeton boys who had prepped at Deerfield, really got under his skin, thinking they were the only ones worth talking to.

"I didn't know he'd disappeared," Ransom said.

Lou felt the leaves of a tall rubber plant in the corner, to check if it was real, stuck his thumbnail through the skin to see if it pierced. It did. "Living plants, even in Silicon Ville," Lou muttered. "Very nice, very nice."

"The truth is, Dresner had a drinking problem. That's why we had to let him go. So it doesn't surprise me that you can't find him. A lot of these people hold themselves sort of in check while they have their high-powered jobs, but the minute they're found out they fall into the bottle."

"Is that where he went?"

"I haven't any idea," Ransom said.

"I haven't any idea," Lou echoed his words as though it was wine he was tasting, moving it across his palate. "Very nice, very nice. Here all my life I've been saying,

'I don't know.' '' He went to the door. ''Thank you for your time. I'll be in touch.''

''What do you think really happened to Masters?'' Ransom said.

''I haven't any idea,'' said Lou, and went out the door. After that he had his friend at the *L.A. Times Book Review* get him together with a sharp financial reporter at that paper for a quick education in corporate raiding.

''Well, it's true what Ransom told you,'' the reporter said. He looked at Lou more like a dean in some graduate school than a reporter, with close-cropped dark hair and serious eyes—heavy glasses attesting to all the hours of research—and a lined, thoughtful face. The two of them were sitting at the counter at the Kosher Burrito, a couple blocks away from the Times Building in downtown L.A. ''They were in negotiation to buy back Masters' stock at the time of his death, so they had nothing to gain, really, if that's what you're thinking.''

''And the *Wall Street Journal* and all you other guys had turned up that it was Masters trying to move in?''

''Well, it all starts earlier than that, these days,'' the reporter said. ''The waters are full of takeover sharks, ready to devour or dismember a company, or hold its shares hostage for greenmail. Visible aggressors like T. Boone Pickens, Carl Icahn, the Belzbergs, Irwin Jacobs. There's a lot of paranoia ever since the takeover of Gulf Oil showed that no one is invincible. So a lot of companies are getting into 'stockwatch' programs.

''Stockwatch programs can monitor a company's stock on an hourly basis, for unusual movements in price or volume. Large block trades can be traded daily. Flushing out a possible raider in the early stages of accumulation gives a company the best commodity of all in a hostile situation—time.''

''Ransom says Fred Masters didn't have hostile designs on the company.''

''Maybe he *was* just trying to drive up the price, I don't know. But there's no question MicroTel knew who their adversaries were, even before the *Journal* and the rest of us flushed out Masters and his group. It sure looked to me like he was trying seriously to involve himself in another business besides publishing, that this wasn't just a maneuver. Did you ever meet him?''

"No."

"He was sniffing around the *Times* for a while there, like there was a chance he could get in. Or at least pick up a little laid-back style for the rag he bought in the valley. He took me to lunch and said great newspapers were only because of great reporters, and then he made me an offer I couldn't refuse. Only I refused it.''

"Why?"

" 'Cause his papers suck, as my kid would say. Citizen Kane he wasn't. I think it bothered him, really, knowing he wasn't taken seriously. His face actually fell, you know, like they say in the novels, when I turned him down. You ever see him?''

"Only pictures.''

"Well, there was a hangdog expression Masters had. If you had pity in your heart, you couldn't help feeling it for him, for all his bluster. He looked kind of like the Pillsbury Dough Boy, gone all flat, when I said no. Not like the tough, insensitive raider he was pictured as. 'But I gotta have pros,' he kept saying over and over again, like a little kid. 'I need pros.' It's my guess—and I don't like to guess, because what I do is based on facts and research—that he was moving into MicroTel because there at least, in computer-chip land, things are cut and dried. Nobody can turn their nose up at the *tone* of what you're doing. Nobody can call your microchip 'sensational' or 'scandalous.' ''

The waitress brought their kosher burritos, pastrami rolled up in a soft flour tortilla shell. "I hope you don't eat this stuff too often," Lou said.

Later that afternoon, Lou went to see Hap Mitchel out at MercerCorp. It impressed him that Mitchel agreed to see him without an appointment, even though most people opened their doors right away when you said you were homicide. Mitchel struck him as strictly a no-bullshit guy, with a lot of things on his desk and his mind. So the fact that here he was the president of this aerospace company, not to mention a national hero, and he still let Lou in right away made Lou like him more than he was already ready to.

"I don't know anything about business," Hap told him in answer to his questions. "So I can't tell you what was going on. All I know is the business of aerospace, not this stock market stuff. I wish I could be more help to you."

"I believe you," Lou said, and got up to go. "Thanks for your time."

"You know, you look familiar to me," Hap said, shaking his hand.

"We were in the same elevator one time. Last October, in New York. Coming down in the Waldorf Towers."

"Nice of you to remember."

"I was there checking out the Masters-Miranda case. Did you know Fred Masters?"

"I was with him a couple of times. I didn't really *know* him. I stayed over to see him that last night, though."

"What did you talk about?"

"He never got there," Hap said, walking him to the door. "So I guess whatever it was he wanted will have to remain a mystery."

"He wanted to talk to you about something special?"

"Seemed like it. He made it sound really urgent."

"Well, thanks again. A real pleasure." Lou handed him a card. "Call me if you need a ticket fixed."

Leaving Hap's office, Lou felt like he'd completed his business education. Not all of it a crash course at Wharton. Some aspects of the case had been regulation police work, like finding out what had really happened to Marty Fontaine. The coroner's investigation had revealed an excess of potassium in the IV bottle beside Marty's bed. It was concluded that a lethal dose of potassium stopped Marty's heart, leaving no traces in the body.

But who exactly had administered it? The staff at the hospital, carefully questioned, recollected shadowy figures seen around that night, someone caught unexpectedly in the washroom disappearing into one of the toilets. Who-ever she was, she hadn't turned around; it was only her back that anyone saw. One of the nurses, the one who remembered seeing the intruder, thought, on reflection, that the shoulders in the nurse's uniform had been much too wide for a woman's.

Lou still hadn't pinpointed, even in his own gut, the reason for the put-away. Was it the tie-in with MicroTel? Were they mad because he unloaded his shares? Had that fucked up the takeover? Or was he dead because of whatever was in the wall safe in his apartment? Was it that, the unlucky coincidence of his having lived in Miranda's apartment?

Lou had tracked as much as he could of Miranda's L.A. history, checking out the agency that represented her in modeling, finding out the jobs she'd had, talking to photographers, commercial directors. Nosing out where she bought her clothes and had her hair done. So part of his work on the case was boring detail, part was college, and part was what his friend at the *Book Review* would call serendipity—when things just seemed to happen, to fall into place, like Lucille reading Suzy Jenks' column at breakfast.

"Damn," she said, hunched over the paper the way she always was in the morning, her hair rolled up in its soft pink curlers, netted over. The flowered cotton duster she usually wore to breakfast fell open to show her nightgown, and the breasts Lou still found appealing after all these years.

"What's the matter?"

"They're having this big Arabian auction at Luke Ben-jamin's ranch in Santa Barbara."

"Who's Luke Benjamin?"

"The theatrical director, for God's sake. How could you not know Luke Benjamin?"

"Tell me who Kenneth Bianchi is," Lou said, putting his bagel in the toaster oven.

"I can't remember," said Lucille.

"He's a murderer," said Lou. "Murderers are *my* business. Celebrities and socialites I leave to you."

"Well, they're all going to be at Luke Benjamin's next Thursday." Her voice was heavy with yet another event that she hadn't been invited to. "They're coming in from all over. Tia Papadapolis is jetting in from Greece, Bunyan Reis and Lily Masters from Gotham, Tracy Fine, the movie star, Gordon Grayson, the writer . . . All the Beautiful People."

"All except one," said Lou, and went to the table, lifted her chin, looked into her face. "And I'm sure you would have been invited if they knew how beautiful you were."

She smiled at him. "You always were a sucker for glamour," she said.

Right after Lou left Hap's office, Hap put in a call to Secretary Jonah. He had been having a frustrating time trying to get through, waiting for callbacks, meetings that never materialized, showing up for appointments that were canceled on the spot. It was a kind of behavior that Hap wasn't used to, particularly not from Dwight Efram Jonah, who was as meticulous about conduct as he was about his appearance. So when it seemed established beyond a shadow of a doubt that Jonah was ducking him, Hap decided to write him a letter.

Letters made him uneasy. He was not a writing man. Besides, he knew that unwelcome opinions in government were best expressed orally. If he wrote too much detail there could be security problems. So he decided to make one last effort to reach Jonah by phone. When the operator at the Wilshire told him that Jonah was unavailable, Hap knew there was no other recourse. Still, before he wrote the thing, he put in a call to Zoe.

"In the middle of the morning?" she said, delight audible in her voice.

"I never got flowers from a woman before." He reached out and touched the arrangement she had sent him, delicately at odds with the coldness of his office, cymbidia and tiger lilies, hot pink and white and yellow, several to a stem, set into a basket of thick wooden sticks arranged to look like logs. Exotic and folksy at the same time, like she was.

"High time," she said. "How come I'm the first to know you deserved them?"

"You're smarter than the rest."

"For that I owe you another arrangement."

"How about you, on a bed?"

"I like the sound of that," she said.

"Maybe you could sneak out for lunch and we could meet somewhere."

"Sounds even better."

"What time?"

"I've got some final loose ends to tie up for Marty. What's your schedule like?"

"Jonah's in town. I'm trying to get through. If he'll see me, I have to go there, but I think we're safe. It looks like he's ducking me."

"Why would he do that?"

"Maybe he knows what I want to talk to him about."

"What do you want to talk to him about?"

"Government business," Hap said, cutting her off, his tone suddenly cold. No matter how much you trusted them, you couldn't trust them. It was as simple as that.

"You think I'm with the KGB?" she asked, amusement in her voice.

"Never can tell."

"Are these the thighs of a Russian spy?"

"I'll have to look into them. What time?"

"Twelve thirty. Is it a nice arrangement?"

"What?"

"The flowers. What do they look like?"

"Delicate, but with guts," he said. "Like you." He reached out and touched an orchid petal. "They feel silky. Like the skin just below your collarbone."

"Stop. I won't be able to concentrate."

"There's a Marriott near the airport. Is that too far for you to come?"

"I have an answer for that, but you might not think it was ladylike."

He paused for a moment.

"How do you tell somebody what they don't want to hear?"

"You have something to tell me?" she asked, the vibrancy in her voice gone, suddenly, the timbre flat, deflated. "Is this our last time?"

"Oh, Zoe," he said. "We're just beginning."

"Swear?"

"Boy Scout honor."

"Well, if I can't trust that in you, I can't trust anything."

"So how can you tell someone what they don't want to hear?"

"A man or a woman?"

"A man."

"Why are you telling him if he doesn't want to hear it?"

"Because I have to."

"Well, it's my experience that people don't usually hear what they don't want to hear. So you should just straightforwardly tell him what you need to tell him. That's what I do. And leave it up to him whether he hears it or not."

"You're wonderful," Hap said.

"I like you, too."

"I didn't say I like you. I said you're wonderful."

"You don't like me?"

"I don't think like is the word."

"What word is it, then?"

"I'll have to think about it and straightforwardly tell you what the word is."

"I can't wait," Zoe said. "Twelve thirty."

"Twelve thirty," he said, waited for her to click off the line, and buzzed his secretary. She looked a little flustered when she came in, because Hap didn't usually ask her to take dictation, the formality of business being something he normally skirted around. But she had her pad in her hand, pencil at the ready.

"Going to the Honorable Dwight Efram Jonah, Secretary of Science and Technology," Hap dictated. "You know the D.C. address. Copy to the Beverly Wilshire Hotel, by messenger, marked 'Personal and Confidential.'"

"Yes, sir."

"Dear Mr. Secretary," Hap began. "I've been trying without success to get through to you since our meeting at the polo matches." Hap paused, looked strained.

"Our meeting at the polo matches," his secretary prompted.

". . . I know how important the welfare of our nation is to you. I share the same concerns, the same love of country." He stood now, the words giving him energy.

"At that last encounter, you kindly expressed . . ."

"You want this to be a new paragragh?" Rachel asked.

"Yes. Okay. New paragraph. Where was I?"

"You kindly expressed . . ."

". . . concern that MercerCorp had lost the R&D contract. But to tell you the truth, I was relieved. Much as we would have benefited financially from the research and development job, I have grave doubts about the whole Star Wars program, lasers and weapons systems in space.

"You said you would give us the inside track on the second stage, but I'm not going to participate, and I'll tell you why. I'm convinced the whole thing will be a great waste of effort and energy and money on the government's part. Trillions of dollars with no benefit to humanity, and of questionable value for defense.

"If the program could put us ahead of the Soviets, I'd savor it in spite of the cost. But I don't believe a hundred-percent shield is possible, my scientists are in agreement, and anything less, even a ninety-nine-percent shield, will serve only as an incentive to speed up the arms race, to put both sides in a hair trigger situation. Driving them and us closer to confrontation.

"New paragraph. So it makes no sense. I'm enough of a conservative to see this, and as an American I have to say it. Very truly yours. What do you think?"

"That's how you want to end it?"

"No, I mean what do you think? You, Rachel."

"Oh, I'm sorry, sir. I wasn't listening. I was just taking it down." She read it over. "I think it's fine."

"You think it's straightforward enough?"

"Straightforward?"

"Type up a rough," Hap said. "I'll show it to my adviser."

Well, it was far from the easiest thing he'd ever done, packing his clothes for the Arabian auction at Luke Benjamin's ranch in Santa Barbara. Packing for Bunyan was like making a collage: inspired selection, impeccable placement, imagining how it would look when all put together. But his concentration wasn't really working; his focus wasn't clear enough.

Now he was getting obsessed, as when Kennedy had been assassinated, and the conspiracy theorists started coming forward, and there were all those mysterious "passings." People "walking" through plate glass windows and having their throats cut, for example. A reporter following a lead given him by Jack Ruby's lover, dead of a karate chop to the throat as he got out of his shower, his murderer never found. A sheriff who had sworn to friends in their living room that the testimony he'd given the Warren Commission about the direction the bullets came from was deliberately changed, shot in the head by an unknown assailant. Dorothy Kilgallen, after an exclusvie interview with Ruby, telling the makeup man on "What's My Line" that she was going to blow the whole case wide open, dead of an "accidental" combination of booze and barbiturates. So many critics of the commission's conclusion that Oswald acted as lone assassin, destroyed, discredited, dead. The woman who saw the puffs of smoke from across the grassy knoll run over by a hit-run assailant. People with seemingly remote connections to the tragedy in Dallas felled as though by a cosmic flyswatter.

Not that Bunyan compared what had happened that November morning to the deaths of Miranda and Fred Masters. Except, of course, that he disbelieved the official conclusions and wouldn't have been surprised if the same organizations had been behind both. Big business. CIA. Mafia. The military. Although the last might have been a bit of a stretch, as he couldn't imagine what connection the military might have had with Fred and Miranda. Unless of course she had something on MercerCorp, some secret swindle Lenrahan had been involved in. How strange that the wisest president should turn out to be Eisenhower, who'd warned, "Beware the military-industrial complex." What a tapioca man to issue such a smart caveat. The possible military link to Kennedy's death was of course clearer. Bunyan knew from some of his fixated friends that Kennedy had told Mike Mansfield that after he was reelected he was going to get us out of Vietnam. Once he was dead, combat troops went in.

" 'Murder though it have no tongue will speak,' " the best of poets had said. But Shakespeare hadn't had in mind a world where crime was organized, people emotionally paralyzed, unwilling to think what might have been behind a death. More anxiety to be created by the truth than by covering it up. Oh, but Bunyan was obsessing again, something he had promised himself not to do, two decades before, when he saw how many of them were going mad, making themselves ill, losing their jobs, their anger and frustration eating deeper into them than grief had the country.

People with proof that the wound in the throat had been an entry wound, so could not have come from the Depository, dismissed as raving, their careers ruined. Mafia overlords commissioned to kill Castro, shot to death in their kitchens, cooking sausages, comfortably relaxing, backs to an intimate assassin who might or might not have been CIA. Oh, how overloaded with plot detail the Master would have been, never having to consult the Holinshed Chronicles for shadowy events. How much simpler, livelier, the days when little boys were kept in towers, and had wicked uncles, and murderers would come, and everyone knew to blame evil Richard. How much more complex a world where the victims were a whore and a newspaper tycoon in a chic West Side apartment and the official verdict was double suicide.

Bunyan had darkly suspected differently all along; he'd known better. But what about the others who were dying? First Clarie Avery, the day she'd made her television pitch to Miranda's girlfriend Stephanie. Stephanie had probably made off with whatever was in the box. What had it been? Letters from Victor Lenrahan? Some high-level organizational creep who'd gotten involved with Miranda and the games she was rumored to play? Bunyan had heard select whispers that Lenrahan enjoyed sharing his mistress' special talents with intimates, making them intimate in reality. Irretrievably. Greater men than American politicians had committed career suicide with their cocks. Higher-ups in government were rumored to be trying to suppress certain revelations about Miranda, involving hanky-panky with close associates. Was there in the box some proof of that?

Had Claire gotten that evidence from Stephanie? Had it been in the briefcase found empty in her car when they pulled it from the river? Could it have been pornography, the way Sheikh Tackey said? He wished he could believe the slimy little Arab, but it was hard to take seriously a people who still shit in bidets, a report he'd gotten from a friend who owned a hotel in the South of France.

Now, added to the celebrity bones was poor Marty Fontaine. He'd really liked Marty, found him pleasant and sharp, if a little sad, the way all Hollywood people of taste were sad in the presence of someone genuinely accomplished, of measurable gifts not on celluloid, who lived in a city where sidewalks were walked on. Poor Marty Fontaine, whose only sin, as far as anyone had determined, was occupying an apartment last tenanted by Miranda Jay.

The press had really jumped on that one. Not to mention Gordon Grayson. Ready to tie himself to yet another star-studded death. Just as he had rushed to the drowning of Robin McKay, claiming her for closest friend before the body was even dry. Poor Robin, like the rest of Gordon's sepulchral cast of intimates, no longer alive to issue a statement that she hardly even knew the man.

Oh, it all made Bunyan age visibly. More spleen provoking than even the suspicion of hidden conspiracy was the thought that Gordon would be benefiting from all this. Getting more publicity in advance for his wretched book on the deaths of Fred and Miranda. Planning a press conference at the Beverly Hills Hotel, as Bunyan had read in the trades, passed on to him by Tia. Oh, why was his spirit so flinty and small where Gordon was concerned, that he wished he could prove how tenuous were the threads of connection, Marty's death to Miranda's. But Bunyan knew in his *gedarem,* a Yiddish word he'd learned from Tony Curtis when still curly-haired and adorable, meaning something past guts, a little before soul, that Marty was dead because of some link with her. Murdered by person or persons unknown. Gordon Grayon's publisher?

After all, the focus of the work and audience up to that point had been mainly East Coast. In New York, Gordon's friends, and fascination with Fred Masters, had assured a riveted audience at Elaine's, a heavy-breathing browsing crowd at Rizzoli's. But now to the cast was added Hollywood, and with it, all those people who didn't read, couldn't read, really, unless it was about them, or someone they knew, if it was in the guise of fiction. So they could call each other on the phone and say, "Who is that, really?" Here there was no need for disguise, since facts were facts and everybody was dead. And now to the glittering lineup was added Marty Fontaine. So Gordon's book would be Number One at Hunter's on Beverly Drive, among all those women who hadn't read anything since the Jackies. And men who hadn't read a book since *Indecent Exposure*.

Bunyan packed some of his casual grays, the sportif mode that would serve him well enough in California, without making his West Coast beloveds feel self-conscious. He understood how much on edge he put them already, gifted as he was. He knew how hard it had to be for them, sacrificing mind for weather, sensibility for success, living in the constant shadow of earthquakes and people who couldn't converse. Not that he liked to make generalizations. Of course there was a mind or two out there. My God, even Thomas Mann had lived in California, saying that every writer needed an island of boredom. At least he'd made the most of it, turning boredom to productivity. Boredom had killed as many people as conspiracies had.

Of course, not in this case, Bunyan was sure. No way boredom was the villain what done in Fred and Miranda. Bunyan lifted the lid to his suitcase and was just about to close it when he noted he hadn't taken a tie. A tie. Symbol of all that was formal, pulled together, businesslike, the antithesis of California. How could he do it to them, flaunting how worldly he was, how Beau Brummelish? Well, maybe just one, in case they asked him to do the 'Tonight Show.' Maybe he should go on and talk about his conspiracy theory, and that way—oh dear, could they be after him too? Was that the two men that were coming around, with hats on? They wouldn't dare do him in. Not when it would risk incurring the wrath of Johnny Carson.

For a while, when the madness flashed through her like fire, when melancholy ate at her edges and torpor deadened her, Lily considered being a slut. She dreamed of tropical balconies, fine hotels in the Caribbean where she danced naked with a towel around her hair, her mons close to the railing for the marimba players down below to gaze at, never losing the beat while wondering whose beautiful pussy it was. There was a lunacy to these dreams besides what she was doing in them, a blistering illogic where she imagined none of the musicians would be able to find out who she was, even as she understood all they had to do was locate her room and find out who was registered there. Still, she didn't think any of them would have that much enterprise. The one really enterprising man in the world was dead. So she spread her legs fearlessly, lifting one up on the railing so they could get a good look into her vagina, gaping and mawing like the jaws of death, playing with herself at the same tempo they played the marimba, a feverish exhibitionism that exhausted her, even while sleeping.

Awake, she wasn't that sure she was healing. Tia Papadapolis sent a masseuse three times a week, as a kind of funeral gift, a soothing offering, comforting, consoling. Other people sent books, food. That was the oddest part of Lily's reawakening: her realization of how many people there were only waiting for the opportunity to be kind. People she hadn't even considered her friends, reaching out to bring her back from the grief which was the survivor's own death.

She no longer thought of the fact that Fred had betrayed her. She remembered only that he was dead, that the smell on the pillow was now just fabric softener. She supposed, when she could think again, that all the consolation was being offered because she had known a love deep enough to mourn. All around her were those getting through by the grace of the cover notes of *Cosmopolitan*: "How to Keep It Sexy and Alive," "Less Is More," "Hold Out for the Big O." Lily at least had loved; Lily at least had lost something.

So they brought her back, each in his or her own way, Steve with his hairdos, Tia with her surrogate massages. Mostly Lily missed the laughs, though, the funny things Fred had said that no one imagined his saying but her, no one knowing how comic he was at home, it being only out in the world that he took himself so seriously.

"I could use some laughs," Lily said as Steve wove little threads of her hair with the tail of a comb, setting them onto aluminum foil, brushing them with thickened, peroxided hair color, folding the papers closed.

"Well, laughs you will get, my darling," Steve said. "That's what Arabian auctions are for. You don't imagine for a minute they're about horses."

The doorbell rang. "That's probably Goodwill," she said. "I finally called them to take away his clothes."

"Good girl." He leaned over and kissed her cheek. "You can start life afresh now."

"I'm not mad at him anymore. Or Miranda either. He never felt he was dashing. So I guess she gave him that, and I'm grateful to her. The feeling he was a conqueror with women.''

"He could have gotten that with you."

"Yes, but how could he have known?" she said, and tried to smile. "He never saw me dancing naked."

"Mrs. Masters?" the maid was in the doorway of Lily's dressing room. "The people are here from Goodwill."

"Yes . . . well show them Mr. Masters' closets and tell them they can have everything . . ." She turned to Steve. "Unless you'd like some of his clothes."

"Not my style, thanks."

"But you are his size," she said. "Maybe just his new suit. The one he was going to wear that last night. He never put it on. It's a shame to give it away. Savile Row. Hand tailored."

"What color?"

"I'll show it to you." She got up from the petit-point Louis XV bench that Fred had had copied from the palace at Versailles and went into Fred's bathroom. She came back carrying the suit, still on its hanger.

"Well, it is *great* looking," Steve said. "The fabric looks fabulous."

"Touch it."

"I have peroxide on my hands," he said.

"I can send it to the cleaners first, if you want," Lily said, and still with the ingrained habits of a wife, checked the pockets. From the right front jacket pocket she pulled a little plastic bag, filled with thin, square, metallic-looking wafers about an eighth of an inch thick. "What do you suppose these are?"

"I haven't a clue," Steve said. "Sit down so I can finish the color."

"He was going to wear this suit to dinner that last night," Lily said, hanging the suit on the closet door and sitting down.

"Don't wrinkle your forehead." Steve recommenced the weaving.

"I remember because he specifically asked me not to touch it, not to have it pressed or steamed or anything, just to leave it there. That he'd be home around seven to change."

"I don't care what advances they say they've made in collagen, you don't need those wrinkles."

"Whatever these are, they must be really important."

"Don't wrinkle your forehead, sit up straight. We have to make a plane," Steve said. "*That's* what's really important."

Hap sent the letter to Jonah at the Wilshire by courier so he knew it had been received. There was only silence for an answer. He started calling Jonah in Washington, once he'd returned there, but the secretary stonewalled him. Hap started making a game of it, calling every morning and every afternoon, so there was no way Jonah could pretend he hadn't got the message.

Hap supposed he'd *really* gotten the message. Obviously one he was unwilling to accept. Still, there was no point in giving up on it. He reached for the phone to put the call in again.

There was a buzz on the intercom. Hap put down the phone and pressed the button. "Yes?"

"There's a Mrs. Masters here to see you," Rachel said.

"Mrs. Fred Masters?"

"Lily Masters."

"Have her come in." He went to the door to greet her. For a minute he almost failed to recognize the woman who stood in the doorway. Her posture looked elegant, more sure. Her hair was lighter, streaked into a honeyed shade. She was slimmer, but with a tightness to her, as though she had spent time confronting life like a Jane Fonda workout tape, developing muscles she never suspected she'd be called on to use. "Lily. What a nice surprise."

"I apologize for coming without calling. But I thought it might be important, what I have to show you. I came straight from the plane."

"You look wonderful."

"I know." She sat down. "Isn't it a surprise how much you're capable of pulling yourself together? With the help of friends, of course. You have no idea what support there was. People I thought were just interested in Fred. Rallying round. As if they were just waiting to be needed, to come forward and be kind. Imagine. We work so hard to be cynical so we can survive in the selfish world it seems to be. And all of a sudden there's genuine caring. All these people waiting for the opportunity to rise to their true nobility.

"It's just a shame that it takes something like that for people to show how good they really are. Life would be so much easier if we were kind to each other before husbands killed themselves with another woman." Lily sighed and opened her purse.

"I found this in one of his pockets." She leaned across the desk and handed Hap the little plastic bag. "It was in the suit he was going to wear to dinner with you that night. So maybe it had something to do with why he was so anxious to see you. Do you know what he wanted to talk to you about?"

"No."

"Well maybe it was that. What are those?"

"Microchips. Computer chips."

"That's all?"

"Well, *all* depends on what kind of chips they are. Some very complex electronic circuits can be printed on chips this size. *All* could also depend on what kind of computer they were going to be used in. For example, if they were for a weapons system, then *all* could have some pretty shattering consequences."

"Then I did a good thing to bring them to you?"

"You did a good thing. Thank you for bringing them all this way."

"Well, I was coming this way anyway. I'm going to an Arabian auction. Horses that is, not people. Though I imagine you could get those, too, for the right amount of money." She stood up, held out her hand.

He stood and took it, looked into her face. "You're a surprising woman."

"Yes, I am. But we all have it in us to be unusual. It's

only the image you have of yourself that limits you. That's what my therapist says. You'd be surprised how strong you can suddenly discover you are. Not you, of course, you've always been on top of things. But it never occurred to me I could be there, too.

"We all have it in us to be victor, or victim, that's what my therapist said. Or maybe it was the masseuse. No matter. Positive is positive. Victor or victim, that's the truth about life. I think Miranda volunteered to be a victim."

"Maybe she didn't have a choice," Hap said. "Some people are luckier than others."

"Without a doubt." She walked to the door. "But sometimes you make your own luck. Miranda didn't have to live the way she did. Or die the way she did, either. She didn't have to be a victim. She could have avoided it."

"You think so?"

"Of course," said Lily. "She could have been a man."

Bunyan absolutely loved Montecito. He could imagine spending his waning years there, with the collie dog he'd never had, a tomato plant, the accumulated dreams of an orphan: homey self-sufficiency a leapfrog away from a cotillion, with a full bar. Extravagant ranches. With a full bar. That seemed to be the common denominator of the area. A signpost, as mezuzahs were on the doorways of Jews, so the Angel of Thirst would know not to strike those that dwelled within.

The Santa Ynez mountains rose massive, surprising, as though just over his right shoulder, with the clear suddenness of a painted flat, rolling and green, an eye blink east of the ocean, an immediate, spectacular contrast to the shore. There had been a cartoon a few years before, by Conrad, a humorist and artist Bunyan genuinely admired, of President Reagan, his arm around Nancy's shoulders, looking out to sea at the offshore oil drilling, sighing wistfully, "Isn't it beautiful?" It was the saddest and funniest cartoon Bunyan had ever seen, because the truth was Santa Barbara was as close to paradise as any place on

the planet, and now they stood like an invading science
fiction army, those gawking, horrific metal tripods, like
giant pinned grasshoppers along the horizon. You could
not walk on the beach without great blotches of sludge
sticking to the bottom of your feet. Industrial herpes. To
be generous, Bunyan thought, they probably did consider
it beautiful, the view from the beach, those whose greatest
passion was business.

But the mountains were still there, unmolested, like
great outcroppings of stubborn spirit, steadfast, startling to
the eye. Especially the eye that had just seen the mountains of Los Angeles, clouded and indistinct in their veil of
smog and haze. The air in Santa Barbara was as clear as
the ocean was now murky, offering up the hills as a visual
feast, an instant variation on the flat repetition of the
sands. Railroad tracks ran just above the beaches of
Montecito, separating not the rich from the poor, but the
rich from the other rich, those who had elected not to have
beachfront property. In the foothills random driveways led
through private groves of trees and caverns and gardens
that might have been mistaken for national parks. These
were the estates of the great Midwestern families. Heirs
with physical defects and mental handicaps who did not
enhance the images of their families in Chicago, bundled
west and enrolled in special schools, where they could be
educated while elegantly hidden among gingerbread lat-
ticework and miles of eucalyptus trees. And then they
could marry each other, and the line continue, in haunted
Henry Jamesian splendor, couples who passed their lives at
long, formal dining tables, entertaining Lindbergh, or any
social person of note passing through. Hosts and hostesses
who during the whole of their marriage never ate a single
meal alone. Oh, if Bunyan had only been a writer, what
tales he could have written of Santa Barbara, especially
now that the Gothic novel was back in vogue.

Patches of bottle-brush, bright blossoms, edged the road
up to Luke Benjamin's ranch, scratching the air like
vermilion Brillo pads. Bunyan felt possessively proud of
Luke for locating himself there, even part-time. As de-

lighted as if Luke were a clever nephew instead of related by virtue of being a fellow artist. Now that he was unmistakably back in favor, acknowledged universally as the best director in theater, arguably one of the better in films, there was more than panache in his breeding of horses. How sad were the Russians that the most their theater people could do to express disdain for the state of their art, and the lack of artistic freedom, was defect. How much more George Sanders, stylishly contemptuous, to do as Luke had done, surround himself with genuine horseshit to recover from the show business kind.

Prestige was its own kind of remission, like love was to loneliness. Luke seemed to hold no store of bitterness for the time he had fallen out of grace. His passon for Arabian horses had kept him occupied and in balance during his temporary decline. Like a monarch restored to his rightful throne, he carried with him the ermine certainty that talent will triumph, if you have enough money to hold out till the good times.

Now that Luke's career was once again the most glowing, there was more radiance than usual surrounding the annual auction at his ranch. Collectors flying in from all over the world. Show business luminaries motoring up from Beverly Hills, Lear-jetting in from New York and Park City, Utah.

Bunyan maneuvered the pebbled pathway between the softly rolling, manicured lawns in his gray Western boots, bought especially for the occasion. It was the perfect location to be a pioneer, a ranch, didn't you know, although in the part of his being that was a frontiersman, he might have preferred some rockier passages to go through, some Indians, more brazenly hostile than people who simply met with his disfavor.

He walked to the ranch house where Luke had invited close friends for a snack before the proceedings. Understated and airy, Nouveau Hacienda, Bunyan considered it, white stucco walls, sparsely furnished, decorated in California sunset colors, mauves and pinks and eggshells, pale Kirman rugs softening terra-cotta tile floors. Terra-cotta pots bril-

liant with red geraniums cornered the rooms, livening up
the pastel vistas of David Hockney paintings, hung spare-
ly on the walls, like blown-up postcards from an elegant
and costly vacation. Stars of some of Luke's more successful pictures, accompanied by current lovers, helped themselves to shrimp and crab from giant shells, set into
oversized lettuce and cabbage leaves in barrels of ice. Over
by the barrels was Tracy Fine, one of Bunyan's screen
favorites. Straw yellow ringlets circled her face, her pert
features rising from the petals of her curls like an alert
flower, her clothes the casual wrinkled wear of last season's look in Saint-Tropez. She was covered in silver and
turquoise, bands on her wrists and arms, snaking up over
her elbows, necklaces around her throat. Her skin was
tanned, a little too darkly, as if she'd just driven up from
Newport. Her porcelain-nailed hand was strung through
the arm of a good-looking dark man in his early thirties,
who seemed to be intent on observing even more than
Bunyan, his eyes coal black as he took in the gathering.

"I'm sorry," Bunyan said, as Tracy introduced them. "I
didn't quite get the name."

"Nick Zetta," the young man said.

"Bunyan Reis."

"Oh, I know that," Nick said. "Heavy lure."

"I beg your pardon?"

"I was supposed to go fishing in Vancouver this weekend. Tracy offered you as better bait. She told me everyone
was going to be here, and I told her I wasn't interested in
everyone, and then she mentioned you."

"I'm flattered that I was . . . bait." He looked at the
young man interestedly. He was slender, obviously self-
possessed, moving among the preppie blazers garbed in a
worn beige windbreaker and faded jeans. "Are you in the
art world?"

"I'm a teacher," Nick said.

"He teaches creative writing at UCLA," said Tracy.

"However do you manage that?" asked Bunyan. "That's
one of the things I've been dying to ask someone for
years. How can you *teach* somebody to be creative?"

"Well, obviously you can't. But if they've got creativity in them, you can bring it out. Did you ever teach art?"

"I'm too selfish," Bunyan said. "Nobody taught me, so why should I help anybody else? It's all I can do to even encourage them. Of course that's not quite as mean-spirited as it sounds. It would be cruelty to set loose a race of artists in a world that seems dedicated to destroying them. Where are our grants? Where's the support? What's become of the Medicis?"

"I worry about that, too," said Tracy. "What's going to happen to the old people if they don't get their benefits?"

It took Bunyan a minute to process through his brain the fact that she was speaking of Medicare, and another moment to wonder whether she was making a joke. Rather than laugh at what might have been unintentional humor on her part, he gave her a show business hug, catching a piece of her jewelry on his jacket pocket before he managed to, quite literally, tear himself away.

All around him were members of Luke's staff, jacketed in oyster white, polo-shirted in pale green button downs, with pink ties and old, tight-fitting Calvins. Blooming as fresh flowers would have in the East, before there were cocaine scandals at Choate. Bunyan's quicksilver eyes tracked the movements of the boys, uniformed in high-fashion casual, Ralph Lauren doing stylish battle with Sergio Valente. Luke himself was dressed like a banker, one who was secure in several generations of banking history, and so did not have to worry if his suit was baggy, because clothes made the man no more than occasional failures did. He was talking to either Bo Derek or a ringer for her, a bold-breasted, round-assed blonde in chamois buckskin, her face unlined, animated only with awareness of its own radiance, pink shell ears alerted for praise.

And, shit, Gordon Grayson. Oh, Bunyan had been having such a good time. How could Luke, with all his class and style, have invited Gordon Grayson?

"What are you doing here?" Bunyan asked him. "Did some celebrity die?"

"Not yet," said Gordon. "But my money is on you."

"I shall give it out officially in my will, to be read to the press at the moment of my passing, that we were never friends, no matter how much you carry on. You are not allowed to write about me, or say that we were intimate, or related, or even enemies."

"And here I thought you only pretended not to like me," said Gordon.

"I consider you a cormorant. A scavenger. A man who preys on the living by marketing the dead. A commercial ghoul."

"That's no reason we can't be friends," said Gordon, smiling.

Bunyan went out the terrace door. Crowds were already gathering on both sides of the road, getting set for the evening. There were three full bars on the lawn, under yellow- and white-striped canopies. Everywhere were limousines. Bunyan started up the road. "Beloved," he heard someone cry out, and recognized Tia's voice.

"Precious," he said, opening his arms wide even as he turned, steeling himself for what would be the latest aberration in her wardrobe. He gazed for a moment directly into the setting sun, as people were warned never to do, in the hope he would be temporarily blinded against her terrible radiance. She was dressed in neon chartreuse, wouldn't you know. "How evil you look!"

"That's the meaning of my name, did I ever tell you? Tia is short for Amartia. Greek for sin."

"Well, no one would ever suspect, except for your pornography collection."

"Speaking of which, I got the most fascinating phone call." She put her arm through his as they walked up the road. "Someone who claims to have pornographic writing by Miranda Jay."

"Do tell!"

"Very mysterious and expensive. They asked for a quarter million in cash."

"Pin money to you, dear."

"Not right now. Right now with the oil, and the problems in the Gulf, I'm poor as a church mouse."

"Of course, with you the church just happens to be the Vatican."

"You wicked thing," Tia said delightedly, and kissed the top of his white hair.

In front of them rose the domed arena, like an airplane hangar, with aluminum roof and sidings. At the entrance, draped with red velvet, was a giant cameo painting of the head of an Arabian chestnut with white markings. The crowd started to move inside. To the rear were bleachers, each place furnished with a little plastic picnic plate of the variety served on airplanes, in each one a croissant and what looked to Bunyan to be bologna. Sections to the front near the stage, set with tables covered with white linen, were roped off for celebrities and people with money.

To the right of the stage, the orchestra readied, fifteen members dressed in black tie. Strips of Mylarlike substance hung from the ceiling, obscuring the stage, coming together to make a semitransparent gunmetal curtain, dark tinted, like deco mirrors.

With Tia clinging to his arm, Bunyan tracked his way through the sawdust, noting all manner of people, some of them in double knit pants, bell-bottoms, plastic jewelry. Bunyan reminded himself not to judge by appearances. The ones with real money to buy at Arabian auctions seldom looked the part.

"Look over there," Tia said. "Lily Masters. Can you believe her? She's positively restored."

"Who's that with her?"

"Steve Holt," Tia said. "Her hairdresser."

"Tia!" Lily signaled, patting the chairs beside her. "Sit with us."

"You look absolutely wonderful," Tia said.

"Thanks to you. And Steve."

"Oh, I remember you," Bunyan said, and smiled at him, sitting down, flashing back to the party at Trump Tower and Sylvia Kranet's good-looking escort.

"Is it all right if we join you?" Tracy Fine asked, sun-browned fingers clutching Nick's arm.

"But of course," Bunyan said. "Does everybody know everybody?"

"Steven Holt." Steve got up and held out his hand.

"Tracy Fine."

"You don't have to tell me *that*."

"And this is Nick Zetta."

"Pleasure," Nick said to those at the table.

Men in black tie were stationing themselves at strategic places in the audience. ready to pick up bids once the auction started. The orchestra casually struck up a rock and roll beat. Bunyan could hear the handlers backstage, gentling the horses, calling out their "Whoas," clapping them into place. Through the darkly transparent Mylar curtain he could see a young handler in workshirt and tightly fitting dark trousers easing a renegade Arab back into the wings.

Behind him Bunyan heard the protesting voice of a security guard, saying the section was reserved. "Reserve this," a man said. Bunyan turned and saw Detective Lou Salerno, showing his wallet and the badge inside. The guard made a gesture of apology and let him through.

Like street people, Salerno looked more conspicuous in California, where there was less piled-up garbage to hide him. To Bunyan's delight, he made his way toward their table. Was the murderer here? Among them? Oh, it was just like being Agatha Christie, only with sex—if he got his nerve back, and Steve was willing.

"Detective Salerno!" Bunyan said, getting to his feet, offering his hand as the band struck up a drumroll.

The Mylar curtain parted; an announcer's voice over the loudspeaker welcomed the audience. A smoke machine started at the rear of the stage. Out of the smoke danced the ranch's star stallion, Araby, up for syndication, according to the talk, to be divided into thirty-two shares, total value of the horse a couple of million. Head arched, tail straining, his hooves kicked up red sawdust filled with glitter, while his trainer sat on his bare back in black tie and tails. The audience burst into cheers and applause.

"What an unexpected pleasure!" said Bunyan, indicating the chair beside him for Salerno.

"Is it?"

The band was playing at full pitch now, the evening officially started. Horses paraded onto the stage, some of them followed by their colts, a mare in foal with a foal beside her, jumping and kicking, shimmering the air with brilliant red spray.

"*Is it?*" Bunyan repeated, clapping his hands together. "How *odious*. Did you hear that everybody? *Is it?* Well, why wouldn't it be, unless I was the murderer. Am I? I can hardly wait to hear. Why would you come if not to bring us dark and terrible news? What else could we be but glad to see you?"

Two Mylar-mirrored podiums moved on tracks to the sides of the stage as the auctioneers in black tie took their places on the platform. "You're still working on the Masters-Miranda case, I assume?" said Bunyan.

"You assume right."

"I thought it was closed," said Lily, stiffening.

The auctioneer started the bidding on the first horse, a dark Arabian. Assistants in black tie in the audience nodded and signaled almost imperceptibly, receiving bids, passing them on to the men on the podium.

"Not for me it's not," Salerno said.

"Eight hundred thousand," said the auctioneer, and brought down his gavel. "Going once."

"Did you find out what was in Miranda's box?" Bunyan asked Lou.

"Not yet."

"Going twice."

"What do you know about Marty Fontaine?"

"He's dead," Salerno said.

"Oh, I get it," Bunyan said, disappointed. "You don't want *me* to know. But it's all been in the newspapers. The potassium. The wall safe being broken into."

"Sold for eight hundred thousand to Mr. Khashoggi," the auctioneer announced.

The curtains parted at the rear of the stage. Off in the

near distance, amidst floodlit green hills, glowed a panorama of galloping Arabian horses. The audience gasped and whistled.

"You don't have to be so cagey," Bunyan said as the curtains closed behind the stage and a handler brought in the next Arabian. "You can let us know what's going on. We won't tell anybody."

"Okay," said Salerno, and turned to Steve Holt. "How come you never came forward, Stephanie?"

Bunyan drew in a breath, like a whistle. "The name of the game is Camouflage! You put the clue out in plain sight where everyone can see it, only nobody can find it but those who know how to look!"

"How did you figure it out?" Steve said.

"I tracked Miranda back to Elizabeth Arden's. They had you down as her beautician. I just put it together. A long friendship. What was in the box?"

"Papers."

"Where are they?"

"I gave them to Claire Avery."

"Were there any other copies?"

"Miranda told me she kept a xerox in a hidden wall safe in her old apartment. She left it there when Masters brought her to New York."

"Who else did she tell?"

"I don't think anybody. She didn't trust many people."

"Then who else would have known?"

"How do I know? Maybe Lenrahan told somebody."

"But why would they have to kill Marty?" Bunyan said. "I mean, all they had to do was get the papers when he wasn't home. They could have broken into his safe anytime. They didn't have to kill him."

"Unless," said Tia, "the safe was already empty when they got there. And they figured he'd found the papers."

"What was in them?" Salerno asked Steve.

"Letters to her daughter. Pornography."

"Only a little pornographic," Nick Zetta said. "And that only for effect."

CENTURY CITY

◊

"Are you crazy?" Victor shouted. "That you would write this down?" He was holding the sheaf of papers that Miranda had left on the dresser, waving it at her, his normally tanned skin beet red now, bleeding up to the white roots of his hair.

"Oh, please, Victor," she said, wrapping the terry cloth robe tighter around herself, toweling off the remnants of her shower. "It's written roman à clef."

"What the hell does that mean?"

"I didn't use real names."

"Real names?" His eyes were wide, his big, square teeth shining grayish white in his unaccustomedly slack jaw. "You think you need real names to sink people? Oh, my God. Why did I ever get you that typewriter?"

"Relax," she said, and wound a towel around her dripping hair, twisting it into a turban. "Nobody will know it's you. I didn't describe your cock. Nobody's going to jump up and say, 'I recognize that cock!'"

"Don't you smartass me about this one, missy. Bad enough I let you write those letters to your daughter..."

"*Let* me... *Let* me!" She wheeled on him, heat rising to her face, rage taking the moisture from her lips. "Those letters kept me alive! What did you ever really do for me? Where's my daughter?"

"You know I've got lawyers..."

"Lawyers! Lawyers talk. If you wanted me to have her, I'd have her."

"That's not true! I've done everything..."

"And now you don't even want me to be able to express

338

myself." Miranda sat on the edge of the bed and started to cry.

"Of course I do." Victor put his arm around her. "I love it when you express yourself."

"The letters are all I have," she wept. "Those letters are my life."

"There are too many names in them." He looked a long way away.

"I'm never going to mail them."

"It's insane to even have them around."

"Then I'll put them in a safe."

"In a bank? Are you crazy? What if someone got hold of them?"

"Then build a wall safe here in the apartment. You're a big man. You can turn the world upside down if you want to. You can build me a wall safe if you're so worried."

"Worried?" The color was gone from his face now, his voice vacant of energy. "I should burn this filth." His hand tightened on the papers.

"Filth?" Miranda got to her feet, rasped at him. "You didn't think it was filth when it was happening."

"But the way you wrote it . . ."

"I thought I wrote it very stylishly," she said, and taking the towel from her head, started to rub her hair dry. "I doubt if anyone else in the class could do it better."

"Class? You turned this in to your class?"

"It's all right," Miranda said. "Nobody sees it but my teacher."

"Oh, my God," Victor said, and put his head in his hands.

"I'm sure he'll think I made it up," she said. "He'll think it's fiction."

"Oh, my God. Oh, my God."

"Nobody would believe it, anyway," she said. "They'd have to think I was making it up."

"What kind of woman can he think you are?"

"Oh, I love this. I love this that you're suddenly

worried about my reputation. All these years you've kept me your slut, and suddenly you're worried about my social standing.''

"You've never been a slut. You've never been anything but a great girl in my eyes," Victor said. "I only want to raise you up, lift you. Show you off. If I could, I would get you a job in campaign headquarters."

"Then do it," Miranda said.

"If I do, will you stop this writing nonsense?"

"Do it first," said Miranda. "Then we'll talk."

When he gave her back her paper, Nick told Miranda he wanted to see her after class. "I'm not surprised," she said.

She was wearing a loose T-shirt that slipped off one softly rounded shoulder, and her skin was tanned to the color of rich coffee with heavy cream. She held her head tilted slightly so her honey-colored hair fell to one side. Her slight overbite, the overlap of the left front tooth onto right, gave her smile an unexpected poignance. Nick found himself gripped by feelings that surprised him. She had the loveliest body he'd ever seen, long, with extraordinary breasts, not big, but aggressively shapely, very round she looked, in spite of how long she was. But it wasn't just the beauty of her breasts that struck him. It was her delicacy, and the long, amazingly shapely legs. Sometimes she would come to class wearing a skirt with a slit in it, which seemed to be a favorite fashion, cut nearly up to her right hip. But even tonight, in jeans, he could see the full outline of her thighs and lower legs, the firm apple roundness of her ass as she walked away from him, looking for all the world like she was in white sequins, wearing a dress that was painted on. She sat down in the wooden captain's chair, put her sandaled feet up on the conference table, and smiled at him again, a mocking smile, but with sadness in it, her teeth so white against the mocha of her skin he was literally dazzled.

He had been touched right away by Miranda's letter to

her daughter, enchanted by the woman herself, titillated by her presence in his class. There was no question in his mind she was intelligent, maybe even gifted. But the question he had now was about himself, and what it was exactly he was feeling. How much he wanted from her, how much he was prepared to give.

After class she agreed to go with him for coffee. She sent the driver of the limo away, giving him a fifty-dollar bill, telling him please not to tell Mr. Lenrahan. "He doesn't like me driving myself at night," she explained to Nick. "That's why he sends me in the limo."

"You don't owe me any explanations," Nick said, opening his car door for her.

"I know that." She got inside.

He took her to the Good Earth Annex in Westwood. "That was a fascinating piece," he said when they were comfortable in the dark wood of the booth, the heavy scent of orange spice tea almost palpable against their skin.

"You didn't give me a grade."

"I didn't feel I was in a position to. My objectivity went out the window. I feel like I've gotten to know you through your assignments, and I wasn't ready for this."

"You asked for it," she said, and looked at him, steely-eyed.

"I guess I did," he said, and told the waitress he wanted a frozen yogurt.

"I'll just have coffee," Miranda said.

"The yogurt is great here."

"I wouldn't want to have anything that's good for me."

"You really do all that stuff?" Nick asked when the waitress was gone.

"It's creative writing," she said. "Don't you think I have any imagination?"

"The details are a little too sharp. Some of it, if you made it up, would be too outrageous. I mean, it's hard to believe people really do these things, but I guess it goes on."

"I guess," said Miranda, and sat back as the waitress put coffee in front of her. She took a sip. "Did it turn you on?"

"A little, I have to admit. I mean, I know a lot of the 'throbbing' was in there just because you were sticking it to me . . ."

"That's right," she sort of singsonged.

"But what was really exciting was that you're talented."

"Oh, come on."

"No, I mean it. You set the scene, you evoke some real feelings . . ."

"You're stroking me," Miranda said.

"Well, there's that too. I admit I'd really like to do that. I've felt something for you all along . . ."

"And now that you've seen me in leather, you find me irresistible."

"Don't try and make it ugly, Miranda. Now that I've seen you in leather, I want to get you out of it."

"Maybe I don't want to get out of it. Maybe I really enjoy it."

"Maybe. But I have to try." He reached into his pocket, took a card, and handed it to her. "This man is a good friend of mine. A psychiatrist. I've asked him if he'll help you, and he's willing to."

"You have some fucking nerve."

"Maybe that's what you have to have when you care about somebody."

The waitress brought his yogurt, set it in front of him, and went away. He spooned some of the creamy vanilla onto his spoon and held it out to Miranda. She shook her head.

"What did you tell him about me?'

"That I love you. That I need him to help you. That you're in trouble."

"Well, you're wrong. I'm not in trouble. My life happens to be very safe and very full and the only trouble in it is that I troubled to take your trouble course, and you're a troubled guy, and you're trying to make your trouble my trouble."

"Okay." Nick scraped the spoon across the yogurt, ate some.

Miranda looked at her coffee, turned the cup around several times in its saucer. "You have a lot of balls."

"Thank you."

She tried to set her face into a sneer. "You're playing with yourself, you know that? You know what this stuff is really about? Masturbatory fantasy. Did you pick that up, in between my setting scenes and evoking real feelings?"

"Mostly the feeling I got was anger," Nick said.

"Well, how clever of you. You'll have to hang up your shingle right next to your friend. What insight. Let's get back to what this is really about." She touched the paper on the table in front of her. "The reason why the owners of *Penthouse* and *Playboy* are multimillionaires. The only thing that's bigger than big business in this country, teacher dear. Masturbation.

"And this is *your* masturbatory fantasy; that you can come into my life, someone who isn't hip enough or rich enough to even be a John, and turn it around and try and make me into something I'm not. Something I haven't been since I was a girl, maybe not even then. Make me into that, and make me yours. You really know how to play with yourself. Why don't you just fantasize about me and leave it at that? Don't try to make it into anything else, or anything more. Why bother?"

"Because masturbation is very lonely," Nick said.

She let him drive her home, telling him to forget her address. She said she didn't want him coming around, didn't want him thinking he would be welcome there. At the last, he moved to kiss her, and she was momentarily set off balance by how strong he was. She had always thought that his slenderness under the windbreaker would mean he was weak, and like Victor, she equated too much thinking with weakness. Surprised by the power of his grip, she let herself be held by him, and kissed. And his lips were soft against her mouth, the outside of her lips, and then the tenderer inside. It was hard to move away.

"Don't take it personally," she said as she managed to pull herself free. "A kiss doesn't mean a hell of a lot."

"It does to me," he said.

"Well, get over it." She got out of his car and didn't look back at him as she walked away. She knew she wouldn't go back to his class anymore. But she kept the psychiatrist's card. And the next time she ran out of coke, and thought about suicide, she called him.

All the psychiatrists in Los Angeles looked to Miranda to be in Century City, in the vast complex of high rises, a sterile, seemingly endless stretch of mirrored facades, from Santa Monica Boulevard to Olympic, on either side of wide boulevards with fountains in the middle. A minicity that appeared to have been erected solely for the benefit of the distraught and the divorcing: offices not listed on the directory as doctors seemed to be lawyers, the price of parking alone making it the province of the privileged. One dollar for every twenty minutes. Eight dollars maximum.

The doctor was a pleasant-looking man in his fifties, who greeted her by name, introduced himself, showed her inside, offered the choice of chair or couch. She took the chair. He reached for a little notebook.

"Will this be just between us?"

"Of course. Everything is confidential."

"Then why are you taking notes?"

"There are certain things I might want to go over."

"But you're not going to show them to anyone?"

"No."

"How about if the government breaks in and steals your files like they did with Daniel Ellsberg?"

"You think there's something of vital national importance that will come out in our discussion?"

"You never can tell!" Miranda said, smiling, and crossed her very long legs.

He took out some papers from a folder then. She saw it was the piece she had written for Nick. "How come he gave that to you?!"

"I suppose he thought it would make . . . certain things . . . clearer for me." He spoke in halting sentences, as though thinking out every word before he would let it leave his mouth, measuring the impact it would have on her.

"He has a hell of a nerve!"

"I . . . know he wants to help you."

"He could help by getting off my case."

He looked over the pages. "This is the way you make your living?"

"Certainly not! I don't get paid for these things. I enjoy giving pleasure. And these things are very pleasurable for Victor and his friends."

"Victor?"

"My friend, Victor Lenrahan."

"What's your relationship with him?"

"He's . . . well . . . I guess you could call him my gentleman."

"He's the one who's Mr X? The one in the maid's uniform?"

"I could kill Nick. God, I wish I smoked."

"Do you get sexual pleasure out of what you write about here?"

"Sometimes."

"Because from my knowledge of this, most women don't enjoy it. They do it to please the man."

"Have you talked to most women?"

"Well, no, I suppose I haven't . . . But from the literature . . . the things I've studied, and some women I've talked to . . . well, it's my understanding that most women don't enjoy it, they just do it to please somebody. Have you been enjoying this kind of activity for a long time?"

"I've been into it for about eleven years."

"And do you like making love in the ordinary fashion?"

"Oh, I enjoy making love. You have to understand this is not really sex we're talking about here. There's no real sex involved."

"By sex you mean intercourse?"

"Well, what do you mean by sex?"

"I mean any contact of a sexual nature."

"Well, then, I suppose we could call this sex. What you and I are having. I mean, from the literature . . . the things I've studied . . . and some women I've talked to . . . well, it's my understanding that you guys pin everything on sex."

"You have a very good ear," he said, smiling. "All my words back again. Very clever."

"I didn't come here to get graded," she said, trying to like him less than she actually liked him. "I went to Nick to get graded, and here I am, because of him, getting graded by you."

"You really consider there is not sex involved in what you do?"

"That's right."

"You like feeling pain?"

"No. That's not what I do."

"You never go through the pain part?"

"Oh, in the beginning I had to. You have to go through being a submissive to understand what's really involved in dominating. You need that experience. I didn't enjoy that. But it's part of . . . the education. You have to understand what the other person is feeling." She sat up, suddenly brighter, putting her spine straight against the back of her chair, so in fact she was a little higher than he was. "That's what all this is *really* about: compassion."

"Would you mind telling me some of your history?"

"I'm from Ohio. The first time I had sex, I didn't even know it was sex. I was ten. I had this uncle, a real redneck, and he came in in the middle of the night and fell on me."

"He fell on you. And what was done sexually?"

"Well, I guess he went inside me. He hurt me, and I was bleeding."

"Into your vagina?"

"Yes."

"And when did you have your next experience?"

"I was twelve."

"And was there any problem with your boyfriend?"

"He wasn't exactly a boyfriend. He was somebody's father." She sighed deeply, a sigh that surprised her with its depth and resonance. Quickly, she pulled herself back. "Does it give you pleasure to say words like vagina?"

"Does it upset you that I used that word?"

"I'm just interested. Just like you say you want to know if it gives me pleasure what I do, I want to know if it gives you pleasure what you do. Especially saying dirty words."

"You think vagina is a dirty word?"

"I think you tiptoe around the edge of it, like it makes you nervous. Do vaginas make you nervous, or just dirty words?"

"You seem upset, Miranda. What's upset you?"

"I'm pissed he gave you my piece. It was for my writing class. I mean, I didn't expect him to submit it to the *New Yorker*, and I didn't expect him to show it to you."

"Do you think Nick likes you?"

"Yes, he likes me. I think he had me write this piece because he's as big a pervert as the rest of them, and that was his way of getting off."

"So he would read it and have sexual pleasure?"

"Yes."

"Then why would he send you to me?"

"Well, maybe he's a moralist, as well as a teacher and a pervert."

"You think all men are this way? That they have to betray you? Disappoint you?"

"If he really cared about me, he wouldn't have made me write this . . . shit."

"*Made* you?"

"Assigned it, the way he did, so he could get his rocks off."

"And you feel betrayed?"

"I *am* betrayed."

"Do you feel that men have a tendency to betray you?"

"Everyone except Victor. And Harry Bell, of course, but he died before he had the chance. Maybe that's how to have the perfect relationship with a man. They should die at the end of the weekend.''

"But Victor takes good care of you?''

"He pays all my bills. He'd pay you, if I wanted to have some kind of treatment. But I don't want to. And he's paying the lawyers, and he'll buy me a house when I get my baby back.''

"Baby?''

"I have a little girl in Paris. I gave her up for adoption when she was born. Victor's paying the lawyers, giving them money to get her, and then he'll buy us a house in the country.''

"Who's the father of the baby?''

"Some Austrian queer I met in Paris.''

"You don't sound like you've had very good luck with the men in your life.''

"Well, not till you and Nick,'' Miranda said, with a very sharp edge.

"What kind of man was your father?''

"A bully.''

"A bully. What sort of things did he do?''

"He made my mother afraid. Afraid to think. Bullying her into being stupid. He didn't want anybody around who was more alive than he was.''

"So you have a lot of feelings identifying with your mother. Feelings about your father . . . And then this boy, when you were ten, assaulting you . . .''

"My uncle. My uncle wasn't a boy. This isn't a boy network we're talking about, doctor. We're talking about grown-ups.''

"Many of whom still have the feelings of boys.''

"Have you talked to 'many of whom'?''

"Well, yes, in this case I have. But it sounds to me with the asault when you were ten, and your friend's father . . . and the 'Austrian queer,' as you describe him . . . it sounds to me like there's a lot to the feeling of men betraying you. And I would wonder whether you didn't develop a sense of anger or resentment toward men from the earliest age on. That somehow involves you still on an unconscious level."

"And you think that's why I have so much fun with my Plexiglas buggy whip?"

"You understand that, then?"

"Well, in spite of all my daddy's efforts, I'm not stupid."

"That's right. Like your mother, you're not stupid. And many of the things she felt, part of her sense of resentment or injury, you understood. You could sense, even though you were a child, what your mother was feeling. And so this . . . anger . . . well, you're aware about the buggy whip. And some pleasure you might get out of it?"

"It's not a question of pleasure," Miranda said stubbornly, even while she wondered if it was. "It's my . . . Art." She leaned her head back and looked at the ceiling. The holes in it were to absorb the sound, she supposed, so when they went mad and screamed their despair, it wouldn't disturb the insane people in the office upstairs. "Everybody has to have something they do well. I would have liked to do . . . oh, I don't know, maybe something different, better. Did you enjoy my piece?"

"I think it's well written."

"Really?"

"It's very expressive. A lot of power in it. It's . . . uh . . . revealing."

"You don't think it's sick?"

"No."

"Then Nick must be very pleased. Because he says the difference between pornography and erotica is that erotica is a key to character. You consider this piece a key to my character, doctor?"

"Well, these women in here . . . they inflict pain . . . they do some of the things you've been involved with in some way."

"In some way? Don't you understand fiction? Fiction is the truth the way the writer perceives it."

"So this piece is the truth?"

"The truth disguised. Naked with a mask on. The only way people can really handle the truth, don't you think?"

"I don't know."

"What do you think about women like Misty?" she asked him.

"They seem to enjoy the suffering, the humiliation."

"You think that's so different from what's going on in regular people's houses?"

"You mean people like your mother?"

"Well, don't you think she submitted? Pretending to like it. Pretending to enjoy being a drudge, being a slave."

"And what about you? Abused as a child, when you had no control. With this, you're in control of the male now. You can beat *him*."

"You think there's anything wrong with that, if it gives him pleasure?"

"I can't advise you on that level. But I think it has directly to do with the assault on you as a child."

"Let me ask *you* something. Does this give you pleasure?"

"Trying to understand?"

"Talking to people about this. Do you get pleasure from it?"

"I'm interested in finding out why people feel the way they do."

"Hey," Miranda said, and popped up from her chair. "It's the same way with me." She started walking around the office, looking out the window, checking the books on his shelf. "You really stay on top of this stuff, huh?"

"It's like a mystery," Dr. Ehrens said. "Solving a mystery. But in a mystery, once you find out who did it, that's usually the end. Here, though, as you find clues . . . you can learn something that could be important to the people you're trying to help. So . . . you think every man you've known betrayed you . . ."

"Except Victor."

"Except Victor. Is there a part of you that's getting even with *all* men by these activities?"

"I certainly hope so," Miranda said.

"So even while you're getting even with them, you're gaining some pleasure for yourself."

"Well, it's more than pleasure and pain," Miranda said, and perched on the edge of the sill, so she was definitely above him now, the strange specter of the oil well outside the window behind her, as she crossed her arms and smiled down at him, making him swivel around in his chair to face her. "It's the *mind*. We're sort of in the same business, doctor. It's a mind game, what I do. Bondage and domination. A mind game. What people do to themselves when they're afraid, that's what gets them excited. What they imagine is going to happen to them. Imagination. That's what brings about the intensity of their orgasm. And that's what it's all about. The perfect orgasm. The most intense orgasm. The Great White Orgasm." Miranda laughed. "It's sort of *my* version of *Moby Dick*."

"And you consider it your job to help them get this?"

"My *Art*. I'm not doing anything they don't want done. They're eager to take the risk. You know about the carotid artery. That if you press it hard enough, orgasm is intensified. That men, when they're hanged, get an erection? And people have been found hanged who didn't mean to hang?"

"Exactly," Dr. Ehrens said. "Auto-erotic death."

"Because it went too far."

"That's right. I'm part of a suicide prevention clinic, and there have been several incidents of adolescent boys who hanged themselves."

"Pursuit of intense feelings . . . Freedom . . . A release they need so they can get on with what might not be so wonderful in their lives. It's the highlight of a lot of these men's lives, you know, what I do for them."

"Well, maybe they're paying the price for this sometimes forbidden sexuality."

"Sometimes forbidden? For Christ's sake, when Victor was a little boy his mother used to tie him to his chair with her apron if he didn't behave, if he wasn't quiet, if he wasn't a good boy."

"Or if he played with himself?"

"He doesn't remember that part," Miranda said. "Or if he does, he never told me."

"Sometimes, when you've suffered, you don't feel so guilty about pleasure," Ehrens said. "You've paid a price, so you're entitled. That may be a motive for some of the men you deal with. When they're little boys, they're forbidden to masturbate, or touch themselves, so sex assumes a forbidden quality. If they can suffer like that, they don't have to feel guilty."

"Sounds like a pretty sick world out there." Miranda slid off the sill. "How come you have so many children's magazines in your waiting room?"

"I work with a lot of children," Dr. Ehrens said.

"The nerve of him. Not even sending me to a grown-up shrink."

"I'm that, too," he said. "Try not to feel offended. I'm afraid we'll have to be stopping now . . ."

"Expecting some heavyweight eight-year-old?"

"But I would like to talk to you again."

"I bet you would. Why, there can't be a ten-year-old in the land has the stories that I do. Do you get off on this?"

"I beg your pardon?"

"You think you're any different from Nick? Any different from the people who like to watch? You're just a voyeur, like the rest of them."

"You're probably right," Dr. Ehrens said, and laughed. "That's a particularly male characteristic."

"Well, much as I'd like to help you," Miranda said, moving toward the door, "I have a very heavy schedule. I'm helping out at party headquarters in the presidential campaign."

"Very impressive." He got up from his chair.

"I'm not doing it to be impressive. I want to help. Why shouldn't I help?"

"No reason," Dr. Ehrens said. "I'm sure you'll be very helpful."

"The way you'd like to be to me?"

"Exactly," Dr. Ehrens said, opening the door for her. "I'm here if you feel like talking."

"Well, thanks a lot. But I wouldn't want you to hang till you hear from me."

"A psychiatrist!" Victor screamed. "Are you crazy?"

"I don't know," Miranda said. "He didn't act like I was."

"What did you tell him? Did you tell him my name?"

"Whatever I told him it's confidential."

"Sure, that's what they tell you. But these intellectuals are all Bolsheviks, and Bolsheviks don't know how to keep their mouths shut. They're just waiting to be able to use this stuff."

"For what?"

"The overthrow of the country, what do you think? What else did you tell him?"

"That I wouldn't be coming back, because I was going to work in party headquarters."

"You told him *that*? You told him *that*?"

"I'm doing it. What's wrong with saying it?"

"Why would you draw attention to it? Isn't it enough I got you a job there? You have to be advertising it around town?"

"I thought you didn't want me to hide my light under a bushel!"

"That isn't exactly a bushel, party headquarters. What can he think of me, that I'd take such a chance, putting you there."

"What can he think of *you*? Who the fuck cares what he thinks of *you*!!"

She started throwing things around the apartment, because it was coming up on Colette's birthday. She was going to be eleven years old, and Miranda understood now that he was only playing with her, that she was never going to get Colette back.

"Control yourself," Victor said, ducking. "Maybe you do need a psychiatrist."

"I need my daughter!" Miranda screamed. "I want my daughter!"

"You're going to get her. May I drop dead if you're not going to get her."

"What if that happens?" she cried, setting down the ashtray she had been about to hurl at him. "What if you die and I'm left with nothing?"

"I've made a special will. Enough for attorney's fees in France, and bribes for the officials over there, plus enough money for the house, and a separate trust fund for Colette—plenty to see her through the best college. With extra for her wedding. My only regret is that I won't be here to see it."

"You'll be here," she said. "You'll live forever. I just wish you'd come through for me now, so I can pray for your continued good health."

"You would, anyway," he said, and touched her hair.

"Whores don't pray."

"Don't speak of yourself as a whore," he said, and pressed her close to his still impressive chest. "Don't even think it."

"The psychiatrist asked me if that's what I do for a living. What we do. Mistress Elizabeth and Jessica."

He let go of her. "You told him about *that*?"

"Is it something that I should be ashamed of?"

"It's just so . . ." He paled. "Private."

"Not the way we play. And after all, he is a doctor."

"What all did you tell him?" he asked, visibly panicked now.

"I told him about your mother tying you up with her apron when you were a little boy."

"Jesus Christ," he said.

"Well she's not going to hear about it . . ."

"My sainted mother . . ." He sat down.

"Some saint, tying you up."

"She thought it was good for me," he said. "How could you desecrate the memory of my mother?"

"I didn't tell God," she said. "I told a psychiatrist."

"Don't you know what you've done? How can I be considered for a government post if there's this kind of garbage floating around? Don't you remember what happened to Eagleton?''

''No.''

''You know what goes on if there's a *hint* of any kind of mental problem? If they ever knew I had been talked about in a psychiatrist's office? How they dump you if there's any talk of trouble? How you drop out of consideration for a post?''

''He isn't elected yet.''

''My God, it's one thing setting you up in Beverly Hills, even letting you help out at party headquarters. But it's another thing your running off at the mouth to a liberal. What else did you tell him about me?''

''I told him you were the only man who hadn't betrayed me.''

''And I never would,'' Victor said. ''Did you call me Victor to him, or tell him my whole name?''

''I don't remember,'' said Miranda.

Nick wrote her letters. She sent them back unopened, marked ''Addressee Unknown.'' ''Addressee Deceased.'' She didn't even steam them and read them before she sent them back, afraid he might not be a really good writer, or that he might be even better than she hoped he was, with the power to change her mind. After a while he stopped writing.

Fall came, several times, a season she could only tell was there if she walked on Carmelita, where there were deciduous trees, maples, with leaves that turned red on silver branches before they dried and fell. It shocked her when she noticed it was that time of year again, three years having passed since she made her last try at being something other than she was, registering for the writing course, her last creative act, if you didn't count the spoon of snow in the mornings.

And a Christmas passed where Victor gave her her own Mercedes, with a big red ribbon tied around it, delivered to her driveway, the same as he had done with his daughters on their ''important'' birthdays. And as an original gift, the following Valentine's Day, rather than candy or flowers, he bought her a fabulous mask from Trashy's, a red and black feathered owl mask that the owner told him was a replica of the one O had worn in *The Story of O*, where she'd gone to a ball with a leopard on a leash, and the leash attached to a ring through her labia.

"Now you try it on," Miranda said to Victor after she took it off. It was very heavy and hot, the best grade of feathers. Sequins around the eyes and the metallic form of the nose made it weighty.

"All right," he said, and took off all his clothes first, so it would have the most effect. His body was still surprisingly good for his age, the little workouts he put himself through having kept his arms and chest in enviable shape for a man of his years. "I'm getting old," he said sadly as he looked at his naked reflection. "Really old."

"Not here," she said, and touched it. "Here you're still young and pink. As good as new."

"My angel," he said.

"Put it on," she said.

He did. "I love how I look in this," he said.

"So does this love how you look," she said. "Look how it loves it."

"You keep a man young," he said, and started dancing around the apartment, with his mask and his hard-on. Then he fell over.

"Victor?" She ran to him, touched his motionless form. "Victor?"

She took the mask off him and moved close to his mouth. There was no breath. "Victor, will you stop clowning?"

He didn't move. She leaned on his chest and listened for his heart. "Help," she murmured, her throat constricting. "I've got to get some help." She ran to the phone and started to dial the operator, for emergency. Then she realized he was on the floor, and saw how naked he was, and how it would look. And maybe he wasn't really dead and then he'd be mad at her for not handling it better, putting his post in jeopardy. So she ran back to him and awkwardly pulled his trousers on, so maybe they'd think he had only been relaxing in her apartment.

When the paramedics got there, they worked him over with a resuscitator. She wondered what they would tell his wife. If they would tell the papers. They put him on a stretcher after a while and carried him out to the fire truck.

"You want to come with us?" they asked her.

"Is he dead?"

"Afraid so."

"Then there isn't any point," she said, and handed them his shirt and jacket, with his ID in the pocket, and his socks and shoes. "Anyway, we were just friends."

There was no formal funeral service. Miranda needed at least the chance to say good-bye, so she wormed it out of his lawyer that Victor was buried at Westwood Memorial Park. He was reluctant to give her even that information, but he had to tell her something, because she was ragging at him about the will, and when it was going to be read, and it already had, and there was nothing in it about her.

"What about the special will?" she asked him finally. "The one about me and my daughter."

"There isn't any," he said.

"But he told me. He wouldn't lie to me."

"There isn't any other will. No special will. Only the one that's already been read. And there's no mention of you in that."

She went to an attorney, one who'd gotten a lot of publicity for helping women who'd been fucked over. He filed a creditor's claim for Miranda and followed it up with a long, legal letter to Lenrahan's lawyer, with various proofs of how long they had been together, recalls of promises he'd made, dates, places and times he had asserted his plans to take care of her. Plus a copy of the correspondence with the French lawyers as proof of Victor's intention to help her get her daughter back, with an additional adviso stating that during the twelve years preceding the demise of Mr. Lenrahan, Ms. Jay literally devoted her exclusive services, full-time attention and dedicated application to the business affairs of Mr. Lenrahan, all at the request of Mr. Lenrahan. That everyone involved wished to avoid a costly and damaging litigation, but that Ms. Jay had applied herself to the exhausting demands of Mr. Lenrahan to such a degree that she was required to, and did in fact, relinquish the pursuit of her own occupational calling. Needless to say, it went on, Mr. Lenrahan's demands were extreme, if not never ending. He had also made repeated promises to her that he would provide for her the means to reclaim and reacquire custody of her child. As the Creditor's Claim indicated, the lawyer cited, the amount required for that purpose would be $400,000. He concluded that her claim was meritorious, his client had a very strong case. It was his hope that it could all be settled amicably.

They wrote back no. The Creditor's Claim came back rejected.

"What do we do?" Miranda asked him, the hand that held the lawyer's letter shaking.

"Now we sue."

"Oh, no. Victor wouldn't like that."

"Victor was the man who screwed you."

"It's a mistake," she said. "I know there's a simple explanation."

"The simple explanation is he lied to you. You've got to become more trouble than it's worth to them. That's the only way they'll pay you off. You have to make them nervous that you'll drag his dirty laundry through the courts."

"Victor is a very private man. I couldn't do that to him."

"He's dead. Do you understand that? He's dead. He didn't do what he promised. You owe him nothing. You've got to take them to court."

"It wouldn't be ladylike," she said. "Victor wouldn't like it."

There was a pharmacy downstairs in the arcade of the lawyer's office, just across from the building where Dr. Ehrens was. A couple of times she'd thought about calling him, but never had. She still kept his card in her little plastic case of credit cards, all canceled now, cut off by the estate, useless to her. It was one of only three business cards she'd gotten in her life, because in the circles she spun through, people didn't hand out their business cards. The second was Fred Masters', who'd given it to her the last time he left the yacht. The third was her lawyer's. She tore it into little pieces as she left his office, because she didn't like him anymore. He wasn't classy enough to deal with Victor.

She felt lightheaded as she pushed open the door to the pharmacy. It was one of those wide, airy, glassed-in stores that seemed to proliferate in Southern California, with racks of greeting cards, stuffed animals, perfume, candies, a kind of Get Well shop for the depressed, showing what a world of alternatives there was to despair.

"Do you have something like smelling salts?" she asked the pharmacist.

"That's such an old-fashioned request. We hardly even stock it anymore. A lot of people . . ."

"Please," she said, "I think I'm going to faint."

He went into the storeroom.

On the shelf directly on the level of her eyes a few feet away were some waiting, filled prescriptions. Because of her farsightedness she could read the labels clearly. One bottle read "Dalmane—Do not take with Placidyl." The other read "Placidyl—Do not take with Dalmane." Both were for the husband of Alicia Farrell, who when she saw starving children had had to think twice before buying another jewel. Miranda moved behind the counter and slipped them into her purse.

"Hey," the pharmacist said. "What are you doing behind the counter?"

"Looking for you," Miranda said. "I was afraid you forgot about me."

"Forget about you?" He grinned. "A man would have to be dead to forget about you."

"Ain't it the truth," she said.

Most of the restaurants in the area were closed. She

went into the Hamburger Hamlet on the corner and sat at the counter, asking the waitress for a glass of water.

"This section is closed," the waitress said.

"I'm not asking you to cook anything. I'm asking you for a glass of water."

"The booths over there are open."

"How about you give me a glass of water, and I carry it over there?"

"How about you sit over there, and I have the waitress bring you a glass of water? I'm off duty."

"Thank you for your graciousness," Miranda said, getting up and going over to the booth, wondering why it was when you thought about leaving life, the people you met were such an affirmation of what a wise decision that was.

When the waitress brought her the water, Miranda took ten Dalmane and ten Placidyl. "Have you decided on your order?" the waitress asked, returning.

"I'm not really hungry." Miranda handed her a five-dollar bill. "But thank you for your trouble."

"Thank *you*," the waitress said, and pocketed the tip.

She was hardly out in the street when the dizziness hit her, a sudden dullness, like someone had struck her in the eyes and tongue. She started to cross the street to get to the garage where her car was parked. But she just made it into the crosswalk.

When Miranda came back to full consciousness, she was in Century City Hospital. At her feet, standing, looking down at her, was Dr. Ehrens.

"How do you feel, Miranda?"

"Stupid."

"I wonder why you tried it."

"He didn't leave me any money," she said. "He promised me he would take care of me, and help me get my baby back, and it was all of it a lie."

"Victor Lenrahan?"

"Victor Lenrahan," she said, and started to cry. "I'd have to sue. I can't go through that."

"So Victor, too, betrayed you."

"Well, I don't guess you have to be a psychiatrist to understand that." She choked on her tears. "I'm sorry. I don't mean to give you a hard time. I know you're trying to be kind."

"Do you?"

"There just doesn't seem to be any point . . . All the dreams I had for my daughter . . ."

"You know, Miranda, I wonder . . . since you haven't seen your daughter since she was born, if maybe she represents more than just your daughter. If maybe she wasn't the chance to give a better life to another little girl."

"You went to school all those years to figure that out?"

Dr. Ehrens smiled. "I don't always come to conclusions this quickly. And they aren't necessarily correct. But you're a very bright woman, and I have the feeling with you that I better say what I have to say, because you might not give me much time."

"I don't mean to put you under such pressure," Miranda said, and they both laughed, the end of her laugh combining with a nose blow into a Kleenex he handed her. "How did you know I was here?"

"The hospital found my card in your purse. They thought maybe you were a patient of mine."

"I can't believe he did this to me," she said, and started crying again. "I just can't believe it."

"You think it was an oversight on his part? A plan he didn't finish?"

"Victor wasn't a liar. He might have been crafty in his business dealings, maybe even a little devious, because that's how it is in business. But he was always straight about money. You know, the reporter from *Forbes* magazine came to interview him for the issue on the 400 Richest People in America, and the reporter was stunned because Victor told him everything he wanted to know. He said most of the time the first thing rich people try to do is hide their assets, and you have to investigate, you know, speak to clerks at banks, uncover real estate holdings, and here was Victor handing him everything but his financial statements. Why would he be so open with a reporter and so deceptive with me?''

"I don't know," Ehrens said. "But I do think I know, or at least have an idea, what you were trying to do for your daughter."

"Yes?"

"Give her a mother who'd be aware of what a girl has to go through. Protect her. Help her not to be hurt by men. Not to have to live a life of pain and humiliation the way you did as a child. Could that have been part of your dream?"

"Yes," she said.

"Probably that dream began as long ago as when you were ten, when your uncle took advantage of you.'

"Oh, this is all a crock of shit," she said. "Does Nick know I'm here?"

"I called him when I got the call," he said. "He wants to see you. He really cares about you, and I can understand why."

"You can?"

"Yes."

"Why?"

"Because you're an obviously intelligent person who had a difficult childhood, a difficult adulthood, who dreamed about making a better life for your daughter. A dream you had for so many years. An idealization. Maybe some of it was an illusion, because you've been away from her for so long. But there's no doubt you really care for your daughter. That your caring is genuine. And so maybe was the hope that you could live some of your life through your daughter. And maybe with understanding in these areas you can live a better life."

"How?"

"By examining . . . the fantasy . . . and understanding what you were trying to do for yourself. And since you can't be both the mother and the child in this instance, maybe you can be the mother to the little girl inside yourself. The little girl longing for something better than she has. Investigate and see and understand and be a good mother to the little girl, and help her be a different person. One you could admire.

"Or maybe . . . it might be possible to begin to understand there are some men who could really care about a woman and not exploit her."

"You really believe there are men like that? That they'd be looking for *me*?"

"I know at least one man who genuinely seems to care about you."

She sat up in bed, a burst of energy suddenly ridding her of her torpor, anger driving the cobwebs from her head. "Is that why you're here? Is that what you're playing, John Alden?"

"John Alden?"

"The Puritan who went to plead his friend's case.'

"Nick has in no way sent me to plead his case. I came because I was interested in you, and because he is my friend and he cares about you."

"Well, it's a fantasy on his part," Miranda said. "As thick a fantasy as mine about Colette, because he doesn't know me, he doesn't know who I am, or what I am, and he hasn't even seen me for three years."

"That doesn't mean he hasn't thought about you," Ehrens said.

"Why do you men always think the solution to a woman's problem is a man?"

"That isn't what I said," said Ehrens. "I only spoke of Nick in answer to your query, your doubt that decent men exist, and if they do, what they could possibly want with you. And, if I can take off my doctor hat, I'd like to say the answer could be everything."

"You really think that?"

"I really think that," he said.

"Well, okay," she said, and her eyes were bright again, the light back in them. "Maybe I'll give it a try."

About three o'clock that afternoon, Fred and Lily Masters arrived in their private Lear jet and took a waiting limousine to Century City Hospital. Fred Masters' card had been in Miranda's credit card case, along with the doctor's, but it hadn't been the hospital that called him. It was a stringer for his scandal sheets who got paid by the gossip tip, twenty dollars an item for advance news on who was in the Betty Ford Clinic detoxing, what celebrity had flunked out of there and was back freebasing, twenty-five dollars per suicide attempt, etc. This man ran from hospital to hospital, checking out with various informants if there was anybody in there ODing or D&Cing. All he had been looking for that day was maybe a quickie abortion, called a curettage. So the news about Miranda Jay had come like a windfall from a relative he hadn't known died.

On the plane coming in, Fred briefed Lily about Miranda, what a delicate, funny, special creature she was, how close she had been to his favorite friend, Victor Lenrahan. Fred was still in a kind of outraged mourning over Victor Lenrahan's death. It was one of the best filthy tips he'd ever gotten, the circumstances of how Victor died. But he'd admired the man too genuinely to use it in any of his papers, where God knew it belonged. Things like that didn't happen to people unless there was a God-given reason, and the reason was surely increased circulation; who wouldn't have picked that story up off the stands? But he didn't, wouldn't use it, when all the conservative papers wrote about the death at length, only stopping at speculating on what exactly he'd been doing when he died. But all of them included the information that the call to the paramedics was made by Miranda Jay, a frequent "companion" of Lenrahan's. They also noted there was some discrepancy in time between his having been stricken and Miranda's making the call, giving rise to the speculation—not printed—(he wouldn't use that either) that she'd spent some time trying to get his clothes back on.

There had also been a clever court reporter who made note of the Creditor's Claim filed against the Lenrahan estate by Miranda's attorney, and the subsequent fact that the claim had been refused. So it was now a matter of public record what had passed between the civilized combatants of the law, and that Miranda seemed to have been treated most unfairly. Many were the women who argued that Miranda was entitled to a great deal more than she had asked for, most of them, surprisingly, wives, not mistresses, who took yoga class together, didn't much care for Lenrahan's wife, and argued the injustice of the whole affair on the way to workouts in Malibu.

As for Lily, her emotions being so close to the surface anyway, her love for her husband, her knowledge of how highly he'd esteemed Victor being in the forefront of her sensibilities, she'd wept all the way to the hospital in the limo for the girl who lay in the hospital. Without ever having seen her, she loved Miranda, just because she'd meant so much to Victor, and Victor hadn't taken care of her, and Fred hadn't printed anything. Lily knew she herself was a pushover, but Fred was anything but. So this welling up of nobility in him refreshed her long fallow adolescent admiration for her husband. And that gave bud to affection for Miranda, who was, after all, the reason behind his unexpected gallantry. She could feel how deep was his affection for his fallen comrade, that he wanted to go to the cemetery, and had printed nothing.

"What you've got to do," she said to Miranda, brisk as the new penny she'd once been, "is get very busy. Busy hands have no time for sorrow." She held Miranda's hand now, its skin still tanned, manicure slightly chipped, the feel of it slightly colder than Lily's own flesh, as if she had come, quite literally, back from the tomb. It thrilled Lily's heart that she could be part of a rescue, a restoring. The girl in the bed looked so frail and touching, pale beneath her tan. Maybe, Lily thought, this was the daughter she'd never had. And fate had given her what the gynecologists never could.

"Busy with what?" Miranda said, curiously warmed by this full-faced, bright-eyed woman, the softness of her voice, the sweet cloud of her perfume. It was a feminine presence stronger than any she'd experienced, and she felt prepared to listen, to join, to turn her life over. Why not?

"Well, what are you interested in?"

"What is this, an interview for Chrissake?" Fred said, sitting in a chair by the window, wondering why nobody had sent flowers, wondering what kind of crappy burg this was that a package as adorable as Miranda could just be dumped like an old bale of garbage, wondering where the fuck they put Victor when he croaked, so he could pay a courtesy call. "What kind of doctor they got on your case? Is he a pro? You want me to make some phone calls? Find out who the biggest guy is in suicide?"

"She didn't commit suicide," Lily said patiently. "It was probably an accidental overdose."

"It was an accidental underdose," Miranda said. "I should have taken more, and not keeled so close to a hospital."

"You're not a quitter," Lily said, and squeezed her hand. "Anyone can quit. I know from Fred, and what he tells me about Mr. Lenrahan's feelings for you, that you're a very unusual young woman."

"Well, Mr. Lenrahan's feelings for me turned out to be shit." Miranda started to cry again.

"You don't know that," Fred said defensively. "It just might be the lawyers for the estate fucking around. The man worshiped the ground you walked on."

"Then he should have gotten me new rugs," Miranda said, and started to laugh.

"I've got a million committees I need help with," Lily said. "A ton of charities. People that are really in need. We want you to come back to New York with us. You can help me. Stay with us. There's plenty of room in our apartment. We just got this triplex at Trump Tower, and there's a whole guest wing you'd be happy in."

"That's what you need," Fred said. "A change of déjà vu."

After Dr. Ehrens left Miranda's room at the hospital, he put in a call to Nick, brought him up-to-date. "Maybe if she could learn to love herself," he said, "she can come to see that a decent man could love her. It doesn't need to be the same with you as it was with the others."

"You better believe it." Nick was saying, all the while turning on the water in his shower, and being glad he had finally let himself be seduced into the California crap of having a twenty-five-foot extension on his phone so he could run around his bedroom taking the right shirt out of his drawer, checking if his trousers were clean, because it would be wrong to go to her in jeans. This was serious business. The most serious business of his life.

"At least she's starting to be a little aware about her past. Starting to learn about herself. So maybe more of her future will be in her own hands."

"And mine," Nick said. "Don't forget mine."

"Well, yes, that would be good," Ehrens said. "But she's got to understand what she's worth to herself, not just in someone else's eyes."

"But beauty is in the eye of the beholder, don't forget that one. Don't get so medical on me that literary doesn't count. Literary sometimes sees the truth as well as doctors. We'll be Eros and Psyche." He was elated now, taking the shirt out of the drawer, his hand not even feeling the motions, he was moving so fast. "That's who she is, you know. The dewdrop that fell on the land that gave rise to spirit and beauty in women."

"That's a Jungian myth, I think. I'm not too familiar with that one."

"All you need to know is that it has a happy ending, even after she had to go to hell. And we'll have a beautiful daughter and name her Pleasure."

"Don't *you* start getting carried away by fantasies."

"Why not?" said Nick, pulling out a clean pair of socks, dark, like a serious man wore, not the white tennis socks of California. "What's better than a fantasy fulfilled?"

"Life lived." Dr. Ehrens said.

"Well, we're going to do that, too."

Nick stopped for flowers on the way to the hospital, and that took him an extra five minutes. When he got to Century City, he was told Miranda had just checked out.

An orderly on the floor told him he wasn't sure who the couple were she'd left with, but one of the attendants said they had a limo waiting.

EAST HAMPTON

◇

"I need to go to New York one more time," Lou Salerno told his commander. "There's one more piece of the puzzle. If I put it in place, everything fits. If my hunch is right."

"Your hunch is wrong," his commander said. "Your hunch is too expensive."

"I don't get it," Salerno said.

"We already spent too much money on this case. Get busy with something else."

"What's the matter?" Lucille asked him that night at dinner.

"I asked to go to New York and the chief won't send me. He says we're over budget."

"Send yourself. We have a travel fund."

"That's for the Greek islands."

"So far I haven't been invited," she said. "Niarchos must have lost my number."

"You really wouldn't mind if I used that money?"

"You'll make it up to me."

"You want to come?"

"There's nobody left in the city," she said. "It's too late in the season. They'll all be in the Hamptons."

He called ahead to make sure Lily Masters was still in town. Reluctantly, she agreed to see him.

He took the Red Eye to New York, because even though Lucille had told him to enjoy himself, carte blanche, he didn't like to spend more than he had to. You always had to spend more anyway on short notice. He took a cab into the city and hung around the lobby of Trump Tower till a decent hour. Then he went upstairs.

"I'd like to go through your husband's canceled checks," Lou said to Lily.

"Couldn't you have called his accountant, or his attorney?"

"Sure. But I like you."

"I could do without your esteem," she said, but she was smiling. She led him into Fred's study and switched on the light. "They're all in those files."

It took him a couple of hours to find it. He closed the files and went inside to say good-bye to Lily, sort of poising himself on tiptoe at the threshold, his knocking tentative, like he didn't want to intrude, even though he knew he was intruding. She was in her dressing room, a new hairdresser weaving color through her hair, a plastic cape around her shoulders, protecting her dressing gown. In a funny way, she reminded him of Lucille. He saw the same kind of basic goodness in both of them, although he wasn't sure Lily would've let him dip into the travel fund.

"Did you find what you were looking for?" Lily looked up into the mirror, caught his eyes reflected there.

"I did, thank you."

"What was it?"

"You sure your husband was only fooling around with Miranda?"

"Let's not start that all over again. Please. What can possibly be the object of that kind of question, except to hurt me?"

"The farthest thing from my mind," Lou said. "I just want to make sure he wasn't screwing around with Connie Garrett."

"I don't even know who that is," Lily said.

"A woman in L.A."

"He hardly ever went to L.A. I told you. Fred didn't have that much time or energy, except for business."

"Just checking," Lou said. "A pleasure to see you again." He tipped the hat he wasn't wearing.

"The pleasure is all yours," Lily said.

"You don't really mean that."

"I guess not. Though why I should be glad to see a policeman is beyond me. Especially one who's responsible for having my hairdresser arrested."

Lou shrugged. "Concealing evidence. What could I do?"

"You could look for real villains," Lily said. "You could try and find genuine bad guys. Not some harmless stylist. You could uncover the true forces of darkness."

"I'm doing my best," said Lou.

He took a plane back to L.A. early that afternoon. Because of the time difference, it was still afternoon when his plane landed. So there was time to photocopy the check and go down to the precinct and put the original in the Connie Garrett file.

"I got what I needed," he told his commander. "A check from Fred Masters to Connie Garrett for twenty-five thousand dollars. He paid her off for a tip, for one of his newspapers, most likely. She put it into her checking account before she took the bullet in her eye."

"Why don't you get off this, Salerno?" the commander said. "You wasted enough time. We had eighteen other murders last week. Use your energy on those."

Lou knew not to take it personally, much as it rankled him not to get encouragement, now that he was so close. Too many crimes passed through the precinct for the commander to care what was murder or suicide. Dollars and cents was what crimes meant to him, budgets for how much he had to spend in his department. So how could he encourage a guy working eight, ten, twelve hours a day on what he probably still thought was a suicide? If he thought about it at all.

"But it's all tying in," Lou said. "All the threads. Garrett wasn't a suicide any more than Fred Masters was. She had a boyfriend, Chuck Dresner, in the Quality Control Department at MicroTel. He must have told her something that she told Masters. A tip for his sleazy newspapers. Some big scandal that was about to break. That's why she died. And why Masters died."

"Masters isn't my province," said the commander. "That's New York. And that case is closed."

"Well this one isn't," said Lou, and went home to tell Lucille.

Hap flew the MercerCorp company jet to New York and arranged for a smaller plane out of LaGuardia to East Hampton. He'd found out Jonah was staying there from his wife.

"Oh, yes," Edith Jonah had said on the phone. "I know your name. You were an employee of Victor Lenrahan, my husband's *good* friend."

"That's right."

"And *his* good friend, Miranda."

"Well, I didn't actually know her," Hap said.

"Are you really sure she's dead?"

"I beg your pardon?"

"Did anybody check out the bones, make sure the flesh is rotting?"

"I don't understand," Hap said, although now that he listened harder, he could pick up the slur of whiskey around the edges of her words.

"Because they didn't fool me for a minute. Not for a minute. I knew everything that was going on, and death isn't good enough for her. So are we absolutely sure she's dead, or was that some other whore's body they put in the ground?"

"It's urgent I locate the secretary," Hap said uncomfortably.

"He's in East Hampton. If we're really positive she's dead, he must have found a new and livelier tart." She gave the address where Jonah was staying.

Jonah had never answered Hap's letter, except to send a brief, annoyed note that it sounded like sour grapes to him, since MercerCorp had lost the contract. Hap continued to try and call him, but the secretary was always out to his calls.

Now with the urgency of the discovery Hap made about the microchips Lily had given him, there was no time to waste trying to get through on the phone. He flew to East Hampton and took a taxi to the address Edith Jonah had with such vindictive graciousness given him.

A butler, white-coated, black, resonant of an earlier, grander time, answered his ring at the front door of the shingled gray house. "Who is it, Raymond?" a woman called out.

"It's a Mr. Hap Mitchel, Mrs. Kranet."

"Oh, yes," she said, coming in from the lunch she was serving outside. "The astronaut. Of course." She smiled at him and held out her hand. "How nice you could drop by."

"I'm sorry to come without calling, but I have some urgent business to discuss with Secretary Jonah."

"Was he expecting you?"

"I'm afraid not. I was hardly expecting to be here myself."

"Well, come along. Join us. It's always nice to have an extra man, especially when he's been to the moon." He followed her outside. Six chairs were arranged neatly around the white-painted wrought-iron table on the lawn under a big green-and-white-and-red-striped umbrella. Matching seat cushions pulled in the colors of the countryside. In one of the chairs sat Jonah, his face expressionless at the sight of Hap.

"Here's a friend of yours, Dwight," Sylvia Kranet said.

"An even better friend than I thought," said Jonah. "Since nobody knows I'm here."

"Well, *somebody* knew." Hap smiled. But the secretary's face was grim.

"I've asked Mr. Mitchel to join us for lunch."

"You didn't have to do that," Jonah said.

"Oh, we have plenty." Sylvia signaled the butler for another chair and a place setting. "I believe you and the senator know each other." She gestured toward her husband.

"Pleasure to see you again, sir." Hap shook hands with him.

"And do you know Allen Hewitt?"

"Of course," Hap said, shaking hands, smiling at the palely freckled young redhead who sat beside him, whose name Allen didn't give him. On the other side of the woman sat Stan Dobson, who sprang to his feet with the introduction.

"Sure I know Mitchel," Dobson said. "We met last year on a plane. Finished that autobiography yet?"

"Haven't started it," Hap said. "I'm not much of a writer."

"We'll get you together with a writer, that's the least of it," Dobson said. "We got Dwight here together with a wonderful writer. Don't you like him?"

"Crazy about him," Jonah said blandly, his face still set this side of a scowl.

Hap sat down.

The butler brought his lunch plate, lettuce leaves and asparagus spears framing an egg in aspic. Hap picked up his fork and tried to look happy about it.

"Tell me the truth, senator," Dwight said. "Did you secretly invite Mitchel here so you two could sandbag me?"

"Excuse me?" asked Senator Kranet.

"Because, as I'm sure you're aware, Hap, the senator's been giving your line practically verbatim to the committees. Although I must admit it's a little more predictable coming from an opponent of the administration than an aerospace man."

"I didn't come here to discuss any of that."

"You're not in favor of the laser in space bullshit?" Senator Kranet asked Hap.

"No, sir, I'm not. I said it to Wilbur and I said it to Orville: this thing will never leave the ground."

"In 1938," said Jonah, sitting up rigid in his wrought-iron chair, "bombers took to the air. No one could see them at night. Then someone invented radar. Radar saved the Brits. It's the same kind of mind-leap as lasers in space. A fresh mind could come up with it. You're just too old, Mitchel."

"Could be," Hap said. "As I said, I didn't mean to intrude, and I know you don't want this discussion."

"Makes no goddamn sense," said the senator. "He's not a bad man. Has good intentions. But doesn't know what the hell he's talking about. Benighted. No scientific input. And all the other guys around are afraid to tell the boss he's made a mistake."

"Eat your aspic," said Sylvia. "We promised no politics over lunch."

"You call this lunch?" asked the senator.

"We've got to take the high ground," Jonah said. "Like the Indians and Custer."

"It's a mistake," Kranet said, piercing the yolk, watching it run onto his plate.

"Well, then, I'll ask Hilda to make us a salad," said Sylvia, and went toward the back of the house.

"Highly provocative and ineffective," Kranet continued. "An immoral mistake. We've already got mutually assured destruction. What's the point of this? Fielding weapons in space to protect strategic missiles. Not even to protect the civilian population. To protect the goddamn weapons. What's the point?"

"We've got to stay ahead. It's the only way to keep 'em in their place. To give our people hope."

"If I may . . ." Hap said. "I believe hope is the worst of it. You make people think you have laser beams out there to destroy enemy missiles, it gives them hope we can avoid being destroyed."

"Nothing wrong with hope," Jonah said.

"There is when it's a false hope. A lie. Where's the ethics in that? Giving people a false hope, when maybe there's something better they could be doing."

"Like what?"

"How about making peace?" Senator Kranet asked.

"There's no chicken," yelled Sylvia, from the back door. "How about tuna?"

"Tuna will be fine," the senator called back, with not quite the vocal strength of his wife. Time had apparently taken some of the energy out of his physical presence, if not from his convictions. "I suppose. Mitchel, since you spent a little private time in space, you feel some attachment to it."

"Well, it was a different kind of space then, senator. Filled with infinite visions, better possibilities."

"What's out there now?"

"Four thousand pieces of orbiting debris, burnt-out rocket casings, shrouds, besides the fifteen hundred satellites."

"For the good of mankind," Jonah said.

"Sure, some of them are. Weather and tides and communications satellites."

"Try to remember," Jonah said, "you're living in a world where Commies arrange to assassinate the Pope. If they were using space as a way to advance, to solve medical puzzles, to explore, we wouldn't have this kind of race."

"Not to mention the good betting for gamblers." Allen Hewitt had a pleasant smile on his face, as if he had just been waiting for the right moment to make the discussion lighter, filling it with a little P.R. pastry. "You know, Lloyd's of London has a group of rich underwriters who take bets on whether or not satellites are going to get lost in space. They handicap that instead of spending the afternoon at the races."

"What fun," said the young redhead beside him, as though she'd just heard about a new ride at Epcot.

"I'm sorry," Hap said. "I didn't get your name."

"Misty," she said.

"Well, yes, Misty. I guess it is fun for them. But for me, you see, space is . . . well, I don't mean to put anybody off, but . . . can I use the word holy?"

"This is making me sick," Jonah said as Sylvia returned to the table.

"I'm so sorry. The salad will be here in a second."

"I wasn't talking about your food," Jonah said.

"We were talking about the rape of space," said the senator. "And this insanity of more weapons."

"Eric, shame on you." Sylvia sat down. "A promise is a promise. And Dwight is our guest."

"But this involves him, too," the senator said. "The true sadness is that the word 'peace' has begun to take on connotations of being un-American. To mention arms control in certain quarters is made to seem unpatriotic. As if life and death, the future of the planet, were a national issue, a partisan issue, not a universal one."

"Hilda has a wonderful little trick with tuna salad," Sylvia said, patting Dwight's forearm. "I'm sure you'll like it."

"The understanding has to be," the senator continued, "that it isn't just the liberals who are going to be destroyed in a nuclear confrontation. The Ku Klux Klan has to realize if the bomb falls, there will be no more Ku Klux Klan. In which case they won't want it either."

"Now, enough," Sylvia said.

"Very well," said the senator. "I yield you the floor."

"Thank you," said Sylvia, and smiling a rather uncertain smile, took quick little gasps of the humid air, as if there might be contained in it some fix for the conversation. Silence. "I see in today's *Times* where Horace Hallowell, the famous food writer, killed himself," she managed, finally.

"Fed up, I suppose," said the senator.

"No taste for battle," said Dwight.

"No appetite for life," said Hap.

"In a stew," said Misty, and clapped her hands in delight at having understood and joined in the game.

"Actually," said Sylvia, "the article said he was depressed at deteriorating health. But what did he expect from all that sauce béarnaise?" She took a piece of lettuce with her fork and turned it, slowly, examining it. "What choices we have to make, in a world where alfalfa sprouts may cause cancer."

"I haven't heard about that," said Misty.

"Well, apparently, they manufacture something in their green to protect themselves from being eaten by bugs, and it may be carcinogenic."

"No!"

"So too much of a good thing may be as bad for you as the bad."

"I've always felt that," said Misty.

"No end of things to worry about." sighed Sylvia.

"I used to think that, too." Misty leaned forward, her creamy, lightly freckled skin slightly aglow with perspiration. "I used to worry about my future. But since they passed the Nerve Gas Bill, I'm living my life Moment-to-Moment."

"You notice it wasn't me who said that," the senator smiled. "It was Mr. Hewitt's guest."

"Did I say something wrong?" asked Misty.

"Not at all," the senator assured her. "It's just we weren't supposed to talk politics."

"Is that politics?" Misty asked.

Dwight smiled. "Mr. Hewitt, your friend is truly delightful."

"Thank you, sir."

"Oh, good," Sylvia said. "Here's the salad. I asked Hilda to put nuts in it, so we could enjoy the crunch."

"I've been enjoying it all along," said Hap.

After lunch, Hap met with Secretary Jonah in the library. "I'm sure you'll have some good explanation for this breech of etiquette," Jonah said, closing the door, backed with leatherbound books.

Hap reached into his pocket and took out the plastic bag of microchips. "You remember the Fred Masters suicide?"

"Of course."

"Well, you'll recall that Masters was involved in the attempted takeover of MicroTel. The crown jewel of MercerCorp. Our most profitable business unit. Supplier of all our computer chips, and a number of other companies'.''

"I know all that," Jonah said.

"Lily Masters, Fred's wife, found this in the pocket of the suit Fred was going to wear the night he died. We were supposed to have dinner. It's part of a multimillion-dollar shipment of silicon semiconductor chips that are highly suspect.''

"Suspect?''

"Insufficiently tested. Not meeting the standards of quality assurance. Apparently, MicroTel was under the gun to meet a revenue target date, and there was a failure to conduct proper tests.''

"How do you know that?''

"I found out from a subordinate of the division manager, a guy named Dresner. Dresner apparently blew the whistle to somebody before he disappeared. But I imagine we'll all find out easy enough pretty soon, when satellites start falling out of the sky.''

"Nothing's going to start falling," Jonah said. "We have no real evidence the chips are faulty.''

"No real evidence? Insufficient tests are insufficient tests. This is a recurrence of the same lack of discipline that's plagued a number of microchip suppliers.''

"You have no hard evidence of that either," said Jonah. "Certainly there have been a few cases of lack of discipline. But what happened with United Semiconductor involved falsifying records, the Chinese were getting paid by the piece. They were marking it up for individual benefit, and the company tried to cover it up by passing off bad parts. That's one instance. But look what happened with T.I. That was the press again, blowing things all out of proportion the way the press loves to do. Really all it was was protocol, Mitchel. The Air Force has its protocol, the testing procedure it demanded, and they didn't make it clear to the company.'' His gray eyes were lifeless, his lips moving in a flat rhythm, as though it was a speech he knew he would be called on to make several times and had already put on automatic. "Sure there might have been some cutting corners, but there was nothing really wrong with those chips. And there's probably nothing wrong with these." He took the bag from Hap. "I'll have them checked into."

"Checked into might not be good enough, sir. They ought to be recalled."

"You don't understand the politics of business, Mitchel. You get people all worked up, excited about what they don't need to get excited about . . . well, the domino theory applies. Heads start to roll. There's panic. Kingpins topple. We're not even talking about the fortunes of money that can be lost . . ."

"I'm glad about that, sir," Hap said. "Because it's my opinion that's probably why Fred Masters died. It would have sent the MicroTel stock into the toilet if it had come out that the chips were suspect and slated for possible recall."

"Nobody said they would have been recalled," Jonah said testily. "And why would Masters have wanted to clean up anything? He was hardly one of nature's noblemen. Not exactly a patriot. Not so pristine."

"Well, sir, we all have a point we won't go beyond. Where we become better than we thought we were. Or at least I hope we do. And maybe even a man who was not exactly a patriot would pause at potential catastrophe. Maybe, like the senator said, he might have realized that it wouldn't be just the enlightened people who were going to go."

"No chips have fallen out of the sky," Jonah said. "I'm sending up two satellites on Friday equipped with some of those T.I. chips. I have no qualms about them. There's been no military accidents from so-called suspect chips in the past. No loss of life."

"If you don't count Fred Masters and Miranda."

"That's just nervous speculation on your part, Mitchel. Fred Masters was a smut peddler who died with a beautiful whore. Don't try to make it more than it was."

"Well, as long as I'm speculating nervously, sir, let me speculate nervously about a few things. Let's speculate nervously about chips that haven't been shielded, hardened against electromagnetic impulses for high altitudes. Let's talk about the disasters that could occur, with chips brought in from Taiwan and Mexico that don't come up to our standards. Let's talk about the flaws and flare-ups in computers fed with these untested chips, that could trigger a nuclear holocaust."

"I'll look into it," Jonah said.

"Sir, you can't be so sanguine. We're not talking about men who can reason. We're talking about computers."

"You mean men who can reason like you?" asked Jonah. "I'll put my money on a machine."

Sometimes, Gordon Grayson couldn't watch all of it. It was like a porno "snuff" movie, where part of the sexual excitement was the actual murder of the participants, usually some far-out druggie prostitute in Chile. But here, he knew the cast. Often he had the feeling he was dreaming it—that free-floating angst you experienced when you came to a cliff in a nightmare, pursued by demons, or critics for the *New York Review of Books*. And in that sweat-soaked, screaming moment before you went over the edge, all you had to do was sit up in bed, and shriek aloud, and wake yourself up, and they were gone. And you were still alive. Not so Fred and Miranda.

Still, when he watched, he now and then had the feeling he might be able to intercede, to stop the murders. That he could break in and say to the team of assassins, "Don't!" Somehow work his way into the videotaped action and let them know they were being observed, so they'd better change their plans. Once he had read a wonderful book called *Kidnap*, about the Lindbergh case, and all through the first half of the book he hoped against fact that the baby might still be alive. So passionate and present was the writing, that in spite of what he knew, what was historically recorded, he still had the glimmer of optimism that somehow the deed had not yet actually taken place and there might be some merciful intercession. But the only intercession for Fred and Miranda, the only thing that could stop the murder, was for Gordon to turn off the tape.

It had been his new favorite toy, the video recorder. Ever since watching horses at sexual play at Coventry Hall, he had been a voyeur on some level or another. As he himself had once paraphrased it, nothing in his life so became him as the watching of someone else's.

He had read a recent piece in the *New York Times* about feelings, about emotional capacities in children. Pleasure, surprise, disgust, and distress were present at birth, he was surprised to discover. Joy appeared at six to eight weeks, anger at four months, sadness and fear by nine months, and tender affection by a year. Shame appeared at eighteen months, half a year before pride, which Gordon found particularly interesting. But what had impressed him most in the article was an account of an eleven-month-old infant who saw another child fall and start to cry, which started the watching child crying as though he himself had been hurt. Primitive empathy, the examining psychologist had called it, a distress as though the other child's pain had been his own. The explanation was that children of that age felt no sense of separation. Gordon felt nothing but. He was a watcher, not a be-er, he understood that about himself, especially on the sexual level.

So it had come quite naturally, matter-of-factly, the video recorder, as a natural extension of his personality, such as it was. He had read with fascination of the video equipment the police had turned up in Sharon Tate's house at the time of the Manson murders, and of the tape of her and Polanski making love. There had been a pathos to it in contrast to the rest of the events, a kind of fleshy innocence compared to the brutality of the slayings. Sex, even voyeuristic sex, had a radiant, healthy quality when so juxtaposed. Right after reading about that, he'd bought himself a video recorder and concealed the camera above the alcove.

It was not long before he began letting people use his apartment for assignations. As desperate times called for desperate measures, so desperate people had a desperate lack of discretion about where they met. So even those who were not really close to Gordon—but then, who was?—accepted his seemingly discreet hospitality. It was tacitly understood, with only a few people passing the information along, and then in very soft voices, that he could be trusted, that the bed was comfortable. It was his one restriction. They could bring food and wine, or cook what he had in his refrigerator, as long as they restocked and cleaned up afterward. But they could never use his bedroom. Only the bed in the alcove was the rule, being very careful of the handpainted silk coverlet.

With Fred and Miranda, Gordon had experienced his greatest voyeuristic bonanza. Miranda brought a level of innovation and imagination to Gordon's tape collection that he'd never dreamed of. Except for her occasional fits of weeping, her passage into the dark, hysterical emotionalism of other ordinary women, she was a star, a vedette, una estrella, a presence so unique he could see her billboarded above the important avenues of all the capitals of Europe, shoulders squared, her remarkable body arched in a posture of domination that appeared more mythic than physical. As if she were indeed the beautiful mother of the earth, and men were allowed only because she birthed them, permitted them to exist.

It was this mother thing that Gordon hated most, even while he honored it. It was the mother thing that kept toppling her from her chariot, hurtling her back to earth, annoying him with reminders of her humanity. How she would weep about her child, this lost child promised her for so long and still denied her. Dissolving suddenly from her certainty into a wounded little girl, she would howl her pain, her disappointment that Fred, like Victor before him, had promised and let her down.

"I didn't let you down," Fred said. "I showed you the papers. You're in my will. Not like Victor. All the money you'll ever need to get her back, and keep her, and do what's right for her, and send her to tennis camp."

"But what if you don't die?" she shrieked at him

angrily that one time, her face suddenly a harridan's face, the mask of beauty torn aside to reveal the anger and the grief and the loss.

"Alive I can do better," he said. "You don't know who you're dealing with here. There's nobody in the world without something to hide. Trust me. We'll come up with something on those Frogs. Sometime, the wife did something she thought nobody would ever find out about. *I* will. Once the man fucked around, or killed, or cheated, and thinks it's a buried secret. Not from *me*. I'll find out, and they'll give you your kid. There's nobody clean, Miranda, and it's me who can get the garbage. It's having the goods on people in this world that gets you ahead."

"Nice place," she said.

Fred looked around the apartment. "Yeah, it is," he said. "The guy really knows how to decorate."

Gordon tried to feel good about that, that it was his apartment that had served for their meetings, offered them their mise en-scène. Like the fumbling friar in an older, more corrupt version of *Romeo and Juliet*, he had at least tried to bring them together, offered them their chance. Giving them whatever happiness there was, although there appeared to be precious little on Miranda's part. From time to time she would get all weepy about Lily, tell Fred what a good woman she was, that it was sick to betray her.

"Yeah, well, she's not that interested in sex anymore," Fred said. "You're doing her a favor."

"She doesn't act like I'm doing her a favor," Miranda said. "She looks at me like I've hurt her."

"That's curiosity," Fred said. "She probably wants to know what you're doing. Lily doesn't go that deep."

"Yes, she does. How can I do this to her?"

"You're not doing it to her. You're doing it to me. And in your way you're helping her. When this is over between us I'll have more to offer her."

"When will it be over?"

"Soon, kid, soon. It's just something I need to get out

of my system. I've never felt like this about anybody before."

"So I see," Miranda said, and tied a ribbon around it, and pulled him around the alcove. But when she turned her face away Gordon could see that she was crying.

How terrible that the most unexpected people had their own pain and sorrow. Heartbreaking that this gorgeous doxy who now lay awhile dead had had worms of conscience eating at her, a terrible longing for her child. It tore Gordon's heart out, the one he didn't think he had, to see how she bled for the return of her daughter, so desperate that she would practice her bizarre craft on Fred.

The earlier tapes were art pieces of their kind. Besides Miranda's beauty, enhanced by her cleverness, there was a feline quality to her lovemaking, once she'd passed the fine points of the game technique. So it was like his own little stash of classics, like those at the Museum of Modern Art: The Fred and Miranda Show. With the hidden camera in the ceiling and the video recorder concealed in a bookcase to the side of the alcove, all Gordon had to do was adjust the built-in timer mechanism to go on automatically at the hour of the rendezvous. He had made the place off-limits to anyone else once he'd seen the quality of their performance. Returning home, he would simply rewind the tape and watch them.

And, as she brought Fred to life, so in her way Miranda nurtured Gordon. Making him almost really care for a woman, certainly desire her, want her for himself. So when he'd come home that October night after Lily's hysterical phone call to him, he'd felt a sense of personal loss. With shaking hands he'd phoned the police, turned off the recording equipment, set a few more books and plants in front of it before they got there.

The police were fairly thorough in their check of the apartment, scouring for traces of blood in other places than the alcove, making sure the bodies had not been dragged from another room and been so arranged, testing for fingerprints, etc. But they had not discovered the recorder.

It wasn't until after they'd gone, and the bodies were removed at five o'clock in the morning, that Gordon had a chance to rewind.

What he had seen transfixed him. Fred was in an unexpectedly agitated state, talking from the minute he came in the door. "You see, if I could find this out about MicroTel, we'll find out about your Froggies. So cut the crap how I'm not going to get you your daughter."

"It's a fantasy," Miranda said morosely. "I should have listened to the doctor. I should have made my own life instead of counting on you."

"Well, it's no fantasy about MicroTel," he said, closing the door. "They've been rushing to meet deadlines, and the chips haven't been tested."

"What are you talking about?"

"The computer-chip company I been trying to take over. They been shipping improperly tested microchips, supplying them to defense manufacturers. So the whole fucking world could catch fire by mistake."

"Why would they do that?"

"More orders than they can supply." He sat down on the bed in the alcove and took off his shoes. "We're talking tens of millions of microchips, jelly beans they call them in the trade, that's how fast they get gobbled up. Not enough time to do real quality control. They're under the gun to meet delivery dates, so who has time for checking?"

"What are you going to do?" She slipped out of her shoes.

"Expose them, of course. What's the point of being the world's best collector of garbage if you can't also clean up from time to time? I could do it at great personal sacrifice, because the stock will take a dive. But I'm unloading my shares before the chips hit the fan." He laughed at his pun. "They're real eager to buy me out."

There was an echo of his laugh, a strange, remote echo. Fred and Miranda turned to locate the source and Gordon saw the terror on their faces. Terror he felt with Miranda, as the two men moved from the bedroom into the picture. Probably they had come in through the old dumbwaiter shaft to the servants' quarters this apartment had been once. One was small enough to have ridden the dumbwaiter, squat and stocky and dark. The other was tall and fair. Both wore coats, gloves and felt hats, a soft detail that strengthened the air of the sinister.

Watching that first time, Gordon felt his whole life changing, even as he pitied her, even as he felt terror for her. He could visualize the book he would write moving instantly to number one on the national best-seller list. Never was there a better publicity hype than this, that such a couple should meet their end, and Gordon would have it on tape. As in the thirties' adaptations of literary classics for the screen, he could see the pages of the book fluttering before his eyes, the riveting nonfiction epic he would write about the two of them. Their lives. What led up to their deaths. And finally, how it took place. In his apartment. On his video recorder.

In an age of television. He who had never really believed in God experienced his own instant Revisionism, the kind of numinous experience Tolstoy might have joined him in, given such a dark and desperate story. Like a shadow of the Almighty, the dark underside of awakening belief loomed in him.

There was nothing he could do to stop the murders. If they had to die, which they did, and had—and would over and over again on the tape he watched—at least they hadn't died for nothing. Some great truth would emerge from his writing, Gordon was sure of it. Truth, and a book that was Number One.

Once he started work on the manuscript, there remained one moral dilemma: what to do about the tape. He discussed it confidentially with his agent, Stan Dobson, skirting what the real legal issues were, not telling him that he had the actual tape, making it hypothetical, a for instance, a fiction he was playing around with. On his own, Gordon understood a few of the legal questions. During the fall of Richard Nixon, when Gordon, like many of his friends, scoured the evidence piling up, looking for what might be the charge to bring the president down, he had learned about misprision of a felony, concealing knowledge of a crime. But that was mainly punishable with a fine, and God knew Gordon was going to have plenty of money.

He was under no obligation to love the law. Letters were his beloved, words his alma mater, the same school his father had gone to. The classmates he brought home from the Algonquin had been Gordon's spiritual uncles and aunts, their writing and wit his only legacy. So he gave himself to the book with an almost religious devotion, consecrating himself to telling this dark and terrible story the best it could be told, piercing the shadow with insight, as much as was given him.

Now, at last, the manuscript was finished. He was on the very last page. He had already told Stan Dobson it would be ready Sunday night. Stan had promised to come in from East Hampton to pick it up from him that evening. Sunday evening, the night most Americans stayed home to watch TV.

So craftily had Dobson negotiated the deal that even without reading the full contents, the publisher was set to rush the book into an enormous first printing, having announced it long enough in advance to create the necessary stir, to get the orders from Waldenbooks and B. Dalton, and display tables at the fronts of stores that weren't part of chains. And just to ensure its instant success, the rocketing rise to Number One Best-Seller, it was Gordon's intention, the Friday before publication, to give the last Fred and Miranda tape to "60 Minutes."

"60 Minutes." In an age of television it was like an anthem, something press agents sang with more feeling than the "Star-Spangled Banner." "60 Minutes." Twenty million households. Thirty-three million viewers, on a Sunday night. The bookstores would sell out on Monday morning. The largest viewer share conceivable. America, as one pair of eyes, watching the crime.

Of course, the one remaining legal question was the Federal Statute Section 2510, 2511 of 18 U.S. Civil Code—Gordon wasn't above looking up things in libraries—that said it was a crime to use an illegal recording device.

But there were all kinds of things that were against the law in America, including oral sex in some states—from time to time Gordon would imagine a battalion of police surrounding a farmhouse in Maryland, shouting through their bullhorns, "Come out of there with your tongues up!" But they didn't use the law unless they were after you. His chances of being indicted were small. Turning it over to "60 Minutes," the criminal implications were not that great, especially as he was bringing a crime to the public awareness. He could always give it to the police and "60 Minutes" at the same time, so the authorities didn't have to learn about it by watching the show.

So he considered all bases covered. He would insist on a shot of the book jacket. Maybe the producer would even be willing to grant an armchair interview with the author, as in the last resurrection of Richard Nixon. Never had there been a better promotion plan or gimmick.

So, though it might have been true before that Gordon did not allow himself to feel deeply, the pathos of it overwhelmed him when he watched Miranda's murder. Great convulsive sobs shook him, and he wept along with her as she pleaded with the two assassins not to kill her.

"Oh, please," she begged. "Don't kill me. I'll do whatever you want."

"What do you guys want?" Fred Masters said, his face pale even through the graininess of the tape.

But the men didn't answer. The short stocky one held the gun to Miranda's head.

"Please," she said. "I have a little girl. She needs me. I love her. I want to see her again. Just give me that. A chance to see my baby again. I'll do whatever you want."

"Where are they?" the fair one said to Fred. "What'd you do with the microchips? Who'd you show them to?"

"Nobody," Fred said. "Honest to God."

"Please," Miranda wept. "My baby."

"Make yourself comfortable," the stocky man said to her. "Stretch out and relax."

"Oh, please." She stretched out on the divan.

"Pull your skirt down," the fair one said, and covered

her knees with the fabric of her dress. "We wouldn't want you to look indecent."

"I'm begging you," she said. "My baby. Please don't kill me. I want to see my little girl."

"Sorry," the dark man said, and holding the gun in front of her right eye, pulled the trigger.

Even now, after all the times he had watched, Gordon felt a terrible convulsive pull as her head snapped forward, a rising in his gorge. Sometimes he would rewind the tape a little, so she would be alive again. Stopped it before the shot was fired, gave her that instant with fear and hope on her face to be frozen in.

But truth was truth. Reality was reality. Things were how they were. There was no way she wouldn't be dead, like the Lindbergh baby. No matter how well the book was written, facts were facts. So when Gordon had drunk in enough of her still alive, he let the tape go forward.

Fred touched her lifeless form, keening, pressed his fingers to her hair, asking them why they'd done that.

"She didn't do anything," he cried. "I didn't do anything. I don't know what you're talking about."

They worked him for nearly an hour, holding the gun on him. "The chips," the short one said. "What did you do with the chips Connie Garrett gave you? Who did you tell?"

"Nobody," Fred said. "Honest to God. Even if I knew what you were talking about and I could tell you, why would you let me live?"

"The contract's very specific," said the stocky man. "It doesn't say we should kill you. It only says we should get you to talk."

"Really?" Fred said.

"Really. So you got anything to tell us?"

"How do I know you're telling the truth?"

"You gotta trust somebody," the fair one said.

The dark one took the gun, emptied out the bullets, and pressed it into Fred's left hand. "I'm not left-handed," Fred said.

"Sure you are," said the dark man. "We don't do sloppy work. Pull the trigger."

"Oh, Christ," Fred said.

"Pull the trigger," said the fair one, and held another gun on him. Fred pulled the trigger.

The dark one took the gun back from him, and with gloved hands put the bullets back in. He held the gun to Fred's temple, and fired.

Fred slumped over. The dark man dropped the gun near Fred's left hand. Then, with a decorator's touch, the killers joined Fred's right hand with Miranda's, pulled the hand-painted coverlet up to the couple's knees, and exited back into the bedroom.

In Gordon's soul now, the one he hadn't realized he had, Miranda echoed like a sorrowful song. Well, the way to rescue oneself from sadness was to put it over to the creative side, use the energy for something positive; for example, planning the rest of the book's promotion. After "60 Minutes," "Phil Donahue." All those callers phoning in, asking about bondage, and was it true, what Gordon wrote in his book, that that was what Miranda practiced. Maybe they could get four or five girls from a B&D club, in their corselettes and boots, to come sit in a semicircle across from him, and explain how they got into it, and how their parents felt about what they did.

Poor, beautiful Miranda. What a gift she had given him, not only in the book, but in letting him know he could have those feelings. He would dedicate the book to her. Deepened by his experience of her, strange as it had been, he was more alive than before. Feeling love, in a way, really. Although with her gone, there was nothing for him to love, except for the books he had always cherished. And since he couldn't save her (Too late! Too late! Rewind the tape!) at least he could breathe some life into the book business. Hard times had come. The price of paper was up. Readership was down. Sales were off. A man had to do what he could.

He called Stan Dobson. His wife said he was on his way in from East Hampton and gave Gordon the number of

Stan's car telephone. Stan said he was stuck in traffic on the Grand Central Parkway but he'd be in within an hour.

"I finished it!" Gordon said.

"Congratulations," said Stan.

"I suspect it's wonderful," Gordon said.

"I suspect you're right," said Stan. "I'll be there to pick it up."

Waiting, Gordon rewound the tape and watched it one last time. And so caught up was he in Miranda's beauty, her curiously wistful charm, that he didn't even hear the door to the bedroom opening. Didn't see the two men, in overcoats and hats, come into the room until they were nearly on top of him.

Now and then, when Hap dreamed, he had visions of outer space, where miracles occurred, where all the agonies were removed, where doctors could make perfect crystals and cure disease, and the infinite became the truly infinite, filled with resources that never ended, and chances that always began. In his conscious mind, he knew that wasn't idle dreaming. Because there was no gravity, laboratory science could create perfect crystals and find the cures. In his realistic mind he understood that if the money that was spent in one day on weapons was available, they could probably find the cure for cancer. Money bought talent, and the top people in the graduating classes of medical schools went into private practice because they couldn't afford to go into research. What America was about besides freedom and opportunity, was making money. So Victor Lenrahan had turned out to be smarter than Einstein.

Still, sometimes Hap would fly through space in his dreaming and be open, and free, and airy, the way space had been, the way the spirit was meant to be. And he was soaring, the way man had been given his chance to soar before he opted for profit. In his dreaming, Hap could be fully a dreamer.

This one night, this night of dreaming, he shared with Zoe. Because of the test in the morning, and the decision he'd just about made, he slept with her, something he'd never done in all the time their affair had been going on. No matter how deeply she stirred him, no matter how softly her skin moved against his, the specter of Claire loomed over their coupling. So even while most of him spun joyfully through Zoe's secret places, a part of him had sat back, checking for betrayal.

But that was over now. He felt suspicion gone from him, sapped, sipped from his lips. So he'd given in, let go, closed his eyes and surrendered to her mattress, the warm aroma of her, and slept. And in the midst of his dreaming, she pressed her silky cheek against him and sighed. He stroked her hair, rubbed it with sleepy gentleness. He felt her tense.

"What's the matter?" he asked her.

"Don't you want to make love?"

"We did. Weren't you here?"

"Oh, I was here. I was very much here. I just thought . . . you're usually gone by now."

"Are you uncomfortable that I stayed?"

"Uncomfortable?" She held him, pressed herself closer. "I've never felt so secure."

"Don't overdo it."

"That's what I'm afraid of. Saying too much. Wanting too much. I thought that's what was scaring you away."

"I didn't stay because I was afraid I'd talk in my sleep."

"As simple as that?"

"As simple as that."

"What could you possibly say?"

"Secrets. Classified information. That I love you."

"It took you long enough to get around to it."

"No, it didn't. I have for a long time."

"Why didn't you tell me?"

"I only said I loved you," said Hap. "I didn't say I trusted you."

She laughed, and he rolled over gently, moving himself on top of her. And she was already ready for him, opening like a flower facing the sun.

"I want to be all the way inside you," he whispered, moving.

"You are."

"I want to get lost in you."

"This is a dream I'm having," she said. "Men don't talk in bed. I'm having a fantasy."

"You're entitled. You've been a good girl."

"That's the truth. Still, this can't really be happening." She kissed him, ate his lips gently with the sharp points of her teeth and her tongue, made a meal out of his mouth. "Not all this, and you say things, too. I wouldn't have expected it."

"Why?"

"Men aren't verbal. Women are verbal. I'm a very verbal person."

"I would have said oral," Hap said, and kissed her, moving.

"But other men . . ." she said.

"I don't want to know about you and other men."

"Good. Then I won't tell you. But whatever they were, they weren't verbal."

"Neither am I. I just have a lot to tell you."

"I love you, Hap."

"I believe you," he said, and kissed her, moving.

"Oh, God. Can this really be happening? Pinch me."

"My pleasure," Hap said, and did, where it would do the most good.

He was out of bed before four in the morning, soundless, so he didn't wake her. But in her sleep she reached out for him, and finding her arms empty, her fingertips touching only warmed sheets, she sat bolt upright, her eyes coming open. She switched on the lamp, saw him dressing. Looked at the clock.

"Did you change your mind?" she said. "Is that all the sleeping with I get?"

"I have some things to do," Hap said, and stepped into his trousers, zipped them up.

"Is anything wrong?"

394 ◊ *Gwen Davis*

"There's a new plane being tested," he said, not telling her he was the one testing it. Much as he trusted her, finally, totally, there was no point loading her up with what he was going through. Not till he'd sorted it out on his own and made his decision.

He thought he already knew what that would be. Since his meeting with Jonah, there'd been all kinds of pressure on him from within the company. He'd sent out directives calling back the suspect microchips. These were followed by a flood of interoffice memos, calls, bureaucratic procedures holding up the process, plus some subtle and not-so-subtle suggestions that he should begin to consider retirement, or a kick upstairs. Behind the desk had never been Hap's place, and he knew it. So he thought he would clear his head, and the air, by taking a ride up to where things got easier to see, and make his decision there.

"Why do I feel like you're not telling me everything?" Zoe said.

He sat on the edge of the bed. "I told you I loved you. That's already excessive."

"Say it again."

"I love you."

"Don't leave," she said, and held his arm, pressed her face against it. "Why am I so afraid?"

"That's why you should never make a commitment to a woman. They get all fluttery on you. Even the brave ones."

"Are you making a commitment?"

"Pushy," he said.

"You think I'm brave?"

"I know you're brave."

"Do I have something I have to be brave about?"

"See you tonight," he said, and kissed her lightly.

"What aren't you telling me?"

"I said I love you. What more do you need to know?"

"Everything." She frowned, a deep double line appearing between her thin, arched eyebrows. "Something's going on, isn't it? Are you in trouble? Whatever it is, we can fix it."

"Lawyers," he said, and smiled.

"Tell me," she urged him.

"Well, I was in trouble," he said. "But then I met you."

"Oh, God," she said, and held on to him. "I was always so scared I wouldn't have a great love."

"I'm not anybody's great love."

"That's what you think," she said.

He swung by his house on the way to Edwards Air Force Base, let himself in, switched on the light in the hall outside Kate's room so he wouldn't startle her. She was asleep on top of the covers, in her clothes, a half-empty glass of Scotch on the nightstand beside her. Too drunk to finish her drink, he thought sadly, and touched her shoulder.

"Huh?" She came instantly awake, the deepest part of the stupor passed.

"We need to talk."

"What time is it?"

"Time to talk," he said. "Time to settle a few things."

"Can't it wait till later?"

"Everything's always waiting till later," he said. "Life's too short. We have to talk now."

She reached over and turned on the light, rubbed her hair out of her eyes, and looked at him. "This is serious, huh?"

"Afraid so," he said.

"I can take it."

"I want a divorce."

She sat up against the pillows and took a deep breath of air. "Is there somebody else?"

"Yes. But this isn't about somebody else. This is about me. And you, Kate. There's still maybe some good years. No point in sleepwalking through them just out of loyalty."

"I've been telling you that for a long time now," she said. "What made you listen?"

"I don't know. Maybe I'm getting old."

"Not you. Never you," she said.

"I'll be back for my things," he said, and got up and moved to the door. "You going to tell the kids?"

"They're not kids anymore."

"I keep forgetting," he said. "You won't worry, will you? There's enough to take care of you."

"I won't worry," she said. "I might drink, but I won't worry."

"Why don't you try and get some help, Kate? It isn't too late."

"You're right," she said, and switched off the light. "It's too early."

When he got to the precinct that morning, Lou's commander told him the Garrett case was officially closed. "The coroner's certified it a suicide," he said. "Write up your closing report."

Lou tried not to feel disheartened. He signed the tattletale sheet to get into the file and noticed that the commander had checked it out. It struck him right away as strange. Why would he have pulled it, overloaded as he was, unless someone else wanted to see it? Lou wondered. The guys in charge didn't really give a shit about individual cases. There were too many things going on to care about one, unless you got personally involved, emotionally involved, like Lou had been dumb enough to do.

When he started going through the file to write his report, he saw that the check from Fred Masters to Connie Garrett was missing. He remembered then that he had seen a man he knew to be CIA in the commander's office the day the file was pulled. Another agency, government agencies, CIA, FBI, IRS, always went through the commander, who dealt with agencies as a courtesy. They didn't go to the detective in charge as a brother officer would.

"Something is shitty in Denmark," Lou said that night to Lucille. "I got pulled off the case. There was a CIA guy in the commander's office the day the file got checked out. And some evidence is missing. Two and two don't make four anymore."

"What do they make?" Lucille asked.

"Twenty-two. You put it side by side and it matches up. Only bigger."

"So what are you going to do?"

"I got a photocopy of the check. I photocopied everything. The whole file. If I can't handle this on city time . . ." He looked at her carefully. "Would it be very hard on you if we cut back for a while? I need to take a leave of absence."

"Well, where do you want to take it?" Lucille said. "If we took it in Rome, I wouldn't mind." She was smiling.

"I need time to figure this out. It'll mean dipping into savings."

"Well, that's what they're for, isn't it?"

"You're a lovely woman," he said.

"You're only saying that because you want my money," said Lucille.

To Hap it still meant quitting. He'd been in the service of his country nearly all his life, so there were agonies at the thought of leaving, no matter how right it seemed. Whatever pangs he had about the corporation, about cutting corners, he hadn't lost his pride at the company's highest achievements. That was what the X-101 was for him, something he'd watched and helped develop from the beginning. That was the reason he was testing it out himself, as he'd tested most of MercerCorp's experimental aircraft himself, no matter what the pressures were to keep him behind his desk. The X-101 represented the best of the aerospace industry, a refinement of aeronautical imagination, on order to DARPA, the Defense Advance Research Procurement Agency. Something that fit the technology, but still allowed for the uniqueness of man, to be piloted by a man who could make a decision, not just react, like a flawed microchip.

"Build me something of this nature," the directive came down from the Air Force. "Wings swept forward and fixed, with high speed flight and maneuverability, wings swept forward so it can withstand gravitational forces. And since there's never been a 'skin' for such a plane to stand up to these stresses, make it with Kevlar, the stuff of bullet-proof vests. Cut it out from sheets in yardage, or from filament, wound, like spools of thread. So it will have strength and elasticity. Make me a forward-swept wing thing.''

And they had.

They'd brought it in from the East Coast by boat to San Pedro, loaded it on a flatbed truck to take it out to NASA at Edwards Air Force Base. Now there was nothing left to do but fly it. Dwight Efram Jonah had called Hap, making no reference to their meeting in East Hampton, asking him only when the test pilot intended to try it out.

''I'm thinking of taking it up myself,'' Hap said.

There'd been a silence on the line. ''Aren't you a little old for that sort of thing?'' Jonah asked finally.

''Only if I had a retirement mentality.''

''That might be a good thing for you to have,'' Jonah said, and ended the conversation.

It only fortified Hap's resolve to test the plane himself. He had no worries about the new system. The sins of MicroTel had nothing to do with MercerCorp, really, it was only a profitable subsidiary. Anything MercerCorp built, Hap was not afraid to fly. No matter what his other misgivings, there was nothing under his direct supervision that he wouldn't vouch for. And the X-101 had been very much his baby.

Sam was waiting for him in the flight equipment room, the company's oldest employee, Hap's best buddy on the crew. He helped Hap into the pressure suit, making sure everything fit. His fingers, like his teeth, were stained with tobacco, the lines of his face like a grooved record of the aerospace business. ''How come you're still with this company?'' Hap asked him.

''Who else would take care of you, knows as much as I do?''

''Nobody.''

''So why should I stay at home, counting my pension, when I could be here, worrying about you?''

''Are you worried?''

''We built it.''

''That's what I think, too,'' Hap said.

In the hangar the chief design engineer, a company scientist, and two aircraft designers waited to wish Hap well. Sam gave him a hug, and a hand up into the Jeep already in gear to take him to the remote area where the aircraft was. Mechanics and technicians were still busy checking it out. Two hundred feet away, in a small lean-to, specialists and technicians checked the radio equipment that would monitor the flight. In another small building, engineers who'd worked on the X-101 since inception check out computers, roll charts, and flat sheets that would get the transmission of the plane's telemetry data.

Hap walked around the craft, checking out the Kevlar skin, touching it as if it were the skin of a woman. He checked the rivets, making sure they were riveted, saw that the doors were in working order and the tires well fixed. "Show me the hydraulics," he said to the mechanic, who opened the door to the main hydraulic pump. As with most MercerCorp systems, it was redundant, a second system in case the first one failed. Nothing was leaking. Like the rest of those involved in this particular project, at least, Hap had nothing but good feelings. "It looks okay," Hap said.

"It is okay, sir," the mechanic said.

The crew chief, Frank, a lanky redhead who'd joined NASA Hap's last year as an astronaut and had followed him to MercerCorp, strutted behind Hap, checking his checking. He had been with the X-101 from the moment it started taking form. "Looks good to me," Frank said.

"Me, too," said Hap. "Why don't we try it and see." He climbed into the airplane.

Frank followed him into the cockpit and started removing the safety pins, pip pins with red flags attached. He handed them to Hap, one at a time, counting aloud till there were seven pins. Once in recent history a pilot had tried to eject, and the canopy had failed to open. After the CAA investigation it was revealed that one of the pins had not been removed. It was still jammed in what was left of the ejection lever. "I make it seven," Frank said. "Now you count 'em."

"Seven," Hap said.

"Then we got them all." Frank strapped Hap in, gave him a pat on the back, and got out of the plane. On the ground, Frank faced the cockpit, gave Hap the thumbs up signal, and the little whirl of the finger that signaled him to start.

Hap checked the instrument panel, started the ignition. "Hydraulic pressure fine," he noted. "Fuel flow is good. Engine temperature good. Position good. Inertial navigation system okay. Okay, tower. Ready for taxi."

"Whenever you're ready, Hap," they called back from the tower.

He looked down at Frank, signaled thumbs up, closed the canopy. "X-101 ready for taxi."

"Clear to taxi," came in over the radio. "To runway 25 right. Winds thirty knots from two eighty."

He taxied out, approached the head of the runway.

"Okay, Hap. We see you. You're clear. Take position and hold."

He got into position. Because of the unique design of the plane, he needed only a hundred foot of roll.

"You're clear for takeoff."

"Rolling," he said. Giving it full throttle, he took off, and, at the twenty-five-hundred-foot marker, pulled the stick back. The aircraft climbed vertically, reaching fifty thousand feet in three minutes. "This is some lovely lady," he said. "Requesting clearance to tactical test frequency."

"Go."

"Engineers? You reading the data?"

"We're getting most of it, Hap. Not all of it. Hit the TM switch."

He cycled it. "Okay," they said. "All data now coming down."

He pulled back on the throttle, went into a slow cruise. Around him were the heavens, the glittering silence he too often forgot.

"Okay. Start maneuver number one."

"Going to idle power," Hap said, putting the flaps down, putting everything down except the wheel, going for slow speed flight at high altitude.

"Data's okay," came the report. "Everything's fine. Start maneuver number two."

It was a vertical dive from fifty thousand to fifteen thousand feet, for a planned hard pullout at maximum acceleration. Somewhere between fifty and thirty, Hap noticed the engine hydraulic instruments flutter and start vibrating. He wondered if the hydraulic pump was okay, or if maybe somewhere in the plane was one of those lousy computer chips. Insufficiently tested.

The HUD, Heads Up Display, projecting the information on the windscreen, showed the left engine fluctuating. Something was wrong with the hydraulic display. He was down to twenty-nine thousand feet, twenty-five thousand feet was coming up fast.

"The needles are going crazy down here," they said from the tower. "What's it look like, Hap?"

"I don't know. But I'm about to make the pullout. Twenty-eight! Twenty-seven! Starting pullout. Trying to get it level. Pulling. Pulling . . .

"My left engine hydraulics are gone! Shutting the engine down. Trying to come back to cruise level . . . I can't do anything with her!" He pulled at the stick, hard.

And he remembered that other time, that terrible time when the capsule landed in the ocean and he'd been swept away in a wave of panic, and, yes, he had to admit it to himself, cowardice, and he'd blown out the hatch so he wouldn't sink and drown, and the capsule had been lost. Remembered fear rose up in him, like an undigested meal, and it was in his throat, the taste of his own cravenness. He pulled at the stick, hard.

"I can't control it. Control system is not responding. I can't bring it back. We're in a descending right turn . . . Very fast . . . Trying to pull the throttle . . . Throttle's coming back, but the power . . . Trying to reacquire control . . ."

"Eject!"

"Down to five thousand feet." The panic, the remembered panic eased from him, and he was totally in control, on top of his game, and this was his plane. His baby. Save it he was going to, if he possibly could.

"Eject, goddammit! Get your ass out of there!"

"Not yet . . ."

"Eject, goddammit! It's only a plane, Hap . . ."

"Not yet . . ."

"Eject! Eject!"

When he finally ejected, it was from a height of a hundred and fifty feet, two miles short of the runway. Scared as he might have been once, there was no trace of fear in him now. From the technical point of view he knew there was nothing to panic about, not even that close to the rushing-up earth. The latest ejection seat was good at ground level. This wasn't like a capsule sinking in the ocean, the fear a man had when he was for the first time facing the unknown. This seat worked at zero feet; he himself had conceived of that one. There was a burst of pressure; he was shot clear and carried into the trees.

As he studied the front page of the *New York Times*, a deep sadness washed over Bunyan Reis. The world was becoming an increasingly terrible place. No more stylish gangsters in black suits and gray fedoras robbing banks. Now there were terrorists, child molesters, all manner of unspeakable crimes. As one who had not had loving parents, but never ceased longing for them, Bunyan supposed it was because there was no more nurturing on the planet. No more love. Not many giving it, and, maybe, not that many who even wanted it. Few who looked for caring and kindness, who watered dry flowers and soothed.

It made him uneasy to be philosophic in the morning. So he reaffirmed his posture of no thoughts before coffee and tried to just drink in the news. Ah, but he wished he was not mean-spirited. Even now as his blood coursed with envy and spleen at the story on the lower right-hand corner, he despised how small he was. The way the world was, the *Times* had started front-paging domestic violence. And just Gordon Grayson's disgusting luck, his suicide got a four-column-wide, front-page spread.

Instantly, Bunyan was on the phone to his spy in the Medical Examiner's office to find out the unpublished details. But the facts seemed to be as they were in the paper, black and white. Gordon had been found hanged, in his underwear, all doors and windows locked, an obvious suicide. The obit went on at length, beside much too large a picture, about Gordon's literary accomplishments, echoing those of his father. And still another recap of the tie-in to the fabled Algonquin table. That second-rate leech. And on the front page. Life was just not fair.

That Gordon was dead was absolutely no consolation. One of the few lofty convictions Bunyan had, that he never talked about, especially at lunch, was that there was an afterlife. A continuation of consciousness, mental energy that couldn't be extinguished. So even now Gordon Grayson was probably floating over all the newsstands in town, gloating over his positioning, his only disembodied regret that there was no book to benefit from the publicity.

"That was unquestionably the reason for his suicide," Stan Dobson had told the paper in a telephone interview. "Gordon was becoming increasingly depressed over his inability to finish the manuscript. It was due at the publisher's this Monday. He couldn't pay back the considerable advance, or tell us when he might be finished, if ever. A classic case of writer's block," Dobson concluded.

Bunyan hated himself that he couldn't feel more for a fellow artist who had come up dry. He knew what it was to face the empty canvas, to invent excursions, to carry a passport, ready always for flight, pretending close friendships, eating countless lunches at Le Cirque, eavesdropping while beautiful women babbled of clothes and root canal, the outfit a thousand, the endodontist twelve hundred. Why didn't he have more empathy for Gordon's pain? Because he hadn't been artist enough, that was why. Even the story of a lifetime, dropped into his lap, hadn't inspired him to true enterprise. Even this extraordinary creature, the embodiment of lushness in a woman, couldn't lift him to perform.

Miranda. How many lives had her life touched, and shaped so strangely, even after she was dead? He felt actually cross with Gordon for not finishing the book, so he could have known more about her. Gordon Grayson, dead by his own hand. Oh, why couldn't Bunyan feel love for his neighbor, even if he was on the West Side? How could he not feel pity in his heart for the dead? Hating Gordon Grayson because he had made the front page of the *New York Times*.

What was the matter with Bunyan? He had struggled for a while to be good, to be loving, but his friends had found him dull. Like a witty, eloquent Irish alcoholic who'd joined AA and grown silent. People liked Bunyan better bitchy. What option did he have?

Any more of an option than Miranda? Well, suppose she had developed her light, instead of her shadows. What would have happened to Miranda had she been taken care of, allowed to flower, risen out of herself to become the best she could be, a beacon instead of a symbol of darkness? Would anyone have been interested?

Hadn't men taken the gifts of life and corrupted them? And wasn't the corruption more fascinating than purity? Just as there was no support for art, just as the energy and money of the world went toward war instead of peace, who would have wanted a happy story?

Bunyan wept.

"I'm taking a leave of absence," Lou told the commander. The CIA guy was in the office again. He and Lou had looked at each other without looking at each other, the cloak-and-dagger fellow thinking if he didn't focus his eyes or speak, he'd be invisible, Lou supposed. "I need to work on this case. I don't want to strain your budget."

"I wish I could persuade you to change your mind. We really need you here."

"Well, we all got to do what's important to us," Lou said. "Right, Mr. Sweeney?"

"I'm sorry," the CIA man said. "I wasn't listening to what you said."

"That's okay," Lou said. "You can play it back for yourself." He went out the door.

Zoe was lying on her bed, facedown, her eyes swollen nearly shut from crying. The news about Hap's plane going down had come over the radio just before lunchtime. She had fled the office, tears streaming down her face.

She was in such a grieving, sobbing pile, that she didn't hear the doorbell the first two times it rang. But after persistent buzzing she got up finally, dragged herself from the bed, and opened the door. He was standing there.

"You'll have to give me a key," Hap said. "That way I won't bother you."

"Oh, Hap," she said, and threw her arms around him. "I thought you were dead. I knew all along you were too good to be true. I thought I found the one man in the world who really likes women, and talks in bed, and asks advice. What could he be but dead?"

"How about alive?" he said, and kissed her. "Could you handle alive?"

"Oh, I could handle it," she said, covering his face with kisses. "Oh God, could I handle it."

He told her what had happened. Told her about the chips and the meeting with Jonah.

"Why are you still surprised?" Zoe said. "How can you be such an innocent? What about toxic waste, and the big companies that don't care whether pregnant women drink tainted water or not. And nuclear power plants leaking their poison. Jonah told you. Lenrahan told you. It's *business*. People would lose their jobs, Hap. Powerbrokers would lose their power. They can't make things *right*, they have to make them profitable."

"Not this time," Hap said.

"So you know what you have to do, don't you?"

"In a little while," he said. "First I have to do this."

So Lou was looking out the window, and even though it wasn't much of a view, he could picture himself going off into the sunset with the file under his arm, in search of truth, and justice, and. like Lily Masters had said to him, uncovering the true forces of darkness. Only he felt overwhelmed, because he knew in his gut how high it maybe all went, suspected what might be involved.

"You don't look so good," said Lucille. She was sitting

at the table in the breakfast nook, reading the morning newspaper, though it was evening now. She'd had him at home most of the day, and it had thrown her off schedule. "You look worried."

"That's because I'm worried," Lou said. "I don't know if I can do this whole thing myself. It might go pretty high up."

"So maybe you won't have to do it yourself. Maybe somebody'll help you."

"Who? This is a pretty exclusive club. These guys don't blow the whistle on each other."

"Somebody'll come through. You'll see. The bad guys don't always win. There's still some of us left. The world isn't all evil people, or Beautiful People either. There's good people around, and you'll find each other. Relax. Maybe you should take a little vacation before you tackle it."

"What kind of vacation?"

"Well, the Annenbergs are having a few friends down to Palm Springs this weekend," she said, looking at the paper.

"I'm not much for the desert," Lou said.

"Me either," said Lucille. "Why don't we just stay home?"

The telephone rang then. Lou and Lucille looked at each other. "It must be the Annenbergs, begging us to change our minds," she said, picking up the phone. "Hello? . . . Who's calling?" She handed the phone to Lou. "It's Hap Mitchel."

Lou smiled and took the receiver. "Well, hello. I've been hoping you would call."

So it was true, what Lucille said. There were still some good guys left. And if a couple of them got together, well, maybe it would be like that stuff they said about God, if two or more of you are gathered in My name, whatever, I'll be there. Maybe good could win after all.

Maybe there was no way to beat *all* the bad guys, to vanquish the evil. But at least you could put up a fight. And as long as you fought, you had a chance. Certainly a better chance than Miranda.